The BORDER HOSTAGE

Virginia Henley

The Border Hostage

DELACORTE PRESS

Published by
DELACORTE PRESS
Random House, Inc.
1540 Broadway
New York, New York 10036

Delacorte Press® is a registered trademark of Random House, Inc., and
the colophon is a trademark of Random House, Inc.

ISBN 0-385-31826-X

Manufactured in the United States of America

For Marjorie Hopcraft
my sister-in-law,
my friend.

The BORDER HOSTAGE

CHAPTER 1

Eskdale Castle, Scottish Borders
May, 1514

Yᴏᴜ stole my heart the first time I ever laid eyes on you!"
Heath Kennedy murmured low. Concealed behind a high stone wall,
the tall, dark figure watched the lovely female as she stood in the
deepening shadows of twilight. Her beauty was enhanced by her re-
gal bearing as she lifted her head with pride. She was darkly beautiful, her skin smooth as satin. It was not just her face that was
exquisite; her body too was perfection. Her slender legs were the
longest he had ever seen. When she turned her head and gazed in his
direction, Heath wondered if she sensed the presence of a male.

Heath knew she would put up a fight once she realized what
was about to happen. But it would avail her naught; he had planned
the mating for a sennight, carefully watching her, following her,
stalking her as she frequented her favorite haunts. At twilight she always wandered down to the River Esk, dallying pensively until the
moon rose. This meadow was a perfect place; high stone walls on
three sides, the river on the fourth, made escape impossible.

Heath rode slowly through the gate and quietly locked it behind
him. She saw him immediately, but his presence was familiar and she
trusted him implicitly. As he cantered toward her she tossed her head
in a gesture that was both playful and enticing. She watched him intently as he slid from the stallion's back.

"Tonight is the night, my proud beauty." His white teeth
flashed in his darkly tanned face.

The moment he slapped his stallion's rump, she knew what
would follow. She began to flee like the wind, intent upon escape.
Her pursuer followed, steadily closing the distance between them.

Fear washed over her, making her shudder uncontrollably. Too late, she realized that he had her cornered, and she screamed.

Heath felt a moment's regret that she must suffer fear and pain, but he ruthlessly crushed the emotion. The end justified the means. The male must dominate, the female must submit; it was the law of nature. Cornered and trembling, she was still ready to fight. The moment he lunged at her, she bit him savagely.

Wild with the instinct to copulate, the black stallion reared its powerful forelegs, sank its teeth into the mare's satin neck, and mounted her with brute force. As the stud thrust into her, the lovely Barbary suddenly yielded to his mastery and her scream modulated to a soft feral cry of need. She quivered as the dominant male buried himself deep inside her, surging in and out with a furious rhythm that unleashed his fierce sexual energy.

As the black stallion drove relentlessly toward his goal, he nipped her roughly on the neck and buried himself hard in her sleek heat. Then, finally, a scream was torn from his throat as his body went taut and he spent his seed. The viscid semen erupted into the fecund mare like white-hot lava, and she tightened on him painfully, ensuring that not one drop would be lost.

The stallion, glistening with sweat, released the mare and almost went down to his knees, robbed of his powerful strength. The female Barbary, however, had been invigorated. She brushed against him playfully, nudging him with her nose. They stood together, their bodies touching. She blew temptingly through her nostrils, while his heaving breath ruffled her mane.

It had been a magnificent mating. Heath was momentarily awestruck by its primal beauty. He walked slowly toward the mare and gentled her with his hand. His warm brown eyes clearly showed the deep affection he felt toward this particular horse. "Softly, my beauty. You were more than a match for him. You have got him staggering on his legs. If it did not take, he can serve you again, but I warrant he did his job right the first time."

A month ago, when Heath Kennedy and Ramsay Douglas had ridden north to the Grampian Mountains to bring back the wild, unbroken horses that were allowed to run free in the northern forests to ensure they could withstand cold and severe weather, Heath had seen the black stallion for the first time. He had known immediately that the animal was capable of siring magnificent progeny, especially with the right dams. Ram had laughed and told Heath he could have the horse, if he could capture him. It had not been easy, but when the two men left with the herd, the young stud stallion had a new master, who named him Blackadder.

Heath had worked with him and the rest of the wild horses from dawn till dark, every day for a month, and his efforts were beginning to pay off. He was training the surefooted garrons for Douglas moss-troopers who had to patrol the endless miles of wild, wide-open, rugged carse and moors of the Borders between Scotland and England. Borderers' horses must have strength, wind, and endurance or they were next to useless.

Heath Kennedy stretched an arm above his head as he lay naked in the wide bed. The ache in his muscles was deeply satisfying, for it came from doing work he loved. Heath's passion was horses; he had bought, sold, and traded them all his life, aye and stolen his fair share too, but he had never been able to breed them, because he had never owned any land. This year, for the first time, he would achieve his ambition, thanks to his powerful brother-in-law, Lord Ramsay Douglas. Heath had helped Ram escape from the Tower of London, where the English king, Henry Tudor, had been about to hang him, and in gratitude Ram had offered him the use of the vast Douglas lands to start his horse breeding. With hard work and clever trading, Heath now owned a dozen good breeding mares, and with any luck his new stud stallion would double the size of his herd within a year.

Heath's smile flashed in the darkness as he absently massaged the rock-hard saddle muscle in his thigh. His cock stirred slightly at the arousing memory of the mating, but he willed himself to relax and soon it lay quiet enough in its nest of thick black curls. He could not wait to see the colt his sister Valentina's lovely Barbary mare, Indigo, would produce. At long last, perhaps Fate had suddenly decided to favor him. Branding Heath Kennedy with the bar sinister of bastardy had not been enough for that wicked jade known as Fate. With cruel delight, she also had bestowed Gypsy blood upon him, doubly dooming him from the day he was born. But Heath Kennedy had laughed in the jade's face and thumbed his nose at the world. His proud bearing deceived all into believing he had been blessed rather than cursed.

He felt a sudden premonition of danger. He forced himself to breathe deeply, slowly, focusing on where the menace was centered. Heath could read minds easily and sense things that threatened about him. He had more physical and psychic power at his command than ordinary men. *Valentina* . . . His sister Tina was the only being he loved in the entire world, and suddenly he felt her fear flood over him like a tidal wave.

He slipped from the bed and quickly donned calfskin breeches, then took time to pull on his soft, thigh-high boots that concealed a deadly blade. With the stealth and speed of a predator, guided by instinct alone, Heath stalked through the castle chambers until he reached the Master Tower. When he heard Tina's terrified scream, he took the stone stairs three at a time.

Heath paused at the bedchamber door only long enough to hear a male demand, "Where is Black Ram Douglas?" He kicked open the door savagely and it crashed back against the wall, revealing his beautiful sister with the raider's hands about her throat. It took only three seconds for Heath to take the blade from his boot and use it to separate the man's backbone and pierce his heart. The hulking brute gurgled, and a froth of blood spattered Tina's white night rail.

"Are you all right, sweeting?" Heath's gut was knotted with apprehension for his beloved sister, and for the child she carried beneath her heart. The back of his neck prickled at the thought of what Ram would have done to him had he not protected the wife and unborn child Douglas loved more than life.

"Ye took the bait, laddie; we've got ye now!"

Heath whirled to face the door as six thickset Borderers shouldered their way into the spacious tower room.

"He isn't Lord Douglas!" Tina denied desperately.

"Liar!" The barrel-chested leader bared rotting, blackened teeth in a hideous leer. "None but firkin' Black Ram Douglas would dare enter yer bedchamber—it would mean his death warrant."

"This is my *brother*, Heath Kennedy!" she cried.

"Liar!" The burly Borderer was enjoying himself. "All the firkin' Kennedys have flaming red hair, like yerself, lass."

"Hush, Tina!" Heath warned before her blazing temper ignited. If they thought they had Ramsay Douglas, they would take him and mayhap leave Tina unharmed. The resemblance between Heath and Ram was marked, and it was not the first time that one had been mistaken for the other.

"Och, the laddie's in luv, begod! Willin' tae sacrifice hisself fer a bloody woman." The Borderer shook his shaggy head in disbelief. "Take him," he ordered.

Two brawny men with fists the size of hams grabbed Heath Kennedy and began to drag him from the tower room. Heath cursed himself for an impetuous fool. If he had still been in possession of his blade, he would have taken on all six.

"I'll fetch the knife," a third said with avidity.

"Ye'll fetch more than the firkin' knife; ye'll fetch the corpse too. We can no' leave one of our clan behind, ye thick-skulled clodpole . . . it would identify us, do ye ken?"

Heath's mind flashed about like mercury as he tried to identify the raiders and their intent. Their blunt, heavy features, dark complexions, and burly bodies stamped them as Borderers. Most probably penniless English Borderers, since they had no weapons save their brawn. Kidnapping the powerful Lord Ramsay Douglas would bring them a large ransom, but thick-skulled and lack-witted they must be to risk bringing down the mighty wrath of Douglas upon their entire clan.

One of the raiders threw the corpse over his shoulder while the other five forced the swarthy Kennedy down the castle stairs. Heath did not fight them; he wanted them away from Tina, and decided to preserve his strength and energy rather than squander it here and now. He was wildly curious about who was behind this kidnapping and assumed he would soon learn the man's identity. Whoever it was would be sadly disappointed when he learned there would be no money forthcoming. Though Heath's father was the wealthy Lord of Galloway, Rob Kennedy would not pay one silver penny to ransom his Gypsy bastard. The irony of it made Heath smile.

The chaos outside Eskdale Castle, however, turned his face grim'. Douglas guards and grooms littered the bailey, beaten unconscious or dead by the marauders, a dozen of whom were reiving the horses. To a man they were mounted on shabby ponies, and his captors shoved him toward one they had tethered.

"Tie his hands behind him," the leader ordered.

"Have ye a bit o' rope, Mangey?"

"Rope costs money," came the terse reply.

Heath thought the nickname most apt; their leader looked as if he had a dose of mange. Then Heath felt the leather thong that secured his shoulder-length hair being ripped from his head, and his wrists were bound tightly behind his back. The thought of these swine stealing Douglas horses, along with his own precious mares, made him want to cut off their balls, and he swore he would do it, given half a chance. He gripped the pony with his knees and leaned his body low over its neck. Years of riding bareback enabled him to keep his balance and prevent him from falling. Though it was early May, the night was briskly cold against Heath's naked chest and back, but years of sleeping outdoors had weathered him, just like the horses he had brought south.

The raiders halted at Langholm, where Eskdale joined Ewesdale. Heath Kennedy watched helplessly as the horses were driven east. His six captors, however, stayed with him, heading south. As they urged their ponies across the River Esk, one of them suggested, "Why don't we drown 'im here?"

"Ye brainless sod! We have tae take him across the Border; we'll use an *English* river."

Drown? The whoresons are going to drown me? Suddenly jolted to the marrow of his bones, Heath Kennedy quickly reassessed his captors. They were the lowest of the low, the dregs of the earth, driven by grinding poverty to commit the foulest deeds no others would undertake. Someone was paying them to murder Ramsay Douglas and make it look like a drowning accident. Since the dreadful defeat of King James Stewart at Flodden, the power of Scotland was held by Clan Douglas. So these orders came from England, Heath reasoned. Yet something at the back of his mind kept pricking him.

Heath took a deep breath and allowed his mind to expand, invoking his sixth sense, which seldom let him down. From the deep recesses of his memory he recalled terrible tales of a *Scottish* clan so bereft of morals that they drowned their victims because it was the most frugal method of murder. Every instinct told him these were Scots Borderers, being paid by England, yet cunning enough to commit the foul deed in the enemy's country, so the finger could never be pointed at them.

Though the actual Border was invisible, Heath knew the moment they crossed it. The land had been marked by violence for four centuries. Feuds between and among the Scots and English here were long-standing; the people along the Border lived by despoiling each other. Robbery, raiding, kidnapping, blackmail, and extortion were a way of life. But when Scot murdered Scot for English money, Heath Kennedy realized the lowest point of degradation had been reached.

Heath was familiar with the landmarks as they passed by a peel tower, and knew the first English river they would encounter would be the River Eden. His hands were completely numb from the tight ligature of his own leather thong, and his upper body had been robbed of most of its feeling by the cold night air. When they drew rein and hauled him from the pony, Heath lashed out with a booted foot, kicking the first man full in the groin, then when he bent double with a scream, Heath brought his knee up sharply beneath the lout's chin, making him bite off the end of his tongue.

Two hulking brutes jumped him and felled him to the ground, where he could clearly hear the river was in spate. The threat of the water made Heath double his efforts to free himself. He butted his head into one man's gut, knocking the wind from him, but the other one picked up a small boulder and crashed it down on Heath's skull. The force of the blow drove him to his knees, and the pain shot all the way down his spine.

"Stop playin' aboot—get 'im in the bloody water." The leader was losing all patience. It took three of them to haul Heath Kennedy into the river, but still they couldn't hold him down long enough to drown him. "Help us, fer Christ's sake!" they admonished their companions.

Heath wrapped his iron-hard thighs about one of the men and dragged him beneath the water. Then he wrapped his legs about the swine's throat and clung to him doggedly. If they were going to drown him, he vowed to take one of them with him. In the end it took four of them to hold him down while their hulking leader stomped brutally on the captive's back with the heel of his boot, then sat on him until the thrashing quietened. Even then Heath Kennedy did not release the man he held underwater.

Gradually, Heath's strength ebbed away into the flowing river. He held his breath until he felt his lungs would burst. Slowly a feeling of euphoria stole over him and he began to relive events from his childhood. He saw his beautiful Gypsy mother, Lily Rose, and recognized her instantly, even though she had died giving birth to him. Although it was the middle of the night, he was suddenly enveloped in a brilliant white light and he experienced a feeling of joy. *So this is Death, then,* he thought with wonder, and then there was nothing.

When the five Borderers finally released their victim, his body rose to the surface. Another body bobbed up beside him, and the two floaters were taken by the current. The murderers splashed after them and hauled them up onto the riverbank. The leader removed the thong from Heath Kennedy's bound wrists, then turned him face up with his boot. He shook his head in disbelief, "Christ, they said Black Ram Douglas was tougher than boiled owl an' they were bloody well right." He cast a baleful glance over the other drowned body and cursed, "Another firkin' corpse tae carry home."

Raven Carleton entered the stables silently in the predawn darkness, yet the hunting birds in the mews above immediately sensed her presence and set up their raucous welcome.

"Peste," she muttered, trying her best to ignore them as she stroked the nose of her pony, Sully, and led him from the stable without a saddle. She felt a stab of guilt as she pictured the hawks moving restlessly on their perches, some wearing their little hoods. Raven, however, resolutely cast away the guilt, knowing she must ride away her feelings of resentment that had banished sleep, before she attended her birds. Training raptors required patience, coupled with an inner calm, and Raven hoped that a ride along the shore at sunrise would restore her tranquility.

Because Raven preferred the freedom of comfortable clothes for riding, she wore a divided skirt, topped by a loose shirt that belonged to her brother. The moment she mounted her sturdy Border pony he began to run. Sully needed little guidance to the River Eden, which emptied into Solway Firth. Raven never tired of riding along the shore of the Solway, for it divided England from Scotland and offered magnificent open vistas of the sea and the purple mountains beyond. When the constraints of Rockcliffe Manor and the strictures of her parents closed in to make her feel trapped, Raven's need for freedom was almost always restored by a gallop along the seacoast.

It had been the usual bone of contention that precipitated the argument between Raven and her mother. Breeding hunting birds, in Katherine Carleton's opinion, was downright unladylike. "In fact, it borders on scandalous!" she had told Raven last night.

"Then what would you like me to breed?" Raven challenged.

"That is precisely the problem—a lady should not be involved in *breeding* anything whatsoever."

"Then how did you manage to have three children, Mother?" Raven asked with wide-eyed innocence.

"That is enough, young lady. Lancelot! Can you not hear the defiance and mockery in your daughter's voice? Mark my words, she will end up a spinster if she persists in her odd behavior."

"But my brother Heron breeds hunting dogs, and you never find fault with him," Raven pointed out.

"We have been over this a thousand times, Raven. If you had been born a male, you could breed whatever you wished."

A passel of bastards? Raven thought wickedly. "My gender should have nothing to do with it. If I did it badly, I could understand your objection, but I do it well."

"In theory, she is right, Katherine," Lance Carleton remarked.

"Lancelot, how can you continually undermine me? Raven should not be spending her days in Rockcliffe Marsh, flying those wretched hawks; she should be polishing her social skills and learning how to run a household. Why, she is like some wild creature!"

Sir Lance Carleton winked at his daughter. "In theory, she is right, Raven. Your mother wants me to clip your wings. When you go to Carlisle and visit the Dacres, you will have to *pretend* to be a lady, at least until we get you safely betrothed."

"Christopher Dacre likes me the way I am!" Raven declared.

I'll just bet he does, thought Carleton as he observed his beautiful, black-haired daughter.

"We do not want him to *like* you, we want him to *marry* you. No gentleman wants a wife with a sharp tongue, and a defiant, willful nature. If you do not change your ways—and your attitude—your sister Lark will make a good marriage long before you do."

"I love Lark; don't pit us against each other."

"What a wicked accusation. Seek your room!"

As dawn turned the sky to pale gold, Raven felt her spirits begin to lift. She breathed in the salt tang as if it were the elixir of life, as Sully's galloping hooves dug into the sandy shale along the shore. The pique she felt toward her mother melted away, and the corners of her generous mouth lifted. Raven knew she was willful, with a temper of fire, and admitted that her mother only wanted what was best for her. Her mother had been plain Kate Heron until she made a good marriage and became the wife of Sir Lancelot Carleton, the constable of Carlisle Castle. The Herons were an English Border clan, and it had been nothing short of a miracle to Kate when she had snared an English gentleman in the matrimonial trap. Now Katherine expected both of her daughters to "marry up" and elevate their social status, as she had done. She never tired of warning her girls about Borderers. "Look at my brother and male cousins, uncouth uncivilized louts the lot of them! All Borderers are alike: dark, dominant, overbold, swaggering swine, and a danger to every female they encounter!"

Raven knew her mother would be ecstatic if a marriage could be arranged with Christopher Dacre, son and heir of Lord Thomas Dacre, Head Border Warden of the English Marches. Christopher had been educated in London and had come north less than a year ago to fight with his regiment at Flodden, where the uncivilized Scots had been brought to their knees once and for all.

Raven smiled her secret smile. The union did not displease her; moreover, she would be in Carlisle next week as a guest of the Dacres. She lifted her head and exulted in the feel of the wind whipping her hair about her shoulders and her skirt about her bare legs. Anticipation bubbled up inside her—she would lead Chris Dacre on a merry chase!

CHAPTER 2

Heath Kennedy opened his eyes and saw the stars above him fading with the dawn. *So, I am not dead after all*, he thought, *only half dead by the feel of it!* He lay still, drawing power and warmth from the earth into his hard, well-muscled body, and willed himself to stop shivering. Earth healing was an old Celtic belief. He moved his long, powerful legs apart and stretched out his arms with the palms flat on the ground so that his body formed a pentagram, or five-pointed star. He closed his eyes, breathed deeply, and tried to merge with the earth's energy. He sensed its pulsations and matched his breathing to the rhythm of nature. Slowly he became one with the earth and rocks upon which he lay, taking the power of nature into his own body, and absorbing the beat of life.

Heath did not know how long he lay there, but gradually he felt the pulse strengthen until he could actually hear it pounding. He opened his eyes and rolled over onto his stomach as he suddenly realized that it was hoofbeats he could hear!

Heath Kennedy caught his breath as he saw a girl riding like the wind along the shore. As he focused his whole attention upon her, the aches and pains of his body diminished. The girl's beautiful black hair streamed out behind her like a proud banner, and it was obvious that she had a free spirit and loved nature as much as he did. She rode bareback and seemed not to know, or care, that her skirt had ridden up to expose her long, bare legs. He took her for a Gypsy girl, yet he was sure he did not know her. Such a female would be unforgettable.

Heath got to his knees, then slowly, without taking his eyes from the rider, he stood up. He knew she saw him, for she suddenly tossed her head and urged her mount to a reckless speed. Her black Border pony was surefooted and bred for stamina, yet the wild gallop to the far end of the beach showed a wanton desire to display her riding skill. The female hardly slowed as she pivoted her pony and rode directly toward him at full gallop.

Heath, who had no intention of moving from her path, planted his feet firmly and laughed at her folly. "Where is the rest of the band camped?" he called.

At the last minute she drew rein and slid down from the pony's back. "What band?" she demanded in a challenging voice.

"The Gypsies. You are a Gypsy, are you not?"

Raven stopped dead, four feet away from him. The features of her beautiful face were frozen in outrage. "A Gypsy?" she repeated in disbelief. "You ignorant swine, I have never been so offended in my life! How dare you offer me such insult?" Raven was stunned that the dark Borderer had mistaken her for a ragtag Gypsy. Her contemptuous glance ran over his bare chest and shoulders with their powerful muscles and corded tendons. He was probably looking for a quick tumble. "I am a *lady*! My father is Sir Lancelot Carleton. We own Rockcliffe Marsh, upon which you, sir, are trespassing!"

Now that Heath saw her close up, he could see that she was no Gypsy. Her skin was like roses and cream rather than dusky, and her eyes were a startling lavender-blue. He also could see her aura, which was a matching shade of lavender against her black hair. "An *English* lady." He gave her a mocking bow and winced inwardly at the pain it caused him. "That is too bad."

Raven's chin went up immediately and her temper flared. "Why so?" she challenged.

"Gypsy girls have fire in their blood—English ladies have ice."

She dug her fists into her hips. "Well, there is no mistaking what *you* are: an insolent Borderer, most likely a Scot to boot!" Raven was amazed at her own temerity. An aura of danger surrounded the dark man before her, and he exuded a sense of threat.

Her words did not offend him, rather they flattered him. Heath

Kennedy was indeed first and foremost a Borderer and a Scot. When she looked at him as if he were the scum of the earth, he smiled inwardly, wondering what she would think if she knew he had a little Gypsy blood mixed in there too.

Raven swallowed her fear of the dark and dangerous man who stood before her, and said with bravado, "You had better be off before my brother sets his dogs on you and my father arrests you for trespass!"

Heath smiled wryly. He knew Lance Carleton had once been constable of Carlisle Castle, but thought his years must sit heavily upon him now that he was lame and had been put out to pasture, so to speak. For his service to the Crown, however, he had been appointed an official who sat in judgment at the Border Wardens' Courts, which were held four times a year. "If Sir Lancelot saw you showing off your bare legs so shamefully, he would tan your arse, I warrant."

Raven could not prevent the blush that rose to her cheeks, because there was truth in his words. This, of course, made her so angry she did not trust herself to retort. Instead she shot him a look of scorn, turned her back upon him, and remounted her pony.

The blush told him that she was an innocent lass, despite her haughty pride. He felt an instant attraction toward the spirited beauty, in spite of her disdain. Heath allowed her to ride a short distance away from him before he put two fingers to his lips and whistled. Her pony stopped in his tracks, turned, and trotted back toward Heath.

"Sully! Whoa! Whoa, boy! Sully, stop!" Raven cried.

Sully did stop, but not until he stood in front of Heath Kennedy. The bare-chested Borderer reached out a hand and scratched the pony's nose, and Sully moved forward to nudge him.

"What in hell's name are you doing?" Raven demanded furiously, suddenly realizing the danger was real.

Heath's fingers took hold of Sully's bridle. "My dearest lady, I find myself in dire straits this morning. I am in need of a mount, and like an angel of mercy you have delivered one into my hands. I pledge to return him at my first convenient opportunity."

Raven laughed in his face. "Give you Sully? You must be mad!"

Heath nodded his head. "A mad Borderer, and a Scot to boot! Allow me to help you dismount."

For the first time Raven's eyes revealed that fear mingled with her fury. She kicked out at him, but he deftly caught her ankle and pulled her from the pony's back. He let go of the reins, and Sully stood obedient to his signal as Heath took Raven firmly by the shoulders and looked down at her. "There is something else that I lust for, my proud beauty." His fingers deftly unbuttoned her shirt.

Raven's eyes widened in shock. "You would ravish me?"

"Another time, perhaps, my lady. Today I only desire the shirt off your back."

Raven's mouth fell open as he plucked the shirt from her, leaving her clad in only her feminine undergarment. She began to pant with rage. "You filthy Scots bastard, stealing horses is a hanging offense, and you will swing, so help me God!"

Heath mounted Sully. "I will not cavil at 'bastard,' but I do object to the word 'filthy.' I bathed in the River Eden last night. I bid you adieu, until we meet again."

Though Heath Kennedy would have liked to ride straight back to Eskdale Castle and his sister Tina, he realized one man would be of little aid. Instead, he must find Ram Douglas and tell him what had happened. Ramsay was the Warden of the West Scottish March, with a force of fifty moss-troopers to do his bidding, and at the moment they were patrolling the county of Dumfrieshire. Heath crossed the border and headed west, thankful that his worst injury was no more than a cracked rib. He patted the neck of the sturdy animal he rode, gritting his teeth against the jarring pain, but adding it to the score he would settle with the evil son of a bitch behind the plot to kill Ram Douglas.

The memory of the dark beauty with the fiery temper was far more pleasant to think about. Heath understood that all young creatures had a need to be wild and free. Most respectable young women had it stifled out of them by the time they left childhood, but a few, like his sister Valentina, remained free spirits all their lives. Tina was the only one in the family with whom Heath had ever felt close. He was a by-blow of Rob Kennedy, Lord of Galloway, and his father's legitimate family considered him an outcast, all except Tina. She had married powerful Lord Ramsay Douglas, and as a result, he and Ram had become fast friends.

Heath thought of them now and marveled at what a perfect match they were for each other. Though Tina and Ram had started out as enemies, they had fallen so deeply in love, they were mated for life, and Black Ram Douglas worshipped the ground Tina walked on. They were about to have their first child, and Heath envied them, longing for a family of his own. Then he laughed at his own folly. Before he could have a family, he needed a wife. Heath had no trouble attracting females, but a wife was another matter entirely. Gypsy girls were amoral and did not interest him beyond sex, and any self-respecting young woman, be she English or Scot, would never marry a landless bastard, especially one with Gypsy blood.

Heath rode only a dozen miles before he found Douglas and his men at Annan. The smell of wood smoke was thick in the air, and he could see that the town had been burned. The Douglas men had put out the fires and were now busy tending burns.

"Whoreson English!" Ram cursed. "We got here too late tae catch them. They set fire tae a dozen small villages as well as Annan." Ram took a good look at Heath, and demanded, "What's amiss? Something has happened tae Tina!"

"When I left, Tina was all right," Heath assured him quickly, then went on to tell Ramsay how the raiders had dragged him from Eskdale Castle, thinking he was Lord Douglas.

"Whoreson English!" Ram repeated. "Greedy fer ransom."

"They did not want ransom, they wanted you dead! And I'm not convinced they were English; I have a suspicion they were Scots!"

Ram's heavy black brows drew down in a frown. King James had outlawed clan feuds and put an end to them by bonds of blood and marriage. Cattle were still lifted, but Scots no longer killed each other. "Nay, man, yer wrong! Douglas power is a threat tae the English throne. We need tae get word tae Archie Douglas tae watch his back. The new Earl of Angus will be the next target. By now they may have sniffed out the secret that he intends tae wed our late king's widow, Margaret Tudor." Marriage with James IV's widow would make Archibald Douglas the ruling Regent of Scotland, because King James V was a two-year-old infant.

"I'll need a fresh mount," Heath said. "I don't want to harm this Border pony."

"That's not all ye need by the look of ye." Ram examined Heath, saw the bruised ribs, and used the linen shirt Heath had worn to bind him tightly. Ram gave him a horse and a leather jack, then called his men together. "We are for Eskdale, lads; we've done all we can here."

As the riders crossed from Annandale into Eskdale, Heath said ruefully, "The filthy swine stole all the horses, except for Tina's Indigo. I had her safe in the pasture by the river."

Ram nodded knowingly. "No cattle or sheep; the beasts would slow them down too much, and the horses have more value."

"I intend to get them back," Heath said implacably.

Ram's pewter gaze flicked over him. "They will be miles across the Border by now."

"Maybe," Heath conceded, "but maybe not. They looked like Scots Borderers to me."

Ram shook his head. "Borderers all look alike and sound alike. At the Border Wardens' Court meetings, the only way ye can distinguish English Borderers from Scots is by their clan badges."

"I'd know these scum anywhere. I'll find them, no matter how long it takes."

"Ye don't have tae do it alone—it was me they intended tae murder. How many are we after?"

"Only five—I already dispatched two to hell."

Ram laughed grimly. Heath Kennedy was the only man he had ever met who had more guts than himself.

Raven Carleton was able to reach her bedchamber without anyone seeing her shocking state of undress only because of the early hour. She knew that if she reported her encounter with the Borderer to her parents, they would forbid her from visiting the Rockcliffe Marsh and no doubt curtail her riding and hawking as well. Raven was still seething with anger at the bold devil who had accosted her and stolen Sully, who was so precious to her. She was furious because he had bested her as well. If her father or Heron asked about Sully, she would have to say that she had left him to graze in the far meadow. But God only knew what lie she would have to concoct to explain Sully's permanent disappearance.

Raven caught sight of herself in the mirror and was shocked at her reflection. Her hair was a mass of wild tangles from her ride, and the ribbon from the bodice of her undergarment had come undone, revealing the swell of her breasts. She lifted her chin and set her hands to her hips, to see what she must have looked like to the Borderer. Suddenly her mischievous eyes filled with laughter. "My God, no wonder he mistook me for a ragtag Gypsy!" She sobered suddenly, realizing how lucky she had been to escape unscathed.

The young lady who sat down to lunch wearing a pristine white dress bore no resemblance to the wild creature who had ridden abroad at dawn. Raven listened politely as her mother instructed her and Lark on table manners, dress code, and the ladylike behavior she expected from them both when they visited the Dacres. "It seems that we are not the only guests who have been invited to Carlisle Castle. Among others, Lady Elizabeth Kennedy, your father's second cousin, will be there. No doubt she will be husband-hunting for her youngest daughter, Beth." Raven suddenly became more attentive. Sweet, fair-haired Beth Kennedy was formidable competition in the marriage market because of the fact that her father was the Lord of Galloway, Scotland, who owned vast acres covered with sheep, and a fleet of merchant ships to export Kennedy wool.

Kate Carleton handed Raven an invitation that had arrived that morning. "At the end of the week, the Dacres are throwing a ball. What is this word, dear?" she asked, pointing to one of the words on the card. "I am not sure of its meaning."

"Masquerade," Raven supplied, knowing her mother had difficulty reading. "It means that the guests wear costumes and masks."

"A fancy-dress ball. Why the devil doesn't it say so instead of using a daft French word!"

"Oh, what fun! I am so glad Lady Dacre invited us, especially during Carlisle Fair week. May we attend, Mother?" Lark asked eagerly.

"Of course we are going to the fair." Raven glared at her sister for asking permission.

"Christopher Dacre and your brother may escort you, if you both promise to conduct yourselves with propriety."

"Raven wants to have her fortune told at the fair."

"Of course I don't," Raven denied, aiming a discreet kick at Lark's ankle.

"I should hope not," Kate Carleton said repressively. "Gypsies cannot be trusted; they are all thieves, liars, or *worse.*"

Raven swiftly changed the subject. "It will be a nice chance for you to visit with your friend Rosalind."

"Raven told me that when Lord Dacre was young, he kidnapped his bride and carried her off! Is that true?"

Raven aimed another kick at Lark. Why could she not learn to keep her mouth shut?

Katherine pursed her lips together and gave Raven a look of disapproval. "What an exasperating girl you are." She turned to Lark and explained, "Rosalind Greystokes was a ward of Lord Clifford of Westmorland. Clifford refused Thomas Dacre permission to marry Rosalind, so the reckless young devil carried her off and wed her!"

"What a dreadful, wicked thing to do!" Lark was appalled.

"I think it the most romantic thing I have ever heard!" Raven declared passionately. "Only imagine having a man love you enough to kidnap you!"

Kate gave Raven a quelling glance. "It was indeed dreadful, and caused a horrendous scandal, I can assure you. Poor Rosalind was blameless, but her reputation was ruined."

"What the devil did her reputation matter? She became Lady Dacre, didn't she?"

"A spotless reputation will be paramount for any female aspiring to become the *next* Lady Dacre," Raven's mother said pointedly.

Raven steered the conversation away from her mother's favorite topic. "What costume will you wear, Mother?"

"Some English queen or other is very tempting, if I could get up the courage to wear a crown."

"Boadicea," Raven suggested mischievously. "All you need is a spear!"

Lark had a rapt look on her face. "If Mother is a queen, I shall be a princess. What about you, Raven?"

She had to bite her lip to keep herself from laughing at them. "Oh, something unpretentious, I think. A goddess perhaps." Raven excused herself. She had more important things to think of than costumes. She must instruct the young falconer she was training in the care of her hunting birds while she was away.

Lady Valentina Douglas ran out to the castle's bailey the moment she heard the thunder of hoofbeats. With her hand at her throat, she watched the half-hundred men clatter beneath the portcullis. She felt her knees wobble with relief when she saw her husband and the taller man riding beside him.

Ram vaulted from the saddle and was beside his beautiful flame-haired wife in seconds. "My honey love, are ye all right?"

"Blood of God, I never thought to see Heath come riding in with you. How did you rescue him?"

Ram kissed his wife soundly. "He didn't need me, he rescued himself. What are our losses?"

"Two guards dead, half a dozen grooms wounded. Ada wouldn't let me tend them."

"I should think not, in your condition," the tall, slim serving woman declared dryly. "We spent half the night scrubbing blood from your bedchamber floor!"

"That does it, Tina! Ye go back tae Douglas where it's safe. I never should have let ye come with me this close tae the Borders."

Tina knew better than to contradict Black Ram Douglas before his men, but she would have plenty to say when they were alone. She shrugged a pretty shoulder and looked up into her brother's warm brown eyes. "Blood of God, I feared they would hang you."

He grinned down at her. "Rope costs money." Suddenly, Heath looked at Tina intently. "Are you all right, sweeting?" Her aura had changed. His sister always gave off a golden light, which had not dimmed, but now there was a double ring around her head.

Tina's hand went to her swollen belly beneath her loose cloak. "I am big as a pig full of figs, if that's what you mean!"

"Ye are lovely and lush and more tempting than any married woman has a right tae be," Ram assured her, slipping an arm about her possessively and escorting her to the castle.

"Are you truly all right, Heath?" Ada asked low. She had seen how slowly he had dismounted. Heath and the attractive widow who served his sister had been good friends for years. He brushed his lips across her brow. "I'm fine, Ada; it's Tina we have to worry about. I think she might be carrying twins!"

Ada hurried into the castle as Heath took Ram's mount, along with his own and the Border pony he had "borrowed," to the stables. She caught up with the couple before they reached their bedchamber in the Master Tower, because Tina climbed the stairs slowly. Ada shook her head in disbelief, for already the two strong-willed lovers were arguing.

"The answer is no! Ye'll do as ye're told, Vixen."

"Devil-eyed Douglas, you're not back five bloody minutes and you are tossing your orders about as if you rule the world!"

They entered their bedchamber and stood facing each other like combatants unprepared to give an inch. "I do rule *your* world, Vixen. There is no earthly reason ye can give me that would convince me tae let ye stay here in the Borders."

"How about twins?" Ada interjected.

Ram gave Ada a quelling glance. "Ye've never respected our

privacy before, so I suppose it's too much tae expect it now," he said with heavy sarcasm.

"Twins?" Tina said, her hands going protectively to her belly and her golden eyes widening in wonder. "Ada, I think you may be right! Oh, that would explain so many things."

"Twins?" Ramsay's gut knotted with anxiety for his beautiful wife, yet at the same time hope soared in his heart.

Tina threw off her cloak and began to unfasten her loose gown. "Help me off with this damn dress," she bade them. "When I lie quietly in bed, I can hear and feel two heartbeats, but I thought one of them was mine."

Ada removed Tina's gown and Ramsay placed his callused hands on his wife's swollen midsection. His dark brows drew together in concentration, then he took Tina's hands and placed them on her belly. "What do ye think, my honey lamb?"

Tina first shook her head, then smiled and nodded. "Ada?"

Ada, who was not only Tina's serving woman but her dearest friend, placed her palms on the thin material of Tina's shift covering her mounded belly and moved them all around. "Either you're carrying twins or it's a three-legged milking stool!"

Tina whooped with joy and laughter. "Oh, I'm so clever and cunning; I have really outdone myself!"

"You? I am the author of this grand production," Ram asserted, his heart overflowing with tenderness and adoration for his beloved. He picked her up gently and laid her on their bed. Then he cupped her face and touched his lips to hers.

"Cocksure devil," she murmured happily, "there'll be no living with you now. Of course, this means I won't be able to travel all those miles to Douglas."

"Ah, Vixen, ye always manage tae get around me."

"I'm not staying in bed though." She slanted him an alluring glance. "Unless, of course, you come too."

Ram could deny her nothing. "After I've seen the wounded men, I'll bathe, then we can have dinner abed." He turned to Ada. "Go and tell Mr. Burque tae prepare something special, and be sure tae warn him her ladyship is eatin' fer three."

Two hours later Tina and Ram dined in the expanse of the big curtained bed, taking turns feeding each other and laughing so much, anyone within hearing distance would have thought them naughty children. Afterward they lay entwined in each other's arms, cuddling, caressing, kissing, and whispering for hours. "I still cannot believe it!" Tina said with awe.

"I can," Ram said, stroking the backs of his fingers across her cheek. "Ye do everything with such unique style and fervor, my little firebrand. Ye are feracious."

"What the devil does that mean?" she whispered.

"It means ye are fertile, fecund, fruitful, and well-fu—"

Tina put her hand over his mouth playfully and admonished, "None of your wicked words in front of the babies."

CHAPTER 3

The next day, Ramsay asked Heath if he would like to go up to Douglas and bring back some of the horses from Castle Dangerous, as it was known. "We need spare mounts fer the moss-troopers."

"I would rather you sent Jock. Tonight I intend to start tracking our stolen horses."

"I shall make a formal complaint next month at the Border Wardens' Court fer the raid on Annan, and under the international law of the Marches, we have recourse fer our stolen horses."

Heath shook his head. "Tell me the rules for a lawful trod."

"The trod is a legal, hallowed process of pursuit. A hot trod is immediate pursuit of the thieves. A cold trod is legal within six days of the raid. But remember that under Border Law there is a clear distinction drawn between a trod and a reprisal raid."

"It is not my 'fatal privilege' to recover my property by force and deal with the thieves out of hand?" Heath asked evenly.

"It is, if ye catch them red-handed with yer property," Ram nodded grimly. "A hot trod is a simple breakneck chase. A cold trod seldom succeeds. The reivers could know every fold in the ground. They could lose themselves with ease while ye are faced with a guessing game, lookin' in gullies."

"That is true if they are Scots," Heath said reflectively.

" 'Tis more certain they are English, and if ye cross the Border there are rules laid down fer a lawful trod with horn and hound, hue and cry. Ye must announce it immediately and seek assistance."

"Is it not unlawful to impede a trod?"

Ram laughed. "It seems ye know the rules as well as I do! I

won't join ye—I am sticking close tae Tina for the next fortnight—but feel free tae take Douglas men."

"Thanks, there's sure to be a few attending Carlisle Fair, so if I need help I'll seek them out there." Heath grinned. "I will try to be back in time for the big event."

"Carlisle Fair is a hell of a good place tae find stolen horses."

"My thinking exactly," Heath agreed. "I've sold a few stolen horses there myself."

At midnight, Heath set out from Eskdale with the border pony fastened on a lead behind his roan gelding. He hoped to encounter the beauteous Mistress Carleton alone, and the best odds of that would be to await her at dawn on Rockcliffe Marsh, where the River Eden emptied into Solway Firth. This time he was adequately clothed and well armed with a knife, and a blade in his boot.

Heath's ride proved uneventful, and when he arrived at Rockcliffe, he tethered the two animals to a willow tree, wrapped himself in a Douglas plaid, and fell asleep, knowing the horses would soon awaken him to any danger that threatened. When he opened his eyes at dawn, the first thing he saw was a hawk circling in the sky above him. He watched appreciatively as it began its dive, and by its speed he identified it as a falcon.

Heath turned over onto his stomach and watched the bird rise with its prey: a marsh duck as big as itself. It flew directly to someone who was swinging a lure. Heath put up a hand to shade his eyes and grinned with pleasure when he saw it was the Carleton girl. He was most surprised to find her hawking, a sport usually indulged in by men. It only added to her attraction, and he decided to learn her first name.

Heath untethered her Border pony, let go of his rein, and pointed him in the direction of his mistress. Only when he heard her cry "Sully!" in surprised delight did he untether his roan and move toward her. At sight of him, the pleasure was immediately wiped from her face. "You!" she cried accusingly.

Heath's bow held only a trace of mockery. "At your service, Mistress Carleton." He had her at a disadvantage; she held Sully's reins in one gloved hand and the falcon's jesses in the other.

A tinge of fear made her overbold. "Borderer, don't you dare use my name as an endearment. We are *not* endeared!" Her blue eyes blazed with fury. He was more maddeningly attractive than she remembered; taller too. His proud bearing proclaimed him arrogant.

Heath looked at her with admiration. *What a magnificent challenge she is.* "I returned your pony, as I promised, *English*. A simple 'thank you' will suffice."

"Thank you? You expect me to thank you for stealing him! How do I know you haven't lamed him?"

"I am not in the habit of laming animals, *English*."

"But you are in the habit of thieving them, *Borderer*! From where did you steal that bag of bones?" The roan gelding was a lovely horse. Such animals were in great demand for riding by English ladies, and it annoyed her that he possessed such a horse.

"It would beat yours in a race."

His challenge made her temper explode, and the young falcon, sensing her anger, flapped his wings wildly. "Now see what you've done!" she accused. "Training a bird of prey requires a calm demeanor."

"You are the one with the fiery temper, *English*. My demeanor is calm enough. Let me have him."

"Why the devil would I do that?" she demanded.

"So you can race Sully against my bag of bones."

"By God, I'll do it, you arrogant swine!" She fastened the jesses of the falcon to the low branch of a flowering alder tree and mounted Sully.

"What will you wager? A race is pointless without a wager."

"I would be rid of you, *Borderer*. If you lose, you will never show your ugly face on Rockcliffe Marsh again!"

"And if I win, you will tell me your first name," Heath stipulated. He mounted the roan and side by side they walked their animals to the shore where he had first seen her ride. She did not look at him, but Heath watched her, and saw that her recklessness made her cheeks bloom like pink roses.

The moment Sully's hooves touched the shingle, she dug in her heels and the Border pony shot forward. Heath took off after the girl, carefully keeping a wide berth between their galloping mounts. He came even with her and kept pace. She stared at him for a moment, showing no fear. He saw her decide that though he was a threat, she would ignore the danger. Clearly it excited her to play with fire. She flashed him a look of challenge and raced ahead.

Heath drew alongside once more. He did not want to best her, he simply wanted to enjoy watching her. His roan was larger with longer legs, but the black Border pony was bred for stamina. They galloped neck-and-neck to the end of the beach, and when she saw that he could easily beat her, she purposely turned her mount into his path, forcing him to draw rein.

Heath dismounted, shaking his head at her folly. She had cheated, but it was worth it to see her bare legs and wildly disheveled hair. She had no intention of dismounting, but lifted her chin and stared down at him. He took the folded shirt from his saddlebags, then walked closer and held it out. His dark, intense gaze swept over her, then locked with hers. "You have too much female pride to lose, but I hope you have too much self-respect to refuse to pay your wager."

As she gazed at him she remembered the lithe, rippling muscles of his naked chest. She snatched the shirt from his hand and spurred past him, needing to get away from the subtle threat he exuded. Then she turned her head and called back over her shoulder, "It's Raven!"

The vivid name made Heath's heart miss a beat. *Raven! Splendor of God, how it suits her.* Then he laughed aloud. He could read her mind and knew that she found him attractive. She also was vain, and could not resist flaunting her beautiful name.

Heath arrived in Carlisle early, before the fair opened, since it was only a short five-mile ride from Rockcliffe. Carlisle was the largest city on the Borders and had always welcomed its Scots neighbors from north of the line at its weekly market and annual fair. Inns and alehouses lined the street across from the marketplace, where Scot and English Borderers rubbed shoulders, drank, gambled, and whored. Farmers from both countries offered their produce and live-stock every week, but the annual Carlisle Fair had grown to cover an area ten times larger than the market.

Heath took a room at an inn called The Fighting Cocks, where he had often stayed before, and casually looked over the men in the common room, hoping to spot Mangey or one of his henchmen. When this proved unsuccessful, he made his way to the fairgrounds to look over every horse that was being offered for sale. Though Heath was certain that none of the horses was either his or Douglas property, he was not discouraged. This was only the first morning of the weeklong fair.

When he spotted a cluster of gaily painted caravans, he decided to visit the Gypsies. They followed the fairs from London in the wintertime, up to the burgh of Stirling in the summer, following the royal court. Heath shook his head, sadly remembering it was only last summer that the Gypsies had entertained the king there, before James lost his life at the disastrous Battle of Flodden. Heath had no trouble recognizing his grandmother's red wagon. Old Meg had her fortune-telling shingle hung above her herbalist sign, and pentacles decorated her door.

Meg stared at the handsome man who was so tall he must bend his head to enter her caravan. "Blessed be," she muttered, never tak-ing her eyes from the Douglas plaid that lay across Heath's shoulder. "From whom did you learn you had the right to wear the Douglas plaid?" she asked evenly.

Heath's eyes narrowed. "Do I have the right?"

Old Meg shrugged. "Lily Rose's father was Archibald Douglas."

Heath almost choked at her words, but could not allow himself to believe that the powerful Earl of Angus was his grandfather. Archibald had been dead for two months, so her tale could not be verified. He discounted most of her tales, for had she not told him that his mother, Lily Rose, had been handfast to Rob Kennedy, Lord of Galloway, when she gave birth to him? "That's a bit too much blue blood to be believed." Meg's weather-beaten face resembled wrin-kled brown parchment. *Is it possible that she was once beautiful?* Heath wondered. From the corner of his eye, he saw his grandmother's tortoise with the huge ruby embedded in its shell. He had always believed it was red glass, but now he looked at it through new eyes, and asked himself who was wealthy enough to have given her a jewel that big. It was neither round nor square, but roughly heart shaped, and suddenly it reminded him of the most famous device in Scotland: the bleeding heart of Douglas.

"What brings you? A woman?" Meg asked.

Heath laughed, thinking of Raven Carleton, but he knew Gypsies were shrewd and always guessed the thing that had the most likely probability. It gave them a reputation for foretelling the future, but most Gypsies were charlatans, saying and doing whatever was expedient. Generations of living by their wits had sharpened their instincts. "Horses. Stolen horses," Heath replied.

"And not horses that *you* stole, for once!" She cackled at her own humor, then sobered. "You are seeking men."

Heath nodded reluctantly. "Borderers; one called Mangey, and four others."

Meg's eyes got a far-off look, and she was silent for a minute. Then she said, "Men from Mangerton are sometimes nicknamed Mangey."

Two attractive Gypsy girls draped themselves on either side of Meg's doorway. "Heath! Heath! We haven't seen you for over a year! Come, let us feed you," one implored.

"You always had an insatiable appetite," the other girl teased.

Meg shooed the three of them from her caravan. The females were lusting for Heath, but she knew they would get none of him today. At the moment, Heath's thoughts were consumed by an entirely different raven-haired beauty.

Raven Carleton took her seat in the carriage with her mother and Lark, without protest. Her brother, Heron, accompanied them on horseback, and Raven watched him with longing. She had asked if she too could have the freedom of riding to Carlisle, and had been given a flat refusal from her father, who was now aligned with his wife in curbing Raven's behavior. "I shall come on Friday," Lance Carleton assured his wife, giving Raven a stern glance from beneath bushy brows. In return, she gave him her most innocent look, relieved that he did not admonish her further. In truth, Raven adored her father. When he had been injured, Raven had been the one who mixed poppy and licorice root into his wine, to ease his agony. He was the bravest man she had ever known, for never once had he complained, not even when it became obvious that he would be left with the permanent handicap of lameness. For the three long months it had taken him to recover, Raven had sat and read to him or played endless games of chess to take his mind from his pain. "Be careful, Father," Raven whispered as she kissed him goodbye.

From the moment the carriage left Rockcliffe, Kate Heron began to catalogue all the behavior that she considered unacceptable while they were guests of the Dacres. With difficulty, Raven curbed her tongue, knowing the five-mile journey would not take long. She felt relief as the carriage approached Carlisle's northern gate. They would soon be arriving at the great, square, red castle where she had spent her childhood, when Sir Lancelot had been its constable.

Raven was torn from the moment she stepped down from the carriage. Lady Dacre was there to greet them, but Heron rode his mount toward the stables, the hunting dog he had brought Chris Dacre at his heels. Raven looked longingly after her brother, then obediently followed her mother and Lark inside.

"Kate, you have such beautiful daughters; how I envy you." Rosalind Dacre was small, dark, and still pretty, despite her middle years. She had a gentle, passive nature, unsuited to ruling a headstrong son who was the image of his dominant father.

"When Christopher takes a wife, you will gain a daughter," Kate said pointedly, guiding the conversation in the direction she desired. "Lark and Heron have their father's fair coloring, but Raven is dark like me, and like you, Rosalind."

She is dark, yes, but she is not like me, thank heaven. She has a mind of her own and is not afraid to voice her opinions. No man will ever run roughshod over Raven Carleton, I warrant. "I shall have the steward show you to your chambers. It will give you a chance to rest and freshen up before the other guests arrive. Lord Dacre and Christopher are riding in from Bewcastle. They should be here soon."

Kate's clan of Herons lived near Bewcastle, the English Border stronghold, which lay about sixteen miles to the northeast, but she did not wish to remind Lady Dacre of her humble Border origins.

It was like coming home to Raven. Carlisle Castle had no romantic pinnacles or crenellated battlements, but she had a great fondness for the fortress. She was familiar with every winding passageway, especially those leading to the attics or the dungeons, where she had often played as a child. She needed no steward to show her the way, but she dutifully followed the man who carried up the luggage to the bedchamber assigned to her and Lark. Raven quickly unpacked for her sister as well as herself. "Come on, Lark, let's go to the stables."

"But we're supposed to rest."

"Rest? We've only traveled five miles! Are you feeling all right, Lark?"

"Oh yes, but I did want to change into a prettier dress before . . ." Lark did not finish her sentence, but asked, "You won't drag me up into the mews, will you?"

"Of course not. You stay here while I visit the birds."

The mews at Carlisle Castle was large of necessity for the number of hawks it had to house. Raven spoke to the falconer, obtaining his permission to view the rows of birds. As they walked past the hooded raptors, some screeched and spread their wings in alarm, but when Raven murmured soothing words, they calmed and folded their wings. She stopped before a small merlin, whose plumage was luminous. "Such a beauty," she crooned, using one fingertip to stroke its wing, and watched as the little female ruffled with pleasure. "This is your bird," she told the falconer.

"Her name is Morgana. How did you know she was mine?"

"She moved her head from side to side as she listened, then preened when she recognized your voice." Raven moved across to look at four falcons separate from the others. "Oh, two of these falcons have their eyes stitched closed!" She was unable to keep the disapproval from her voice. "I think that cruel, unnatural, and completely unnecessary. Hoods suffice, until they are tamed, then even the hoods can be taken away, if the mews is kept in semidarkness."

"These two new falcons belong to Lord Dacre, lady. I have my orders," the falconer said quietly.

"Here you are, Raven!" Christopher Dacre walked down the row of perches. "Heron said I would find you in the mews, but I didn't believe him." Lord Dacre's heir was tall and blond, with the aquiline nose of his Anglo-French ancestors.

"Hello, Christopher. I have a great interest in hunting birds. I spent many happy hours up here when I was a child." Raven did not tell him that she bred hawks; he would find out soon enough if their relationship developed further.

"That's strange—hawking is a man's sport."

Raven did not wish to contradict him, so she chose her words carefully. "Ladies, especially at court, are taking an interest. It is becoming fashionable, I have heard."

Christopher ran a negligent hand through his fair hair as his gray-green eyes moved over her with speculation. Court ladies were notoriously promiscuous, and he wondered if she had heard that too. "Would you like to try hawking?"

"I would love it!" Raven took him up on the offer immediately, showing great enthusiasm.

Young Dacre hid a satisfied smile. Raven Carleton was obviously trying to please him. "Ready my falcon," Christopher ordered the falconer, deciding to show off his prowess with the peregrine.

"Allow me to offer the lady my merlin." The falconer handed Christopher Dacre a leather gauntlet.

"You honor me, sir!" Raven smiled with delight as she pulled on a smaller gauntlet, and offered her arm to the small huntress. After only a slight hesitation, the merlin moved from its perch and dug its talons into her leather-covered wrist. She held the jesses securely, then removed the hood. Raven stared into the unblinking yellow eyes for a full minute. "She accepts me," Raven said with satisfaction.

They descended to the stables below with the falconer at their heels carrying Dacre's peregrine falcon.

"Christopher and I are going hawking. I will need your horse," Raven advised her brother.

When Heron looked doubtful, Christopher laughed and assured him, "She'll be all right with me. We are just going into yonder woods for an hour." By way of an inducement, he offered, "Why don't you try my new stallion I picked up at Bewcastle?"

"The black?" Heron asked eagerly. "Thanks, he's magnificent." As Heron handed his sister up into the saddle, he murmured a low warning. "Don't outshine him, Raven."

As the couple trotted their horses toward the woods, their hawks perched on their saddlebows, Christopher inquired, "Do you often ride astride?"

She gave him a provocative glance. "If I answer yes, you will think me a hoyden; if I answer no, you will think me a liar."

"How do you ride at home?"

"Very well. I have a Border pony."

Christopher looked amused at the way she had turned the question. "Would you not like a horse?"

"Of course I would. One just like your new stallion," Raven replied with daring.

"Surely a gelding would be preferable for a lady?" He watched her face to see if she knew what they did to a stallion to turn it into a gelding.

Raven knew exactly what he was doing. "What's the difference?" she asked with wide-eyed innocence.

Chris Dacre had the decency to clear his throat. "They are better behaved, I think."

Unlike some gentlemen, Raven thought, trying not to laugh. "My grandmother lives near Bewcastle. The forests thereabouts are vast, and wildly beautiful."

"Yes, wildly beautiful," Dacre repeated, his hot glance licking over her like a candle flame.

"Would this clearing be a good place to fly our birds?" Raven asked, deferring to him as she knew gentlemen expected.

"Yes." Dacre slid from his saddle. "Let me help you."

The moment he lifted her down, Raven reached for the merlin to prevent his hands from lingering at her waist.

"Let me show you how to thread the jesses between your fingers."

"Thank you," she said faintly, amazed at his male arrogance.

Dacre took his peregrine falcon onto his wrist and directed, "Now watch me." He removed its hood and cast the bird high. He had not waited for the falcon's eyes to adjust to the sudden light, but Raven forbore to criticize him. They watched it soar and circle about the clearing. "Cast the merlin," he directed.

"Not until your falcon views its prey and starts its dive. I don't want it to kill Morgana."

"We have hawks aplenty," Dacre assured her. When he saw her scathing glance, he said, "Perhaps you are too tenderhearted for this sport."

Raven saw the peregrine dive, and immediately cast the merlin. The small brown female had already spotted a mole, and swooped across the clearing, snaring it in her talons, then flew back to present her prize to Raven. "Good girl, Morgana," Raven praised, and gave the mole back to the huntress.

"No! No! Raven, you must never feed a raptor. They won't hunt unless they are hungry!"

She gave him a sideways glance. "A female prefers a reward to being starved."

Dacre laughed. "Birds are different from ladies." His falcon returned with a young peacock from the castle grounds. "Oh Lord, my mother will have a fit."

"Really? You don't have peacocks aplenty?"

"Touché! Will you forgive me for my callous remark, or will you hold it against me?" he teased.

Raven knew a double entendre when she heard one. "Behave yourself, and I may let you take me to the fair tomorrow." She allowed him the privilege of lifting her into the saddle.

"I have to return to Bewcastle next week. If you visited your grandmother, I could continue your lessons."

The corners of Raven's mouth lifted. "Irresistible as that sounds, sir, it is out of the question." Her smile widened. Christopher Dacre had flown to the lure faster than his falcon!

CHAPTER 4

At Carlisle Castle that evening, Raven Carleton's glance traveled down the long dining table. Lord Thomas Dacre sat at the head of the table with Lady Elizabeth Kennedy and her daughter, Beth, on his right. Though Raven was too far away to hear their conversation, she observed Dacre's cordial manner to Elizabeth Kennedy and watched that lady simper and bask in his attention. Raven's eyes flicked over Beth Kennedy, dismissing her as a sweet little nonentity. She would have been astounded had she known the fierce arguments the young girl had precipitated.

Lady Kennedy and Beth had traveled from Castle Doon at the Scottish port of Ayr to Carlisle aboard a Kennedy merchant vessel. Ever since the Scottish defeat at Flodden, Elizabeth Kennedy had made no secret of the fact that she wanted an English husband for her daughter Beth. The face of Rob Kennedy, Lord of Galloway, had turned a congested purple when his wife had received the Dacres' invitation and uttered the blasphemous words "Christopher Dacre would be a perfect match for our daughter Beth."

"God's passion, woman, nothin' good ever came up from England!"

Kennedy's imposing bulk and his loud, grating voice usually intimidated his wife, but that day she was foolish enough to protest indignantly, "Rob, I am English."

"I'm relieved ye take my point, Lizzie! The bloody English have attacked my vessels, stolen my precious wool, killed my king along wi' my youngest son and a hundred other Kennedys at Flodden, and yet my wife has the gall tae suggest a match between my wee lass an' the son of the bastard who is now Head Warden of the English Marches."

It was too painful for Elizabeth to speak of the loss of her son Davey. She blamed her husband for allowing such a young boy to go to war. "You know very well that Thomas Dacre was a good friend of my family in Carlisle."

Rob Kennedy's face turned a deeper shade of purple when he heard his usually docile wife answer him back. "Too bad ye didn't *wed* Thomas bloody Dacre, an' save me from a life of purgatory, listenin' tae yer whining an' yer tears!"

"You have run roughshod over me for years, Rob Kennedy, and I have always been a dutiful and complacent wife to you. But when it comes to the happiness of my precious daughter, I intend to stand up to you. You are nothing but a coarse bully. Perhaps I shall stay in Carlisle permanently!"

"Is that a threat or a bloody promise?" Rob roared. "Ye're no' the only one who can make threats, Lizzie. If Beth gets no dowry, ye'll see how fast Thomas bloody Dacre betroths his heir tae her!"

The altercation between Thomas Dacre and his heir, Christopher, had been a little less fierce. Dacre knew his son was willful as himself and that bullying tactics would not work. "The Kennedy girl's father is rich as Croesus, and her mother is an old friend of the family."

"But the girl herself has the looks and personality of an oatcake. I prefer a little gilt on my gingerbread, Father," Chris Dacre argued.

"I'm not blind, Chris. I am well aware of Raven Carleton's beauty and her tempting pair of titties, but Beth Kennedy's dowry will provide a thick layer of honey to sweeten the plain oatcake."

"Not sweet enough for me to lick! Besides, Raven Carleton is English, while Beth Kennedy is Scottish."

"Beth Kennedy is half English," Lord Dacre pointed out.

"Which half?" Christopher drawled. "The top or the bottom? Father, you could have married Elizabeth Kennedy, but you didn't! You lost your heart to a raven-haired beauty and carried her off. You are the last person on earth to advise me to wed for money."

"Christ almighty, Christopher, try to think with your brains instead of your prick. A wealthy wife's money will allow you to have as many exotic beauties as you want in your bed."

"I want only one at a time, Father; I'm not greedy."

"I warrant you are, if you're anything like me." Dacre's eyes narrowed. "Women are like horses, Christopher."

"Because we ride them?"

"Because you have to let them know who's master, and you always keep a spare one. All I ask is that you think about it carefully before you do anything rash."

Raven felt someone playing footsies with her beneath the table and looked across at Christopher Dacre. He lowered one eyelid in a wink. "Do you have something in your eye?" she teased.

"Yes . . . you," Christopher murmured, not caring that her brother could hear their byplay. He turned to Heron and said low, "I want to be alone with Raven at the fair tomorrow. Would you be a good fellow and escort Beth Kennedy and your sister Lark?"

Heron Carleton's gaze traveled down the table and came to rest on the fair-haired young lady who was his second cousin. Beth must have felt his eyes on her, for suddenly she looked at him from beneath her lashes and blushed. "What's it worth to you?"

Lowering his voice even further, Chris Dacre bargained, "I'll find us a couple of bedmates for later tonight." When he saw Heron hesitate, he added an incentive. "Gypsy girls!"

"Done!" Heron offered his hand with heartfelt gratitude, and they shook on it.

Raven looked with curiosity from one to the other. "Did I hear you say 'Gypsy girls'?"

"Costumes. We were discussing costumes for the masquerade," Chris Dacre lied smoothly.

Heron quickly improvised, "Chris wagered me that none of the ladies would be daring enough to dress as a Gypsy."

Raven's wicked juices immediately began to bubble.

Heath Kennedy, on the second morning of Carlisle Fair, once again rode over the acres, checking every horse that was being offered for sale. He dismounted to examine some mares he wouldn't mind owning that would make excellent dams, but perversely he wanted to get his own animals back.

The day was warming up and Heath unfastened the neck of his leather jack, wondering if he was wasting his time in Carlisle. All of a sudden he spotted his stallion Blackadder. There was no mistaking the magnificent animal that had spent its life in the northern mountains guarding its herd of wild mares. Heath stopped dead in his tracks, legs spread wide, ready for a confrontation with whoever held his stallion's reins.

Heath observed the tall, blond male with the aquiline nose and expensive English clothes, almost feeling sorry for the poor fool. Then his eyes widened in disbelief as he saw that the son of a bitch was escorting Raven Carleton. When she saw him, Heath knew she was shocked by her swift intake of breath.

"What is it, Raven?" her escort inquired.

Raven blinked twice. "The roan," she said quickly, "it is a beautiful riding horse."

"Let me buy it for you." Dacre's glance moved from the horse to the dark Borderer who owned it. "How much for the roan?"

"It's not for sale," came the flat reply.

"Oh, come now, everyone has his price," Dacre said with great condescension.

"Really? How much for the black?"

"Three hundred pounds."

Dacre named the impossible price with such arrogance, Heath Kennedy wanted to slit his aristocratic English nose. Heath clenched his fists to stop himself from reaching for his knife. "Three hundred it is, if you'll throw in the woman."

Raven gasped in outrage.

Dacre said, "You insolent swine, you need a damned good thrashing!" The stallion danced away at the angry tone, and Dacre suddenly found the black difficult to control.

"When you find someone up to the job, I'll be ready and waiting," Heath taunted.

"Damn you both! I know a cockfight when I see one, and I have no stomach for them!" Raven's back, straight as a ramrod, showed her outrage as she walked off.

Dacre suddenly found the dark Borderer so threatening, he felt a prickle of fear at the back of his neck. He reached for the only thing that would shield him. "Obviously, you don't know my name. It is *Dacre*."

Heath was stunned, though the expression on his face hid it well. *Did Lord bloody Dacre order the murder of Ram Douglas?* It was entirely possible. It was Thomas Dacre who had once arrested Ram and sent him to England to be hanged. Heath looked at Dacre's arrogant offspring with loathing, but he knew there was no way he could knife Dacre in the middle of Carlisle Fair and take back his property. "Obviously, you don't know *my* name," he retorted. *But you will before I'm done with you.* His gaze swept over Dacre with contempt, then he turned his back and walked away, with a devil-may-care swagger that was deliberately provoking.

It wasn't long before Heath spotted Raven Carleton near the Gypsy caravans. He smiled knowingly. There wasn't a female breathing who could resist having her fortune told. He tethered his horse and watched. He wasn't the least surprised to see Old Meg beckon the girl and take her inside the wagon.

The Gypsy sat gazing into her crystal ball while holding out her palm. When the girl placed a silver sixpence in her hand, Meg asked abruptly, "Are you a witch?"

"No, of course not," Raven replied honestly.

"I see a Celtic witch, a magic woman," Meg insisted.

"Ah, that would be my grandmother." Raven smiled. "She works spells and dispenses wisdom along with herbal remedies."

"You smile, when you should take her seriously. She has the ancient gifts and knowledge; she is a Diviner. You should ask *her* what you wish to know."

Raven shook her head. "She would bend me to her will."

Meg's shrewd gaze lingered on the girl before her. "She will try, as will others, but it will not be a woman, it will be a man who bends you to his will."

"A man? Can you tell me about my marriage?"

"Every female your age wants to know about marriage," Meg said dryly as she looked into the crystal ball. "You will marry well into great wealth and a title. But the path will be circuitous."

Lady Raven Dacre! The corners of Raven's mouth lifted in a smile. "I intend to lead him on a merry chase."

"A chase indeed," Meg replied, "but he will be the raptor; you the prey."

"Oh, you speak of raptors and prey because I train hunting birds! You really do have the sight!"

Meg stared at her. "You too have the sight. You just do not use it. Ask your grandmother."

"I shall! I intend to visit her soon." On a sudden impulse, Raven said, "I want to buy a Gypsy dress, can you help me?"

Heath watched as Old Meg took Raven to another caravan. In less than five minutes they emerged with the dark beauty carrying a small paper parcel. When his grandmother entered her own wagon, Heath visited the other caravan. "What did the girl want?" he asked the young Gypsy woman.

"I sold her a Gypsy dress." She opened her palm to show him the gold coin.

"You greedy jade!" Heath grinned. "A sovereign for one dress?"

She shrugged happily. "It was red. Red costs more!"

Heath was happy too, as he guessed that the Dacres must be hosting a masquerade ball at Carlisle Castle. All he needed was a costume and a mask! When he left the caravan, he searched for Raven. He saw her at a gaily colored booth, perusing its wares. Heath came up behind her silently. "You will meet a tall, dark, and handsome stranger who will steal your heart," he murmured low.

Raven whirled around angrily. His mocking words told her he had seen her with the Gypsies. "Tall, dark, and ugly, you mean!"

He looked at the merchandise offered for sale and saw that they were silk stockings. "I suggest the black . . . very seductive."

Raven turned her back upon him. "I will have a pair of the flesh-colored stockings, please." She waited for his insolent comment, and when none came, she glanced up over her shoulder. With relief, she realized that he had departed, and turned back to the vendor. "I've changed my mind. I'll take a pair of black, please."

As soon as dark descended, Heath made his way to Carlisle Castle. If his black stallion was grazing anywhere on the castle grounds, it would disappear tonight. He also reasoned that if Dacre was in possession of Blackadder, other animals from Douglas may have mysteriously found their way there. The broad meadow below Carlisle Castle was filled with horses. At first it seemed an impossible task to differentiate between a Douglas horse and any other, but Heath had worked with the animals for a month, and once he began to touch them, he recognized some of them. Moreover, the horses recognized him.

Heath, disappointed that his stallion was not grazing with the other horses, returned to the inn to concoct a plan. He already knew the ideal time would be the night of the ball, but he still had to decide how to get the herd back to Douglas, undetected.

Heath was not surprised to see Ramsay Douglas's two brothers, Gavin and Cameron, when he arrived back at the inn. Both captained Douglas vessels and had taken much-needed food supplies and fodder to Annan and its surrounding villages devastated by the recent raid, before anchoring in the River Eden at Carlisle. The minute Heath saw them, he knew they were the answer to his dilemma. He told them what he'd found at the castle, and outlined his plan.

"Lord Dacre would never raid a Douglas holding. He's Head Warden, sworn tae uphold the law. Are ye sure they're Douglas horses?" Cameron asked.

"Do we care?" asked a grinning Gavin, ready to reive anything that belonged to the English.

"I'd never steal anything that didn't belong to me," Heath swore solemnly, and watched the Douglas brothers fall off their stools laughing. "Tell your crew to get their carousing done tomorrow; they'll need to be sober the night after."

"Then we'd best get started!" Gavin declared.

"Do you have a Douglas dress plaid I can borrow? I need a costume," Heath explained.

"Yer never attending a bloody fancy-dress ball?" Cameron almost choked with mirth.

"We anchored next tae a Kennedy merchant ship. Ye'll likely run into yer father's wife at the party. Why don't ye wear a *Kennedy* plaid and shock the shit outa her ladyship?" Gavin said gleefully.

"I would never put Lady Elizabeth in the position of explaining one of Lord Kennedy's bastards," Heath said gallantly. Though he meant it, the Douglas brothers thought him most droll.

On Friday, as promised, Lancelot Carleton arrived at Carlisle Castle. When he greeted his second cousin, Lady Elizabeth Kennedy, he found her in a rather petulant mood. "Your son, Heron, has been monopolizing my daughter. He has deliberately elbowed Christopher Dacre aside each and every time that young man has tried to pay attention to Beth."

Lance Carleton tried not to laugh in Elizabeth's face. Young Dacre was the wrong sort of man to let anyone elbow him aside, and the only female to whom he was likely to pay attention was Raven. "Surely Rob will want a Scots noble for your daughter?"

"Over my dead body! Beth has too sweet and gentle a nature to be sacrificed to a coarse Scot. I have no intention of returning to Doon. Next week Beth and I plan to move into the old family home in the Rickergate, here in Carlisle."

"Elizabeth, I cannot believe you would jeopardize your marriage to the Lord of Galloway. It is unthinkable."

"It was unthinkable to have married him in the first place. Beth shall not be sacrificed as I was."

Lance Carleton was shocked. His second cousin Elizabeth had somehow managed to snare one of the wealthiest lairds of Clan Kennedy, so blood-proud they claimed they were descended from the Kings of Carrick, and the foolish female was now risking it all by setting herself against Rob Kennedy. It was like pitting a flea against a wily red fox.

In the afternoon, when Thomas Dacre and Lancelot Carleton were drinking whisky, the subject of betrothals came up. Dacre seemed open enough to consider Raven Carleton and her dowry, but he would not agree to a firm commitment between her and his son, Christopher.

"Your relative Elizabeth Kennedy makes no secret of the fact that she seeks a match between Christopher and her Beth," Dacre informed Carleton.

"Lizzie likely makes a secret of the fact that she has separated from Lord Kennedy, however." Carleton did not need to point out that Kennedy controlled the purse strings of his family; Dacre's mind was seldom far from money matters.

"I see," Thomas Dacre said thoughtfully. "Well, neither of us is in a hurry, Carleton. Next week, when we return to Bewcastle, I shall sound Christopher out about a future marriage with your lovely daughter Raven. In the meantime, the young people can enjoy getting to know each other better."

Sir Lancelot knew his wife, Kate, was hoping against hope that a betrothal would be finalized, so that it could be announced at tonight's ball. He tried to cushion her disappointment. "Kate, it's better this way. Dacre and his son return to Bewcastle next week, so it will give Raven more time. I want her to be sure about her feelings before a commitment is made."

"She *is* sure!"

"No, Kate, you are the one who is sure. You have made it clear you expect her to marry someone titled, and you have pushed her relentlessly toward Christopher Dacre."

Kate Carleton laughed. "Lance, if you think Raven can be *pushed* toward anything, you are deluding yourself. Raven will always do exactly as she pleases."

Before the Carleton ladies dressed for the ball, Kate sought out her daughters in the bedchamber they were sharing. "Your father is in negotiations with Lord Dacre for your betrothal, Raven. I have every reason to believe that we will hear wedding bells before the year is out." Kate touched the material of a gold tissue cape Raven had laid out on the bed. "Very pretty. I've been thinking that it has been a long time since you have visited with your grandmother. You have neglected her shamefully."

Raven's eyes widened. Her mother had been trying to wean her from her grandmother's influence for years. Then suddenly Raven realized her father hadn't been able to make Thomas Dacre commit to the betrothal yet, and that Christopher and his father were returning to Bewcastle. Raven hid a smile. Her mother was trying to manipulate her! "I shall do my duty and visit my grandmother next week. Would both of you like to come with me?"

An identical look of horror crossed her mother's face and her sister's at the same time. "You know we never saw eye to eye on anything in our lives! You are the one she loves, Raven."

Raven heaved an inward sigh of relief. She would have a free hand in bringing Christopher Dacre to his knees with a proposal! Dressing for tonight's masquerade, however, presented more of a problem. She had to put on the red Gypsy dress, then cover it with the gold tissue cape that would disguise her as a goddess to her family. "Lark, why don't I help you with your costume? Then you can go along and help Mother while I dress."

It took the best part of an hour to ready Lark for the ball. She had decided to be Princess Elizabeth of York, since she already owned a gown embroidered with white roses. It was her crown of silk roses that took up most of the time; it seemed to Raven that she would never succeed in anchoring it securely to her sister's fair tresses. Lark's eye mask was on the end of a wand, so she could wave it about; she looked more like a fairy princess than a real one.

"Lark, come along and help me with my Queen Guinevere costume. The steeple headdress needs more veiling attached, I believe," Kate Carleton declared, "but I shall take your advice in the matter."

The moment they left her chamber, Raven undressed, slipped into the red Gypsy dress, fastened golden hoops in her ears, then also decided to wear the black silk stockings. She carefully covered all with the golden cape and donned her gold-colored eye mask.

Tucked into the waistband of her dress were a couple of red paper poppies she had bought at the fair. She would put them in her hair later, once she summoned the courage to remove the gold cape and become an enticing Gypsy girl for the night. Raven couldn't wait to see the look on Christopher Dacre's face when he discovered her identity!

CHAPTER 5

Heath Kennedy, garbed in a Douglas dress plaid, tore a strip from his old Douglas plaid, cut two eye slits in it, and fastened it across his eyes as a mask. The short kilt rode on his hipbones, exposing muscular thighs. He wore no shirt but instead draped the dark green and blue plaid across one broad, bare shoulder and tucked it into his belt along with his knife and his dirk.

Heath deliberately arrived late at the ball so that a good crowd would be gathered and he would not receive too close a scrutiny. He had reckoned without the young ladies, however. Word spread amongst them like wildfire that one of the handsome and powerful Douglas lairds was in attendance. They gathered in a group and followed him at a discreet distance, whispering and giggling.

Heath strode over to them and bowed before Beth Kennedy. "May I have this dance, mistress?" He saw the look of dismay on his half-sister's face, so before she could refuse, he swept her into a reel. "It's me, Heath," he said low when they came together.

"Heath Kennedy, I cannot imagine *your* being invited here."

He grinned. "I'll bet you are relieved I'm not a Douglas."

"In truth, I am," Beth admitted ingenuously. "I shall never know how my sister Valentina found the courage to marry Ramsay Douglas. He frightens me to death!"

"Valentina does have an overabundance of courage, and a good thing too. She's about to have twins."

Beth went pale. "Oh dear, please tell her how sorry I am."

"Sorry? She and Ram are celebrating this as if it were a gift from the gods. Anyway, you can let our father know. He'll be like a dog with two tails. He already thinks the sun shines out of Tina's arse, so this will put a halo round her head too."

When Beth didn't reprove him for his coarseness, he knew something was wrong. "What's amiss, lass?"

"I cannot tell Father; Mother has left him," she whispered. "She wants me to marry an Englishman, and he won't tolerate such a thing. We are moving into her family's town house next week."

"Whom does Elizabeth have in mind for you?"

"Christopher Dacre," Beth whispered again. "He frightens me as much as the Douglases."

Heath Kennedy wanted to choke his father's wife. Dacre's heir was no fit match for his sheltered half-sister. Chris Dacre would take her dowry, then wipe his feet on the passive girl as if she were a doormat. "Under no circumstances must you allow your mother to push you into a betrothal. You must assert yourself as Tina has always done. You need a backbone, not a wishbone, Beth."

"There *is* someone here I like," Beth confided with a blush. "His name is Heron Carleton; he took me to the fair." Her hand covered her mouth quickly, as if she had said something wicked.

Heath was surprised. She was talking about Raven's brother. It was a small world! "Sir Lance Carleton, who used to be constable here, is related to your mother. Though English, he's a man of honor and integrity. If you want Heron Carleton, go after him!"

Heath felt a tap on his bare shoulder, and looked through the mask and into the eyes of the man cutting in. It was Christopher Dacre. Since the dance had ended and partners were being sought for the next reel, Heath relinquished Beth without a word.

From across the ballroom, Raven Carleton watched in amazement as the two handsomest men at the masquerade flanked Beth Kennedy. The Douglas laird was giving up the girl to Christopher Dacre. Raven immediately decided it was time to ditch the gold tissue cape. She removed it, scrunched it up, and stuffed it behind a potted plant. She left the gilded mask in place, then took the red poppies from her waistband and set one behind each ear. Raven was intent upon securing the notice of Christopher Dacre.

Heath Kennedy, who had been watching for the red Gypsy

dress, spotted Raven immediately. He stalked around the perimeter of the ballroom until he stood before her. "May I partner you, mistress?"

His deep voice did strange things to Raven's pulse. Rather than refusing him, she quickly decided that the magnificent Scots laird might stir Chris Dacre's jealousy. "You may, my lord."

Heath took a firm hold of her hand and led her out of the ballroom onto a stone terrace.

She felt a hint of danger. "What are you doing?"

"I asked if I might partner you," he pointed out, tightening his hold upon her hand. "I said nothing about a dance."

"Partner you in what?" she demanded, masking her apprehension.

"A little dalliance. A *real* Gypsy girl wouldn't object; a *real* Gypsy girl would have fire in her blood." With the toe of his boot he lifted her skirt to reveal the black silk stockings and winked.

"You may be a Douglas lord, but you are no gentleman! I shall scream for my father if you don't let go of me immediately!"

Heath's white teeth flashed in a grin. "I don't believe you will, Raven. The last thing you want is for your parents to find you dressed as a Gypsy harlot."

The moment he said her name, she recognized who it was. "It's *you*, you devil!" She also knew he had her trapped. "What do you want, Douglas?"

"Pay a simple forfeit and I'll let you go."

Raven tossed back her hair, pulled a scarlet poppy from behind her ear, and held it out to him.

Lust shot through him swiftly as a sword thrust. "If the males of your acquaintance are satisfied with paper flowers, it is time you learned what a real man desires." He swept her into his arms and took possession of her lips in a long, slow kiss that was deliberately seductive.

Raven began to struggle, then stopped. How else was she to learn what a real man desired? His hot mouth branded her as if he were claiming her as his own, now and forever. When he removed his arms and his mouth from her, she felt light-headed, slightly dizzy, and a little disoriented. She swayed imperceptibly, then drew back her hand and slapped his insolent face. "The first time we met, you left me half naked; tonight you have the temerity to manhandle me, you Douglas dog!"

Heath saw her lavender-blue eyes glittering through the mask. "The name is *Kennedy*, sweetheart, and I want you to never forget it. Next time we meet, I promise to do something even more outrageous!" He vaulted over the stone balustrade and was swallowed by the misty darkness.

Raven gasped. The wicked devil wore nothing beneath his kilt! *He said his name is Kennedy; does that mean he's Beth Kennedy's brother?* she wondered. *Nay, there are probably hundreds of Kennedys.* Raven wondered why she hadn't recognized him immediately as the Borderer who had stolen Sully. She concluded that since she had been told he was a Douglas laird, she had believed it. She shivered. She knew he was dangerous and that she was lucky to be rid of him. She went back into the ballroom on trembling legs and came face to face with Christopher Dacre.

His glance took in the tawdry dress. "Don't think you can sneak in here through the balcony doors."

Raven was delighted that he didn't recognize her. "You don't know who I am?"

"You're the Gypsy wench I bought for Heron Carleton last night! This is a respectable gathering; take yourself off."

Raven was momentarily shocked, then thought perhaps he was only teasing her. "Christopher, you do know me, don't you?" she asked tentatively. "It's me . . . Raven!"

A silent moment passed, then Chris Dacre said, "What the hell are you doing dressed like a Gypsy wench? Go and change before someone recognizes you, Raven."

Her chin went up. "I don't take kindly to orders, sir."

Dacre knew he had blundered. "I'm sorry for speaking to you so brusquely, Raven. You are too innocent to realize that this costume could sully your reputation."

Not quite as innocent as you suppose, Raven reflected ruefully. She sighed with resignation. She had only chosen the costume to please Christopher, but since he was clearly *dis*pleased, she might as well give up the idea of being a Gypsy girl. She took the red flowers from her hair and went to retrieve her gold tissue cape from its hiding place. When she saw that Christopher followed her, suddenly her self-confidence returned. "Perhaps you had better go and dance with Beth Kennedy," she taunted.

He fastened the gold cape about her. "I don't want to be with Beth Kennedy, I want to be with you, Raven. Do you know how exciting it is to know that beneath this demure cloak, you are wearing a scarlet Gypsy dress?"

"And beneath that I am wearing black silk stockings? No, I haven't the faintest notion how exciting that is," she teased.

"Then let me take you out on the balcony and show you."

"And risk sullying my reputation? I think not, sir." Though Raven secretly wanted Christopher Dacre to kiss her so that she could compare it with the kiss of the bold Borderer, she was woman enough to know it would be far better to hold him off with one hand while beckoning him with the other. She was in no hurry.

Heath Kennedy returned to the place where he had left his mount, then made his way to where the castle horses were grazing in the broad meadow beyond the walls. His considerable equine affinity had taught him that, like people, horses were clannish. They preferred to gather together in their own herd, which would make tonight's work much easier. He imitated the nasal call of a nightjar and was relieved when he received an answering *peeyah* that told him the Douglas brothers and their crew were waiting.

Heath herded the horses, thankful that the mist and the darkness would conceal all from the eyes of the sentries on the wall. When he reached the men, he did not need to tell them that stealth and speed were necessary. The horses' hooves were silent on the mossy turf as they drove the animals westward toward Carlisle city's Irish Gate. He did not ask whether the Douglases had bribed the guards on the gate or merely rendered them unconscious. All he cared about was getting the horses out of the walled city without setting off a cry of alarm.

The posse herded the animals toward the bluffs that rose above the River Eden, then drove them through a cut in the sandstone to where the two Douglas vessels lay at anchor. The other half of the crew were awaiting them, and in a short time had the horses in the holds and were able to weigh anchor and head toward Solway Firth.

It took only an hour's sail to reach Annan, and before the red fingers of dawn reached up the sky, the horses had been taken off the ships, none the worse for their short sea journey. Gavin and Cameron Douglas were jubilant at the success of the operation, and Heath's only regret was that his black stallion was still in Christopher Dacre's possession. *That won't be for long!* he vowed.

Gavin Douglas opted to accompany Heath and the herd to Eskdale, while Cameron Douglas would take the ships west and up the River Dee to Castle Douglas, their Border fortress, where Ramsay moored his vessel, the *Revenge*.

When Heath returned with the herd of horses he'd been working with for over a month, Ramsay Douglas shook his head in disbelief. "Where the hellfire did ye find them?"

"Carlisle Castle."

"Bones of Christ! I should have known Dacre was behind this."

"I caught Dacre's son red-handed riding Blackadder. My stallion is the only one I couldn't retrieve."

"How the devil did ye manage?" Ram asked.

"I had help. Gavin and Cameron loaded them aboard their ships and we sailed across the Solway to Annan," Heath explained.

Just then, Gavin rode up grinning from ear to ear and slid from his saddle. Ram looked from one to the other and shook his head again. "Ye're enough alike tae be twins. I warrant there's some truth tae the rumor that Angus was yer grandsire."

"Speaking of twins, has Tina made us uncles yet?" Heath asked.

Ram shook his head. "I've not left her side. Sometimes I think she'll never foal."

Gavin laughed. "I would never have credited it if I hadna seen it with my own eyes—Black Ram Douglas domesticated, begod!"

"Your turn will come, laddie," Heath taunted.

Ram grinned. "He'll never be that lucky. He hasn't the faintest notion what he's missing, poor sod. I have a woman in a million! Tina makes me whole, complete; she fills me with life."

Gavin winked at Heath. "His brain's gone soft. 'Tis the other way about—he filled *her* with life."

"We've the best blood in Scotland, 'tis time tae start doubling it, and if ye've no guts fer marriage, I'll do the job myself, two at a time," Ram jested.

Heath envied Ramsay his marriage, if Gavin did not. He longed for a family of his own, but he resolutely thrust the thought of a wife away, thinking it impossible because of the two great obstacles in his path: Gypsy blood and bastardy.

Heath found his sister Tina reclining against cushions on the window seat overlooking the small lake behind Eskdale Castle. She was raptly watching a pair of swans that had arrived two days ago. As she glanced up, Heath saw her aura clearly against the mullioned windows and was glad that it was both vibrant and clear.

"I wish I could find a way to persuade the swans to stay. We've had them before upon occasion, but they always fly away."

"We could catch them and clip their wings. If they laid eggs and they hatched here, perhaps the cygnets would stay," Heath said.

"I would never clip anything's wings."

Heath smiled warmly. "I didn't think so." He straddled a chair so that he could talk to her. "I spoke with Beth last night."

"Beth? Where on earth did you run into her?"

"As a matter of fact, I danced with her at a masquerade ball in Carlisle Castle, and I swear I'm not making this up."

Tina's eyes sparkled with amusement. "I'll believe you; thousands wouldn't!"

Mr. Burque, Tina's French chef, joined them, bringing a cup of chocolate for the mother-to-be. He was accompanied by Ada, who carried a lap robe to tuck about Tina. Heath continued his story, for the four of them kept no secrets from each other. "Beth told me that your mother has left our father and intends to live in the Rickergate house in Carlisle."

"Well, I'll be damned! How did she ever summon the guts to leave him? If there ever was a crisis when I lived at home, Mother took to her bed and left all in my lap."

Ada's glance swept over Tina's middle. "No pun intended."

"Apparently, Lady Elizabeth wants an Englishman for Beth. I can only imagine the shouting and brawling to which our charming father subjected her," Heath said.

Tina dimpled with amusement and sipped her chocolate with relish. "Does she have a particular Englishman in mind?"

"Thomas Dacre's heir, Christopher."

"Blood of God!" Tina exclaimed.

"The crumb de la crumb!" Mr. Burque declared succinctly.

"My mother must be mad. She must know Dacre will forever be my enemy for what he did to Ram!"

Ada said shrewdly, "I know why your mother wants Dacre's son for Beth. She thought Thomas Dacre would ask her to wed him, but instead he carried off Rosalind Greystokes. Elizabeth wed Rob Kennedy just to show everyone she could catch a wealthy husband with a title. You need not worry about Beth. Your father controls the purse strings, and without a dowry for bait, Elizabeth won't hook a Dacre for your sister."

"And a damn good thing. Young Dacre is no fit mate for Beth," Heath said grimly. "Beth confided to me that she fancies young Heron Carleton, whose father used to be constable of Carlisle Castle. I told her to go after him."

"You are the best brother in the world; I am so blessed."

Heath suddenly felt anger on Valentina's behalf. "Your mother should be here with *you* at this time, not suckholing up to Dacre!"

"Blood of God, I don't want my mother descending upon me like a biblical plague. Ada here is worth a thousand Elizabeths."

Ada winked. "That's what your father used to tell me! God's passion, Tina, you're just like him."

The four doubled up with laughter, for Rob Kennedy had often said to Tina, "God's passion, but ye get more like me every day."

"Perhaps Father was right; he always ate enough for three, and now I'm doing the same. What's for dinner, Mr. Burque?"

"Lamb on skewers, the very thing to induce labor, chérie."

"I hope and pray you mean by eating them, Mr. Burque, and not by using them as probes," Ada said with a straight face.

Tina, laughing, held her belly. "You are so droll, Ada. If you don't cease and desist, I shall give birth by mirth."

"Save me some food, Mr. Burque. I intend to start branding the horses I managed to retrieve."

"Good. D for Douglas!" Tina saluted with her chocolate.

"D for Douglas, or D for death to any who dare reive them ever again," Heath vowed savagely.

It took two days to brand all the horses. On the third day Heath packed his saddlebags for another journey. When Ram Douglas cocked a dark eyebrow at him, Heath simply replied, "Unfinished business."

"There's no need tae range alone like a wolf. Ye'll be safer with a dozen moss-troopers at yer back."

"I'm only going fishing."

Ram eyed the sword that Heath was wearing. It was one he had won from him in a dice game. "Fishing with a sword?"

"Very handy for gutting and filleting. If I don't return, you can start the search for me at Bewcastle."

"In the dungeon or the graveyard?" Ram asked tersely.

"If I'm not in one, odds are I'll be in the other."

"Dacre could have bought the horses legitimately."

"You and I are both too cynical to believe that," Heath said evenly. He touched his knees to the roan gelding and cantered off.

Heath rode the dozen miles to Mangerton at a steady pace, then he slowed the roan to a walk and examined the town, building by building, farm by farm, and concluded that poverty was widespread

in the area. He scrutinized the face of every individual he encountered, then he bought a drink at the alehouse and kept his ears open
for the name of Mangey. When he made casual inquiries, the people
looked afraid. It took most of the day, but he finally learned that a
Border clan named Armstrong, outlawed by the late king of Scotland,
terrorized the area. When the Armstrongs had been put to the horn,
they had become vicious marauders and turned against their own.

Heath rode through the fields on the outskirts of Mangerton
looking for signs of a camp. A spiral of smoke above the trees drew
him to the edge of the forest. Beneath the oaks he spotted four mares
and knew immediately they were his. Caution told him to go no
closer. He crushed down curiosity about the men, because it didn't
matter whether there were four or forty within the forest; once darkness fell, Heath intended to retrieve his breeding mares.

He looked up at the sky to gauge the time, and knew it was late
afternoon because the sun was already setting. He retreated about a
mile until he found a stream, then he followed it into the forest, dismounted, and watered his roan. He took a bag of fodder for his
mount from his saddlebags, then with his back against the bole of a
tree, he sat down to eat a couple of oatcakes.

Heath reflected on the men in the forest. Most likely they were
Armstrongs, and the evidence of their being in possession of his
mares condemned them as being the scum who had been paid to
murder Ramsay Douglas. He knew he lusted for their death, but
struggled with his need for revenge, telling himself it was a luxury he
could not indulge this night. Reclaiming his mares must take precedence over vengeance.

The time dragged interminably for Heath, who knew he had to
wait beyond darkness, until the raiders slept. The night was unusu-
ally warm, and the water of the stream was a potent lure; finally he
gave in to the temptation. He unbuckled his sword and laid it on
the ground, then he removed his clothes and dropped them atop
the weapon. He waded into the water, which came to his knees. It
wasn't deep enough for him to swim, but he knelt down and dipped
his head in, then let the refreshing water trickle down his body. It
felt so good, Heath repeated the motion, but this time when he

lifted his head from the water, he was stunned to see four dark, burly Borderers staring at him. Their ugly faces were sickeningly familiar.

Their look of disbelief was accompanied by muttered exchanges. "Christ almighty, Mangey's gone tae collect the money!"

"Don't panic. We'll kill 'im now. Same difference."

Heath cursed himself for a careless fool. Never had his instincts let him down so badly before. The quartet stood between him and his clothes. He decided there would be no more attempts to drown him, so he stood up to his full height. The water cascaded down his limbs, leaving his dark skin glistening as he walked warily from the stream.

"So, Douglas, ye escaped a watery grave."

"The name is Kennedy. I assume yours is Armstrong!"

They exchanged uncomfortable glances.

"Where is Mangey Armstrong?" Heath asked, seemingly oblivious of his naked, dripping-wet state.

One of the outlaws grimaced with glee. "He's selling some of your firkin' mares at Kelso horse fair. We'll save you for 'im."

"Tae lowest hell wi' Mangey," another Armstrong said. "That pleasure is mine, 'ere and now." The shaggy-headed brute drew his lips back to expose rotting teeth. "What's more, I'm gonna kill him wi' his own knife!"

CHAPTER 6

Seemingly, Heath stood mesmerized as the outlaw drew the long knife from his belt, but in truth his rippling muscles were tensing in readiness for the onslaught.

The brute eyed Heath's cock and balls. "I think I'll do a wee bit o' trimmin' before I finish him off. Let's have some fun."

Heath knew that all he had was a split second before three of them grabbed him and held him down. He rushed at them and rolled to the ground within reach of his discarded clothing. Not quick enough to escape a slash from the knife, but at least the cut was across his shoulder and not his groin.

As Heath grabbed his sword from beneath his pile of clothes, his lust for revenge returned with a rush. His first target was the lout who was in possession of his own knife. Heath blocked the brute's plunging arm with his own solid forearm, then thrust the sword into the Borderer's gut and withdrew it quickly. He raised the bloody sword over his head, swinging it in a deadly circle to keep the other three at bay. The trio had no weapons; Heath's knife, which lay beside the dying man, was out of their reach.

They backed off slightly from the naked, sword-wielding figure, but it was apparent they still believed that three could take him. Heath concluded they hadn't the brains of lice. He selected a target and lunged swiftly, taking his enemy in the throat. He swung about and grabbed another by his leather vest, holding the point of his sword beneath the man's chin. The third man took to his heels as if the Grim Reaper were after him.

"Who ordered you to murder Lord Ramsay Douglas?" Heath demanded.

"I dinna ken . . . Mangey knows."

Heath shoved the point of his sword into the man's gullet, just deep enough to draw a trickle of blood. "You said he had gone for the money. Did he go to Bewcastle? Was it Dacre?"

"Dacre?" the reiver repeated slowly, as if such a possibility had never occurred to him until now. "Nay, he went north to Kelso. Mangey's our leader, he's the only one who knows. He does the negotiatin' an' handles the money."

Heath ordered, "On your knees, with your arms behind you." When the thick-set marauder obliged, Heath took the leather thong from his tied-back hair and tightly bound the man's wrists. He stepped over to the two men on the ground and saw that they were dead. Only then did he take the time to put his clothes back on and pick up his favorite knife, with the pentagram etched into its blade. With his sword, he prodded the man to his feet, then took the reins of his roan, and they set off to where the raiders had made camp.

It was dark by the time they arrived, and the embers of the fire were barely smoldering. Heath took a rope from his saddle and securely tied his prisoner to an oak. Then he inspected and watered his mares. He concluded that they were thinner and had been neglected. Likely they hadn't seen an oat since they'd left Eskdale, but the grass had kept them from starving.

The reivers had been roasting a haunch of mutton from a ewe they had stolen, but the stink of the rancid fat almost turned Heath's stomach. He tossed it into the trees, built up the fire, and sat down to plan. He had been forced to kill two men in self-defense and was honest enough to regret that his prisoner also had not died in the fight. The ugly brute was little use to him, yet he could not bring himself to knife a man in cold blood. Heath wanted Mangey Armstrong. Badly. Perhaps all he need do was wait for him to return from Kelso, which was only about thirty miles from Mangerton. Heath decided to wait another day and if Mangey didn't show up by then, he would move on to Bewcastle.

———

At Rockcliffe, Raven Carleton was about to depart for Blackpool Gate to visit her grandmother, Dame Doris Heron. Her brother was accompanying her as far as Stapleton, approximately a dozen miles from Rockcliffe, to help her deliver two hunting birds that she had trained for a friend of her father. But Heron refused to escort her the short distance from Stapleton to their grandmother's, fearing he would be coerced into visiting "the old crone."

Since Raven didn't know how long her visit would be, she also decided to take her two falcons whose training wasn't yet complete. Sultan and Sheba were a pair of valuable peregrines who needed daily attention. She had recently acquired two new merlins, both as yet untrained, but decided this pair could be left at Rockcliffe in the care of the young falconer.

Raven's mother had a private word with her daughter before she departed. "I know you will be spending time with Christopher Dacre and will most likely be invited to Bewcastle. You are a clever girl, Raven; make the most of this opportunity." Kate Heron's tone lightened as she said, "Don't you dare come home until you catch a husband." Though Raven and her mother laughed, both knew she was serious.

Doris Heron was aware that her favorite granddaughter was coming, for that morning a raven had flown to the rowan tree in her garden. It had not come for the bright red berries, for ravens were meat-eaters; therefore she knew it was an omen.

Dame Doris came out of her large stone house to greet her granddaughter. "Raven, my lovely, I knew you were coming."

"Grandmother, I've come for a good long visit. I brought Sultan and Sheba so I can continue their training." Raven dismounted from Sully and lifted two small wooden carrying crates from the pack animal that also carried her luggage.

"Bring them into the stillroom and set them on the perch."

The women entered through the arched doorway, then Raven

removed the falcons from their crates and fastened their jesses to the old perch. "I'll leave their hoods on until they settle."

A large hare sped from the stillroom as soon as he sensed the raptors, and Raven laughed at her grandmother's familiar. "Magick, you must weigh over two stone; my raptors cannot carry you off!"

"Nay, but he knows they would peck out his eye for a delicacy." Dame Heron followed her hare from the stillroom and lifted Raven's bags from the packhorse. Then she called to a lad who was throwing pebbles into the pond and bade him take Sully and the other pony to the stable. "Come and we'll sip some heather mead and have a natter."

"I'll carry my luggage, Grandmother."

"Cheeky young jade, d'ye imagine I'm past it? I can carry you *and* yer bags if I have a mind to!"

"I know you can do anything," Raven acknowledged.

"And so can you—you've the power, my lovely, if you will only learn to use it!" Doris set down the bags in the vaulted living room, then poured her homemade mead into pewter goblets, and Raven sipped it with appreciation, tasting the honey and the smoky-flavored heather. She didn't know it also contained a small amount of rue, which loosened the tongue.

"Tell me, Raven, has your fancy settled on anyone yet?"

"Perhaps it has."

"He's a Borderer, I hope. I want a *real* man for you, Raven."

"I'd rather be flayed alive," Raven said laughing. "I'd be dead of disgust in a week!"

"Better someone wild and fascinating like a mountain ram than someone tame and uninteresting like a craven lapdog." Doris gave her a speculative glance. "Have you found yourself a hag stone yet? The one I gave you as a child won't do; you must find your own to give you great positive power."

Raven hesitated for a moment, then admitted, "Yes, I did find a hag stone." She pulled the stone with the natural hole through it from her pocket and held it out on the palm of her hand. When she had found it, she had hidden it because it seemed silly, but here with her grandmother, there seemed nothing frivolous about it.

"You are old enough to know that the hole in the hag stone is a symbol of your female genitals."

"Is that why it has no power for a man?"

Doris chuckled. "A male needs a phallic-shaped stone, called a god stone." She saw Raven blush and smiled knowingly. "Hold your hag stone to your breast, close your eyes, breathe deeply, and center yourself." She watched with approval as Raven obeyed her. "Now blend with the stone. Feel its heartbeat. Feel its strength and attune yourself with its special life force. It has the power to heal. Never forget to give thanks for its energy and power."

"I really do feel it," Raven said with wonder.

"Over the years, I have taught you all I know of herbs, because you were so adept at learning. Now I shall teach you how to combine herbs' properties with the power of the Craft, to make you invincible as a healer."

"You mean witchcraft?" Raven asked solemnly.

"I never use that word; it is simply the Craft. A Solitary who practices the Craft has such an empathy with nature that she becomes at one with it. You must have a reverence for the sun, the moon, the wind, the rain, the earth, and the sea. Fire, rock, earth, water, thunder—all have energy and power within them that can be harnessed. I believe you have an old soul, Raven. Your soul talks to you; you must learn to listen."

Raven wondered why her family, and her mother in particular, thought Dame Doris babbled nonsense. To Raven, the things her grandmother said made perfect sense.

Doris drained her goblet of mead. "Sufficient for today. Tomorrow, if you like, we can do a ritual."

Raven lifted her goblet in a salute. "I would like that above all things, Grandmother."

When they awoke, early the next morning, it was raining, and Raven, wearing only her shift, followed her grandmother outside. Both were barefoot and they sank their feet into the loose earth of the herb garden, and lifted their arms and faces so that the soft rain could cleanse their spirits and their bodies. The fragrance of mint, mingling with the scent of thyme and rosemary, was heavy in the damp air, and Raven drank in the perfume until her senses swam. She had done these things with her grandmother since she was a little girl, and she found nothing strange in the ritual. She had been taught to revere every plant, insect, and animal, and knew this was the reason she had such an affinity with birds.

In the afternoon when the rain ceased and the sun came out, Raven flew Sultan and Sheba at the edge of Kershope Forest. The falcons explored the vastness of the strange new territory, flying so high they were almost invisible. Raven envied them their ability to fly. She was passionate about her freedom and longed to wheel about the sky. It was a physical impossibility, yet not a spiritual one if she allowed her soul to fly free. Raven was relieved when her beautiful raptors returned, for it was a testament to her training that they were not lured to fly away. She returned them to the stillroom but did not hood them.

Raven took Sully into the stable and had a visit with her uncle Johnnie Heron, her mother's brother, who had a farm adjoining her mother's land and tended her stable. He was a born and bred Borderer to his bones, teasing the life out of Raven, making her laugh until her sides ached.

That night it was a new moon, and Dame Doris decided the time was ripe to initiate Raven into the Craft. She laid out a diaphanous robe of pale lavender with silver threads for her granddaughter. She placed homemade incense into a pewter bowl, then she gathered together the consecrated tools needed to perform a magic ritual. Finally she opened the window as a portal for the spirits of the other world.

Raven donned the robe, aware that her naked limbs were quite visible through the transparent material. She knew that colors had their own power within them. Red was for war and revenge, blue was for fertility and creativity, and silver-lavender was for visions and magic divination. She watched her grandmother roll up the rug to reveal a large circle chalked upon the flagstone floor. Within the circle was a pentagram, or five-pointed star. Raven placed her hand into her grandmother's, took a deep breath, and together they stepped inside the magic circle.

First, Dame Doris lit four golden-yellow candles, but left one purple and two green candles unlit. There also was power in numbers, seven being the most mystical. Then she set the lit taper to the pewter bowl's incense, which was made from pine resin and catnip flowers, sprinkled with milfoil, or yarrow as it was commonly known. She positioned Raven so that the moon was visible through the open window and instructed, "Repeat after me:

> *When I see the new moon*
> *It becomes me to lift mine eye,*
> *It becomes me to bend my knee,*
> *It becomes me to bow my head,*
> *Giving praise, thou moon of guidance."*

Raven intoned the words her grandmother gave her, then waited for further instructions.

"Now pour the milk into the hollow stone and make an oblation to Hecate, the goddess of the dark side of the moon."

Carefully, Raven poured the ewe's milk into the elliptical stone of red agate and watched in wonder as it seemed to turn pink. "Do not repress your subconscious, Raven. The moon rules the subconscious instincts, feelings, dreams, and intuition. It represents the unknown, mystic, hidden aspects of nature, and will shed light on the unforeseen and give you insight to your secret enemies. Open, Raven, like a night-blooming convolvulus."

Raven closed her eyes and breathed deeply, evenly, attempting to open her mind and her spirit to the natural forces of the universe. She opened her eyes quickly when she felt something touch her head, but saw that it was her grandmother's staff. Then Raven felt a rush of energy enter at her crown and flow down her body, until the soles of her feet tingled. Her robe fluttered about her naked limbs, and the curtains at the open window blew about as if taken by a gust of wind. Then, suddenly, all was still.

"The green candles represent love and marriage, the purple is your heart's desire. Light first the green, contemplating upon whom you want for your husband, then light the purple and envision your heart's desire."

Raven took the taper from the burning incense and lit the first green candle. In her mind's eye, she conjured a picture of Christopher Dacre, tall and fair, then set the taper to the second green candle. A picture of the Borderer who had called himself Kennedy came unbidden into her head. His dark visage and long black hair were in stark contrast to the other man. Raven quickly denied him. "No!" But as if he would not be denied, the flame of the first green candle sputtered and died, while that of the second green candle elongated and flamed high. She quickly relit the candle that had been snuffed out and concentrated upon the vision of Christopher Dacre. When her focus was firmly fixed upon him, she lit the purple candle.

Raven had a vision of a falcon like Sultan. The raptor swooped about her in a great circle, then flew up close to the rafters. She caught her breath as she saw a black raven flee from the hunter, but knew the falcon would catch its prey. The great hawk, however, did not kill the smaller bird, but forced it to fly in unison. Raven stood spellbound, watching them until they flew off together, through the window, into the night.

Dame Doris set down her staff and took up a small dagger. She kissed its double-edged blade and presented its haft to Raven. "Once you have drawn your own blood with this dagger, it will belong to you and no other. Always cut your healing herbs with this knife," she instructed. "May it serve you well."

Raven hesitated for only a moment, then took possession of the black-handled dagger, made a shallow cut in her fingertip, and let the crimson drops of blood run down its blade. *It is done, for better or for worse*, Raven thought. She had been inducted into the Craft. She wet her fingers with her tongue and snuffed out the seven candle flames. Then she took salt, a final offering to the goddess, and poured it upon the incense to stop it from smoldering. She remembered to thank the deity, and together the two females stepped from the magic circle.

"Did you experience a vision, my lovely?"

"I had *two* visions," Raven said with awe.

"When you lit the green candles, you saw the man you would love and marry," Dame Doris said knowingly.

"I did. I saw Christopher Dacre, heir to Lord Thomas Dacre, Head Border Warden, whom King Henry appointed."

"Dacre." Doris Heron repeated the name without approval or disapproval. "The young man plays a leading role in your future."

Raven dimpled. "I know. He will come shortly to visit me. And if—no, I mean *when*—he invites me to Bewcastle, I shall go!"

"Good. You need more experience with men; you have been far too sheltered. You have the capacity for great power, Raven, but always remember that a woman's greatest power lies within her sexuality. Never be afraid to explore it, to utilize it. At the moment, you have an innocent sexuality that attracts and tantalizes the male. But as you gain sexual experience, you will be able to attain ascendancy over any mere male." Doris watched her granddaughter's face closely. "What happened when you lit the purple candle?"

"I had a second vision. You know that my heart's desire is training hunting birds. . . . I saw a falcon and a raven flying together. The raven was obviously me. Though my mother strongly disapproves of my training hawks, I now know I am doing the right thing by following my heart!"

"Your heart is the doorway to your soul, my lovely. But always remember that your soul has the final say, not your heart. When your soul talks to you, you must listen."

Raven laughed as she saw her grandmother's hare cautiously emerge from his hiding place. "Did you experience the vision too, Magick?" The furry creature hopped across the floor and sniffed at a black object lying on the flagstones. "It's a feather, a raven's feather! If it was only a vision, how did this get here?" Raven picked it up, then gazed at her grandmother for an explanation.

"The goddess left you a token, a talisman. Objects such as feathers, shells, or horns that come from living creatures have great energy and power within them."

Raven laughed with delight. "I shall sleep with it beneath my pillow tonight, so my dreams will be filled with magic."

It was a long time before sleep claimed Raven, because her mind played over and over the ritual she had performed with her grandmother. She relived every detail, every word, every image, trying to divine their symbolic meanings. She asked herself why on earth the vision of the dark Borderer had intruded when she was focusing her full attention upon Christopher Dacre. Raven felt extremely vexed that the bold devil had insinuated himself into her ritual. He seemed to represent a vague threat, and she vowed to banish him from her consciousness. Gradually she slipped into slumber, yet the images remained.

She was in a castle tower room with Christopher Dacre. She was wearing her brother's shirt. Dacre blew out the candles and took her in his arms. She pulled away, coyly, and relit the candles. "You go too fast, Christopher. We should not be alone together in a bedchamber."

"How else can we get to know each other . . . intimately?" Once again he took her in his arms and looked down at her lips hungrily. Then he blew out the candles and claimed her mouth.

Raven did not resist the kiss, but surrendered her lips up to him, yielding to his masterful arms and mouth, determined to explore her sexuality. Suddenly the candles relit themselves, their flames elongating brightly, and she opened her eyes to look up into the warm, hazel-brown eyes of the Borderer who had called himself Kennedy. He was bare to the waist and she recoiled from his nakedness. "You! How dare you?"

"You enjoyed the kiss immensely, Raven. You cannot deny it!"

"It was Christopher Dacre's kiss I enjoyed, you arrogant swine!"

"You are dreaming, Raven."

"I know I am dreaming, you devil!"

"Do you imagine I would allow Dacre to kiss you, fondle you?"

"Allow? YOU allow?" she demanded scornfully, masking her fear. "I am the one who will allow Chris Dacre to woo me. We are betrothed!"

"I am the one who will woo you, Raven, and if you resist, it will be a bloody rough wooing!" To prove his words, he snatched her into his arms and took total possession of her mouth and her senses. He lifted her and carried her to the bed. Though she struggled valiantly against him, it was in vain. "Cover yourself!" she demanded in outrage. He wore only a kilt and she knew that beneath it he wore nothing whatsoever. Unbelievably, she felt

him unbutton her shirt and remove it. Then he pulled her down into his arms, cushioning her breasts upon his broad chest.

"There is something else I lust for, my proud beauty. I demand a forfeit." He held her against him possessively and slid his hand up her skirt to caress her bare leg.

Desperately, Raven reached beneath the pillow and pulled out the black feather. She watched in amazement as the dark Borderer accepted it, and sagged with relief. Yet she sighed with longing as his image began to dissolve, then moved restlessly in her sleep. Her palm cupped her full breast where the hand of the Borderer had touched her so possessively only a moment before.

When Raven opened her eyes in the morning, the dream was still with her. She was incensed that the bold Borderer had invaded her dream. The thought of him touching her, being in the bed with her, provoked a feeling of fury inside her, even though she had only been dreaming. It seemed so real that she reached beneath her pillow for the raven's feather. When her hand felt nothing there, she lifted her pillow and saw that it was gone. She desperately searched the bed with trembling hands, but the black feather was nowhere in evidence. Raven pressed her lips together angrily and vowed that from now on she would sleep with her dagger beneath her pillow, rather than a useless feather that she had imagined had magic properties. Then she convinced herself that the feather had never even existed. She tossed her disheveled hair back over her shoulders defiantly and swore that the black feather had simply been a figment of her vivid imagination.

CHAPTER 7

Heath Kennedy dozed fitfully throughout the night. Though the sting from the gash in his shoulder kept him from sleep, the shallow wound did not worry him. He knew that once the bleeding stopped, it would heal well enough. At dawn he heard a rustle in the bushes and with great stealth crept to investigate. It was a fox drawn by the smell of the rancid mutton he had thrown into the trees. He unsheathed his knife and pounced, swiftly dispatching the carnivore that would be his food supply for the next two days. He decided to keep the fox pelt. It would produce a fine silver fur once it had been thoroughly cleaned and dried.

Heath built up the fire and spitted the carcass to roast, then he searched for some burdock leaves to cleanse his wound and ease the sting of the knife blade. He was aware of his prisoner's resentful eyes, and was cautious when he unbound the Borderer's hands so that the man could relieve himself. He secured him again, then moved his mares to a fresh grazing spot. When the meat was cooked, Heath doled out an oatcake to his prisoner, then cut a crisp, juicy piece from the animal's small haunch and sat down to enjoy it.

When his appetite was replete, he felt better physically; food always acted as a palliative, yet his mind was restless. Some instinct told him that he was a sitting duck waiting here for Mangey. The leader might not return alone; he could have other Armstrongs with him. Someone in Mangerton must have informed the Borderers of Heath's presence. The only way they had found him at the river was because they were searching for him.

Heath fed his mount, put the meat he had cooked into his

saddlebag, then kicked earth over the fire. When his roan finished the oats, Heath saddled him, then he fastened his mares to a tether rope so that they would be easier to herd. Finally he undid the rope that secured his prisoner to the oak and fastened it to his roan's saddle. He would ride slowly to Bewcastle; his captive would walk ahead of him, where he could see him at all times. If his suspicions were right, and Dacre was the one who had offered money to have Ramsay Douglas murdered, Mangey had not gone north to Kelso's horse fair, he had gone south to Bewcastle.

Heath crossed the Border from Liddesdale into England and headed south. The light was fading from the sky by the time he arrived in the vicinity of Bewcastle. Though surrounded by trees and streams, the English fortress sat almost a mile from dense forest, and Heath made camp within the wooded haven. He watered his horses, then tethered them. He lit no fire, but ate cold meat, and gave some to his prisoner. As darkness descended, Heath decided to go on foot to inspect the fortress. After a moment's consideration he tore a strip from his linen shirt and gagged the stocky Borderer, choosing to take his bound captive with him rather than leave him behind.

Bewcastle's iron portcullis was guarded, so Heath avoided the main entrance, and with his drawn knife in one hand and the rope binding his prisoner in the other, he made his way with great stealth around the massive walls. He stopped dead in his tracks when he saw two men outside the sally port gate in the rear wall of the castle.

The gagged man made a noise in his throat, and Heath threatened him to silence with his knife. Heath knew his prisoner had recognized his cohort who had fled before Heath's sword. The other man was none other than their leader, Mangey. The men were deep in conversation and though they were too far away for Heath to hear what was being said, it was apparent they were having an altercation.

Suddenly, Mangey slammed his fist into the other Borderer's gut and the man went down. Only when Mangey bent to wipe his hand on the grass did Heath realize that Mangey's hand held a dagger. The victim drew his knees up into a ball, then his body went slack. Mangey spoke to someone inside the gate, and a man came out and they dragged the body inside by the heels. Once again, Heath's prisoner groaned deep in his throat, and Heath had to fight the urge to silence the swine permanently.

Heath withdrew to the forest in a murderous mood. Suddenly he heard the call of a nightjar, and shortly after he answered it, he watched Gavin Douglas and four moss-troopers pick their way through the trees where his mares were tethered.

"Don't get yer back up—Ram insisted we come."

"Keep your distance, Gavin, I'm in a foul temper. I just missed catching the only man who can connect Dacre to the plot to dispose of Ramsay. The son of a bitch is safe inside Bewcastle."

"What about him?" Gavin indicated his prisoner.

"A useless piece of offal who swears he knows nothing, but I'll keep him alive for the present. I haven't finished with him yet." Heath added, "Christ, with Mangey safe inside Bewcastle, there's no chance of bringing Dacre to justice. I want to storm Bewcastle and make the son of a bitch pay!"

Gavin said, "I've no doubt at all that you'll find a way to make Dacre pay. But I think it would be expedient tae take the mares you've recovered back tae Eskdale, rather than hang about here."

Heath pulled his knife from its sheath and began to sharpen it. Hatred for the Dacres almost consumed him. Justice delayed was justice denied, yet he knew he would have to curb his impatience. "The rest of my breeding mares are likely inside Bewcastle, and Christopher Dacre still has my black stallion."

Gavin Douglas knew better than to argue with him. Heath's pride, stubbornness, and tenacity prevented him from leaving without his property. With resignation, Gavin removed his saddle from his mount and directed the moss-troopers to bed down for the night.

Heath took meat from his saddlebag, sliced it with his knife and offered it to the men. "It isn't hedgehog," he assured them with dry humor.

"What the hell is it?" Gavin asked with a grimace.

"Fox," Heath said solemnly.

———

The rising sun awakened Heath the next morning. Shortly he saw Christopher Dacre ride out alone under the portcullis of Bewcastle. The arrogant swine was astride Blackadder. Suddenly it came to Heath how he could make Dacre pay, and he smiled with savage anticipation. Sooner or later young Dacre would return, and when he did, Kennedy and Douglas would be waiting for him.

Raven Carleton was delighted when Christopher Dacre came calling. She had known he would come, though not quite this soon. She pretended to be completely surprised at his visit, although she was anything but. Raven had laid out a special riding habit to wear when he came. The slim black skirt was slit to the knee to show off her high calfskin boots, and the crimson velvet jacket was trimmed with black braid at throat and cuffs. The matching red velvet cap sported a black ostrich feather, and her black leather riding gloves were embroidered with crimson beads.

Raven introduced Lord Dacre's heir to her grandmother, and could have hugged her when Dame Doris Heron poured them wine, then excused herself so that the couple could be alone.

"Your grandmother is a most discerning woman."

Raven dimpled. "She discerns more than you ever dreamed, Christopher Dacre."

"Ah, a magic woman, no doubt, who casts spells and brews potions in her stillroom."

"You may laugh, sir, but have a care what you drink."

Chris Dacre held up his wine cup, then deliberately drained it. "You have stolen my senses with your love potion." He set the empty cup down and took Raven's hands in his. "Come to Bewcastle. I want you to be with me."

"What a lovely invitation. I suppose I could come for an hour; 'tis only a three-mile ride," she said lightly.

"I don't want you for an hour, Raven."

"For how long *do* you want me?" she tempted.

"Forever." Dacre's eyes were riveted upon her mouth.

Raven caught her breath. "You are a dreadful tease, Chris Dacre."

"Nay, it is you who are teasing me, Raven. Come for a week, a month," he begged.

"That is impossible!" She tossed her hair over her shoulder in a feminine gesture calculated to belie her words.

"It's not impossible, Raven. If you accept the invitation, I swear everything will be proper. If you'll come for a visit to Bewcastle, all the proprieties will be observed."

"The proprieties would not be observed unless we were formally betrothed, Christopher." She gave him a ravishing smile. "Let me go up and change and we can ride over to Bewcastle. But you must promise to have me back by nightfall."

Upstairs, Raven's grandmother helped her change into the vivid riding habit. "Do you have your hag stone and your knife?"

"I do." Raven hugged her grandmother. "I warrant Chris Dacre will find a way to persuade me to stay at Bewcastle." Raven's eyes sparkled with mischief. "Don't worry if I don't return tonight. All my things are packed. If I do decide to stay, I shall send for my bags."

"Goodbye, my lovely." Dame Heron's voice held a wistful note. "Your life's adventure begins today. Do not forget to use your power, Raven."

As she saw Christopher's reaction to her vivid riding outfit, Raven knew she had chosen well. "I'm sorry I kept you waiting."

"It was worth the wait," he assured her, his eyes lingering upon the swell of her breasts beneath the fitted crimson jacket.

As one of the young Heron boys brought Sully from the stables, Raven gave Chris a provocative sidelong glance from beneath long black lashes. "You don't mind if we take my pair of falcons on our ride, do you, Christopher? They are in need of exercise." Raven knew that if she was to stay at Bewcastle for a week, she must take the valuable hunting birds with her.

"Are these peregrines yours?" Dacre asked with surprise.

"Yes, they are a lovely pair, but still very young."

Dacre gazed at the male bird with covetous eyes. "Your father certainly indulges you."

"Do I detect a note of disapproval in your voice?" Raven asked lightly, taking the raptors from their perches.

He quickly covered the censure his words had revealed. "Envy, perhaps. I would like to be the one to indulge you."

They walked outside into the sunshine and Raven handed him the birds while she mounted Sully. Then she took them back until Dacre mounted his new black stallion. She offered him his choice of falcons, and he picked the male, as she had known he would. Raven smiled inwardly; Christopher Dacre was so predictable.

They rode about two miles in the direction of Bewcastle before they cast their hawks. As the birds soared miles above them, Chris Dacre dismounted and lifted Raven down beside him. His hands lingered at her waist and he drew her close for their first kiss. Raven momentarily closed her eyes, then quickly opened them again and looked up into his gray-green eyes, reassuring herself that the male she was kissing really was Christopher. Then she laughed at her own foolishness.

"Why do you laugh?" he asked huskily.

"Because I am happy."

"Make me happy, Raven. Stay at Bewcastle with me," he implored.

"I long to," she said wistfully to raise his hopes, then purposely dashed them, "but I cannot." She turned from him to remount Sully, but he stopped her.

"Raven, if you come, you may consider yourself betrothed."

She caught her breath. "Are you asking me to marry you?"

He searched her face. "Since that's the only way I'll get you. I've quite made up my mind to have you."

Raven knew Lord Dacre's heir was used to getting whatever he wanted. "How impetuous you are, Christopher. Now you will have to exercise patience while I make up *my* mind," she teased. Sheba returned to her wrist without her prey, and Raven suspected the female falcon had devoured it. She set the huntress on her saddlebow.

"Your falcon needs the firm hand of a master."

Raven tossed her head. "I hope you are not implying that I too need a master. One of the incentives to marry is the freedom it would gain me."

He reached out a finger to stroke Sheba's variegated cream and gray feathers. "Freedom isn't good for a woman, according to my father." *Christ, I'll enjoy taming her, more than the falcon!*

Raven's eyes sparkled. "If I refused to marry you, would you carry me off as your father did your mother?"

"I thought you didn't want a master."

Raven laughed. "I don't! Nevertheless, I think it the most romantic thing I've ever heard."

"Here comes my falcon. Damn, he's flown into that treetop and won't come down."

"Sultan is just not used to men. He'll come to me." When Raven moved away from Chris Dacre, Sultan flew to her wrist and released the snipe he had caught. Raven handed the falcon to Dacre. "Would you like to try again?" Her invitation held a double meaning.

"Let's ride closer to Bewcastle; the game there is plentiful."

Raven agreed, laughing. "You just want to be sure of your quarry. Lead the way!"

Dacre quickly secured Sultan to his saddlebow, mounted Blackadder, and rode heedlessly through the trees, leaving Raven far behind him. Suddenly he saw a horse and rider in his path—it was the dark Borderer he had tangled with at Carlisle Fair. He drew rein, scenting danger, and when he glanced about him, saw that he was surrounded. "What do you want?" he demanded.

"I want my horse." The words were implacable.

The look and the voice of the Borderer held such a threat, fear slithered down Dacre's spine. He saw that they had Mangey Armstrong's brother, bound and gagged, and was careful that no recognition passed between them. Dacre suddenly set his spurs to the stallion's flanks and roweled hard in a desperate attempt to flee. Heath Kennedy was after him in a heartbeat, and the moss-troopers closed ranks to trap Dacre. Blackadder reared in terror, the blood on his flanks clearly visible against his glossy coat. Heath slipped from his roan and grasped the black stallion's bridle. Then he grabbed Dacre, pulled him from the saddle, and smashed his fist into his face. "You vicious whoreson, if I ever see you bloody another horse, I'll take a whip to you."

"Take the damn horse!" Dacre offered desperately.

"I intend to take you both."

At this moment, Raven came upon the scene. When she saw Dacre picking himself up from the ground, she cried, "Christopher! What's going on?" She looked at the mounted moss-troopers surrounding them, and then she saw the dark Borderer who called himself Kennedy. Fear prickled her scalp. She had known from the first moment she had seen him that he was dangerous. She had felt the subtle sense of threat whenever he had drawn close to her, yet she had willfully ignored it. Anger suddenly overcame her fear. "You Scots swine, how dare you attack us without provocation!"

Heath Kennedy stared at her in utter disbelief. "Raven Carleton, what the hellfire are you doing here?"

"I am visiting Bewcastle with Christopher Dacre."

"Scum like him will blacken your reputation," he spat angrily.

"We are betrothed! Christopher Dacre and I are to be married."

Her words were flung at him defiantly, like steel-tipped arrows, and they hit their mark. Never in his life had Heath Kennedy wanted anything as badly as he wanted Raven Carleton. The lust that rose up in him was so strong, he wanted to tear off her fancy clothes, lay her back in the grass, and put his brand on her. The dark beauty was a challenge to his manhood, and the thought that she belonged to Christopher Dacre was unendurable to him. "That's strange," he sneered. "In Carlisle, Thomas Dacre was considering a match with Beth Kennedy for his precious son and heir."

"Things have been settled since then," Raven said loftily. "Christopher and I are pledged."

Not for long, Heath vowed silently. *I took Blackadder from him and I shall take you too!* He was suddenly elated, for here was the means to make the Dacres pay in more ways than one. He could not have planned a more perfect revenge than kidnapping Christopher Dacre and his intended bride! Aloud, he said, "Good! Lord Dacre should be most willing to pay ransom for his son's future wife." Heath said to Gavin, "I'm taking her too."

Gavin Douglas was grinning like a heathen. "I've often wanted tae kidnap a woman, but always thought better of it. They can be one hell of a lot of trouble, especially English females."

"Leave her alone. Let her go!" Dacre cried.

"You shut your mouth," Heath warned, "and while we're at it, I'll have your boots."

After a moment's hesitation, Dacre removed his spurred boots and handed them to Kennedy. Heath flung them into the trees, then told him to mount the roan. "Take him," Heath directed Gavin, and watched with satisfaction as the Douglas men headed west with his prisoners and his mares.

Raven jumped down from Sully's back to confront him. "You must be mad! Taking him to Scotland is kidnapping!"

"I am relieved you understand."

"*I* shan't go with you!"

Heath ignored her and looked about for burdock plants.

Raven was incensed at his indifference to her plight. She reached into her pocket, rejected the hag stone, then closed her fingers over her knife. She withdrew it cautiously and launched herself at her captor. In a flash she found herself on her back with the Borderer astride her. Gone was his indifference as he pried the knife from her fingers. "You, mistress, will do exactly as you are told." As he looked down at her, he wondered if she had allowed Dacre to make love to her. The thought knotted his gut.

As Raven lay panting beneath him, she knew real fear. Her own recklessness had put her in this dangerous position. She expected any moment he would ravish her, and opened her mouth to scream.

Heath covered Raven's mouth with his in a rough kiss that effectively silenced the scream. He withdrew his lips and stared fiercely into her eyes.

She remembered the last time he had kissed her. *The name is*

Kennedy, sweetheart, and I want you to never forget it. Next time we meet, I promise to do something even more outrageous. Raven feared he was about to fulfill that promise.

"Let me go, Kennedy," she begged softly.

For long minutes, Heath fought the sexual hunger her closeness provoked. She was so beautiful and so reckless, her passionate spirit cried out to him. Finally he stood up and helped her to her feet. He moved away from her and bent to cut burdock leaves with her knife. He rubbed the leaves into the bloody gashes on Blackadder's flanks and at the same time spoke softly to the stallion. When he was done, the horse nudged him with his nose.

Raven saw how gently he handled the horse, and some of her fear receded. When he gave her back her small dagger, she was thunderstruck. Did it mean that he trusted her, or was he showing contempt for her futile attack? "You don't really intend to kidnap me, do you?" she asked, clinging to hope.

"Yes, lass, I do. You were in the wrong place at the wrong time. Get Sully, and let's go."

"I cannot go yet," she said desperately. "I have a pair of falcons with me."

Heath glanced up at the tallest trees where he saw the outline of a hawk against the sky. He took a piece of meat from his saddlebag and tied it to a rope, then swung the lure in a wide circle, imitating the flight of a small bird. Sheba flew to the bait immediately, and Heath caught hold of her jesses and fastened them to his saddlebow. He smoothed down her feathers, using a firm but gentle touch, and whistled a two-note refrain that he repeated a few times. Sheba cocked her head and settled quietly.

Suddenly the male peregrine swooped down and landed on Raven's shoulder. She staggered slightly but had enough presence of mind to get a firm hold on his jesses. "Good boy, Sultan."

"You may bring your hunting birds."

"How generous of you! Most likely you covet them," Raven accused as she fastened the falcon's jesses to her saddlebow.

Heath's gaze swept her from head to toe. "I do have a fancy for the female."

His words brought a blush to Raven's cheeks. She could still feel the imprint of his kiss and the rough touch of his unshaven jaw against her cheek. She watched him mount the stallion, then he gestured for her to do the same. She obeyed him reluctantly, and when she was in the saddle, thought about fleeing. She knew he would recapture her in minutes, and almost immediately she realized that if she was to escape, she would have to use subtler means.

Raven rode ahead of him, and she imagined she could feel his dark, compelling gaze riveted upon her. She vividly recalled the vision she had had of the falcon flying into the room, swooping about her in a great circle. She saw the raven from the rafters try to flee. The raptor had not harmed the small raven, but had forced it to fly in unison. She realized that the vision had been a portent of things to come, and that Kennedy was the raptor.

CHAPTER 8

When Heath and his captive caught up with the others, Gavin Douglas nodded in Dacre's direction. "I gagged him; couldn't stand listenin' tae his whining for twenty miles."

Raven wanted to protest their treatment of Christopher, but held her tongue. Anything she said might make his plight worse. She rode in silence over the rugged moors, and realized they must now be in Scotland. As endless miles of wild, wide-open carse stretched before them, she saw that the Scottish Borders were far less inhabited than their English counterpart, making them lonely and dangerous, with treacherous terrain. She obeyed her captor's orders to stay close beside him whenever they skirted a moss or perilous bog, for she feared Sully might sink up to his fetlocks and break a leg.

The weather became overcast and daylight was fading fast by the time they reached Eskdale Valley. Raven was relieved when the small cavalcade headed toward a castle that sat in the valley's sheltered lee. She resented that the dark Borderer was so unwearied. When they arrived at the stables, there were many hands to take their horses, and she realized that most were moss-troopers rather than grooms. Her heart sank, for she knew it would be impossible for Christopher Dacre and her to escape with so many would-be guards.

Kennedy lifted Sheba from his saddlebow. "Bring your falcon to the mews. It is empty at the moment; Lord Douglas left his hunting birds at his other castle."

Raven took Sultan onto her wrist and followed him up five stone steps and through a doorway. "Which Lord Douglas would that be?" she asked loftily, setting the male peregrine on the perch next to Sheba and securing his jesses.

"Lord Ramsay Douglas, Border Warden of the West March, and nephew to the late Archibald Douglas, Earl of Angus."

Raven hid her surprise. Since King James Stewart had died at Flodden, the Douglas clan held all the power in Scotland. And Lord Ramsay was a Border Warden like Lord Thomas Dacre, sworn to uphold the law and keep peace. He could have no idea that Lord Dacre's heir had been kidnapped. She would make a formal complaint to him, if she was lucky enough to find him in residence.

Kennedy secured the wooden door, descended the stone steps leading from the mews, and ordered Dacre to the castle. Raven saw that the other prisoner had been taken away, and she hurried to walk beside Christopher, determined to stay close to him. Inside, there were servants everywhere, and Raven was impressed with the richness of the furnishings. Kennedy spoke to a burly steward, who nodded his understanding and led Dacre toward a studded door. When Raven tried to follow, Kennedy stopped her.

"I want to be with Christopher . . . I intend to share his fate!"

Heath looked amused at her dramatic gesture. "The walls of the dungeon drip with damp, and the rat-infested straw pallet stinks with mold." When he saw her look of outrage, he laughed. "You must think me a barbarian. I am sorry to disappoint you, mistress, but Dacre will occupy a well-appointed tower room until the ransom is paid. And you must not consider yourself a prisoner here; you will be an honored guest, Mistress Carleton."

"You must be mad—we both know I am your prisoner!"

"If you insist." He gave her a mocking bow. "Come, I will escort you to your chamber, so you may refresh yourself."

Raven looked down at her disheveled state in dismay. "You devil, I have only the clothes on my back."

"And very fetching they are," he said, placing a proprietary hand at her back to urge her up the stairs.

She straightened her back and pulled away from him immediately, hurrying up the stairs. "Don't touch me."

"As you wish," he drawled, throwing open a heavy wooden

door that led into a well-furnished tower. "Actually, these two rooms are mine, but since you are my honored guest, you may take the far chamber with the window and the fireplace."

Raven saw that she was fairly trapped; she would have to enter and exit through his chamber. "I cannot sleep in an adjoining room to yours; it would be highly improper!"

"I am concerned only for your safety."

"What about the safety of my virtue?" she demanded.

His bold eyes swept over her, assessing her. "If Dacre is your lover, you have no virtue."

"How dare you! I demand to speak with Lord Douglas."

"I suggest you do something about your appearance before you seek audience with his lordship," he told her bluntly.

Raven wanted to fly at his face, but did not dare. Instead she marched into the adjoining chamber and slammed the door. A huge bed dominated the room, and knowing it was his, Raven averted her eyes and moved toward the welcoming fire in the hearth. On the front of a massive wardrobe was a mirror, and when she stepped before it, she gasped. The black skirt of her riding habit was covered with dirt from rolling about the ground with the Borderer. Her red velvet cap sat at a comic angle, and the once finely plumed ostrich feather hung limp and bedraggled down her back. Her hair beneath the cap was in such a wild black tangle, she despaired of ever getting a comb through it again. Then she groaned, remembering that she didn't even possess a comb.

She pulled off her gloves and dragged the ridiculous cap from her head. She grabbed one of the brushes laid out on an oak chest, ignoring the fact that it belonged to her captor, and firmly brushed the tangles from her curls. Because of the dampness, the brushing made her hair look like a wild blackberry thicket, and she had to take the ribbon from the neck of her shift to fasten it back. Then she took up another brush and removed the dirt from her skirt. Finally she poured water from a big jug into a bowl and washed the travel stains from her hands and face.

Raven heard urgent voices in the adjoining room, then from a distance she heard a woman scream. She threw open the door and saw the Borderer conversing with an attractive woman about thirty.

"Thank God you're back, Heath. She's been in labor for twelve hours, and Ram is mad with worry. He's with her now, making things worse. I need you to calm him down, so Tina and the midwife and I can get on with women's business."

"I'll do what I can, Ada." He ran from the tower room, leaving the women to their own devices. "Who is in labor?" Raven asked.

"Heath's sister, Valentina. She's Lady Douglas. . . . She's having twins, and she's been at it for twelve hours with nothing to show for it but pain and misery!"

Suddenly their identities fell into place for Raven. *Of course, Valentina Kennedy, Beth Kennedy's older sister, was married to powerful Lord Ramsay Douglas, and the man who had kidnapped her was one of Valentina's brothers, no less!*

"Have you tried giving her colewort?" Raven asked.

"Oh, God be praised, you know herbal medicine?" Ada asked.

"My grandmother taught me. Colewort steeped in wine speeds up childbirth."

"I have no idea what it looks like. Go to the stillroom and if you find some, take it to Mr. Burque in the kitchen. He will make a decoction that Tina can drink. I must go . . . please hurry."

Heath ran up to the Master Tower, but before he could knock on the bedchamber door, it was thrown open by Ram Douglas. He had a distraught look on his face, and his black hair stood on end from running his hand through it. "She's ordered me out!" Ram said incredulously. "That's the thanks I get fer hoverin' over her night and day—she's thrown me out!"

"Women like to be in charge at times like this, and rightly so. It is their domain, and you are trespassing. Ada has given me orders to distract you, and that should prove easy enough."

Ram arched a black brow. "How so?"

"I am convinced that Dacre is paying Scots to murder Scots. I tracked down the scum who came for you and took me by mistake. I have reason to believe they are Armstrongs, an outlawed Scottish clan. I saw their leader, Mangey Armstrong, at Bewcastle, where he had gone to collect his blood money. Safe behind the walls of the English fortress, I couldn't get my hands on him. I was so thirsty for revenge, I kidnapped Dacre's son instead, and I'm holding him for ransom."

Ram gave a sharp bark of laughter. "Ye're a Borderer through and through," he said with admiration. "It's a sure way tae make Dacre pay, and at the same time send him a message that we know who's behind these bloody raids." Ram's eyes glittered with anticipation. "Let's go and help the heir write a letter that will put the fear of God in his father, then Jock can deliver it."

"I don't want to put Jock in jeopardy."

"No fear of that," Ram replied. "I'm an old hand at this; let me explain how it's done. In plain language the ransom letter states that if our messenger doesn't return by midnight, Dacre will get his son back in pieces. Then set down the time and place where the exchange will be made, and the amount of the ransom."

Heath nodded. "I'll give him two days, and make the exchange at the peel tower right on the Border at Liddel Water."

"Good plan. Only one at a time can cross the bridge, and I insist ye have two dozen moss-troopers at yer back, just in case."

"Chris Dacre had a young woman with him. I brought her too."

"Double the ransom," Ram said with approval.

Heath shook his head. "I'll not take Dacre's money for her."

Raven went immediately in search of the stillroom. A plump maidservant with a thick Scottish brogue led her downstairs, through the great hall, and past the kitchens to an unheated chamber where milk and butter were kept on stone slabs and dozens of bunches of herbs hung from the rafters. Raven had no trouble identifying the different herbs by their scent and by their appearance. Colewort was a common plant whose seeds were used in cooking to flavor soups or desserts, and Raven was relieved to find a good supply. She took out her knife and cut some dark green leaves with their sticky seeds and hurried back to the kitchens.

The castle kitchens, redolent with delicious smells, were bustling with activity. The chef in charge stood out from his Scottish assistants by his accent and his attractive, expressive face as he paced the kitchen restlessly. Raven approached him and held out the colewort. "You are Mr. Burque, I believe. Ada asked me to bring you this herb to make a decoction for Lady Douglas. When steeped in wine, the seeds . . ." Raven hesitated, wondering how she could speak of childbirth to this stranger.

Mr. Burque plucked the colewort from her fingers and his face became transformed with hope. "Ah, it will help the birthing and soothe her pain, no?"

"Speed it up, yes," Raven confirmed. She watched his graceful hands as he washed the plant, placed it in a copper pot, crushed its seeds, and poured red wine over it. As he brought the mixture to a boil, the air was filled with the scent of colewort, which resembled that of cloves. He added honey to thicken the potion and to sweeten its taste, and in a remarkably short time declared it ready. He poured the steaming wine into a goblet. "Ta-da! I shall carry it for you, chérie, and we will present it together!"

Mr. Burque led the way to the Master Tower, and Raven had to run up the staircase to keep up with him. As he raised his hand to knock on the door, a long wail of distress came from inside the chamber. Burque thrust the goblet into Raven's hands and fled. She knocked loudly and the door was promptly opened by Ada.

"Oh, thank God, you found some. Come quickly."

Raven approached the bed and found herself staring at one of the most beautiful women she had ever seen. She had flaming red hair that fell about her shoulders in wild disarray. Large golden eyes stared out from a pale, heart-shaped face. Her belly, which she clutched with a shapely hand, was grossly distended.

Raven proffered the goblet. "If you will drink this wine with colewort, it should hasten your delivery."

"If any of you give me one more filthy brew, I will throw it in your face!" Tina threatened. "Who are you?" she demanded.

"She is Heath's woman," Ada explained. "She knows all about herbal potions."

"Ah, thank God and all his saints!" Tina sagged against her pillows, all resistance magically swept aside by Heath's name.

Raven swallowed the denial that rose to her lips, and sat down on the edge of the bed, as compassion for Tina's plight filled her heart. She steadied Tina's hand that reached for the goblet, and guided it to her mouth. In the calming voice Raven used with her falcons, she set about soothing the mother-to-be's distress. "You are so brave. Twelve hours of travail is hard to bear, but that is the normal amount of time for a first birth. All will be well." She watched Tina drain the goblet, then she handed it to Ada and reached into her pocket. "Here is a hag stone. It has great magical power. Hold it and take its power for yourself."

Tina desperately clutched the stone to her breast, ready to put her faith in anything that might help. Shortly she rose up from the bed as a great labor pain gripped her body. The colewort was strengthening her contractions to expel the child from her womb. When Tina screamed, the midwife rushed forward and Raven stepped back. In the next moment the first of Tina's twins was born.

Ada took the baby girl from the midwife to wash it, and Tina lay back against her pillows, panting from her efforts. "Rest for a few minutes," Raven advised, caught up in the miracle of birth. "You have the power, Tina. You must decide when you are ready."

"Ah, Tina, your beautiful daughter has black down on her head."

"A girl? Ram Douglas will kill me. Nay, I shall kill him, if he ever comes near me again!" Tina vowed with passion, then she was taken with another agonizing contraction and pushed with all her strength. She clutched the hag stone until her knuckles turned white. "Surely this one is a boy . . . only a male could bring so much pain and suffering to a woman!"

"Ye're right, it's a lad!" the midwife rejoiced, "an' a wee redhead just like yerself."

"Lord have mercy upon us," Ada said irreverently, as tears of joy and relief streamed down her face.

The cries of the new babies brought half a dozen maidservants to the chamber, and Ada put them to work immediately, bathing Valentina and changing the bed linen. Raven helped Ada swaddle the babies, while the midwife, puffed with pride, went to inform his lordship. Though Tina was exhausted, she looked radiant, and glowed with happiness as Ada gently laid a baby in the crook of each arm.

Suddenly the door swung open and Ramsay Douglas swept into the room with the intensity of a summer storm. All the maids stepped back in deference as he strode to the bed. He took one look at his beautiful wife, holding their babies, and slipped to his knees beside her. "My honey lamb, how do ye feel?"

"I feel perfect," Tina declared.

"Lass, ye were so brave; ye were in labor more than twelve hours." His voice almost broke with tender emotion.

Tina touched his face tenderly. "No, no, twelve hours is normal the first time," she assured him, using Raven's words.

He took her hand reverently and buried a kiss in her palm. "So much pain and suffering," he said, riven with guilt.

"Hardly any," she lied gallantly.

"I love ye with all my heart, Vixen. Thank ye for these precious babies." He touched a finger to the downy tufts on their heads, then touched his lips to his wife's brow. "Sleep now, beloved, get some rest while ye can."

Raven was amazed at how tender this man was with his wife. By rumor, Black Ram Douglas had a fearsome reputation. She listened as he thanked Ada and the other women in the room, showering them with gratitude. Raven followed him from the chamber, determined to seize this moment to lodge a formal complaint against her captor.

"Lord Douglas—"

Ram swung about and fastened his pewter gray eyes upon her.

Raven lifted her chin and gave vent to the wrath she felt. "Heath Kennedy has taken me against my will!"

Ram's eyes widened. "He *raped* ye?"

"No, of course not!"

"Ah, I see. That's the root of yer complaint?"

Raven gasped in outrage. "You are as uncivilized as he is!"

"Far more uncivilized," he assured her gravely.

"I believe you, since you are a Scot and a Borderer!"

"Border laird," he corrected. Then his mouth curved with amusement. " 'Tis impossible tae anger me tonight. I have been blessed by the gods. I am the luckiest man alive. Tonight we cele-brate the birth of my twins. As Heath's woman you shall sit in the spot reserved fer a guest of honor."

"I am *not* Heath's woman!"

"Patience, lass," he advised with a devilish grin.

When Raven found herself alone, she knew this was her chance to find Christopher. Kennedy had mentioned a tower room, which she reasoned must be up here somewhere. Her heart hammered as she hurried down the long passageway, which led into another, and before she knew it, she became hopelessly lost. She took some stairs that led up to the ramparts, and though it was now dark, she could see the silhouettes of the corner towers, which helped her to learn the layout of the castle. She descended the stairs and followed the stone wall to a corner tower. She moved close to a studded door and rapped. "Chris, Christopher, are you in there?"

Raven almost jumped out of her skin when the door opened and Heath Kennedy stepped out. "Miss me already?" He locked the door and put the key in his pocket. "Or did you lose your way?"

There was no point in lying; he knew exactly what she was do-ing. "You know damn well I was looking for Christopher."

"Your concern is misplaced. He isn't worried about you. Let me escort you back to your own tower, mistress."

"*Your* tower, Kennedy!"

"If you insist," he said agreeably. "Since we are sharing quar-ters, my name is Heath. Ada told me how you helped my sister, and I shall be forever grateful to you, Raven." They entered the tower chamber and he closed the door. "I believe this is yours."

Raven looked down at the hag stone lying on his palm. Suddenly she felt foolish and expected him to mock her.

"We have more in common than I first realized. I too believe in the ancient Celtic practices such as earth healing." He looked at her intently. "Do you have the power, Raven?"

She was startled. What did he know of the power? Then she felt his magnetism, felt drawn to him against her will. She lowered her eyes to break the spell. "If I had any power, I would not be here!" As she reached for her hag stone her stomach rumbled.

"You are starving. Come down to the hall; we are celebrating the birth of the twins, and we have the best chef in Scotland."

"No, thank you. I prefer to be alone."

He loomed above her. "I could carry you downstairs; I could force you to my will."

Raven knew he could force her physically, but in that moment she wondered if he also could force her mind to obey him. "Does threatening a woman bring you pleasure?" she demanded.

He gazed down into her lavender-blue eyes and saw the smudges of fatigue beneath them. "Nay, in truth it does not. I shall leave you in peace." He opened the door to leave. "For now," he added.

Even after he left, Raven imagined she could still feel his presence. She told herself it was because these were his rooms, but deep down inside, she suspected it was more than that. Her grandmother believed in magic and the power of nature, and since the ritual, Raven was convinced there was such a thing. Was it possible that Heath Kennedy had the power? Heath . . . even his name was strange. It meant earth, which was certainly a powerful element in nature. He had easily charmed Sully. Was it possible that he could cast a spell over her too? She gave herself a mental shake and told herself to stop being fanciful.

She answered a low knock upon the door and was pleasantly surprised to see that it was a maidservant with a tray of supper. The aroma of the food made her mouth water, and she carried it through to the bedchamber and sat down before the fire to eat. Every dish tasted like ambrosia and she was ready to concede that Mr. Burque, the chef she had met earlier, really was the best in Scotland, or England for that matter. Anyone who lived in the Borders ate a steady diet of mutton, but the sauce that accompanied this dish totally transformed it.

There was a syllabub that had honest-to-god strawberries in it. Raven hadn't tasted strawberries since she was a child in Carlisle. There was a flagon of wine and a small silver dish that held chocolate truffles. As the chocolate melted in her mouth and she sipped the rich red wine, she knew she had Heath Kennedy to thank for this. Damn him to hellfire, he had only sent up the food so that she would feel gratitude toward him, and to her great dismay, it had worked!

From behind her she could feel the lure of his big bed and fought it as long as she could. But finally, unable to resist it any longer, she undressed and climbed beneath the warm covers in her shift. As she curled up, her grandmother's words floated about her: *I want a real man for you, Raven, a Borderer . . . better someone wild and fascinating like a mountain ram than someone tame and uninteresting . . . your life's adventure begins today . . . do not forget to use your power, Raven.*

As she flirted with sleep, Raven felt warm and strangely happy. She was glad she had been able to use her herbal power for Valentina and her babies. She acknowledged that she had used other power too. She realized that the secret was to believe and to get others to believe; that was the power. Suddenly she knew that Heath Kennedy also had the power. That would explain the strange attraction she felt for him, when her head told her plainly that she should hate him. As Raven closed her eyes and allowed sleep to claim her, her mouth curved into a smile. What an exciting challenge it would be to pit herself against him—and win!

It was after midnight before the celebration in Eskdale's dining hall came to an end. Every member of the Clan Douglas who resided at the castle, every moss-trooper, and every servant had congratulated Lord Ramsay Douglas and drunk to the health of his twins. When the last song had been sung and the last skirl of the pipes drifted off into the night, Heath Kennedy climbed the tower stairs and entered his rooms. He smiled grimly as he took the letter from his doublet. He had asked for eight breeding mares of good stock and an insultingly low two hundred pounds for Dacre's son and heir. Jock had been back well before midnight with Lord Dacre's agreement to the ransom demand.

He lit the square quarion candle and saw that the door to the adjoining chamber was closed. He would only have her for two more days. The thought propelled him to the door; he hesitated only a moment, then he opened it quietly and went inside. The fire had burned low, so he built it up and set a fireguard before it. Then he moved softly toward the bed and gazed down at the sleeping girl. In the firelight, her black hair lay in a pool upon the white pillow, and her dark lashes shadowed her cheeks. Sexual desire for her blazed up in him, and yet it was not as fierce as his longing for something more, something far deeper. It was her spirit that called to him, making him hunger for a connection with her. If Raven Carleton would look at him the way his sister Valentina looked at Ram Douglas, he would ask for nothing more in this life. In that moment he knew he would not let her go. He would keep her.

CHAPTER 9

At Castle Doon, Rob Kennedy was having one of the most miserable days of his life. He had rolled about in pain most of the night and feared that his heart was the culprit. He summoned Bothwick, the hairy giant who was the castle steward and sometime surgeon. Bothwick had much experience in pulling teeth and lancing boils, but internal maladies were beyond his ken.

"I'm cursed!" The florid face and sagging jowls belied the fact that the Lord of Galloway had once been a handsome devil. His hands massaged his barrel chest that over the years had slipped down into a paunch. "What can ye give me tae stop this pain in ma chest?" he demanded petulantly.

"Whisky!" Bothwick suggested the panacea for all pain.

"Whisky my arse! I've drunk the castle dry since Elizabeth abandoned me. God's passion, women can be vengeful. I'm cursed, I tell ye."

"The Gypsies are back in Galloway Valley. Why don't I fetch Old Meg? She has some powerful remedies."

Rob fixed Bothwick with a baleful eye. He and Meg were bound by old hatreds. For Bothwick to suggest bringing his Gypsy adversary must mean that his steward thought he was dying.

Old Meg took her own sweet time when Bothwick brought the summons. Though she hated Rob Kennedy with a vengeance, she had no thought of refusing the visit. It would bring her more than money; it would give her perverse satisfaction to see him suffer.

She waited until early evening to gather her herbs and para-phernalia for brewing potions. Arriving at this hour should guaran-tee her a good dinner and perhaps even one of the castle's luxurious guest chambers for the night.

Meg went straight to the kitchens when she arrived, and learned to her great disappointment that Mr. Burque, the Kennedys' renowned French chef, had gone with Lady Valentina when she wed the power-ful Black Ram Douglas. The dinner she was served was unpalatable to say the least. The mutton managed to be both tough and greasy at the same time, and the bread pudding that accompanied it was a heavy, soggy mass.

When Meg was shown to the first-floor room where Lord Kennedy conducted his business, her shrewd glance noticed the dust in the untidy room that gave it a neglected appearance which matched that of its owner.

"I'm in a bad way, Meg. There's a gold sovereign fer ye if ye can take away the misery in ma chest."

She watched him rub his distended belly, heard the belch it pro-duced, and concluded that the irascible old swine was suffering from a massive bout of indigestion. It was no doubt brought on by a steady diet of poorly cooked food accompanied by too much whisky. Meg bent close, as if imparting a secret. "You are right, Rob Kennedy, you are in a bad way. I think it's your heart."

He closed his eyes; it was exactly as he feared. He thought fleet-ingly of Elizabeth. A wife's rightful place was at her husband's side to comfort him in such calamitous circumstances. *In sickness and in health*, Lizzie had vowed. Overwhelmed with self-pity, he moaned, "I'm cursed."

"You are right again, Rob Kennedy, you *are* cursed," Meg said with grim satisfaction.

"Remove the damn curse, ye old Gypsy witch, for ye are the one who put it there!" Rob roared, purple in the face.

Meg shook her head regretfully. "I did not put it there, Rob Kennedy. You brought the curse on yourself, as well you know. I cannot remove it. The only one who can remove it is yourself. You know the remedy," she said cryptically.

He glared at her fiercely, fighting the urge to smite her dead. "I *loved* yer daughter, Lily Rose. She was the only lass I ever did truly love."

"And therein lies your shame!"

"The remedy ye hint at is impossible!" he roared.

Meg knew her adversary was stubborn, but at the moment she had him at a disadvantage and enjoyed twisting the knife in his belly. "Is not the Kennedy motto 'Consider the end'? That is exactly what you must do. The curse dooms your entire family, not just you, Rob Kennedy." Meg had been in Carlisle and knew all the gossip. She took out her tarot cards and waved them under his nose. "I consulted the cards; it's all here. Your male line will completely die out; there'll be no more Kennedys. Your own marriage is doomed, and your youngest lass will make a disastrous marriage, as did your other daughter."

Rob gripped his belly. "Nay, Valentina has a happy marriage. She's expectin' a child."

Meg shook her head gravely. "I saw two coffins, dark clouds, and red hair. *Consider the end.*"

Rob was greatly alarmed. He had had no news of the birth, and it was long overdue. God's passion, he must go to Tina, she was his favorite child. "*Two* gold sovereigns if ye take my pain away and get me on my feet!"

Meg rummaged in her big cloth bag until she found a vial of senna and figs. It was a harsh purgative that would open his bowels, but not without him suffering violent gripe and cramp. "I'd better stay. You could get worse before you get better."

If Rob Kennedy had feared death earlier, he now had a change of heart and begged it to take him out of his misery as the endless hours of the night slowly crept toward morning. As well as physical torment, he suffered mental anguish over the fate of his children. His son Duncan should have sailed back from Flanders days ago. What if his ship had been sunk? The old Gypsy witch had said his male line would die out. His other son, Donal, had only produced a girl, and now there was no word about Tina. "I am cursed, cursed," he moaned as he rolled from his bed and made another hurried visit to the garderobe.

By midday, after Meg had dosed him with syrup of wild rhubarb, the flux stopped, and by afternoon the distension of his innards lessened. His bloated belly was no longer putting pressure on his heart, and the pain in his chest had eased considerably.

When Meg came for her money, she saw that her patient looked pinched around the gills, and though he appeared subdued, she knew that wouldn't last long. She pocketed her sovereigns, then proceeded to destroy his peace of mind. "I saved you this time, Rob Kennedy, but my remedy was only temporary."

"Yer bloody remedy felt like poison!"

"That's guilt," she pronounced with conviction. "Guilt is the deadliest poison there is. It will surround your heart, and squeeze until it bursts. If you don't assuage your guilt, you'll be dead within months, but not before you see the curse visited upon the rest of your family."

His mouth set in a hard line. "I'll see Heath. Do ye know where he is?"

"When I saw him in Carlisle, he wore a Douglas plaid," Meg said cryptically, then pressed her point, "The curse can be lifted."

It can be lifted, all right, Rob thought. *I'll see Heath an' order him tae have ye remove the bloody curse, ye evil Gypsy witch!*

After Old Meg departed the castle, Rob Kennedy sat in his chair all night. Dark thoughts and persistent worries chased each other around his brain seeking an escape hatch, but it felt as if he had cut his mooring rope and was adrift. Last night the gates of hell had opened, and he smelled the sulphur as he *considered the end*.

The loneliness of the castle surrounded him and pressed in on him. Where had all the happiness gone and the laughter? They had left him one by one. When his beloved Valentina left, most of the light had gone out of his life. She had even taken Ada with her, who had always been such a comfort to him. He remembered the old days when Kennedy hospitality was legendary and the castle had been filled with guests. The bachelor quarters of Doon used to overflow with red-haired young Kennedys from four different branches of the clan. Every spring they brought the wool from the first shearing to be exported via his Kennedy vessels. Half of those promising young men had lost their lives at Flodden.

Only three had come this year. They had brought the wool and left as if they couldn't get away fast enough. He acknowledged morosely that it was the women who had drawn them, attracted them like lodestones, entertained them and filled the castle with fun and games, love and laughter. Even his bed was empty now that Lizzie had left him. "I'm cursed." He reached for the whisky.

"Father, where the hell are ye?"

Rob Kennedy opened his eyes and tried to struggle to his feet, but he was held fast by the wool plaid Bothwick must have wrapped about him once he had drunk himself to sleep. "Duncan, is that ye, man? I've sat here all night worritin' about ye!"

Duncan found his father in the room where he conducted business, and knew immediately that he had slept there. "The place seems deserted. Where's Mother?"

"Left me . . . gone tae Carlisle. Taken Beth an' all the bloody maidservants." Relief that Duncan was home safe washed over him. "Well, at least everythin's all right wi' ye."

"No, it isn't all right. We ran into a terrible storm. I was near washed overboard. We limped home, taking on more water than we could pump. It'll take weeks tae repair the *Thistledoon*."

Rob Kennedy's face turned ashen. The *Thistledoon* was the pride of the Kennedy fleet, swifter than any other vessel. It was the bloody curse! Hadn't she said the male line of the Kennedys would all die out? Duncan was doomed! Rob surged up out of the chair and crashed his fist upon the table. "It's her that's done it tae me! Well, I'm no goin' tae sit here an' fall tae bits. We'll sail tae Carlisle an' put a stop tae it!"

Duncan mistakenly assumed his father was talking about his mother. "Did they bring the wool from the spring shearing?"

"Aye, it's all loaded aboard my own ship, the *Galloway*. We will weigh anchor tomorrow if no storms threaten. If she thinks I've lost my old ruttin' spirit, she's wrong! After I settle my business in Carlisle, we'll go an' make sure Tina is all right. I've had no word about the wee bairn!"

Duncan eyed the whisky and felt sorry for his mother. Still, she would have a couple of days of reprieve. Before he sailed the *Galloway* to Carlisle, he would have to arrange for the damaged *Thistledoon* to get towed up to the shipyards in Glasgow for repair.

Two maidservants entered Raven's chamber, one bringing hot water and towels, the other carrying a breakfast tray and a message. "Lady Douglas asks you to visit her, so she may thank you."

As she dressed, Raven decided that today she would make her plight known to Valentina. She had already earned the new mother's gratitude, and when Tina learned what her brother had done, she would be outraged. It would gain her sympathy and perhaps lead to Raven and Christopher's release as well.

The Master Tower was a hive of activity. Servants were carrying in two carved cradles, baby blankets, and a mountain of flannel napkins. Embroidered nightgowns and caps were strewn across the big bed where the radiant mother lay feeding her little daughter. A buxom wet nurse had just finished feeding the new Douglas heir and was issuing orders where his cradle must be placed.

"There you are; perhaps she'll listen to you." Ada took Raven's hand and propelled her to the side of the bed. "Tina insists on getting up later today. Kindly inform her that English ladies stay abed for two weeks after the birth of a child."

"Kindly inform Ada that I am not an English lady . . . not a lady at all, as well she knows." Tina gave her a brilliant smile. "I don't even know your name, but I thank you with all my heart for coming to my aid yesterday."

"I am Raven Carleton. I believe that my father and your mother Elizabeth are second cousins. I know your sister Beth; we were both recent guests at Carlisle Castle."

"Then Heath was telling the truth—he did see Beth at Carlisle. She told him that my heartless mother was trying to betroth her to the son of Dacre, my husband's most hated enemy, but that she much preferred Heron Carleton, who must be your brother!"

"Yes, Heron is my brother," Raven acknowledged, remembering that he had escorted Beth Kennedy to the fair. Her heart sank as she learned that Lord Dacre was Douglas's most hated enemy.

"Raven is such a beautiful name; perhaps I will use it for my daughter." Tina lovingly touched the dark down on her child's head. "How lovely of Heath to bring you for a visit."

Raven took a deep breath and plunged in. "I am delighted that you are recovered enough to want to get up, and I am most sorry to give you news that will upset you, but your brother kidnapped me!"

"A stolen bride? I warrant that is the most romantic thing I have ever heard! Ada, Heath is finally in love."

"No, no, he is not in love." Raven avoided the name Dacre because of Tina's passionate response. "I was out riding with my betrothed when your brother took him prisoner, and now he is holding him for ransom. I was in the wrong place at the wrong time, and he kidnapped me too!"

"What an impetuous devil to steal you with only the clothes on your back. Never mind, I have a whole wardrobe of lovely gowns I haven't been able to wear for months. Ada, get Raven whatever she needs. Take anything you want," Tina said generously.

"What I *want* is for you to persuade your brother to free us. Kidnapping is against the law!"

Tina laughed merrily. "Borderers are a law unto themselves. Heath would never take something he didn't highly covet. This is his way of wooing you. I know better than to interfere between a man and the woman he has chosen." Tina handed her baby daughter to Ada. "She's fallen asleep; put her in her cradle." Just then her baby son began to scream. "Give him to me; it takes a special touch to soothe a Douglas male." She dropped a kiss onto the tiny brow, then smiled at Raven. "Ada will bring you the clothes, and you must visit us again. Come and have dinner with Ada and me tonight and you can tell us all the gossip you heard in Carlisle."

When Raven left the Master Tower, she was riven with anxiety about Christopher Dacre. Not only did Heath Kennedy hate the Dacres, but she had just learned they were Lord Ramsay Douglas's most hated enemy. Obviously there was bad blood between them that stretched back before the war when England had defeated Scotland at Flodden. Though Raven felt no danger to herself, the danger for Christopher was very real. She must find a way to help him escape!

Raven assured herself that if she steadfastly believed that she had the power, she would find the means to free Christopher. The best time, of course, would be under cover of darkness, and he would need a mount. With so many moss-troopers frequenting the stables, it would be almost impossible to take horses from there, so Raven decided to go outside and see if any animals were being grazed close by the castle.

Hope soared in her breast when she saw a meadow with about twenty horses in it. Almost immediately she saw Heath Kennedy riding among them. Unfortunately, because of her scarlet jacket, he saw her too, and closed the distance between them. "Were you thinking of going somewhere?"

Raven swallowed the tart reply that rose to her lips in an effort to disarm him. Determined to allay his suspicions, she decided to use her feminine wiles. "I was looking for you. I would like your permission to fly my falcons. They are young and need exercise and training." She looked up at him beseechingly. "Can you and I not set aside our differences and come to an understanding?"

Her sweet voice told him she was sheathing her claws because she wanted something. "These horses here also need training," he said. "We can work together each day. You may fly your falcons in this meadow. The more time we spend together, the closer our understanding will become." He dismounted. "I'll come with you to the mews."

Raven had no choice. She had not been lying when she said her hawks needed to be flown, but she had hoped it would gain her some freedom. Obviously he had no intention of letting her out of his sight, and she was annoyed that once again he had thwarted her.

As they walked toward the stables, the horse he had been riding followed him and nudged him in the back. Heath turned to rub the animal's nose, and the other horses gathered about them in a circle. "How did you learn to charm horses?" she asked.

"You don't teach the horse your language, your ways; you learn his. That is the secret."

"Why, that is what I do with my hawks. Most people make the mistake of trying to master them, but falcons have no masters. At best they tolerate you. With kindness and respect and a potent lure, you can train them to do your bidding, but they can never really be tamed."

In the mews he lifted Sheba from her perch and glanced sideways at Raven. "A potent lure will make the female do my bidding?"

Raven blushed. His words had an intimate connotation, and in his raw linen shirt with his corded neck still glistening from his exertions, he was a most potent lure. He held her glance until she was forced to lower her lashes. Curse him! How was he able to make her respond to him against her better judgment? She picked up Sultan, hurried through the stables, and swept outside into the meadow. She cast the male peregrine and watched him soar into the sky, wishing she could fly after him.

"You forgot something." He handed her a pigeon-feather lure he had picked up in the mews, then he cast Sheba. She caught the breeze beneath her wings and soared after Sultan.

"You did that very well," she acknowledged.

"I watched you closely. You are a good teacher."

She was flattered at the compliment. Most disapproved of falcon training by a female. Then she realized what he was doing: he was offering her respect to gain her trust.

"Come, we'll ride after them. This garron hasn't been trained to the saddle, but you don't need one, you ride like the wind."

Raven hid her amusement as she mounted the garron. He was doing it again! If he thought to train her to do his bidding with compliments and kindness, he was doomed to disappointment. She watched him mount another horse that didn't even have a bridle. He threaded his fingers into its mane and together they galloped across the turf. Then the other garrons kicked up their heels playfully and thundered after them.

Exhilaration bubbled up in Raven as she lifted her face to the sky and watched the pair of gyrfalcons circle together, then drop from the clouds in a double dive. She threw back her head and laughed joyfully, intoxicated by the ride and the wild creatures with whom they shared the glorious afternoon.

Heath's face was taut with hunger as he watched her. "I like the way you laugh, full out, holding nothing back." Would she love this way too? He pictured her in his bed, beneath him, laughing up at him, and he knew that with the right mate, she would indeed.

The falcons returned and presented their prey to Raven as she had trained them to do. She took the snipe from the hooked beaks, praised their efforts, then gave them back the game they had caught. They flew onto the meadow's stone wall to devour their prey. "They hunt for food, so that is how I reward them."

"They have trained you well," he said solemnly.

"Cheeky swine!" Raven tossed back her hair. "Now it's my turn to assess your training methods."

For the next two hours she watched Heath Kennedy work with the garrons. He had infinite patience, walking among them, following them, talking softly to them, then he turned his back, put distance between them, and waited. It took a long time, but finally, one by one, half a dozen horses followed him. These were the animals he focused upon, touching them, mounting them, and finally getting each one to accept a saddle on its back.

As the falcons preened themselves atop the stone wall warmed by the sun, Raven watched the dark Borderer work the garrons. Though he made it appear effortless, she could see the lithe muscles of his thighs ripple beneath the calfskin breeches. The powerful bulge of his forearms as he lifted the saddle brought back the memory of being in his arms, and the thought of his darkly furred chest beneath the shirt made her aware of her own body. She looked away, fighting the attraction. She had been warned against Borderers all her life, but as her eyes slid back to watch him, she realized just how much temptation lay in the forbidden.

He worked until the light began to fade from the sky, then he slapped the horses' rumps and sent them back to the herd. His hand went to his shoulder to massage an ache, and when he took it away, Raven saw blood on his shirt. "You have injured yourself."

Heath glanced at his shoulder. "It's a shallow wound I keep reopening . . . nothing to worry about."

She saw a chance to gain his trust. "After we take the falcons back to the mews, you must come to the stillroom with me for some yarrow. That will stop the bleeding."

"Yes, yarrow is good for that. Who taught you herbal medicine?"

"My grandmother, Doris Heron." She glanced up at him from beneath her lashes to gauge his reaction. "She is a Solitary who practices the Craft."

"Then I presume the two of you have dabbled in Celtic rituals?"

"You may presume whatever you like, Heath Kennedy, and I shall do the same," she promised.

In the stillroom, Raven took out her small dagger, cut yarrow leaves and a few dried blossoms, and placed them in a wooden bowl. Heath took a pestle and ground the leaves into a yellow powder. "Have you drawn your own blood with that knife, so that it will serve you and no other?" he murmured. "Do you believe in the power of magic, Raven?"

Her glance flew to his and held. "I believe in the power of nature." She took a small pot of butter, sprinkled in the powdered yarrow, and handed it to him. "Try this."

He cocked a dark brow. "No magic incantation I must chant?"

"Hocus pocus, fish bones choke us."

His lips twitched. "I deserved that."

You'll get everything *you deserve if I have my wish, Heath Kennedy,* Raven thought with satisfaction.

CHAPTER 10

After Raven left Heath, she entered her chamber and firmly closed the door between the adjoining rooms. The bed was piled high with dresses, cloaks, riding clothes, and undergarments. The female inside her was thrilled, and she was astounded that Valentina Douglas could show such generosity to another woman. As she hung them in the wardrobe, she was surprised at the vibrant colors and rich textures of the gowns. She knew there were far more clothes than she would ever need, for she did not plan to be here much longer. Still, she could not resist removing the clothes she had worn for two days and changing into one of the dresses.

Someone had brought warm scented water and fresh towels, so Raven quickly undressed and took a sponge bath. She donned a fresh white petticoat and marveled at the delicate flowers embroidered around its hem and low neckline. She chose a jade green gown because its vivid color cried out to her. She put it on and ran to look in the mirror. Her reflection both pleased and surprised her. The gown was cut much lower than anything she had ever been allowed to wear before, and the curve of her breasts swelled above the square neckline, making her feel overtly feminine. She brushed her hair until it shone like black silk, then picked up the green cloak that matched the gown. She had decided to accept Tina's invitation to dine and try again to obtain her help.

When Raven opened her chamber door and walked into the adjoining room, she was astonished to see Heath Kennedy standing naked with only a towel about his hips. He had just bathed and was examining his shoulder in the mirror. His discarded clothes lay upon a wooden settle, and Raven's eye fell upon a key that had fallen from his pocket. It was the same key he had used yesterday to lock Christopher in the tower! Excitement surged through her as she realized that here was the means to free Christopher, if she could summon the courage. All she had to do was use her power to distract his jailer.

She casually laid her cloak down over the key and walked toward him showing great concern. "God's passion, that is far more than a cut; it's a knife wound! Let me have a look at it."

Heath's smoldering glance roamed over her, lingering on her breasts so temptingly displayed. Sexual hunger threatened to engulf him and though he turned his shoulder toward her, his gaze never left her. The moment her scent stole to him, his arousal lifted the towel.

His marked response to her gave Raven added confidence. She drew as close as she dared to examine the wound. "It won't stop bleeding until it is stitched," she declared.

He held up the needle and thread he had been about to use. "For once we agree. You have the gift of healing, I believe."

Raven had never stitched a man's wound before. She had watched her grandmother, and she had sewn one of Heron's hunting dogs that had been lacerated by a wild boar. Kennedy, however, willing to put himself at her mercy, handed her the needle. Confidence in her own ability surged into her the moment their fingers touched, and she became sure of her healing power.

Heath did not flinch as her small deft stitches closed the gaping cut. He did momentarily lose his erection, but the minute he felt her fingers gently rubbing on the yarrow mixture, his desire flared up again, hot and hard.

Raven focused on the flesh beneath her fingers, willing it to heal, seeing it heal in her mind's eye, then actually feeling the skin become smooth and firm again. For a few unbelievable moments she merged with the powerful male who stood before her; she felt the stinging pain of the shoulder, then she experienced the flaring desire that consumed him. She released him instantly, as if she had been burned, and stepped back.

"You are beautiful in your witchery," he murmured low.

Raven felt that he was the one casting the bewitching spell. She broke it quickly before he could read her thoughts. "You should rest; put no exertion upon your shoulder. To sleep is to heal." Then she casually changed the subject. "Your sister has invited me to sup with her and Ada tonight; I have been looking forward to the female company."

Raven walked over to the settle and picked up her cloak, and with it, the key. She willed him to let her go, and exhaled a long sigh of relief when he did not stop her from leaving the tower.

The iron key felt heavy in her hand as Raven walked quickly, summoning her confidence, focusing on her power, determined that this time she would not lose her way. She believed her biggest problem would be to convince Christopher to leave her behind; that his chance of escape would be far better if he went alone.

The passageway that led to his tower was pitch dark and Raven had to gather all her courage to keep going. To reassure herself, she felt for her herb knife that she had slipped into the cloak's pocket. Her heart hammered as she desperately clung to the belief that she had the power to free Christopher Dacre. The key would never have come to her hand had it been otherwise.

She felt the rough oak of the studded door beneath her fingers as she found the keyhole, then she turned the lock and miraculously the door swung open. After the darkness of the corridor, the candle-lit chamber seemed bright, and Raven quickly closed the door behind her. Dacre rose up from the bed, and she went into his arms with a sob. "Chris, thank God they didn't put you in the dungeon or mistreat you!"

"Give me the key," he demanded.

She pressed it into his hand. "There are horses grazing in the west meadow. Don't go near the stables," she cautioned.

"I'll have no chance of escape with you along. I can't take you, Raven." His voice was cold, calculating.

She was momentarily hurt that he did not put her safety before his own, then crushed down the ridiculous feminine emotion, assuring herself that he was being both sensible and practical.

"Do you have a weapon for me?" he asked.

"All I have is my herb knife." She put the small dagger into his waiting hand, praying that he would escape without using it.

He held her by the shoulders and looked down into her eyes. "I swear I will avenge myself against him, and against every Kennedy breathing. I will destroy them with fire and sword!"

She had never seen such naked hatred in his gray-green eyes before. "No, Christopher! They have not harmed us. There has been no blood shed. Killing only leads to more killing!"

Suddenly the heavy door flew open and crashed into the wall. Raven jumped guiltily and stared into eyes that were dark with fury. Then Chris Dacre wrapped his arm about her middle and thrust her in front of him, snarling, "Not one step closer, Kennedy!"

Raven was shocked to feel the point of her own dagger against her throat. She was not afraid of the man who held her; she knew that Christopher would never harm her, that his threat was one of calculated desperation. The rage she saw in the Borderer's eyes, however, sent a shudder of fear up her spine. As if from nowhere, he drew a long knife and launched himself through the air with the speed of a raptor. Raven thought she screamed, then realized it was Christopher who had cried out in fear and pain as his arm was bent up his back and her small dagger clattered to the flagstone floor.

"I'm worth nothing to you dead," Dacre babbled.

"Please don't kill—" Raven's words stuck in her throat as Kennedy swung about and pierced her with a murderous glare.

"Go!" he bellowed.

With overwhelming relief she saw him sheath his knife, then she obeyed his order, before her presence goaded him to violence.

Heath flung Dacre against the wall and watched him sink to his knees. "If you ever touch her again, I'll cut your heart out."

When Raven returned to her chamber, she found Tina's woman with a tray of food. Ada surveyed her from head to foot with a look of approval. "Aha, just as we suspected. Tonight you have other fish to fry! In that gown you will have him eating out of your hand. Tina swears that green gives a woman power over a man. I say show him no mercy; drive him to his knees, which is exactly the position he will crave after five minutes alone with you." Ada winked. "Valentina invites you again tomorrow night."

Raven closed the door tightly when Ada left, wishing it had a bolt upon it. Heath Kennedy's power was far greater than hers. She sank to the bed with trembling knees, afraid of what he would do to her when he returned. She looked at the food and knew it would stick in her throat if she tried to eat anything. The wine was another matter, however; perhaps it would give her some much-needed courage. She poured a goblet from the flagon and took several large gulps. Almost immediately she felt its effect. Like magic, it felt as if the petals of a huge red rose unfurled in her breast. She drained the goblet and felt her blood heat as it pulsed through her veins. Ada's words echoed in her head: *In that gown you will have him eating out of your hand . . . green gives a woman power over a man.* Raven realized that she did have power; a woman's power over a man had its own potent magic. He had certainly responded to it earlier; it was her only defense against the dark devil!

The moment she heard him enter the outer chamber, Raven opened the adjoining door and walked bravely toward him. "I know my behavior was reckless. I saw the key and took it. If you expect me to apologize for trying to free him, you will be disappointed."

His glance moved over her, saw her glittering eyes, and her lovely breasts that rose and fell with her agitation. "My only disappointment is that you are as devious as other women."

"We are adversaries! What other weapons do I have?"

"You have many weapons, Raven, as well you know. I should give you a damn good beating for what you did tonight. Your reckless actions almost got you killed."

"I was in no danger from Christopher."

"No, you were in danger from me!"

She ran her tongue over her lips slowly, provocatively. "Danger excites me," she whispered, swaying toward him.

Heath's arms went around her, steadying her. When his mouth covered hers, tasting her, his suspicions were confirmed. She was trying to handle him as if he were one of her hunting birds, using herself as the lure, to make him do her bidding. "Go to bed, Raven, you are flown with wine!"

His rejection stung her pride. She was aghast at her own behavior. "How very noble you are! First, you think to save me from Chris Dacre, then you think to save me from myself!" She retreated into her own chamber and crashed the door closed.

Heath's mouth curved into a smile. He had a vast experience of females, all of them devious. In comparison, Raven Carleton was so innocent, it touched his heart. She possessed great power; she just hadn't learned to utilize it. But once she did, it would be devastating. She was quite right, he did intend to save her from herself. He would never let that swine Dacre have her. He would woo her relentlessly until he won her, then he would flaunt her.

It was hours before his body allowed him to sleep. He lay in the narrow bed consumed by thoughts of her. He knew he desired Raven with all his heart and soul, but at the moment his body was obsessed by a physical need for her. His sexual hunger for her grew hourly. He indulged in a fantasy, forcing himself to go slowly at first, then he would allow his imagination to progress to hot and wild.

Heath stood framed in the doorway, enthralled by the black-haired beauty in the green gown. He held out his hand in invitation. "Come to me, Raven." He could feel his heart thudding in his chest, feel the pulse beat in his throat, feel the shaft of his cock fill with blood, lengthening and thickening, until it throbbed with need. His gut ached with hunger for their first magical touch. She came to him slowly, moving sensually, swaying her hips, breathing deeply, so that the curve of her breasts swelled temptingly above the low-cut neckline of her gown. She stopped inches from his body, then deliberately ran her tongue over her luscious lower lip and whispered, "Danger excites me." He reached out and with one fingertip touched her mouth. The current that ran between them was so intense, he almost came out of his skin. He stroked his thumb across her lip. "I'm going to taste you, I'm going to taste you everywhere." Raven lifted her mouth for his ravishing, needing the kiss as much as he did. He licked her bottom lip, then sucked it whole into his mouth as if it were a ripe cherry. His hands unfastened her gown, then removed it. He teased her with the tip of his tongue while he denuded her of her petticoat. Her mouth tasted like honeyed wine, and he savored the anticipation of tasting the other intimate places of her body.

Heath pulled away from Raven and allowed his smoldering glance to travel the length of her body. Her skin was the color of ivory and smooth as cream; her breasts were full and tipped with bright rosebuds. Her thighs were soft, and the dark shadow between as tempting as sin. He lifted her high, until her mons was on a level with his mouth, then he kissed the tight little curls, and slowly allowed her naked body to slide down his until her toes touched the carpet. He could wait no longer. In a heartbeat, they were naked together in the bed, and his hot mouth was open against her creamy skin, whispering all the things he was going to do to her. His hands threaded into her black silken hair, combing his fingers through the curls, inhaling their intoxicating fragrance that reminded him of purple heather. He lifted her above him, so that her glorious hair pooled upon his chest, then covered her breasts with kisses, and sucked and licked her nipples until they became taut little spears thrusting into his hungry mouth.

Suddenly he was ravenous for the feel of her long, lithe legs wrapping themselves about his body and sliding up his back. Like magic, she was beneath him, writhing, panting, moaning, in a fever to yield everything to him that he had ever desired. Heath rose up, then plunged all the way down, feeling her close sleekly around him. His palms curved over her lush breasts as he began the primal mating dance, plunging, thrusting into her scalding heat until the surging waves of passion rose higher and higher, threatening to drown him in forbidden pleasure. It was a race against time to bring them both to fulfillment before they were engulfed.

After Raven slammed the door, she admitted to herself that the wine on an empty stomach had gone straight to her head. She ate a little food, hoping to diminish her dizziness, and thought about her failed attempt to free Christopher. Try as she might, she could not deny that he had acted cowardly to use her as a shield. She laid the blame at Heath Kennedy's feet, of course, where it belonged. He held the master hand over poor Chris Dacre, whose only weapon was empty threats of revenge. Raven was beset with frustration. She had tried to use her power to help Christopher, but the Borderer's power was far more potent than hers.

She undressed, donned one of the pretty nightgowns that Ada had brought, and slipped into the wide bed, glad that the wine would make her sleep. An hour later Raven did not know if she was dreaming or if she was awake, but she did know that she was not alone in the bed. She turned her head on the pillow and looked straight into Heath's dark eyes.

"You will learn to do my bidding, Raven." He spoke softly, mesmerizing her with his words. "I will train you to my hand." He reached out and touched her, stroked her, smoothing his hands over her bare shoulders, combing his fingers through the black curls that lay upon her breast. Then he moved away to the far side of the bed and waited with infinite patience.

She saw that he held her knife in his hand, and it was a potent lure. Slowly, inexorably, she moved toward him until their bodies touched. He had an irresistible power that she could not fight, did not even wish to fight.

"Tell me what you want, Raven."

"I want to drive you to your knees."

"That is exactly the position I crave!"

In a heartbeat, she was between his powerful thighs. He knelt above her, naked, and lowered the blade to her breast. She was not afraid of the man who straddled her; Heath would never harm her. With tantalizing slowness he slid the point of the dagger into the fabric of her nightgown and slit it from her body. She shivered with delicious anticipation, waiting for the moment when she would be completely naked and he would cover her body with his.

"First, you must pledge to me, Raven." He took her knife and made a cut on his thumb. Then he took her finger and pricked it with the dagger's point. "Merge your blood with mine."

They pressed their hands together so that their blood mingled. Then their mouths fused and they unleashed the fierce desire that had been mounting since the first moment they had encountered each other and their destinies were joined.

Raven's eyes flew open. She turned her head on the pillow

expecting to see Heath Kennedy beside her, but she was alone. That was impossible; she could still feel the heat of his firm flesh on her skin and feel her lips swollen from his passionate kisses. Somehow he had enchanted her, cast a spell upon her. He had come to her bed and taken her into his power!

Raven jumped from the bed and ran into the adjoining chamber. She blinked with disbelief, for there on the narrow cot lay Heath Kennedy in a sound sleep. He had flung off the covers and lay naked, but there was no doubt that he was fast in the arms of Morpheus. She looked down at her own body and found it still clad in the nightgown without any knife slits whatsoever. Slowly she realized it must all have been a dream. She cast a guilty look at his lithe, well-muscled body and felt her cheeks suffuse with a blush. God's passion, what if he opened his eyes and found her there, hovering at his bedside?

She crept back into her room and stood before the fire to warm herself. She had never experienced a dream so real in her life. She turned to the bed, and there upon the pillow lay her black-handled dagger. Raven lifted her finger, and by the glow of the fire, she saw the cut upon it. Her heart began to hammer, then she remembered she had deliberately made the cut herself, during the ritual she performed with her grandmother. She told herself that she was being fanciful, but somehow she was not convinced. This was the second time he had come to her in a dream. Last time he had stolen the raven's feather from beneath her pillow as a forfeit; this time he was determined to steal her heart.

CHAPTER 11

Raven stayed in her room for most of the next day. When she finally emerged into the adjoining chamber, she was relieved to find it empty. She decided that for her own peace of mind she would avoid Heath Kennedy at all costs and make sure they were never alone together. She went to the mews to feed her falcons, but since they did not need flying every day, she did not take them to the meadow. Instead, she returned to the castle and sought the company of Valentina. She found her reclining against the cushions of the window seat in the solar, writing letters. The babies lay in their cradles at her feet, while the young maids rocked them and sang to them.

"Raven, come and join the family circle. Heath tells me you train hunting birds. I find it interesting that Heath's passion is horses and yours is falcons. I saw the two of you yesterday, from my windows. When you ride together, it is easy to see that you both share a great love of nature."

"Your brother is holding me captive against my will," Raven said quietly. "He permits me to fly my hawks only in his presence."

Tina stroked her chin with the feather quill as she studied Raven. "Between a man and a woman, it is difficult to know who is the captive and who is the captor. Their roles change back and forth, in my experience. A clever woman can always gain the upper hand, then hold it by wearing a velvet glove."

"You make it sound like a game."

"Between a man and a woman, it is always a game. You have been playing two men against each other. I have only just learned that one of them is a Dacre. You must know that Heath will do everything in his power to save you from such a fate."

The families were old enemies, a classic case of Scots against English, and Raven realized she could say nothing to change Valentina's mind. It also was plain that Tina would not take her side against her brother Heath's. Raven felt a pang of guilt for trying to involve Tina in her problem. The new mother had enough on her plate at the moment. "I cannot fault you for being loyal to your brother."

"Heath and I are very close. He always accepted my willful, reckless behavior. I suppose it's because our temperaments are similar, completely unlike our other siblings'. I am writing to my brother Donal and his wife, Meggan, to give them the news about the twins. He's a dear soul, and I love him, but he is such a simple, uncomplicated man with no passion in his blood. He is quite content to live quietly on his land and graze thousands of sheep. He has no ambition, yet someday he will be Lord of Galloway."

"And your other brother?"

"Duncan. He helps my father run the merchant shipping business. They export Kennedy wool to Flanders. He used to be good-natured, but he turned bitter after Flodden. He's quite avaricious; thinks everyone is out to cheat him, especially women. That's why he's still unmarried. He is fully convinced that he should have been the heir, rather than Donal."

Raven could not help liking Valentina. She was so frank and honest. Before she was married, she had been known as Flaming Tina Kennedy, but that hadn't hindered her in making a powerful marriage. She had radiant beauty, but she also had great magnetism, and something else, which Raven realized was the sexuality her grandmother had spoken about. She had the power to hold any man in the palm of her hand and enslave him. Raven gazed at the lake outside the window, wishing she could acquire the same confidence as Valentina. A movement on the water caught her eye. "Oh, you have swans. How beautiful they are!"

"You know all about birds. What can I do to make them stay?"

Raven remembered a trick her grandmother had taught her.

"You must put grain out for them. Then get a rope with a bell on it and hang it from this window. When you throw out the grain every day, you ring the bell, and the swans will learn to come for it."

"Does it really work? It sounds like a magic trick!"

"No, it is training. Most birds can be trained."

"Oh, we must try it. Ada, do go and get one of the stewards to get us a rope and a brass bell." As soon as Ada departed, Tina said, "Raven, will you teach me how to fly a hawk? I must get back in the saddle if I am to regain my slim figure."

"Don't you think it's too soon?"

"Oh, now you sound like Ada. I am determined."

Though Raven didn't believe she would be at Eskdale much longer, she nodded. "Whenever you feel up to it."

Ada arrived with the steward, who fastened the bell to the rope and lowered it from the window, as she instructed him to do. Then Tina scattered the grain he had brought while Ada rang the bell. As Raven watched, it was brought home to her that here was another woman who had great power over men. The steward would have gladly lowered *himself* into the water, to please Ada.

Ram Douglas arrived on the scene and listened with amusement as Valentina explained what they were up to. "I came tae see if ye would grace the hall with yer presence tonight. Everyone is clamoring fer a glimpse of the famous Douglas twins."

"I shall be delighted. Will you carry their cradles down to the hall for me?" When Ram immediately lifted one, Tina began to laugh. "No, no, I must feed them first, unless you want everyone in the hall to glimpse the other famous Douglas twins."

The reference to her breasts brought a smile to everyone's lips, including her husband's, and Raven saw the look of intimate adoration on his face that told everyone he was deeply in love.

"Darling, I've written letters to my family, telling them about our amazing blessed event. There's one for Donal and Meggie, one for Father, and a third for Mother and Beth in Carlisle. I want them to have the news right away so they won't be worried."

Ram kissed her hand that held out the letters. "I will see that they are dispatched immediately, my honey love."

Raven avidly watched the interplay between the lovers. He granted Tina's every request as if she were a goddess, and if he didn't have a swift messenger available, looked ready to call upon the god Mercury to do her bidding!

Raven thought about her own family and was vastly relieved that they would not be worried about her, at least not yet. Her mother believed she was staying with her grandmother, who in turn thought she was at Bewcastle. She hoped they would never learn the truth, and prayed that Lord Dacre would ransom them soon. She had no idea how long it would take, and resolved to confront Heath Kennedy tonight and demand some answers. She had been patient long enough.

The hall was lit with a hundred torches. It was the first time Raven had dined there, and she found it fascinating. Valentina and the two cradles holding her babies were elevated upon a dais displayed like treasure. The hall was filled to capacity by the men and women who served Douglas. Some of the moss-troopers were married, some were handfast, others completely unshackled, but every male had a female companion by his side. Most belonged to Clan Douglas and were connected by bonds of blood, marriage, or loyalty. All took great pride in the fact that Lord and Lady Douglas had produced twins.

Mr. Burque, the French chef, presented the dishes he had prepared to Lady Douglas for her admiration. He made a great show of serving Valentina first, then Lord Douglas. When they enthusiastically nodded their approval, Burque clapped his hands and the servitors carried similar dishes to the other tables.

Raven's glance traveled around the hall searching for Heath Kennedy. She had successfully avoided him all day, but fully expected that he would dine in the hall tonight. Where was he? She was eager for the confrontation, but now the exasperating devil was nowhere in sight and seemed to be deliberately avoiding her! It occurred to her that now would be a good time to search his chamber. Perhaps she would find notes about the ransom demand, or even the key to Christopher's tower room, if her power was strong tonight.

Raven waited until all the toasts to Valentina's health had been offered and acknowledged. Then when everyone formed a long line to visit the dais and view the celebrated babies in their carved cradles, she slipped from the hall.

Upstairs in her own chamber the fire blazed cheerfully, and she used it to light all the candles in both rooms. As she moved toward the table beside his narrow bed, she drew in a swift breath. She picked up the black raven's feather with fingers that suddenly trembled. She dropped it quickly, scolding herself for being ridiculous. Anyone could have a black feather. It meant nothing.

She opened a drawer in the table and was amazed to find that it held tarot cards and a peculiarly shaped stone. Though she had never seen one before, Raven immediately knew what it was. Its phallic shape proclaimed it a god stone. Here was proof that Heath Kennedy practiced the Craft, and Raven's worst suspicions were confirmed. The dark devil *did* have the power!

She was careful not to touch anything. He must not know that she knew his secrets. Raven moved to the wardrobe and began to search the pockets of his clothes, looking for the key. The scent of his garments stole to her as she touched them. The masculine smell of leather was mixed with something else, something exotic like sandalwood that stirred her senses.

"Is this what you are looking for?"

Raven whirled around, angry that she had been caught, furious that he could move with such silent stealth, and incensed that he was dangling the key from his fingers. "I am looking for *answers*! I absolutely refuse to be kept in the dark from now on. I demand to know how much longer this will take. No evasions! I want you to be straight with me, Heath Kennedy."

"Ask your questions, Raven. I will tell you anything you wish to know. Come and sit down."

She took the chair because her knees felt like wet linen. He sat down in the chair facing her and waited for her questions. She took a deep breath to calm herself, wondering where to begin. "I know nothing about holding someone for ransom. What are the steps involved? How long does it take? What happens if the ransom is not paid? I am racked with worry for Chris Dacre's safety."

"The procedure is quite simple; let me explain. I took Chris Dacre prisoner, then sent a letter to his father demanding ransom. It set down the time and place where the exchange would be made. Lord Dacre agreed to my terms immediately."

Raven moistened her lips with her tongue. "Where and when?"

"On the Border at Liddel Water. You can stop worrying over Chris Dacre. Tonight the ransom was paid and my prisoner turned over to his father. By now he will be safe at Bewcastle."

Raven was stunned. "You released Christopher? What about me? Didn't Lord Dacre pay my ransom too?" she asked in disbelief.

"I did not ask him to ransom you," Heath said quietly.

She jumped up from the chair and flew at him with her fists. "You vile devil! How could you release Christopher without me?" She pummeled his chest with her fists as hard as she could.

Heath covered her hands with his and forced them to be still. "I wouldn't take Dacre's money for you, Raven," he said with stiff pride. "That would be like selling you to him."

"So, tomorrow I am free to go?" she asked cautiously.

"Not exactly. If I let you go now, you'd run back to Dacre."

"No, I would not!" she denied. "I would go home. When I told you Chris Dacre and I were betrothed, it was a lie!"

"In that case, my beautiful little liar, I am free to woo you." With a great whoop he picked her up and held her in the air, laughing up into her face.

"You ugly Scots brute, if you try to keep me captive, I will make you rue the day you were ever born! I will make your life so miserable, you will beg me on bended knee to leave this place!"

Heath laughed. "You are irresistible when you are angry. I love a challenge, Raven; I will woo you relentlessly. You already enjoy my kisses, and before I'm done you'll enjoy everything else I do to you. Passionately!"

She bent her head and fastened her teeth into the hand that held her in the air. The moment he set her feet back to the carpet, she picked up her skirts and fled to the sanctuary of the adjoining room, slamming the door with fury. Then she pushed and struggled with the heavy oak chest that stood against the wall until it was wedged against the door. Her temper was high as she stood panting from her exertions, and she experienced a heady feeling of triumph that she had thwarted his advances.

All was quiet as she stood catching her breath, but shortly a strange scraping noise broke the silence. It sounded like metal against wood, and she puzzled about what he was doing. All at once, the door was no longer between them; only the tall chest separated them. Her short-lived triumph dissolved as she realized with dismay that he had removed the iron pins and lifted the door off its hinges. Then effortlessly he moved the heavy chest back to where it belonged.

"You have slammed the door for the last time, Raven. It was most tiresome; from now on there will be no barriers between us."

"You cannot do this! My God, I will have no privacy! How will I bathe, how will I dress?"

He grinned. "It is time I kept a closer eye upon you."

Another frightening thought occurred to her. How on earth would she be able to sleep with no barrier between them? He had the power to invade her dreams and make them seem real. Without a door, what would prevent him from invading her bed while she slept? Raven's resolve hardened against him. More than anything in the world, she wanted to wipe the grin from his face. She lifted her chin and said coldly, "I wish you *had* sold me to Dacre."

She watched his grin fade, then without another word, she turned her back upon him and withdrew from the doorway. She pulled a chair closer to the fire, armed herself with the iron poker, then sat down. Under no circumstances would she undress and lie down in the bed. She would sit up all night, and every night until he put the door back where it belonged.

Raven managed to stay alert for the next two hours, but after that her eyes began to close and her head began to nod. She fought against sleep with a vengeance, shifting about in the chair and focusing on the bright flames of the fire. Gradually she became hypnotized and finally succumbed to slumber. Two more hours passed before her eyelids fluttered. *This chair is amazingly comfortable.* Raven turned over and felt the sheet brush against her bare legs.

She opened her eyes and was utterly confounded to find herself in bed. Then she realized that only one person could have put her there. She lifted the covers and it confirmed what she suspected. She was completely nude; Heath Kennedy had undressed her!

At Bewcastle, Christopher Dacre paced the vaulted chamber, venting his anger, while his father questioned him about the kidnapping. He made no mention whatsoever of Raven Carleton. If it became common knowledge that she had been carried off to Scotland, her reputation would be blackened and his father would never negotiate a betrothal. But after what had happened, Chris Dacre was absolutely determined to make Raven his wife. Kennedy had humiliated him beyond endurance. He had taken his horse and even his boots; there was no way in hell Chris Dacre would allow the whoreson to take his woman. When he had learned the Borderer had only asked for his mares and an insulting two hundred pounds ransom, the black hatred he felt toward Kennedy deepened to untold depths, making him lust for revenge. He had vowed to destroy him and the rest of the Kennedys with fire and sword, and needed his father's aid for this retaliation.

"There are Kennedys aplenty we will avenge ourselves upon, never fear. We will start with the father and his prosperous shipping empire. Rob Kennedy will rue the day he turned his nose up at a marriage bond with the Dacres. Then we'll hit his son and heir's vast landholding in Kirkcudbright. But there will be no revenge taken at Eskdale," Lord Dacre declared. "It is a Douglas holding. We cannot afford retaliation that would point the finger at us. As things stand, there is no way that anyone can connect us with the Armstrongs."

"There is a way!" Christopher informed his father. "Kennedy has Mangey Armstrong's brother safely locked up at Eskdale!"

"Son of a bitch! That puts a different complexion on things. The fucking Armstrongs must have piss for brains; they botch everything they put their hand to. Well, we have to get him out of there, fast. Dead or alive makes little difference."

When Raven opened her eyes in the morning, the first thing she saw was a grinning Heath Kennedy leaning against the doorjamb.

"It is a good thing I decided to keep a closer eye on you, my beauty. You fell asleep in the chair and almost did yourself an injury with the poker."

"If you don't remove yourself, I will show you a bloody injury!"

"Can't I watch you get up?" he teased.

"No! Absolutely not! If you remain in that doorway, I shall simply stay in bed all day."

"Mmm, if you stay in bed all day, I assure you that I won't remain in this doorway. I've seen what you are hiding under the covers." He rolled his eyes suggestively.

"You devil, this is just a game to you!"

"A game I want you to play, Raven."

"Even games have rules!"

"All right, I'll let you make a rule, and then I'll make one."

"You will let me get dressed without watching me!"

"Agreed. You will stop avoiding me. Sully needs exercise."

"Agreed. I will bring him to the meadow today."

He grinned. "Give and take. See how easy it is?"

"Then give me back my freedom!"

Give me back my heart, Raven. "I shall give you the freedom to get up and get dressed. I'll see you in the meadow."

The moment she heard the outer door close, she jumped from the bed, opened the wardrobe, and took out an amethyst velvet riding dress. She immediately heard the door reopen. "You filthy liar!" she cried, grabbing the dress to cover herself.

Ada came in carrying a breakfast tray. She glanced at Raven, then glanced at the door that had been removed. "Sorry to disappoint, but it's only me."

"I thought it was that maddening devil Heath!"

"Filthy liar? Is that how you talk to him?" Ada glanced at the door again. "It must be a rough wooing."

"Oh, Ada, I'm at my wit's end. The ransom was paid, but last night he freed Chris Dacre without me, and I am powerless to do anything about it."

"Powerless? Heath wants you for his woman. Don't you realize that gives you all the power in the world over him?" Ada wanted to shake Raven. She would have given anything to have Heath want her.

"Ada, I am woefully ignorant about men. I watch you and Valentina and am absolutely amazed at the way you both use your female power to get whatever you want. Please give me some advice, and tell me your secrets."

Ada sighed with regret. If Heath had set his heart on this young woman, so be it. "Come, I'll share your breakfast and impart my worldly knowledge, as I once did with Tina before she was wed."

Raven slipped on her petticoat and the two of them sat down on the bed with the food between them.

"The Borders of England and Scotland are harsh lands that teach men harsh lessons. Might is right; wolves survive, sheep perish. Gentle, biddable women are soon crushed, because men will ride roughshod over any who let them. If you make a doormat of yourself, men will wipe their muddy boots on you. But a real man admires a woman who has the guts to stand up for herself.

"When two volatile personalities come together, sparks are bound to fly, but any man can be managed if a woman is clever enough. A real woman can defeat any man breathing. Raven, you possess a vibrant beauty, but beauty is only a small part of it. I'm speaking of your sexuality. Most women can never utilize it because they never achieve it. The only time they get their way is by nagging or by tears; but, oh, how men resent them for it. Men don't want tears, they want laughter. Life is harsh, and the only fun a man ever gets is with a woman.

"Sexuality is in the way you dress, to lure him and please him, inflaming his desire. The eyes are for flirting, and teasing, and promising him paradise. The mouth is for laughing, and kissing, and sighing, and whispering soft, sweet words that will make him melt with longing. It pays to use a man softly. Sexuality starts up here in your brain, then moves on to the rest of your body.

"To become a woman, you must lose your virginity; it is of no use to a real woman. Some things can only be learned from a man, but once you gain sexual experience, it will give you complete confidence over him. But only if you learn to love sex. If you can abandon yourself, and truly enjoy the feel, and the taste, and the smell of your own sexuality, you will hold a man in the palm of your hand. You will own him body and soul, and he will be able to deny you nothing."

Suddenly, Raven heard the echo of her grandmother's words: *You need more experience with men; you have been far too sheltered. You have the capacity for great power, Raven, but always remember that a woman's greatest power lies within her sexuality. Never be afraid to explore it, to utilize it. At the moment, you have an innocent sexuality that attracts and tantalizes the male. But as you gain sexual experience, you should be able to attain ascendancy over any mere male.*

"Thank you for being so frank with me, Ada. You have certainly given me much food for thought."

"Then I will let you digest it, along with your breakfast. Tina wants to know if you will give her a lesson in falconry today. She is determined to get back into the saddle and ride again."

"Yes, yes, of course I will," Raven said absently as her mind tried to absorb the shocking advice Ada had so freely dispensed.

CHAPTER 12

Raven brought her falcons down from the mews to the bailey. While Sully and a surefooted garron were being saddled for them, she introduced the birds to Tina, warned her of their razor sharp talons, and showed her how to thread the jesses through her gloved fingers. She demonstrated how to cast a hawk and, when the birds took flight, taught Tina how to swing the lure to entice the hunters to return. Tina was familiar with the rudiments of the sport, and as soon as she felt comfortable handling a bird, they mounted and rode out into the meadow.

Heath joined them immediately. He was in high good humor, since Dacre had paid the ransom with seven of Heath's own breeding mares; the eighth horse he had never seen before. If he was disappointed not to have Raven to himself today, he did not show it. "I'm so glad you are recovered enough to ride again, Tina."

"I couldn't stay cooped up indoors any longer. Besides, I intend to ride to Hawick next week for the wedding."

"Why did they chose Hawick over Edinburgh?" Heath questioned.

Tina shrugged an elegant shoulder. "Symbolic, I suppose. It's a Douglas seat of power, and therefore safer, I warrant. You and Raven must come, of course."

"Who is to be married?" Raven asked.

"Margaret Tudor is to wed Archibald Douglas, the new Earl of Angus," Tina replied.

"The queen?" Raven's look of astonishment amused Tina.

"Well, I suppose technically she's the dowager queen. She's the mother of our new king, Jamie Stewart, and because he's only two years old, Margaret is the regent."

Heath explained, "The Scots would not long tolerate an Englishwoman being the regent of Scotland, especially not the sister of England's King Henry Tudor. The King of England would do anything to get his hands on our little king so he could control both countries. Archie Douglas is marrying her to prevent a power struggle and safeguard King Jamie with the might of Douglas."

"Are you suggesting our English king would harm his own nephew?" Raven asked indignantly.

"He killed James Stewart because he was Scotland's king; he wouldn't hesitate to kill another King James Stewart."

" 'Tis the sport of kings!" Tina declared. When she saw Raven shudder, she steered the conversation to a lighter vein. "The wedding will be a great diversion. The queen and her court ladies are the homeliest creatures you've ever seen, Raven. You and I shall put them in the shade, even though I'm still plump as a partridge."

Heath looked at Raven with speculative eyes. "Will you allow me to escort you to Hawick, mistress?"

Instead of putting him in his place with a cold refusal, Raven smiled. "Why not?" Surely an English queen would be her ally!

Tina gave her a look of approval. "Where is Indigo?" she asked her brother. "I want to show her off to Raven."

"She's grazing in her favorite haunt, by the river. I put my own mares down there with her."

When the hawks returned with their prey, Raven and Tina cast them again in the direction of the river and rode after them, along with Heath.

"Oh, she's purple!" Raven exclaimed. "That's why you called her Indigo. I've never seen a more beautiful animal." The ladies dismounted and Indigo greeted Tina by blowing softly through her nostrils and tossing her mane in a playful manner.

"She's a Barbary. Heath gave her to me."

"Wherever did you find her?" Raven asked Heath.

"I'll let you explain that one," Tina said, laughing.

"I won her from Ramsay in a knife-throwing contest. How was

I to know he had lifted her from the head of Clan Kennedy, the Earl of Cassillis? And how was either of us to know the earl intended this fancy female for the king?"

Tina laughed. "I was mounted upon Indigo the morning that the earl and Ram had a terrible fight over the filly's ownership. The king witnessed their barbarous behavior and bade me keep the mare to make up for their atrocious manners."

"Don't Borderers realize that taking something which belongs to another is theft?" Raven asked sweetly.

"They realize it." Tina swept her with an amused glance. "They simply believe that if a man cannot hold what is his, he doesn't deserve to keep it."

Sultan and Sheba returned with wood ducks from the river. "I shall give these to Mr. Burque and ask him to prepare them especially for you two tonight," Tina said. "It is obvious you have many differences to resolve and would benefit from time alone together." Before Raven could protest, Tina declared, "I am going to walk back. That saddle has paralyzed my bottom."

"Leave the ponies with me," Heath suggested. "They'll enjoy being out in the pasture overnight."

The ladies readily agreed. Though Raven had qualms about being alone with Heath Kennedy, she had none about leaving Sully with him. Heath's love for horses, and their affection for him, was plain to any who saw them together. Raven cast the hawks in the direction of the stables, and the two women enjoyed their walk back through the long, sweet-smelling grass of the meadows.

Raven opened the wardrobe and carefully considered what she would wear for the intimate dinner alone with Heath Kennedy tonight. She planned to put some of Ada's suggestions to the test to see if they had any effect upon him. Raven blushed; naturally she had no intention of having a sexual experience, but she would dress for him, and laugh with him, and use him softly, rather than pitting her will against his. Instinct told her she'd get more from this man by appealing to his senses than by making demands.

She decided to wear a pale peach dress made from taffeta. Its pastel shade was a pretty contrast to her dark hair, and the rustling sound the material made as she walked across the room was deliciously feminine. She wondered if it would serve her better to openly await him in his chamber, then decided against it. No, let him come to her. It would be the first test, to see if just the sight of her alone could lure him over the threshold.

She also decided that they should eat in here before the fire. The setting and the atmosphere were warm and conducive to soft words. The big bed looming behind them in the flickering shadows would be as tantalizing as an unspoken promise. Raven smiled as it dawned on her that she was planning to seduce him. Not physically, of course, but in every other way a woman could seduce a man.

When she heard him enter the tower room, she remained out of sight. She heard him splash water into the bowl and from the other sounds realized that he also was shaving. She saw his shadow pass across the doorway, heard the rustle of garments, and knew that he was changing his clothes. She counted to one hundred, took a deep breath, and showed herself in the doorway. He was tucking a linen shirt into his breeches, which gave her an excuse to murmur a brief apology and quickly withdraw.

Raven's pulse raced as Heath's tall figure filled the doorway. She allowed the hint of a smile to touch her lips. "Thank you for attending Sully; he has taken quite a fancy to you." Her soft words worked like magic, drawing him across the threshold and into the chamber. She bent down and picked up the poker. When she saw his wary look, she laughed and held it out to him. "Would you tend the fire? We could have dinner in here, if you like."

His fingers touched hers as he took the poker. "I would like."

His touch and his voice played havoc with her senses, and she hoped she was having a similar effect upon him. As she moved toward a small table that sat in the corner of the chamber, the peach-colored taffeta whispered deliciously against her legs. She knew that he could hear it by the way his glance followed her. "Could you set this table before the fire?" She could easily have lifted it herself, but it gave her pleasure to have him respond to her smallest requests.

He moved the table, and as she came back across the room, he stared at her, entranced.

"Why are you staring?" she asked breathlessly.

"I can see your aura tonight. It is a lovely shade of deep lavender. I first saw it the day we met."

Raven knew there were such things but that only certain people could see them. She smiled at him. "And what does it tell you about me?"

"It tells me that you are in a receptive mood tonight, perhaps even playful." He drew close and lifted his hand above her head. "It surrounds your hair like a halo." He moved his hand lower. "The light even plays about your shoulders." His fingertips brushed across her taffeta sleeve in a tentative gesture.

Raven smiled up into his eyes. She knew he had been unable to resist touching her and knew she would test her female power further. She ran the tip of her tongue across her upper lip in a provocative gesture that invited him to kiss her. She saw the pupils of his eyes dilate, and as he dipped his head to take possession of her mouth, tasted the sweetness of victory.

The knock upon the outer door forestalled the kiss. She heard him curse beneath his breath and knew she had won the first round of the male/female game they played. "That will be dinner. Are you not hungry?"

"Ravenous," he admitted. "There is nothing like an interrupted kiss to whet the appetite."

"Perhaps we should save the kisses for dessert, unless Mr. Burque offers something more tempting."

Heath opened the door, thanked the servant, then brought the laden serving tray and set it on the table before the fire. He held Raven's chair for her, but could not resist cupping her shoulders and dropping a kiss on her hair when she sat down. She waited until he was seated across from her before she lifted the covers. "Smoked salmon," she said happily.

He sniffed appreciatively. "With dill."

"You have a considerable knowledge of herbs."

"Something else we have in common."

She reached for another silver cover and thrilled when his hand covered hers, so they could lift it together. Tonight, whenever he touched her, he evoked a wild sensation deep within that made her want to scream, yet she could not resist tempting him, luring him to touch her.

The skin on the wood ducks was crisply brown, and the cherry sauce was a perfect complement for the game. Playfully, Raven dipped her finger in the sauce, then held it out to Heath. He lifted her hand to his lips and licked off the sweetness. Beneath another cover was a panache of fresh greens and a dish of artichokes with drawn butter. Heath immediately broke off a leaf, dipped it in the butter, and offered it to Raven. As her lips took it from his fingers, she deliberately bit him. "Did you know the part that we eat is the flower of the artichoke?"

"Did you know that the artichoke is an aphrodisiac?"

Raven blushed, for indeed her grandmother had taught her all about the plants that provoked lust, and now she was beginning to experience the effect firsthand. The food was so good, they both ate with gusto. When Heath poured them wine, he warned, "Drink sparingly; Mr. Burque may have brewed us a love potion."

Raven smiled, knowing she held him in the palm of her hand. She was most confident that when she asked him to put the door back on its hinges to give her privacy, he would rush to do her bidding. To do otherwise would be churlish.

Heath was secretly amused that Raven had done an about-face and changed her tactics. Until today, they had been fencing. Every time he had tried to thrust, she had parried. Now she pretended that she had laid down her arms and was ready to surrender. She was using her feminine wiles to seduce him into a giving mood. Her behavior pleased him, for her game of enticement told him that she was beginning to enjoy the wooing and welcomed his advances.

Suddenly, Heath raised his head, like an animal who scents danger on the wind. Then they both heard shouts from somewhere below and realized that cries of alarm were being raised throughout the castle. Heath ran for his sword and as he opened the tower door heard the terrifying cry, *"Fire! Fire!"*

Raven, her hand at her throat, followed Heath as he descended the tower stairs to join Ram Douglas, who was hastily gathering his moss-troopers. When she learned that the fire was in the stables, she clutched Heath's arm and cried, "Sully!"

"Sully's safe in the meadow, Raven—go back up to the tower!" Heath shouted above the pandemonium, before he was swallowed by the swarm of men surging through the castle doors into the bailey.

She offered up a quick prayer of thanks that Heath's mares and the herd he worked with every day were safe outdoors, but knowing the stables held the mounts of fifty moss-troopers filled her heart with dread. Ada, in a hastily donned bed robe, was organizing the servants to set up a table in the hall to treat the burns and other injuries that would be inevitable. Raven vaguely remembered seeing Ada and Gavin Douglas emerge from the same bedchamber, but realized how insignificant dalliance was in the face of the danger and destruction that threatened. The laundry women brought sheets and Raven joined them to prepare bandages, when suddenly she remembered Sultan and Sheba!

Her peregrine falcons were tethered to a perch in the mews, and she realized that none would even attempt to rescue them when the lives of horses were at stake. Raven ran out into the bailey and saw the flames from the stables burning bright yellow and orange against the dark sky. She reasoned that the stable itself was built from stone and could not burn. It must be the wooden stalls filled with hay, and the thatched roof, that were on fire.

Men were bringing out horses as fast as they could. The crackling and roaring of the fire mixed with the terrified screams of the animals, and clouds of acrid black smoke billowed everywhere, causing both men and beasts to cough and choke. With only one goal in mind, Raven entered the stable and ran up the five stone steps that led to the mews. The wooden door at the top of the steps was smoldering, but without hesitation she pushed against it and cried out as it burned her hands. The screeching falcons were moving back and forth across their perch, flapping their wings in a panic of fright. The heat was intense because the thatched roof above them was entirely in flames. Raven's heartbeats thundered in her ears as she grasped hold of the jesses in an effort to untie them from her falcons' legs. Her fingers hurt so badly they fumbled again and again as she attempted to undo the cords. She murmured soothing words to calm the birds, and perhaps to calm herself, but they seemed to have little effect.

Finally the jesses fell from Sultan's legs, and he flew in a circle, then returned and perched next to Sheba as Raven struggled with the jesses that held the beautiful creature captive. At last she pulled the tangled cords from the female's claws, still not realizing that her hands were badly burned. "Fly, fly!" she cried, but as she looked up, watching them rise toward the flaming thatch, her cries turned into a scream. Then, like a miracle, a huge section of thatch fell away in a shower of sparks, and a circle of dark sky became visible. As Raven watched them fly to freedom, relief overwhelmed her. She sank to her knees, then stared at her hands in disbelief. Her fingers were burned black, and her palms were swollen red and blistered. She knew the terrible danger she was in and knew she must get outside fast. The moment she stood up, however, Raven felt the full impact of the searing, agonizing pain that enveloped her burned hands, and she went down in a faint.

When Heath Kennedy arrived at the burning stables, he rushed inside and went directly to the corner box stall with the iron-barred door, where his Armstrong prisoner was incarcerated. The wooden walls of the stall were ablaze, but there was no one trapped inside. The Borderer was gone. Heath cursed as his suspicions hardened. This fire had been deliberately set to get Armstrong away from Eskdale.

He had no time to worry about it now. He grabbed the manes of two horses, who were kicking their burning stalls apart, and ran with them into the bailey. As he returned for more horses, he saw a small figure dressed in pink run up into the mews on the far side of the stables. "Raven! No!" Fear snaked through his gut. He knew immediately that she was going up there in a reckless attempt to rescue her falcons. The rows of stalls between them were all ablaze, and the floor was thick with burning wood and flaming hay that flew up into the air as it caught fire.

Heath made his way across the stables, trying not to impede the men who were still desperately rescuing horses. He bounded up the stone steps in two strides, then used his booted foot to kick open the blazing wooden door. For a moment he couldn't see her amid the smoke and smoldering thatch that was raining down in clumps of sparks. Then he saw her small figure, huddled on the floor, and his heart turned over in his breast.

He swept her up in his arms, and when he found she weighed no more than thistledown, the lump in his throat threatened to choke him. He carried his precious burden through the bailey and into the castle. Only when he set her limp body down in the hall did he see her burned hands.

Heath left her with Ada, while he ran to the kitchens, where Mr. Burque and his staff were boiling water and making poultices that could be applied to the burns of either men or horses. "Burque, I need that pot of alkanet ointment I made you for kitchen burns."

Burque knew exactly which cupboard held the alkanet.

"Do you have any syrup of poppy?" Heath asked hopefully.

Burque shook his head. He had given the last of it to the midwife when Valentina was suffering through twelve hours of labor.

Heath filled a bowl with cold water and carried it back to the hall with the jar of alkanet. He lifted Raven into his lap and very gently lowered her hands into the cold water. She regained consciousness immediately and tried to snatch her hands from the water. "Hush, Raven, the cold water will take the fire from your burns." Though she struggled frantically and cried out from the pain, Heath gripped her legs with his powerful thighs, holding her immobile, while he held her hands beneath the water.

"Feel the burn leave your hands, Raven, feel it!" His voice was so compelling that she wanted to believe it. After he held them beneath the water for a full five minutes, some of the heat dissipated into the cold water, and she imagined they were cooler. However, when Heath lifted them from the water and the air touched them, the pain was once again excruciating.

Heath knew that if he dried her hands with a towel, it would peel off her blistered skin. He let the air dry them, then coated them with the ointment Mr. Burque had given him. "This is alkanet, Raven. I know of nothing that works better on a new burn."

Though she was sobbing in agony, she nodded her understanding. Ointment made from alkanet was the best treatment for burns. He took up a roll of linen bandage and gently wrapped each finger and then the palm of each hand, and tied the ends securely about her wrists. Then he lifted her high against his heart and carried her upstairs to their tower.

He sat her down in a chair away from the hearth. "The heat of the fire will increase the pain of your burns. I have no syrup of poppy for you, Raven, but I do have whisky." He poured a half-cup of the amber liquor and, kneeling at her feet, held the cup to her lips. "You may sip it slowly, but you must drink it all. It won't take the pain away, but it will help you endure it and perhaps make you sleep." He crouched before her with infinite patience until she drained the cup.

He threw off his once-cream linen shirt, now blackened and ruined from the fire, and Raven saw that against his naked chest he was wearing the god stone. He looked for all the world like an ancient pagan Celt. He knelt before her once again and looked deeply into her eyes. "Raven, I can take away your pain. I have the power to take it; you have the power to give it. You must merge with me; you did it before when you treated my wound, and you must do it again."

She looked at him with frightened eyes filled with pain, and Heath saw that her aura was no longer a vibrant lavender color but had faded to an unhealthy gray. "Let's get this blackened dress off." His fingers were so gentle, he was able to remove the gown without touching her bandaged hands. Then he brought soap and water and washed the black streaks from her face and neck. He lifted the hem of her shift to remove her shoes, then explained before he did it that he was going to remove her hose. When he examined her feet and ankles and found no burns, he quickly washed them and dried them with the towel.

"Now, are you ready to give me your pain?"

Raven nodded, but her voice caught on a sob. Heath lifted her and carried her across the chamber to a rocking chair, then sat down holding her in his lap. He enfolded his arms around her waist and bade her rest her arms upon his.

With his lips against her ear, Heath began to murmur, "Don't focus on your pain, Raven, focus on me. Listen to my words and do as they bid you. Open your mind and let me come inside. Trust me, Raven. Yield your will to me, just for tonight."

Her pain was so acute, it filled her body and her mind. How could she not focus upon it? Desperately she tried to focus on Heath. He was so darkly beautiful, with his black hair curling about his ears, and his sabre-sharp cheekbones so prominent beneath his darkly tanned skin. His eyes were a warm brown, his eyelashes long for a male, and the cleft in the center of his chin held her attention for long minutes. Raven suddenly wanted to dip her finger into the cleft and trace the dark shadow of his beard that was still visible even though he had recently shaved.

"Good, Raven. You have focused on me. Listen to my voice and obey my commands. Open your mind to me; merge with me, Raven."

She did listen to his voice, she heard its gentleness and its kindness, but underneath she heard its determination and its power. She did allow her mind to merge with his, but she was too afraid to yield her will to his and allow him to take complete control of her. Gradually she began to hear his thoughts inside her head. *I love you, Raven, I vow I will never harm you.*

"Suspend your own thoughts, suspend your will, my love, and yield your inner self to me." *Sully trusts me completely, and you can too, Raven.* "Pool your will and your healing energy with mine, Raven, and our combined power will be invincible."

Suddenly, Raven felt her will and her control floating away from her, but miraculously, the agonizing pain in her hands also was floating away to another place, just beyond her reach. "It's working," she whispered.

Heath began to rock her, and the soothing words of a lullaby surrounded and protected her. "When your eyelids become heavy, don't fight sleep; slip down into it like a warm pool. Sleep heals. I won't leave you; our spirits will be enjoined all night."

Raven sighed deeply and gave herself up to his keeping. He rocked her for a long time, but when the chamber became chilled, he carried her to the big bed and, with her still enfolded in his powerful arms, lay down beside her. Heath curved his long body around hers, spoon fashion, making sure that her bandaged hands were safely cushioned upon a goose-feather bed pillow.

Finally, Raven did sleep, but it was a fitful rest, and occasionally her body was taken by a great spasm that jerked her awake. Heath's arms closed about her when this happened, and the heat of his big body seeped into hers as his whispered words calmed, soothed, and lured her back to the painless haven of sleep.

Heath had never felt so protective of a woman in his life. He knew this was the woman he wanted for the rest of his days. He believed that with patient wooing he could seduce her into sharing her body with him, but it wasn't enough; he wanted more. Heath wanted Raven to share her heart, her soul, and her spirit with him. He closed his eyes in quiet desperation, knowing he wanted the impossible.

CHAPTER 13

Duncan Kennedy piloted the *Galloway* up the River Eden at dusk, just as the torchlights along the docks of Carlisle were being lit. His father, Rob Kennedy, stood on deck, scrutinizing the other vessels that lay moored at anchor. He was on the lookout for the *Revenge* or one of the other Douglas vessels that might be able to give him news of Valentina's baby or news of Heath's whereabouts.

Rob saw none of the vessels he was looking for, and walked back to inform Duncan, who was at the ship's wheel. "Dock her over there, where there's plenty of light," he ordered. "I dinna trust the thievin' English around our superior Scottish wool. Tell the first mate tae post a double watch tonight."

Duncan ground his teeth. His father still treated him like a boy who was wet behind the ears. "Go and get us a carriage; I'll see that everything's shipshape and give them their orders."

A short time later, both men climbed into the carriage and gave the driver their destination. "The Rickergate," Duncan directed. At the same moment, Rob Kennedy said, "The Fighting Cocks." Rob looked at his son angrily. "What the hellfire are ye aboot? I ha' no desire tae spend the nicht wi' a disobedient, disloyal wife!"

"Well, I'll be damned! Ye couldn't get to Carlisle fast enough the other night. I thought you were going to confront Mother and lay the law down to her about deserting you!"

"Aye, and maybe I shall, when I've attended tae ma other affairs. But I ha' no stomach fer any discourse wi' the Englishwoman tonicht!" He tapped the driver with his walking stick. "Take us tae The Fighting Cocks."

When they arrived, Duncan soon rid himself of his father and went off to visit the amenable widow of a captain who used to sail a Kennedy merchant vessel. If he was in luck she would offer him dinner, and he would satisfy two appetites for the price of one.

At the inn, Rob Kennedy made inquiries and learned that Heath had been there with two of the Douglas brothers during the week of Carlisle Fair, but they were now long gone. Rob reasoned that they would all be at Castle Douglas, the Border fortress that stood guard over the River Dee on Solway Firth. He cursed his luck which was all bad, for they had sailed past the mouth of the River Dee earlier in the day.

It made sense that Ramsay Douglas would want Valentina to bear his son and heir at the impregnable Douglas seat of power, and odds were that Heath would be there too. Castle Douglas was in Kirkcudbright, less than ten miles from the tower castle of Rob's eldest son, Donal Kennedy. The Douglas and Kennedy landholdings ran together and were so vast that their acres of curly-horned sheep were too numerous to count. Rob was filled with foreboding, not only for Valentina, but for his son Donal as well. If the evil old Gypsy witch *had* put a curse on him, his heir would not be spared.

Rob hadn't made up his mind what to do about Lizzie, but one way or another he decided he would deal with her while he was in Carlisle. Then he would get Duncan to sail back through the Solway to the River Dee so he could visit both Donal and Valentina and ease his worried mind.

His decision made, Rob took himself off to the taproom, where a buxom lass served him with a tempting dish of tripe and trotters. He enjoyed it so much, he even broke open the knuckles of the pigs' feet to suck out the jellied marrow. Feeling adventurous, he decided to have some haggis. That fancy, prancing French chef of Tina's had always refused to make haggis. Rolling his eyes, he had condemned it as "all ears and arseholes"! Well, it took a proper man to tackle haggis, and he told the buxom lass to bring it on.

Rob washed it down with malt whisky and bade the serving woman bring a jug. Feeling frisky, he tickled her between the rolls of flesh that encircled her waist, spun two guineas across the table, and invited her up to his room.

She pocketed the money, squeezed his thigh, and picked up the jug. "Lead the way, me old cock!"

By the time they climbed the stairs to his bedchamber, Rob's face was already beet red and his breathing labored. He sat down on the bed and began struggling with his clothes.

"Here, let me help you, I can see ye're in a great hurry." She removed his coat and folded it neatly, but left on his linen shirt. Most older men didn't appreciate getting completely naked; it made them too vulnerable. She knelt down before him to remove his boots and laughed up at him when he reached into her bodice to fondle her overripe breasts. "Do ye want me to undress?" she asked matter-of-factly. Some men did and some didn't.

"Aye, ye're a fine figure of a woman, let's 'ave a look at ye," Rob said as he struggled out of his breeches.

She sat naked on his knee while he fondled her, and certainly did her part to stimulate him, but no matter what she did, Rob Kennedy remained flaccid and limp. She reached down to cup his huge sac, and playfully rolled his balls, one against the other. Though Rob groaned with pleasure, his cock remained small and soft.

"Lie down an' let me on top," he directed. The desire for sex was certainly present, if the ability was not. He mounted her and tried a dozen times to penetrate the generously endowed female, but in his unresponsive state it was physically impossible. His breathing became labored from his exertions, and his face turned from red to purple. He rolled off her onto the bed in defeat. " 'Tis the curse," he muttered, " 'tis the bloody Gypsy curse!"

The serving woman slipped back into her smock. "Let me get ye some whisky, luv. This happens all the time."

"Not to me it doesn't," Rob said hopelessly, massaging the pain that was suddenly squeezing his heart. He lay all night with the premonition of death shadowing his doorway, and knew that he must get the curse lifted.

In the morning, there was another calamity for the Kennedys

to face. The first mate of the *Galloway* pounded on the bedchamber door at The Fighting Cocks, not knowing which Kennedy he dreaded to face most. Duncan was likely to dismiss him on the spot, but Rob Kennedy, the irascible Lord of Galloway, had an explosive temper, a cutting tongue that could clip tin, and fists like wooden clubs. When Duncan opened the door, the seaman's knees knocked together with relief. "There was a terrible fire, sir. Started in the hold amongst the wool. We fought it fer hours, but tae no avail."

"The winter wool's all gone? The whole cargo?" Duncan demanded.

"Aye, sir, the wool's all gone . . . an' the rest."

Duncan ran his hand through his red hair until it stood on end. "The rest? What do ye mean, man? Is the ship damaged?"

"The *Galloway* is no more, sir. Every plank an' spar burned like tinder wood. 'Twas a conflagration!"

"Christ almighty! Who the hell will tell Father? Ye'd better wait while I get dressed. Did we lose any of the crew?"

"Not sure, sir . . . there were two lads sleepin' in the hold."

Duncan pulled on his boots. "Come on, we'll face him together."

Between Duncan and the first mate, they conveyed to Rob Kennedy the disaster that had befallen the *Galloway* in the night. He grabbed his chest and sat down heavily in a chair. Then he shot out of it and lumbered about the room like a loose cannon rolling about the deck of a ship, inflicting damage upon all in its path. He booted a stool across the room and bellowed in agony at the pain it brought to his big toe. In turn, the stool tipped over the chamber pot, sloshing its contents over his leather boots, lying on the floor where the lass had dropped them last night.

With a purple face he poured the piss from his boots and jammed his feet into them. "Carlisle!" he bellowed. "God's passion, how I loathe an' hate this bloody English town! Carlisle is where all my misfortune began. Carlisle is where I met her; Carlisle is where I wed her. The curse follows me, no matter where I go!"

"We guarded the cargo wi' our lives, my lord. We know the

English canna be trusted. They must ha' thrown a lit torch down the hold."

"Nothin' good ever come outta England; the evil swine are no' satisfied tae steal our superior Scots wool; nay, they'd rather destroy it and my merchant vessel that puts their scows tae shame."

Duncan ran his hand through his hair again. "We'll have tae buy another ship. What the hellfire will that cost us? The crew can forfeit their wages fer a month."

The first mate began to breathe easier; he had expected to be fined a year's wages at the least.

"Never fear, we'll take this tae the Border Wardens' Court when it sits next month. Ramsay Douglas is Warden of the West March; he'll get us compensation fer our vessel *and* our fleeces!" Rob vowed. "Bloody Dacre is Head Warden of the English Marches, and his job is tae keep the peace!"

"What use is he when Scottish merchant vessels are burned right under his nose?" Duncan demanded.

"An' yer muckle-headed mother wants tae wed ma wee lass Beth tae Dacre's arrogant son! Duncan, you go an' see aboot gettin' us another ship. I'm off tae the Rickergate tae issue yer mother an ultimatum; it's high time Lizzie was brought tae heel!"

When Raven awoke in the morning, she found herself alone and immediately began to panic. Heath had treated her burns and kept her pain at bay; she couldn't manage without him! She looked at her bandaged hands, and the moment she lifted them from the pillow, they began to throb. The sound of the tower door opening filled her heart with joy. When Heath came through the adjoining doorway, Raven realized she had never wanted anyone as much as she wanted him at that moment. She held up her hands. "The pain is back," she said helplessly.

"I know. That's why I went out early to cut some hemlock. The bruised leaves laid on your burns will have a cooling effect. They will take away the pain and inflammation as well as prevent the blisters from becoming infected."

Raven heard the compassion in his voice and sighed as he propped her up against the bed pillows. She held out her hands trustingly so that Heath could remove her bandages.

"Don't look down at the burns; look at me, Raven." He dipped the hemlock leaves in cold water, bruised them with his fingers, then laid them over her palms. "See how cool that feels?"

"Ohhhh, ohhhh, that feels so good," she whispered. "My grandmother warned me that hemlock can be deadly if taken internally, but she didn't teach me its benefits."

Heath thought, *My grandmother is an authority when it comes to poison.* "We'll leave these on for an hour and redip them to keep them moist. Then we'll put on a fresh layer of alkanet ointment and rebandage them. Perhaps as early as tomorrow we can start coating the burns with honey."

"Honey is reputed to heal without scarring. Does it work?"

"We shall use our combined power to make sure that it works," Heath assured her.

"I can still taste and smell the terrible smoke."

"It is in your hair, Raven. When you are feeling up to it, I will wash it for you."

She was about to protest, when she realized that he would have to do everything for her—wash her, dress her, feed her. She knew that she should insist upon a maidservant to tend her, but in her heart she did not want one; she wanted Heath.

"I was able to let Sultan and Sheba fly to safety; were they lucky enough to get all the horses out?"

Heath hesitated. Raven had given him her trust, and he decided that he could not lie to her. "A couple died from the smoke, a few had their hair singed, but the men did a miraculous job. It will take some gentle handling before the horses get over their fear; they'll spook easily."

"How did it start? Was it an accident?" she asked hopefully.

"I doubt it. I believe it was set."

Raven closed her eyes. *Dear God, Chris Dacre swore to avenge his kidnapping with fire and sword!* She pushed the horrendous thought away from her. Christopher had only been released the night before the fire; there was no way he would risk returning to Eskdale. *No, but the Dacres are powerful enough to hire henchmen to do their dirty work for them.* Raven forced her mind to cease all evil thoughts. She would most likely become Chris Dacre's wife within the year. Ugly, unfounded suspicions could ruin any chance their union had for happiness.

Heath had just finished rebandaging Raven's hands when Valentina and Ada came to see how the patient was faring.

" 'Tis easy to see why my brother has lost his heart to you. It is because you have identical reckless personalities. Where did you find the courage to save your falcons?"

"I had no choice. I knew the men couldn't spare them a thought when the lives of their horses were at stake."

"No good deed shall go unpunished, Raven. Is the pain very bad, love?" Ada asked with genuine sympathy.

"It was . . . but Heath has made it bearable," Raven admitted.

"He has the power to heal," Tina said proudly. "You have identical personalities; perhaps you are even soul mates."

"Stop wishful thinking, Tina. I know you'd like her for your sister-in-law, but I have to woo her and win her before there's any chance of our becoming soul mates."

Though Heath's tone was light and teasing, Raven suddenly realized that they all wanted her to stay. She felt gratitude and guilt at the same time. Gratitude because they had made her feel like one of the family; guilt because she intended to leave.

"Ram is off to Glasgow for some of the gold he has on deposit. Not only do the stables need immediate repair, but he wants money to recruit more moss-troopers." Tina bent and kissed Raven's brow. "I hope you feel better soon, love. Come and see the babies when you feel up to it."

As they were leaving, a serving maid brought a breakfast tray. Heath took it from her and asked her to bring enough food for two for the next few days. Then he sat down, put the tray on the bed, and lifted a cover. "Traditional Scots breakfast. Do you like porridge?"

Raven wrinkled her nose and shrugged. "Porridge is porridge."

"Porridge is porridge except when Mr. Burque makes it. Then it is ambrosia, fit for a goddess."

There was a jug of yellow cream and a dish of golden syrup which Heath poured liberally on the oatmeal. Then he dipped in the spoon and lifted it to Raven's lips. The act felt so intimate that she blushed when she opened her mouth for him.

"Ah yes, I can clearly see what you had for dinner last night. I see a salmon and a wood duck swimming about."

Raven laughed and the awkwardness was gone. "As well as feeding me, you are going to entertain me. And you were right, this is ambrosia. No, no, don't take the spoon away so quickly, let me lick off the syrup."

He held up the spoon and smiled into her eyes. "Lick away."

Her blush was back. Her thoughts were sensual. Now that she was deprived of her tactile sense, she suddenly had an urge to touch things and experience what they felt like. Her glance roamed over the dark shadow on Heath's cheeks, and she wanted to run her fingertips across his morning beard. Her glance lowered to his cream-colored shirt that was such a contrast against his tanned skin, and her fingers itched to feel the rough linen. Then, from beneath her lashes, her glance slid across the smooth black calfskin that covered his thigh. She licked the syrup from her lips and swallowed hard.

Beneath the next cover was a platter of eggs, potatoes, and lamb kidneys. Raven shook her head. "You eat it, please." She watched Heath with pleasure as he devoured the food. He had a man's healthy appetite, and he appreciated the artistry of the chef's superior talent in both the cooking and the presentation. Mr. Burque also had sent up freshly baked scones with strawberry preserves, and when Raven saw how much Heath was enjoying them, she decided to try one.

Heath offered her a bite of his, and she took an extra-large mouthful. "Greedy wench," he teased, delighted that she felt well enough to eat at all. When the food was finished, he set aside the tray and said matter-of-factly, "Do you want to get dressed?" The look of apprehension on her face told him clearly that she was not yet ready to have him remove her night rail and put her clothes on for her. He opened the wardrobe, selected a garment, and brought it to the bed. "Instead of struggling with a dress today, why don't you put on this bed robe. It's quite respectable enough to wear while you visit the babies."

Raven rewarded him with a look of gratitude, which gave him pleasure, but he knew that shortly she was going to have to get over her modesty. "Your hands should be pain-free for the next few hours. I have to see to some of the horses, but I will go to the still-room and mix you some poppy and licorice root for later. When you are in pain, the hours of the night can be endless."

Raven felt a stab of fear at letting him leave, but crushed it down. She would need him much more throughout the long hours of twilight, dusk, and night. "Heath, thank you for helping me."

"You make me feel quite gallant," he teased, then he sobered. "We will get through this bad time together, Raven."

When she was alone, her thoughts seemed to chase each other in circles. She thought about Christopher Dacre and how unchivalrous his behavior had been on the night she had tried to free him; however, she refused to believe that the fire was in retaliation for holding him to ransom. It must have been an accident, though Heath had made it clear that he thought otherwise. And Ramsay Douglas intended to recruit more moss-troopers, so he too must believe it was a deliberate act of arson. She wished with all her heart that the English and the Scots would cease their hostilities and put an end to their mutual acts of violence. Since she had been here in Scotland, she had come to realize there were absolutely no differences between Scot and Englishman. Nationality did not matter one jot. People shared the same hopes and fears, felt pain, envy, jealousy, and love, no matter their heritage, their age, or even their gender. Human beings were human beings the world over.

Raven's thoughts were interrupted by two maidservants who carried in a slipper bath and a pile of fresh towels. They both expressed sympathy about her burns, and one of them picked up the singed and blackened gown she had worn. "Is it true that Heath Kennedy rescued ye from the fire?"

"Yes, he saved my life," Raven confirmed.

"He is so courageous, and so handsome." Both maids sighed as if the mere thought of the dark Borderer made them weak with longing.

"I apologize for not making my bed or tidying up the chamber." She held up her bandaged hands, feeling completely useless.

"Heath has informed us that you must do nothin' but rest for the next few days." The maids looked at her as if she were the luckiest female in the world to be in his keeping.

After they left, Raven felt her cheeks burning. Not only had he instructed them to bring the bathing tub, it must have been obvious that he had removed the door from its hinges, and quite apparent that he had not slept in the other bed last night. *Splendor of God, what must they be thinking?* Her inner voice answered her: *They are thinking that Heath Kennedy is my lover, and would willingly trade places with me, burned hands and all!*

CHAPTER 14

Raven spent the early afternoon hours with Valentina and the twins. As she had foretold, when they rang the bell that hung from the window overlooking the lake, the pair of swans came gliding up, eager to be fed.

"Oh, I am so glad the fire didn't frighten them away," Tina said happily, then quickly looked at Raven with sympathy. "But I am sorry your falcons are gone. It must be most upsetting for you."

"I am infinitely thankful that they escaped the fire, so I am not unduly upset. They know how to hunt for their food, they have their freedom, and they have each other. Sultan and Sheba will soon revert to their wild ways."

When Tina declared that it was feeding time for her own little swans, Raven went back to her chamber to give Tina privacy. She was surprised, yet secretly pleased, when Heath returned in midafternoon. Her pulse became erratic when she thought of his promising to wash her hair, and wondered just how they would go about the business. She half hoped he had forgotten, but almost immediately the servants arrived with hot water and filled up the bathing tub.

Heath closed the door behind the servants when they left, then turned to Raven, studying her with intense eyes, as if trying to read her thoughts. When he saw her look of apprehension, he realized immediately that she would decline, and knew he would have to firmly take the decision upon himself.

"Washing your hair will rid it of the offensive smoky odor, and the easiest way will be to bathe you at the same time."

"Heath, I don't think I can," she said faintly.

"Raven, don't turn all prudish and prim on me. I know how shy you are feeling at this moment, and I will do my very best to preserve your modesty, but I am giving you absolutely no choice in the matter." He went to his trunk and removed a garment. "Since you once very generously lent me your shirt, I am now going to return the favor and let you wear one of mine."

Very deliberately, his fingers unfastened the neck of her bed robe, then he took her to the bed, bade her sit, and sat down behind her. He reached his hands around her and slowly drew off the robe, taking extra care with her bandaged hands as he pulled off the sleeves. Raven was now down to her white night rail, and without hesitation, Heath reached to unfasten the row of tiny pearl buttons that ran from her neck to her navel. When he tried to lift it off, she held her arms close to her body, preventing him.

"Raven, don't you think I've imagined what your body looks like a thousand times over?" he murmured.

She drew in a swift breath and her heart skipped a beat. His words disarmed her. He was a man of the world and a woman's body probably held little mystery for him. It was different for her, who had so little experience of men. Sitting on a bed, being undressed by Heath, while their bodies were inches apart was most disturbing. She could feel the heat of his broad chest and the warmth of his arms as they reached around her. His murmured words slithered down her spine in a frisson of pleasure, while his male scent enveloped her, evoking feelings that were new and strange.

At the same time she felt vulnerable and helpless, and completely in his power. To Raven's utter amazement, she liked the feeling. He was fiercely protective of her and she felt that she could rely on him for anything, everything. He was her rock, her bastion, her protector, and her healer. She lifted her arms and symbolically yielded herself to his tender care.

The night rail dropped from Heath's fingers as he looked down at Raven's naked back. It was like cream satin, and the warm, smooth flesh curving down to her round bottom was sensual and feminine. He longed to lift the black curtain of hair from the nape of her neck and brush his lips across the intimate, private place. He wanted to

put his mouth against her naked flesh and whisper dark, erotic words
that would arouse her and make her feel beautiful. She smelled of
smoke and woman, and it made him smolder with an insatiable longing to taste her.

Heath was fully aroused by the lovely female who sat before
him. Though her back was turned to him, he was quite tall enough
to look down over her shoulder and watch her delicate breasts rise
and fall with every breath she took. He fought his desire to caress
her by concentrating on getting his shirt on her without hurting her.
He gave her no time to change her mind, but lifted her from the bed
immediately and deposited her gently in the water, reminding her to
keep her bandages dry.

Raven carefully draped her arms over the edge of the tub to
keep her hands from getting wet. She had no idea that the water had
turned Heath's shirt almost transparent and that her pink nipples
were completely visible through the wet material. She watched him
lather his hands with soap, and her lavender-blue eyes widened as
she realized that he intended to rub them all over her. The material
was thin enough that the soap would penetrate through to her skin,
and she realized that she would feel every touch, every stroke, every
caress of his hands as they slid over her wet body.

"Some things take precedence over modesty, Raven. Just keep
reminding yourself that cleanliness is next to godliness," he said with
a perfectly straight face. Heath placed his hands firmly upon her
shoulders and rubbed his palms in circles, then as soon as that part of
her was soaped, he moved his palms down to her breasts and gently
massaged and stroked the lovely round globes until each of her nipples was decorated with a peak of white lather.

"Oh!" Raven gasped. "That is the first time a man has ever
touched my breasts!"

"There is a first time for everything, my beauty, and earth-
shattering as it may seem to you at this moment, I can certainly
promise you it won't be the last time."

Though his actions had not yet made her blush, his words did.
Then when his hands reached into her armpits, it felt so personal
and intimate that her blush deepened. When he moved down the

tub slightly to soap her feet and legs, she was able to breathe again. However, that lasted only a moment, for without warning, Heath lathered his hands again and reached between her legs. Raven cried out her indignant protest, but it was too late.

"All done but the shouting, milady." He winked outrageously and said, "If it will make you feel any better, I'll let you bathe me when your hands are healed."

"When my hands are healed, I shall slap your face, Heath Kennedy!"

"Well, if I'm going to get my face slapped, I might as well do something to deserve it." He waggled his soapy hands at her and laughed with delight when she shrieked.

"You wicked devil, you are enjoying this!"

He grinned at her. "The question begs: Are you?" His lips twitched. "You needn't answer if it makes you feel unladylike."

"It makes me feel *shameful*!"

His teasing grin vanished as he bent toward her and looked deeply into her eyes. "I can read your thoughts, Raven. You don't feel the least shameful. You feel a little shy, slightly breathless, and a tiny bit afraid. But danger excites you, you told me so yourself."

She licked her lips. "*Am* I in danger?"

"I hope so, Raven," he murmured intensely. "I hope you are in danger of losing your heart."

She did not dare to examine any feelings that concerned her heart, and quickly changed the subject. "You promised to wash the smell of smoke from my hair."

"Let's do it before the water cools. Can you move down so that you can dip your head back into the water? Don't grab the edge of the tub; I'll ease you down." Heath placed his strong hand at her back and lowered her very gradually until all her hair was submerged, then he eased her back up again. He lathered her hair thoroughly with the rose-scented soap, then brought the water jug and rinsed it. He wrapped a towel about her head in turban fashion, then bade her wrap her arms about his neck, so that he could lift her from the water.

She wound her arms about him and was acutely aware of where

Heath put his arms. One was about her back, the other was beneath her knees, but she could feel her bare bottom cheeks brush against his flexed arm as he lifted her and set her down before the fire. Raven stood there helplessly as he wrapped her in a large towel and rubbed her vigorously. His fingers moved beneath the towel to unfasten the shirt buttons, then, holding the towel about her with one hand, he peeled the wet shirt from her body with the other hand. He then proceeded to dry her thoroughly.

He brought her bed robe and held it out for her. She turned her back demurely, allowing the towel to slip to her feet, while Heath wrapped her in the warm gown and gently pulled her bandaged hands through the sleeves. "What a team," he murmured.

"You are my magic man," she said breathlessly.

He raised her chin with his fingers until their eyes met. "Hocus pocus, fish bones choke us."

A knock on the door was the maidservant with their supper. Barely above a whisper, Raven said, "I'm not really hungry. The pain is coming back."

"I've been expecting it; we were lucky it stayed away this long. You must eat something, Raven, because I'm going to give you some poppy and licorice and it's not good on an empty stomach. Gradually it will take away your pain and put you into a sleep that will be mercifully deep."

Raven decided she would try the mutton-and-barley broth, which Heath fed her one spoonful at a time. Then he built up the fire and brought the sleeping draught. He held the syrup of poppy to her lips and waited with endless patience until she took every drop. Then he picked up the hairbrush, sat down in a chair before the fire, and motioned for Raven to sit on the rug and rest her back against his knees. He unwrapped the towel from her head and began to brush her long, wet tresses.

Almost immediately the dancing blue flames of the fire, combined with the gentle stroking of the hairbrush, hypnotized Raven. The repetition of the long, firm strokes put her into a trancelike state where she had no will of her own. She wanted only to yield herself into his powerful, possessive hands, all night. As she sat curled against his knees she gradually became euphoric, drifting in a warm sea of delicious sensation. She noticed absently that the pain in her hands had receded to a place apart, where it could not touch her, and she longed for Heath to go on brushing her hair forever. Her eyelids finally closed, she half turned toward him, gently lowered her head into his lap, and gave herself up to sleep and the warm haven of Heath Kennedy's body.

He held absolutely still, savoring the trust she had placed in him. A pulse beat erratically in his throat because her soft cheek was pressed into his hard thigh. Each stroke of the brush through her silken black curls had aroused him further. It had been unbelievably erotic for the dark Borderer to brush Raven's hair as if he were her body servant. If she ever became his, how sensual it would be to play with her ebony tresses before he made love to her. There was no denying that she had craved his touch tonight.

Heath set the brush aside and stroked her shining hair with his callused hand. He was infinitely glad that she slept and could no longer feel any pain. "You enthrall me, my beauty. I never believed I would find a female as innocent and as lovely as you, but I was wrong. I want you for my woman, Raven. Tell me you feel the same." He closed his eyes, crushing down the raging desire he felt to brand her as his. Tending her needs tonight had been a combination of the pleasures of paradise and the agonies of hell.

He carried her to the wide bed and gently covered her. He stood watch over her for a long time, savoring her delicate beauty. He marveled that one with such black hair could have skin like cream and roses. Her eyelashes formed crescent shadows on her high cheekbones, and her soft, pink mouth begged for a man's kisses. With difficulty, he moved away from the bed, then sat before the fire to eat his dinner. When he was finished, he leaned his head back, closed his eyes, and tried to think of other things. But her presence cried out to him, tempting him, luring him, beckoning him back to the bed. Heath fought his desires valiantly, but he knew it was a losing battle, and finally he gave in to temptation and returned to her. He undressed slowly, quietly, then slipped into the bed and drew her against him with tender yet possessive hands.

The narcotic effects of the poppy not only induced Raven to sleep, they took her to a mystical place, where colors were brilliant, creatures were magical, and every sense was heightened. A ring of orange and yellow flames danced about her, but she was not afraid because Sultan was beside her, guarding her. She loved him so much, she cried, "Fly, save yourself!"

He flew in a wide circle, then came back to her. "I won't leave without you. We will get through this bad time together, Sheba." Suddenly they were caught up in a spiral of smoke that carried them higher and higher, away from the flames, away from the terrifying darkness, into a cloudless blue sky, brilliant with sunshine. Freedom! There was no greater feeling in heaven or earth; it was intoxicating! Sultan and Sheba clasped talons and cartwheeled through the sky as one being, joyful to be alive, to be free, and best of all, to be together.

She could hear the rhythm of something beating steadily, and thought it was the sound of their wings. Almost immediately, however, she realized it was the beat of their hooves as they galloped across the springy, emerald green turf. An azure sea lay before them, and when they came to its shore, they began to race each other with a wild and reckless abandon. Their long black manes streamed behind them like banners in the wind, and the glorious freedom they felt was so exhilarating, they kicked up their heels in playful rapture. When they ran out of beach, they plunged joyously into the sea and began to swim.

Raven looked down at herself and saw her breasts clearly outlined through the wet material. "You devil, Heath Kennedy! You purposely gave me your shirt because you knew the water would make it transparent! I feel absolutely shameful!"

"You don't feel the least shameful. You feel a little shy, slightly breathless, and a tiny bit afraid. But danger excites you, Raven, you told me so yourself!"

She dived beneath the water, hoping he would pursue her and follow where she led, but he was suddenly before her, waiting for her with outstretched arms, and she went into them willingly, eagerly, knowing that she felt more complete when he held her against his heart. With one arm around her back and the other beneath her knees, he lifted her and carried her from the sea. With his every step, she could feel her bare bottom cheeks brush against his flexed arm. Heath laid her down upon the warm sand and stretched out beside her. Slowly he unfastened the buttons that ran down the front of the wet shirt from neck to navel, then he removed the garment altogether. While one palm cupped her breast, the other caressed her body in all the most intimate, feminine places a woman possessed. His powerful hands stroked down her body from her breasts to her thighs, and she shuddered at the callused roughness of them on her soft skin. Raven reveled in his touch, longing to stroke his darkly tanned, naked flesh with her palms and trace her fingers over all the hard, muscular, male places a man possessed, but her hands were somehow held immobile by an invisible force.

As Heath made love to her with his hands and his mouth, the world receded until they became oblivious to everything around them. They did not notice the tide edging its inevitable way toward them over the sand until it engulfed them. Raven clung to him desperately as they went down, down, into the midnight blue depths; then, like a miracle, his powerful strokes took them up to the surface. She knew that he was her rock, her bastion, her strength. He had the power, and she wanted him to hold her safe against life's dangers forever.

They swam together, two black swans with their feathered wings touching, gliding across the lake toward the castle and the irresistible ringing of the bell. The church bell pealed forth its joyous notes telling the world that two people were about to be joined in holy matrimony. Raven's eyes widened with disbelief as she saw the priest standing before the altar with Heath, ready to do his bidding and perform this forced wedding without her consent. Her bridal gown was a white shirt, the only garment he had allowed her since he kidnapped her and imprisoned her in his tower.

The dark Borderer had total control over her. He knew her thoughts, knew her every action. He fed her by hand as if she were a falcon and he her master. He was training her to do his bidding, allowing her to fly occasionally, but always luring her back, then securing her jesses between his all-powerful fingers. She had no will of her own; he had taken it from her as easily as he had taken her clothes and her freedom.

"Raven, focus on me. Suspend your will, my love, and yield your inner self to me. Listen to my words and do as they bid you."

She did listen. She heard his gentleness and his kindness, but she also heard his determination and his power.

"Open your mind and let me come inside. I am giving you no choice in the matter. Repeat the sacred wedding vows after me."

She felt vulnerable and helpless, and completely in his power. In a trancelike state, she promised to love, honor, and obey him, and heard the priest pronounce them man and wife.

Heath swept her up in possessive arms and strode up the stairs to their tower. He put her in his wide bed, slipped in beside her, and pulled her into his powerful arms. "You must merge with me, Raven. Yield your will to me, just for tonight."

She laughed up into his dark face, feeling happier than she had ever felt in her life. "Darling Heath, thank you for forcing me to wed you. It took all the responsibility out of my hands and gave me my heart's desire." She lifted her mouth for his kiss. His mouth on hers felt glorious. She had never experienced anything to equal the deep pleasure she received from the touch and the taste of him. When he enfolded her in possessive arms and pressed his hard body against hers, she thought she might die of joy.

"You are dreaming, Raven."

"I know I am dreaming, you devil." But suddenly, Raven did not feel like she was dreaming. Was it possible that she was awake? She could not tell what was real and what was imagined. She knew she was in bed in Heath Kennedy's arms, and the last thing she remembered was marrying him!

"Close your eyes, Raven, and let sleep take you back to your dreams. It isn't yet morning and the effects of the poppy will lull you back to slumber if you remain still and quiet."

Her eyelids were indeed heavy and sleep beckoned her. She felt warm and safe and exceedingly grateful that her hands were without pain. She took a deep breath and relaxed against him. Her cheek rested against Heath's chest, and his heartbeat lulled her back to sleep. This time, however, it was peaceful and dreamless.

When Raven awoke in the morning, she was alone in the bed. Her mind was filled with questions about the night, but she was reticent about asking them when he brought their breakfast, because she was afraid of the answers. Heath fed her, then selected a wide-sleeved blue gown for her to wear. She had no choice but to let him dress her, but he did it in a way that allowed her to preserve a modicum of modesty. Then he unwrapped the bandages from her hands.

"They are much improved, Raven. I am going to wash off the ointment and coat them with a mixture of honey and balm, then re-bandage them. Two more days might be all they will need."

She saw that her fingers were no longer black, and the blisters were gone, though her palms were still red and tender. As Heath bathed her fingers and palms, then coated them with the soothing honey and herb mixture, she focused on his hands. They were beautiful hands, strong and capable, yet so gentle it brought a lump to her throat. When her bandages were in place, he picked up the hairbrush and, with long, rhythmic strokes, untangled her curls. She closed her eyes at the sensual pleasure it brought her, and broke her silence. "I dreamed that you compelled me to marry you."

"Yes, I know."

"How could you possibly know my dreams?"

"You thanked me for forcing you to wed me. You said it took all the responsibility out of your hands."

So, you did sleep with me . . . I did awaken in your arms!

"You wouldn't really force me to wed you?" she whispered.

"I won't lie to you, Raven. It is a distinct possibility. You know that I want you for my woman, and I cannot deny that a forced marriage has much to recommend it."

CHAPTER 15

Freedom is the most precious commodity on earth. Without freedom, my life would be meaningless. If you forced me to wed you, Heath Kennedy, I would hate you forever!"

"Raven, there is such a fine line between hate and love, I am quite willing to take the gamble."

"You are so damned cocksure of yourself and your powers of persuasion. Why don't you give me the choice of staying or leaving?" she challenged.

Heath set the brush down and turned her to face him. "If you will give me a week to woo you, I *will* give you the choice."

She searched his dark face, trying to discern just what he meant by wooing. Her pulse beat a rapid tattoo and her blood warmed perceptibly as it flowed through her veins. He meant wooing in every sense of the word, with no barriers between them and no holds barred, and she wondered wildly what it would be like to have Heath Kennedy make love to her and teach her about passion. Was she woman enough to take up his challenge? She wavered on the brink. He had promised to give her the choice of staying or leaving if she agreed, and she knew instinctively it was the only way he would ever let her go. "Three days," she bargained, "I will allow you to woo me for three days."

Heath's dark eyes gleamed. "Three days it is, but they will start after your hands have healed for two more days. I don't want you to accuse me of taking advantage of you, my beauty. In two days you should be up to a rough wooing." He winked and his white teeth flashed in a smile that showed his supreme male confidence.

When Rob Kennedy rapped impatiently on the door in Carlisle's Rickergate, Lady Kennedy's maid, Kirsty, opened it and almost fainted when she saw it was the irascible Lord of Galloway. He pushed past her immediately, treating her like a nonentity as always.

"Her ladyship is indisposed," Kirsty whispered timidly.

"She *will* be indisposed when I'm done wi' her," Rob bellowed, and had the satisfaction of watching Kirsty flee in trepidation. He rolled into Elizabeth's sitting room like a barrel of whisky down a gangplank, his face congested with fury, and his salt and cayenne pepper hair standing in sparse tufts. "Lizzie, Carlisle has been an accursed place tae me since I set foot in it, tae come courting ye. The bloody English have burned ma vessel, the *Galloway*, along wi' her precious fleeces. This is the last time Carlisle will ever see me or mine again!"

"Oh, Rob, that is terrible," Elizabeth murmured.

"I'll tell ye what's terrible, Lizzie, a willful wife who doesna honor an' obey her lord! This is an ultimatum, Lizzie. The choice is yers: Ye can come or ye can stay, I don't much care either way. But young Beth comes wi' me, and if ye choose tae stay, ye'll never see her nor any of the childer again."

Elizabeth felt faint and nauseated; her husband always had this effect upon her when he exercised his authority. Her hand fluttered to her throat and she closed her eyes to block out the fearsome picture he made. "I . . . I think it best I come home."

"Home? I said naught about goin' home, woman. As soon as Duncan buys us another vessel, we're sailin' tae Kirkcudbright tae see Donal, then Valentina. Ye're an unnatural mother, Lizzie. Ye shouldha bin wi' Valentina while she had the wee bairn. There's bin no word, an' I'm worritin' mysel tae death aboot it!" He looked about the chamber and bellowed, "Where's Beth?"

"I'm here, Father." Beth had known of his arrival from the first word he uttered, but his grating voice had rendered her paralyzed until summoned.

"Tell that Kirsty woman tae pack yer bags. There'll be no be-trothals tae no bloody Englishmen, Dacre or otherwise!"

Though Beth was vastly relieved about Chris Dacre, her heart did yearn for another handsome, young Englishman by the name of Heron Carleton. But she decided that discretion was the better part of valor, and kept her mouth wisely closed.

Five miles north at Rockcliffe Manor, Heron Carleton thought fleetingly of pretty Beth Kennedy and was tempted to visit Carlisle. His mother placed an obstacle in his path, however, when she said, "I wonder how Raven is faring with my mother? I believe it is time that you visited your grandmother, Heron; you have neglected her shamefully this past year."

"She takes as little interest in me as I take in her, Mother. It is Raven whom she dotes upon," Heron objected.

Kate Carleton could think of nothing but Raven and how she was progressing with Christopher Dacre. Her daughter had been gone for only eight days, but to Kate it felt like a month. "You need spend only a few hours with your grandmother, Heron, then you will be free to visit with your friend Chris Dacre at Bewcastle. The hunting in Kershope Forest is the best in the Borders. As well, I be-lieve Raven will benefit from having her brother along as a sort of chaperon. It will remind Lord Dacre that Raven comes from a highly respectable family who will not tolerate dalliance."

The mention of Bewcastle erased Heron's reluctance. He had always had ambitions to belong to a Border patrol as his mother's clan of Herons did. Even his father had started this way, before he had become constable of Carlisle Castle. His mother, however, had insisted he go to school in London and learn to be a gentleman. Heron had met Christopher Dacre at Eton, and when his friend had gone to fight the Scots at Flodden, he had been green with envy. His mother, however, had put her foot down, insisting that her only son was far too young to fight in a bloody war against the uncivilized Scots. When Heron got to Bewcastle, he fervently hoped that Chris Dacre would take him on a Border patrol.

Heron timed his visit so that he would arrive at Blackpool Gate in the late afternoon. That way he would only have to spend one evening with dotty Dame Doris, before moving on to Bewcastle the next morning. When his grandmother told him that Christopher Dacre had taken Raven for a visit to the great English Border fortress, he readily agreed to take the baggage his sister had carelessly left behind. By the sound of things, Heron deduced that he and his friend Chris would be brothers-in-law before the year was out.

As Heath had predicted, Raven's hands were healed enough to leave off the bandages after two more days of coating them with honey and balm. She was vastly relieved to be able to use her hands again to bathe and dress and feed herself, for the closeness which had grown between her and Heath when he had done these intimate things for her evoked a longing she could no longer suppress. Now that she was healed, she knew his wooing would begin in earnest, and Raven wondered wildly what she would do if she succumbed to his dark, potent persuasion. It was the first time that she had admitted to herself that such a thing was within the realm of possibility, and she knew she must guard her heart with every fiber of her being.

Raven was glad that when she had awakened before dawn, Heath was gone from the tower. Early today they were riding to Hawick for the wedding of Queen Margaret Tudor to Ramsay's cousin, Archibald Douglas, Earl of Angus. While Heath was tending his mares, Raven would take her bath, then pack a bag. They were not staying away overnight, because Valentina would not leave the twins that long, but Raven had decided to pack the gown she would wear at the wedding, and ride there in her own red and black riding dress.

She swore beneath her breath as she heard Heath enter the outer chamber of the tower, and hastily reached for the drying cloth.

"Raven, are you ready yet? I've saddled Sully for you . . ." His voice trailed away as he walked into the adjoining room and caught sight of her in the bathing tub. He moved with the swiftness of a predator after its prey, grabbing the towel that she had just picked up. It stretched between them as they both vied for possession, but Heath managed to snare the coveted cloth.

"You wicked devil; I desire my privacy every bit as much as I desire my freedom!"

"Speak not of desire, Raven; it would be sheer folly at this moment." Her wet skin was translucent as if it had been dusted by powdered pearls. Her lashes were black, tipped with gold, over eyes that changed from blue to lavender to deep purple. Her nose was small, yet her nostrils flared sensually, as if they caught his scent and found it disturbing. Her mouth was full and lusty, and colored deepest rose. Her throat curved beautifully, drawing his eyes to lush breasts of alabaster, crowned by buds of dark rose, the color of her mouth. "I'll dry you," he said hoarsely.

"I will dry myself," she said firmly.

His teeth flashed. "With what, my beauty? You will have to walk about naked for long minutes if you would have the air dry you. You allowed me to dry you yesterday, why not today?"

"Yesterday my hands were bandaged."

"Your bandages were your protection; they had me at a complete disadvantage."

"When I am naked, you have me at a complete disadvantage!"

Heath grinned. "I know. If I'd thrown all your clothes through the tower window and kept you naked all week, we'd be wed by now."

"Cocksure devil! We will *never* be wed. You delude yourself that I burn for your touch and long for your kisses, when in reality you have no effect upon me whatsoever."

"If that is the truth, Raven, you can have no objection to my drying you." He moved purposefully toward her and lifted her from the water, wrapping her in the soft linen. He drew her close and gazed down into her eyes. Then he dipped his head and tentatively brushed his lips against hers. When she opened her mouth, he stopped her protest with a deep kiss that was deliberately sensual.

Before he released her mouth, his hands began to circle across the linen that covered her curves. He dried her back in this manner, then his hands moved around to the front. He cupped her breasts on his palms and weighed them, then he splayed his fingers around them and caressed their lush fullness through the fine material. With his mouth, Heath caught the soft sounds she made, then he touched the corners of her lips with the tip of his tongue.

Again his hands moved behind her, but this time they were much lower. He cupped her bottom cheeks through the linen and lifted her against the fullness of his erection. When she gasped, he took full possession of her soft mouth and kissed her thoroughly.

With his powerful hands upon her, Raven felt warm and wantonly weak. There was no question that his hard body responded to hers, but she knew she must stop hers from responding to his. She turned from him, though he still held her fast in his hands. Then she felt the full hard length of him pressed into the valley of her bottom cheeks, while he cupped her plump mons with the palm of his hand and began to circle and stroke her over the rough linen.

A frisson of pleasure shimmered through her to her woman's core, then it came again and again. Her response was so instant, so hot, it shamed her. She longed for his fingers to stroke faster, and bit down on her lip to stop herself from screaming with excitement. His fingers, however, moved with a deliberate slow rhythm that made her aching need spiral tighter and tighter until she thought she would shatter into a million shards. The bud inside the pink folds of her center began to swell with passion, and just when she thought she could bear no more, it burst open like a rose coming to full bloom in the hot sunshine. She cried out, "Heath!" and sagged back against him. Raven was again wet, where she had been dry.

His arms enfolded her, and he dipped his head to nuzzle her neck with his lips. He felt humbled that this was the first time her body had known carnal pleasure. Heath knew that if he did not stop now, he would take her to his bed and keep her there all day. The hour was yet early, and their day would be long, but Heath vowed that before midnight he would make love to her.

Raven and Heath joined Valentina and Ramsay on their ride to Hawick. They followed the River Te into the dale of Teviot, which was reputedly the most beautiful valley in all Scotland. It was surrounded by the highest craggy hills Raven had ever seen. "The vistas take my breath away and the air is as intoxicating as wine," Raven said passionately to Tina.

"The first time I saw it, I couldn't believe that Clan Douglas owned as far as the eye could see," Tina said. "I loved the late Earl of Angus; he was both fierce and canny. It was *his* plan that his son Archie marry Scotland's widowed queen, Margaret Tudor. Ram is very like old Angus; they shared an infallible shrewdness. If the earl could have had his way, I warrant he would have preferred that Ramsay be his heir, over his own son."

Raven looked at the two dark men who rode side by side. The resemblance between them was marked, though Ram's features were harsher. She had felt extremely shy when Heath had helped her mount, and his possessive hands had lingered about her waist, but he had let her ride beside Valentina, and her shyness was floating off on the heather-scented breeze. Her glance moved from Ram to Heath. *Death and damnation, why am I so attracted to him? His hair is black until the sunlight strikes it, then it takes on the same blue-black sheen as the stallion he rides. . . . In that leather jack, his shoulders are impossibly wide.* Raven blushed at her own thoughts. She had seen him without his shirt and knew his well-muscled arms and chest revealed an unmistakable raw strength. A spiral of desire descended from her belly to between her legs, and she suddenly refused to feel shame. Instead she tossed back her hair and smiled inwardly; at long last she was becoming a woman.

Ramsay Douglas rode beside Heath Kennedy, deep in thought. Finally he broke his silence. "When I was in Glasgow, Samuel Erskine, the goldsmith, said something that has made me ponder. He informed me that Angus had left a huge sum of gold on deposit for me, and all I had tae do was produce a copy of the will."

"Have you seen the will?" Heath asked.

"Nay. Though he's been dead two months, there's been no readin' of the will tae my knowledge. Strange," Ramsay commented.

"Who's the earl's attorney?"

"Moses Irvine. Angus said there was always a job for a whore or a lawyer, and he dealt with only the best of both." Ram grimaced. "I'll quiz Archie and see what he has tae say."

As they rode down the lee side of the Teviot valley the air was filled with the heady scent of wild hyacinths, or bluebells as they were commonly known, and when the carpet of blue came into view, beneath the spreading branches of the trees, they saw a Gypsy camp. "I hoped the Gypsies would be here," Valentina said happily. "They follow the royal court because they know there is money to be made from love potions, spells, and abortifacients, to say nothing of occasional doses of poison."

"I had my fortune told at Carlisle Fair. A Gypsy foretold I would marry well, into great wealth and a title." *She also predicted the path would be circuitous,* Raven suddenly recalled.

"When I had a Gypsy read the tarot cards about my marriage, I refused to believe anything she predicted, but every word she uttered came true." Tina laughed, and glanced at her husband. "And I thank God and his saints every day of my life."

"Your king died less than a year ago. Don't you think it scandalous that his queen is marrying again so soon?"

"It wasn't a love match. James Stewart never wanted Margaret Tudor. He was mad in love with a raven-haired beauty called Maggie Drummond. Only after she died did James send for his bride."

"How did she die?" Raven asked compassionately.

"She was poisoned. Don't look so horrified; it was likely the English who did the dirty deed. The political marriage to Margaret would never have been consummated had someone not expediently removed Jamie's beloved."

"Is power always corrupt?" Raven asked abruptly, thinking of the rumors she had heard about the Dacres.

"Of course, but it is the degree of corruption that matters. A man worth having has his own noble code of honor, but remember that a man's honor is different from a woman's. Personally I prefer a man who is a little wicked, though I abhor evil."

Yes, Valentina is right. Wicked is most attractive, while evil would be anathema. Raven shuddered, hoping evil never touched her.

The men spurred forward to ride beside their partners. "How are ye holding up, my honey lamb?" Ram asked Valentina.

"I am absolutely bursting with energy and vitality. Let us hope the nuptial ceremony is brief so we can enjoy the dancing."

"Are you cold, Raven?" Heath inquired.

"No." She knew he must have been watching her if he had seen her shiver. His closeness enveloped her and she felt precious to him. She wondered wildly if he was using his power to enchant and snare her. Then she smiled. Had she not power of her own?

Just to the east of the town of Hawick sat Cavers Castle. It was a fortified tower castle, and only its lovely setting prevented it from looking threatening. The dozen Douglas moss-troopers who had ridden a mile ahead of them were waiting outside Cavers. When the two couples crossed the moat, the moss-troopers clattered after them. The moss-troopers elbowed aside the grooms who came out to assist the guests, knowing that Ramsay and Heath preferred to help their own ladies to dismount. Usually, Cavers Castle had only a skeleton staff, but today it was bristling with servants. Royal footmen came forward to take their baggage, and Valentina led the way into the castle. They were met by a gaggle of ladies-in-waiting, most of them English, Raven realized.

The men were shown to another chamber where they could change and quaff the dust of the road from their throats. When Ramsay's cousin Archibald Douglas, the new Earl of Angus, joined them, he was wearing his wedding finery. His skintight red silk hose were saved from looking obscene only by his rich surcoat that ended just below his groin. It was white satin, embroidered with huge red lions that constituted the arms of the Earl of Angus. Ram slanted a dark brow; he had never seen old Angus in anything save black. Ram himself donned a black velvet doublet with the Bleeding Heart of Douglas device, pricked out in small rubies.

Archie narrowed his eyes. "Do ye know, in the list of Douglas jewels I received, there was mention of a ruby in the shape of a heart, that was big as a plover's egg, but I've seen none such. I dinna suppose my father loaned it tae Valentina?"

"Anythin' Angus gave tae Tina was a gift," Ram said. "Women are not in the habit of considerin' jewels as loans, as ye'll soon learn when ye acquire a wife of yer own. However, tae put yer mind at ease, Tina owns no ruby big enough tae choke a horse!"

A picture of Old Meg's tortoise came full-blown to Heath, and he chuckled at the sheer audacity of his grandmother. If Angus had given it to her because he had sired Lily Rose on her, she had stuck it on the tortoiseshell to show her contempt for noble blood.

"Did ye receive the list of jewels when the will was read, Archie?" Ram asked casually.

Archibald blinked rapidly. "My father died without a will."

"Nay, he did not. Angus made his will with Moses Irvine in Glasgow, and added a few codicils last year, after Flodden."

"Did ye no' hear? Moses Irvine died a fortnight after Father. His younger partner took over the law practice. Goldman assured me there was no will. It makes little difference, since I have always been my father's legal heir."

That gives ye the title and two castles, Archibald. Ram managed to smile and thump his cousin on the back. "Earl of Angus is a noble title tae live up tae, Archie, and costly too," he added to twist the knife. *If Angus left most of his gold tae me, I warrant ye'll stoop tae any foul deed tae line yer pockets.*

As other Clan Douglas members arrived in the chamber, toasts to the bridegroom became continuous. "We'd better get ye tae the church while ye're still on yer feet, Archie. Ye should not keep a queen waiting, man; she could change her mind."

Inside Cavers's chapel, Ramsay slipped into the pew beside Tina and bent his head to kiss her brow.

She smiled up into his pewter eyes. "Archie didn't ask you to be best man, because it is too obvious you are exactly that, my love."

Ram shook his head. "He doesn't want me that close. I might uncover a few secrets."

Heath caught his breath when he slipped in beside Raven. She was wearing a gown of palest sea-foam green, and Tina must have supplied her with a jade necklace and carbobs that enhanced her lovely dark coloring. His heart constricted momentarily, because he knew he could never afford to give her jewels. Yet Raven enthralled him. Her image was ever before him, night and day. He had an unquenchable thirst for her. Whenever he glimpsed her across a chamber, he drew close, then when he was close enough, he must touch her. Her fragrance filled his senses; he would never get enough of smelling her and tasting her. Both the sound of her voice and her laughter aroused him instantly, no matter who was there to see. Heath covered her hand with his, and she jumped as if she had been burned. *You too feel the fire*, he thought. He stroked her hand with his thumb, then curled his fingers about her wrist and rejoiced in the feel of her rapid pulse beats.

Raven craned her neck when the bride entered to join her bridegroom before the altar. Margaret's gown was cloth of gold and she was wearing an ornate crown, but the woman herself was a disappointment. Her figure was rather dumpy; her hair was a faded gold, her face square, her mouth hinting at self-indulgence.

"She lives at the top of Mount Dotage," Tina whispered, and Raven had to bite her lip to keep from laughing aloud. Her eyes ran over Margaret's plain-faced bridesmaids, and it was obvious why they had been chosen. The thick-tongued Scots bishop who officiated spoke in Latin, mangling the language as badly as he did English, and Raven's attention wandered. She could smell the dank dampness of the chapel in spite of the scented candles and burning incense. Margaret, sister to King Henry Tudor, was marrying a Scot. Raven wondered what her mother would say when she found out. Kate would be scandalized. Raven glanced at Heath Kennedy and quickly banished the thought about marrying a Scot, before it could form in her head. Then she very deliberately removed her hand from his and edged closer to Valentina.

CHAPTER 16

The voices of the choirboys rose in a crescendo as the triumphant bridegroom led his new bride down the aisle of the chapel, past the pews filled with their honored guests. Raven thought the bride looked amazingly smug for one who had just stepped down in rank from queen to countess.

The bridesmaids followed with baskets of rose petals. "A perfect English rose," Valentina murmured.

"Aye, Archie must have a cast-iron gut tae stomach her," Ram commented.

Valentina glanced archly at Raven and Heath. "Don't let this put you off marriage; we highly recommend the institution," she told them.

By the time the guests filed outside into the sunshine, the bride was mounted upon her husband's gift to her: a white palfrey. Heath's grin was immediately wiped from his face as he looked at the horse. It was his; the only one of his breeding mares that he had not recovered.

"Judas Iscariot, that's my bloody mare!" he blurted to Ramsay.

"So it is," Ram confirmed. "Don't tell me that whoreson Dacre has been here, ingratiatin' himself with the new Earl of Angus!"

"It could be the other way about; perhaps Archie has been visiting Bewcastle!"

"Christ-all-fucking-mighty!" Ram cursed. If that were true, Archibald Douglas was playing a very dangerous game. And it would certainly explain why they had chosen to get married in Hawick!

Cavers's great hall, on the second floor of the castle, was

brilliantly lit and ostentatiously decorated for the bridal reception. Margaret Tudor Stewart Douglas sat upon a padded throne up on the dais next to her husband and surrounded by her courtiers. She was waiting to receive her subjects' obeisance as mother of Jamie Stewart, the new King of Scotland, and wife of Archibald Douglas, the new Earl of Angus. The earldom had been the most powerful in Scotland when old Angus was alive.

When Raven had donned the sea-foam green gown earlier, she had been self-conscious about its low-cut neckline. Now, however, she saw that all the ladies of the court were vying with each other to see who could expose the most. Of course, Valentina won hands down, for her breasts were lush and lovely from feeding her babies.

Tina took Raven's hand. "Come, I will present you to Margaret. She is shallow, greedy, vain, immature, petulant, and demanding. I am speaking of her virtues. Dip your knee, but don't give her a full curtsy." As the two beautiful young women ascended to the dais, every eye in the hall was upon them.

"Your Highness, it gives me the greatest pleasure to present my kinswoman Mistress Raven Carleton. I was most fortunate that she was visiting when I gave birth."

"Ah, Lady Douglas. Your child was delivered safely, I trust?" Margaret could not hide her envy of Valentina's radiant beauty.

"Children, actually. I had twins, a boy and a girl. The thought occurred to me to bring them to Hawick to be christened, so that you and Angus could act as godparents, but then I didn't want to up-stage the bride," Tina said sweetly.

As Raven dipped her knee, she saw Margaret's eyes glitter with venom, and realized Valentina had just destroyed any hope she had of persuading the English queen to aid her. When they left the dais, Tina said, "When I mentioned the twins, did you see her hand go to her belly? By God, I warrant she's breeding again!"

"That would mean he has been her lover for some time?" Raven realized she was naive to be shocked.

"Margaret's been rutting with Archie since she presented the late king with an heir. Once Jamie did his duty, he never darkened her bed again." Tina laughed. "Did you not think English ladies could be promiscuous? The royal court is like a dead mackerel on the beach—it shines and it stinks. The English court is even worse; I've attended both."

Ramsay used the time the banquet was being served to connect with the lairds of the many branches of the Douglas clan. The Western Marches of both England and Scotland were the cockpit of the Border and home to the most predatory clans. When he was done, he tallied pledges for thousands of Douglas moss-troopers who could be put in the saddle if the English raiding of their frontier got worse.

The banquet had eight courses, and each was successively more sumptuous with richer food and sauces. Raven thought wistfully of Mr. Burque's delectable offerings. Beside her, Heath's sexual hunger increased by the minute. Valentina tapped her feet and fingers impatiently to the music and wished they would clear away the food and the trestle tables, so that the dancing could start. Heath too was impatient for the dancing, when he could legitimately take Raven in his arms before the entire company.

When the dancing did begin, Raven was taken aback. She and Valentina were immediately separated from their men by the other guests. The male courtiers surrounded them, begging to partner them in the dance, which was rather flattering. But it was the behavior of the ladies which surprised Raven most. Margaret immediately attached herself to Ramsay Douglas, blatantly touching him and inviting him to take whatever liberties he fancied. Two ladies-in-waiting laid claim to Heath Kennedy. They hung on his every word, as well as his arms, begging him to partner them in the dance.

"Isn't it a heady feeling to make a roomful of women hate you?" Tina whispered. "These English ladies cannot resist our dark, dominant, and dangerous Borderers. They are positively panting for a look or a touch from the swaggering devils."

"Don't you resent their wanton behavior?" Inexplicably, Raven realized that she certainly resented it.

"Nay, let them touch away . . . I'm the one who shares his bed."

The bridegroom bowed before Raven and asked her to dance.

She smiled her assent and received a leer from Archibald in return. The moment he drew her into his arms, she could smell the whisky fumes, and realized the drink had banished his inhibitions, if he'd ever had any to begin with.

"Raven, is yer father Sir Lancelot Carleton, one of the judges at the Border Wardens' Court?"

"Yes, the very same, my lord earl."

"And ye are kin tae our beauteous Lady Valentina?"

"Yes. My father and Valentina's mother, Lady Elizabeth Kennedy, are cousins." It easily explained why she was with the Douglases. Whatever would he do if she blurted out that she was not their invited guest, but a kidnap victim? Raven decided it was too preposterous to be believed.

He leered down at her and bent his head to impart a confidence. "Lizzie Kennedy hates the Douglases wi' a passion, and Black Ram Douglas, who wed her daughter, most of all."

Raven blinked and wondered what he expected her to say. He sounded pleased that Ramsay was hated. "I was recently in Lady Kennedy's company in Carlisle. We were guests of the Dacres," she said, apropos to nothing whatsoever.

"Ye know the Dacres?" Archibald seemed startled.

"Very well indeed. Lord Dacre's son, Christopher, is a particular friend of mine."

The new Earl of Angus clamped his lips together as if he had said too much, and allowed his hands to wander down Raven's back. Heath Kennedy's tall figure loomed beside them. "This is a galliard, I believe. The lady promised the dance to me."

"Och, aye, take the lass. I'll have at yer sister."

Heath very much doubted that Ram would trust Archie to lift his wife into the air for the galliard, but left the matter in the capable hands of his brother-in-law.

"I promised you no dance," Raven challenged.

"Ah, but you did," Heath insisted, enfolding her in his arms. "Dancing is part of wooing . . . and wooing is a mating dance." He murmured intimately, "The male and the female move their bodies together in the same rhythm, imitating what they really want. Their long, drawn-out eye contact is a copulation look." The music quickened to double tempo and Heath lifted her in a high arc.

Raven's jade green petticoat and black silk stockings became visible for all to see, and suddenly she didn't care. The rapid beat of the music had entered her blood, and she wanted to be more alluring to Heath Kennedy than any other woman in the great hall. She laughed down into his warm brown eyes, and when he set her feet to the floor and pulled her close, she felt him quicken against her. At the feel of him, threads of desire ran from her navel to her woman's core, vibrating and rippling, until she became dizzy and breathless and aroused.

Raven looked up at him as he towered above her. Beneath heavy brows his dark eyes caressed her and made love to her, and promised he would soon possess her. His long black hair had lost the leather thong that tied it back, and it fell to the shoulders of his black doublet, making him the very image of a predator that had marked his prey. Raven had never felt more beautiful or more powerful in her life. When the tempo of the music changed to triple time, and Heath again lifted her high in the air, she wanted to scream from excitement.

As he held her almost upside down, her breasts threatened to spill from her bodice. When she intercepted his hot, appreciative glance, Raven winked down at him. She saw his white teeth flash in a grin and was almost overcome with the need to feel his mouth upon hers. He read her mind, and as the dance ended, he lowered her feet to the floor and lowered his lips to hers. She clung to him to keep her balance, and because it made her feel small and deliciously feminine.

The music changed dramatically to a Scottish reel, and a whoop of appreciation came from all the Douglases in attendance. There seemed to be miles of dark green plaid in the hall as partners were chosen. Raven should have welcomed the separation, but rather, she felt deprived. After the reels came "The Gay Gordons" and "Strip the Willow," country dances that were familiar to both the English and Scots who were celebrating. Raven found herself longing for the moment when Heath would become her partner again, even though it would be only briefly. As the music accelerated, the sweat dripped and the kilts flipped. The raucous laughter and shouting grew apace with the accidental falls, interspersed with a few deliberate trips. The company grew so bawdy, it sounded like a brawl or a rape, and threatened to degenerate into one or both any minute.

Though the hour was relatively early, Ramsay and Valentina sought the newlyweds to bid them good night. Archibald, drunk as a proverbial lord, encouraged them to stay for the bedding. Ram cocked an amused brow. "Ye've done it so often, I'm sure ye'll get it right without me."

Raven had been thoroughly enjoying herself, and Tina saw she looked reluctant to leave. "The night is young; trust me," she murmured low, then used the excuse of the twins to Margaret. "I brought us warm cloaks so we don't have to change our gowns for the ride back." Tina handed one to Heath, who quickly wrapped it about Raven and led her into the bailey, where their moss-troopers awaited them with their saddled mounts.

As they rode from Hawick the fires of the Gypsy camp lit up the sky. "Are you game?" Tina asked her brother.

"Careful how ye answer her; she'll tell ye tae stick a feather up yer arse and start crowing!" Ram jested.

Heath grinned. "I'm game."

As they galloped toward the camp they could hear the Gypsy fiddles and tambourines mixed with merry laughter, and Raven's pulse quickened with anticipation as Heath tethered Blackadder beneath an elm and turned to lift her from Sully. He slid her slowly down his hard body until her feet touched the ground. Momentarily, the world receded until there was only the two of them. "Sweetheart," he murmured, and brushed his lips against hers. Then they clasped hands and ran toward the fire.

Raven was in a reckless mood. She had made up her mind to abandon herself to pleasure for just one night. She turned a deaf ear to the inner voice that whispered caution, for every female instinct told her that if she did not seize this moment, she would regret it for the rest of her life.

She was surprised at the easy camaraderie that Tina, Ram, and Heath had with the Gypsies, then realized that they must be familiar with each other. She watched Ram exchange coins for two wineskins and hand one to Heath, who immediately squeezed an arc of wine into the air and caught it in his mouth. Heath's glance moved from hers down to her mouth, then back up to her eyes. "I don't suppose I could tempt you?"

Tonight everything about the dark Borderer tempted Raven. She flashed him a smile, unable to resist his challenge, and opened her mouth. She did a credible job of catching the stream of wine, but then she began to laugh and sprayed it everywhere. "No more," she said, gasping, "we'll ruin Tina's lovely gown."

"I'll show you how to drink without spilling a drop," Heath offered as he squeezed the wineskin and filled his mouth. His arm shot out and drew her close, then he set his mouth to hers and fed her the wine.

Raven licked her lips. "I believe it's more potent that way."

His heart soared at the seductive quality he detected in her voice. Was it possible that desire was awakening deep inside her? He slipped his arm about her and hugged her to his side, then he drew her toward the music. Heath felt his hot blood throb and pulse wildly in his throat. Then the rhythmic beat of the music seemed to enter his bloodstream and his cock lengthened and hardened as he became fully aroused. Heath curbed some of his sexual hunger, knowing that if he let it rage out of control, he would be in an agony of need.

Heath's dark beauty was so magnetic and compelling it drew Raven like a lodestone. Tonight his maleness was blatant, primal. His unleashed energy was tangible as he dominated the space around them. As well as the heat from the fire, Raven imagined she could feel the heat from his body and smell his male-scented skin, which was acting like an aphrodisiac upon her. She licked her lips with a provocative tongue and began to slowly undulate to the music. She let the cloak slide from her shoulders as she moved her hips to the dark, erotic rhythm of the Gypsy music.

Heath followed her movements in the dance, and she suddenly

realized he had been speaking the truth when he said that the male and female move their bodies in the same rhythm, imitating what they really want. Her movements became sensual, as did his, then as the tempo of the music quickened, they became overtly sexual. It was a mating dance in every sense of the word, teasing and taunting, advancing and retreating, inviting and withdrawing. Luring on, then moving away, yet gradually they drew closer and closer until they were almost touching, as their bodies swayed and swelled and yearned for each other. The male must dominate, the female must submit; it was the law of nature.

From the corner of her eye, Raven saw Ramsay and Valentina withdraw from the circle of dancers toward the meadow that was carpeted with wild hyacinths. Her heart skipped a beat, knowing it was too romantic for them to resist, but knew she must not be lured into following their example. She danced away from Heath, moving around the fire. When he followed, she danced away before he could draw close. Suddenly all eyes were upon them, and the other dancers began to clap and stamp their feet in rhythm to the music. As the tempo accelerated, going faster and faster, rising in a crescendo, Heath leaped across the flames and caught her before she could retreat. Cheers and applause erupted from the Gypsy dancers as he took her in his arms and bent her backwards in a triumphant kiss. Then, playing to his audience, he took a bow. Raven decided she too could play-act and deliberately turned her back upon him. She immediately realized it was a tactical mistake when two Gypsy girls rushed to take her place as Heath's partner.

Raven watched him dance with both, leaping back and forth between them, across the fire, and when the music came to a climax, it was they who kissed him, in blatant invitation. It was a game Raven decided to win. With hands on hips she sauntered up to the females, pushed them aside, and claimed her prize. A great shout of approval rose up from the Gypsy men, and they laid claim to their females by dragging them from Heath's side.

Raven laughed up at him. "You've done this before."

"Many times," he admitted, "but never with a prize like you at stake, my beauty."

His words made her feel special, yet it was brought home to her that Heath had probably made love to some of these females. She envied them their freedom to take a man they desired, for in her world such a thing was highly immoral. For the first time, Raven became aware of just how tempting the forbidden really was, as she admitted to herself that she longed to know what it would be like to have Heath Kennedy make love to her and teach her about passion.

When Valentina and Ramsay returned, the Gypsy men pressed Heath and Ram to join them in a knife-throwing contest, but both laughingly declined, pleading the lateness of the hour. With reluctance the two couples bade their hosts good night and made their way to where their mounts were tethered. The moss-troopers had been fed and entertained by Gypsy girls, and before they departed, Ram paid them for their hospitality with gold. He addressed his moss-troopers quietly, directing two of them to stay in Hawick to report on Archibald Douglas's activities, and ordering two more to Bewcastle to keep an eye on Thomas Dacre. Then he mounted and took Tina before him in the saddle, secure in the knowledge that his moss-troopers would tend her horse.

Heath did not ask Raven if she would ride with him, for he knew she would likely demur. He gave her no choice in the matter, but lifted her before him on Blackadder. When Raven opened her mouth to protest, Heath silenced her with a kiss and tucked her cloak about her. "Hush, sweetheart, I want to keep you warm."

Raven was acutely aware of his desire. She also was aware of her own. She felt an unbelievable physical attraction for the dark, dominant devil. She had tried to build a wall against him, but knew deep down that the edge was crumbling, for tonight she found him absolutely irresistible. She leaned back against his hard, well-muscled chest, looked up at him, and sighed. In the darkness his face was in shadow, but when he looked down, his white teeth flashed in a smile. His male scent made her nostrils flare, and she nestled against him listening to the strong, steady beat of his heart. She was honest enough to admit to herself that tonight there was nowhere else on earth she would rather be than galloping through the velvet darkness of the Borders in Heath Kennedy's powerful, possessive arms.

As Raven nestled against his body, he became aware of how small she was. Desire pulsed at his groin with a savage ache that was almost unendurable. Resting between his thighs he could feel the warmth of her body mingling with his. Her delicate scent aroused him further and he shifted in the saddle to ease the pressure of his swollen cock and the tightness of his balls. His arm brushed against her breast, and he knew he had reached his limits of restraint. He took a firm grip on Blackadder's reins with one hand and slipped the other beneath Raven's cloak. His knowing fingers found their way inside her bodice, and he cupped her bare breast with the palm of his hand and stroked over her nipple with his rough thumb.

She gasped as a frisson of purest pleasure shot from her nipple, spiraling down through her belly to her woman's core. As he continued to fondle and caress her, the rippling sensations of pleasure increased. The fiery touch of his fingers on her naked flesh almost burned her. She shuddered and suddenly fire turned to ice and she shivered uncontrollably until ice turned back to fire.

"Almost there," he murmured against her ear, and the ache his words evoked became an unbearable, sweet torture.

CHAPTER 17

When they arrived at Eskdale Castle, Heath jumped from the saddle and lifted Raven to the flagstones of the bailey. A moss-trooper stepped forward to take Heath's horse, while another took Ramsay's. As the two couples walked to the castle, Raven broke the silence. "Thank you for a lovely day, Tina. I wouldn't have missed it for anything."

"It isn't over yet." Tina winked at her. "We made it home well before midnight."

"Stop meddling, Vixen." Ram picked her up, carried her to the Master Tower, and chided her again. "I know ye want tae aid and abet him, but Heath can lift the lass's skirts without your help."

Raven and Heath paused at the bottom of the stairs that led to their tower. Their eyes met and held for long minutes; hers were shy, his directly bold. She lowered her lashes and without a word they clasped hands and ascended the steps. Anticipation of what was to come made Raven breathless and weak at the knees. Inside, her excitement built with every step she climbed. One heartbeat after he closed their tower door, Heath had her in his arms. His lips told her of his raw desire, and his dark glance promised her forbidden delights and tempted her to recklessness.

Raven opened her lips and yielded the hot, sweet cave of her mouth to him. She tasted wine on his tongue and became intoxicated. She clung to him, loving the taste, the smell, and the feel of him as she pressed her soft curves against the hard length of his body. Raven loved his strength and his power; it made her feel small and feminine, and took all the responsibility for what he did to her out of her hands.

Heath swept her up in his arms, carried her through to the inner chamber, and sat her down upon the wide bed. He removed her cloak, then dropped to his knees and removed her riding boots. His hands slid up her legs beneath her petticoat to take off her stockings, then he changed his mind. He had imagined those silk stockings since he'd urged her to choose black at Carlisle Fair. So instead, he removed her white cotton drawers. Then he took her small foot in his hand and kissed her instep. A savage impatience to bed her had ridden him all the way from Hawick, but now he found that he wanted to savor every second of the loving he would give her.

Heath drew her to her feet, unfastened her gown, and slipped it from her shoulders. Then he traced her collarbone with one fingertip and anointed it with tiny, quick kisses. The pale green gown pooled on the floor, leaving her clad in the jade petticoat and busk. His fingers unfastened the ribbons at the waist of the petticoat, and it too pooled at her feet, revealing her slim legs clad in the black silk stockings. The tops of her thighs were naked, her creamy flesh contrasting with the black curls on her mons. As she stepped from her undergarments, Heath removed the busk, and his mouth went dry at the sight of her luscious, upthrust breasts, crowned with delicate pink crests. He kissed his fingertip and touched it to each nipple, watching them tighten into hard little buds. Then he touched his lips to them and tasted her with his tongue.

As he undressed her, Raven felt like she was in a warm, delicious trance, but the moment his mouth touched her breasts, she almost came out of her skin. She arched against his tongue sensually, and when he took her nipple inside his mouth and sucked, she cried out her pleasure. Raven had a wild desire to do the same thing to him, and her fingers sought to open his doublet. She knew he read her every thought when he stripped off his doublet, then his linen shirt, and lifted her back into his arms. The coarse hair on his chest abraded the sensitive tips of her breasts, and she dug her nails into his shoulders, reeling from the delicious roughness. He let her slide down his body until her feet touched the carpet, and she felt her cheek brush across his male nipple. Her tongue snaked out to lick and taste and tease, then in a little frenzy of passion, she took it between her teeth and bit down.

Heath watched her closely, enjoying her arousal and the sensual look it brought to her face. His hand covered her breast and gently squeezed, then he stroked his palm down across her belly and cupped her hot mons. He was rewarded by her cry of pleasure, and watched her eyes turn smoky with feral need as she arched her hot center into his hand. His fingers felt her wetness start, and he knew he could wait no longer to taste her.

Heath picked her up and laid her back on the bed. He spread her glorious black hair across the pillows and his eyes dilated at the beautiful picture she made. He opened her legs and traced his fingers up the black silk stockings to where they ended on the inside of her creamy thighs. Then he moved his head between her legs and tasted her.

"No!" she cried, shocked at what he did.

He raised his head and looked into her eyes with an intensity she'd never seen before. "Raven, don't deny me all I hunger for. Don't deny yourself." He kissed her mons reverently, then blew gently on the triangle of black curls and inhaled her scent. Very deliberately he touched the tip of his tongue to her tiny pink bud and felt her quiver at the strange, new sensations he evoked. When she made no further protest, he slowly thrust inside and, with a tantalizing rhythm, began to stroke her with his rough tongue.

Raven thought she must be dreaming, for surely it was impossible that she was yielding herself to Heath Kennedy and allowing him to make love to her with his mouth. The exquisite pleasure she felt was far too real for a dream, and she threaded her fingers into his hair to make sure it was really happening. She felt his thumbs open her wider, then felt him thrust deeper. She began to writhe, wanting to enjoy this arousal to the full, wishing the dark erotic sensations could go on forever. She began to pant with need, then heard him moan; it took more than a moment for Raven to realize the moan came from her throat. She held his dark head to her hot center, then the pleasure became too intense to bear, and she arched up off the bed and cried out his name, "Heath, Heath!"

He stripped off his breeches and, naked, came up over her. He held her possessively against his heart, then he lowered his mouth to hers, knowing she would taste herself on his lips. He began with tiny, quick kisses, then he kissed the corners of her mouth. His lips traced along her cheekbone to her ear, and he kissed her temples and her eyelids, before he returned to her lips. Then his kisses lengthened. They exchanged hundreds of kisses. For a whole hour they lost themselves in the bliss of slow, melting kisses. He caressed her tongue with his, tasting the nectar of her honey-drenched mouth. His senses reeled and his mouth became harder and more demanding. Their kisses went on and on; fierce kisses, wanton kisses, savage, sensual, and erotic kisses. Heath knew he would never have enough. His cock, harder than marble, pulsed and jerked. He felt her press her soft thighs against him and knew her need almost matched his.

Heath was in the throes of an agonizing dilemma; he had wanted her to be his bride when he consummated their union. To be honorable, he should wait until they were wed, but a mocking voice told him there may never be a wedding. He had nothing to offer her, no title, no wealth, no castle of her own. All he had to offer her was his love, and for most women, love was not enough. Christopher Dacre flashed into his mind and Heath made his decision. There was no way he would allow his enemy to take Raven's virginity.

He rose above her and gazed down at her lovely face. Her avid eyes devoured his rampant male shaft, jutting from its black nest of curls, and she reached out to caress the solid slabs of muscle that ran from his chest to his groin. The tantalizing touch of her fingers almost undid him. He positioned the head of his phallus against her cleft and, with one powerful stroke, thrust through her hymen. Raven cried out at the sudden pain and fullness, so he held himself absolutely motionless, allowing her to become more accustomed to the intrusion. She was so hot and tight, a primal cry erupted from his throat, and he knew he could remain still no longer. Fire flamed through his belly and groin as he slowly slid in and out of her satin sheath, completing the mating dance he had begun hours earlier.

She clung to him fiercely, sweetly, trusting him to erase the pain with exquisite, heart-stopping pleasure. Raven yielded her body to him generously and was rewarded a thousandfold as he brought her to blissful fulfillment. Heath withdrew before he allowed himself to spend. He would not take the chance of getting her with child. He enfolded her in his arms and held her against his heart. His lips brushed across her temple. "Raven," he whispered against her skin. Heath buried his face in her fragrant hair, closed his eyes, and prayed. *Let love be enough.*

Raven lay in the circle of his arms, enjoying the languorous afterglow that made her body feel warm and replete. Her mind, however, slowly separated itself from her physical being and stood apart. Tonight, Heath had solved for her the age-old mystery of the male-female sexual ritual, and in doing so, he had empowered her. She knew that what had happened to her was cataclysmic and that she would never be the same again. She had exchanged innocence for female knowledge, and knowledge was power.

If there were only the two of them in the universe, how easy it would be to isolate themselves in their tower, indulging every whim while their attraction for each other lasted. But that was make-believe, and Raven knew she must live in the real world. It was impossible to think only of herself; she had her family to consider. They loved her and wanted only what was best for her. They had high expectations, and she had a duty to her parents to marry well. Raven could see the crescent moon through the chamber window, and silently spoke to the goddess Hecate.

> *When I see the new moon*
> *It becomes me to lift mine eye,*
> *It becomes me to bend my knee,*
> *It becomes me to bow my head,*
> *Giving thee praise, thou moon of guidance.*
> *Give me the means to attain my freedom;*
> *I have the power, and know how to use it.*

When Duncan Kennedy sailed the new ship *Doon* into the mouth of the River Dee in Kirkcudbright, his father, Rob, almost collapsed with relief when he saw with his own eyes that no grave disaster had befallen his son Donal. Rob graphically catalogued the foul deeds the English had perpetrated upon him in Carlisle, and without mentioning the "curse," warned Donal to be vigilant.

"Is there news of Tina? Has she delivered the babe yet?" Rob could not rid himself of a sense of impending doom and disaster.

"I've heard naught," Donal said, "but ye mustn't worry about Tina, 'tis only a bairn."

"Only a bairn?" Rob roared. "A bairn that could be my grandson! A bairn that'll keep the male line of Kennedys from dyin' out! When ye heard naught, did ye no' think tae ride tae Castle Douglas?"

Donal looked contrite. "I've been busy with the shearin' and then the lambin' . . . three thousand ewes lambed this month alone."

Somewhat mollified that the wool they had lost would be replaced by Donal's fleeces, Rob shook his head. "Ye're a good lad, just thoughtless like all young men yer age."

When Rob announced they would sail up the Dee to Castle Douglas on the morrow, Elizabeth balked. "I'll not set foot in Castle Douglas; I shall stay here with Donal and Meggie."

Rob's face turned a dangerous purple. "Ye'll do as I bid ye, Lizzie. Tina needs her mother!"

"Tina has Ada; she won't welcome my interference, nor want my advice. You go, Rob. If Tina asks for me, naturally I will come."

At mention of Ada, Rob changed his mind about forcing Lizzie to accompany him. Ada would give him the comfort he so badly needed. Without Lizzie there, he also would be able to lay the law down to Heath about his witch of a grandmother. "Aye, well, I suppose Beth can accompany me in yer stead."

The following day when they dropped anchor at Castle Douglas, they found only Cameron in residence. He informed the Kennedys that Ramsay and Valentina were at their castle in Eskdale, as were his brother, Gavin, and Heath Kennedy. "I dropped them off at Annan, with the horses they recovered from Carlisle Castle."

"That whoreson Dacre raided Eskdale?" Rob roared.

"Nay, he didn't do the reivin', but he ended up with horses that belonged tae Douglas, accordin' tae Heath, and he knows horses."

"Has Valentina had her bairn yet?"

"I'm assuming she has, but I've had no word."

"I've learned not tae assume aught in this bloody world!" Rob stated flatly. He turned to Duncan. "Ye can weigh that anchor and sail tae Gretna. We'll ride tae Eskdale from there."

Heron Carleton approached the great English Border fortress of Bewcastle with relief. As he had ridden through the area of wild fell and moor, so close to Scotland, he had become nervous when the light began to fade. At the gate he was challenged by Bewcastle's Captain Musgrave. The name Carleton was familiar to the captain, and when he learned that the youth had come to visit Christopher Dacre, he ordered that the portcullis be raised to admit him.

Heron found Christopher in the dining hall, which was filled with men. Only a handful of the servitors were women, and Heron began to feel uncomfortable about his sister's visit. He devoured the mutton on his trencher and said, "I don't think it's proper for Raven to be here."

"She isn't here." Chris indicated he had something to tell him in private, so Heron quaffed his ale and followed his friend from the hall, up to his bedchamber on the third floor.

"Where the devil is she?" Heron asked with a frown.

"She's across the Border in Scotland, at Eskdale Castle. Don't get in a lather; she's perfectly safe. It's a Douglas castle."

Heron looked at him blankly. "Douglas?"

"It's the Douglas who's wed to a Kennedy, kinswoman to your father," Christopher prompted.

A picture of pretty Beth Kennedy filled Heron's head, and it took him a minute to sort out the connection Chris was alluding to. "But I understood Raven was visiting you, here at Bewcastle."

Dacre didn't want to overly alarm Heron Carleton, for he needed him to go to Eskdale and get Raven away from the hated

Kennedy. "That was my intent, but on the ride here we were captured and taken to Eskdale for ransom."

"Captured? She's a prisoner?" Heron cried in alarm.

"No, I was the prisoner. . . . Raven's more like an honored guest!"

Heron shook his head. "I don't understand."

Dacre sighed with exasperation. "It was a Kennedy who kidnapped me for my new black stallion, then the bastard demanded that my father pay ransom, and I was released."

"You left Raven behind?" Heron stared at him in disbelief. "Bewcastle must have a force of over a hundred men. Why didn't you attack Eskdale and rescue her?"

"For Christ's sake, Heron, I intend to make Raven my *wife*! I don't want my father or anyone else to know her reputation has been blackened by being dragged off to Scotland. She is not being treated as a prisoner, she is being treated as a guest. It is better for everyone, especially Raven, to pretend she's been visiting her kinswoman." Dacre paused for a minute so that Heron could digest what he was saying. "All you have to do is ride to Eskdale and escort her home."

Heron looked at Christopher Dacre through new eyes. He had never thought him a coward. He also suspected Dacre wasn't telling him the whole story. Riding alone into Scotland filled Heron with dread, but he knew he had no choice in the matter. "I don't suppose you'll be coming with me, so you had better tell me how to get to Eskdale."

In the morning, when Raven opened her eyes, everything that had happened yesterday came flooding back to her. It had been the most adventurous and eventful day of her life. She relived the wedding, then the exciting time with the Gypsies, the romantic ride home, and finally what had happened here in this tower room. Heath was not in the bed with her, and for a moment she wondered if she had dreamt it. She threw back the covers and had immediate proof that it had been no dream. She was naked except for one black silk stocking. Raven blushed. After Heath had removed the first one, they had both been too impatient to even think of the second.

She heard the outer door open and pulled the covers back up to her chin. It was a maidservant bringing her breakfast, so she asked if she could have hot water for the bath. When the servant left, Raven arose from the bed and went to examine her reflection in the polished silver mirror, anxious to know if she looked as different as she felt. She quickly removed the stocking, then stared at her body and her face with curiosity. On the surface she looked exactly the same, but when she took a step closer to the mirror and looked deeply into her own eyes, she perceived the difference. Her eyes reflected an age-old wisdom, and subtle self-confidence that could only be gained through experience. The corners of her mouth lifted; she was a day older and a thousand years wiser.

Raven dallied in the bathing tub, enjoying her time alone with her thoughts, then she selected a lavender-blue gown and pinned her hair up in a style that made her look both taller and older. Raven thought herself very worldly-wise as she descended the stairs and made her way to the hall, where she could hear voices. Tina was there with her baby daughter in her arms, while her baby son was being held by a burly, barrel-chested man whose florid face was wreathed in smiles. "God's passion, he's the spittin' image of me!" He paced back and forth, vigorously jiggling the little redheaded twin with a look of overweening pride that smacked of sheer arrogance.

"Rob, it's a baby, not a butter churn," Ada admonished, and shook her head in exasperation when Rob Kennedy beamed at her and told her how he had missed her.

Young Beth Kennedy turned and, with a look of genuine surprise, said, "Hello, Raven! I didn't know you were here."

Valentina passed her daughter to Ada. "Raven, my family arrived this morning. You already know my sister; come and meet Father. This is Sir Lancelot Carleton's daughter, Raven; this is my father, Rob Kennedy, Lord of Galloway."

"My lord, I am honored." Raven took in the craggy ruined face and saw that he had once been a fine figure of a man.

Rob looked Raven up and down with a baleful eye. "Yer father is Lizzie's second cousin." It was a statement rather than a question. He followed it with another. "Naught good ever came up from England."

"Be damned to you, Rob Kennedy," Ada declared with amusement.

"Ah well, lass, ye are the exception," Rob declared fatuously.

"And so is Raven. We owe her a debt of gratitude. If it wasn't for her help, Tina and the babies would have been in dire straits."

Rob's face blanched as he turned to his daughter. "Ye told me all went well! I knew there was trouble! Felt it in me bones! I've had a bellyful of trouble lately!" He was suddenly reminded that Old Meg had foreseen two coffins and mentioned red hair. "Where's Heath?" he demanded petulantly.

"I shall be pleased to find him for you, Lord Kennedy." Raven was secretly amused that Heath's father was here. They were different as chalk from cheese, and she couldn't wait to see the two of them together. As she turned to leave, Tina winked at her.

"If you run into an ugly redhead, it will be my brother Duncan."

Raven decided that Heath was most likely outdoors. A frisson of excitement spiraled inside her. She couldn't wait for the moment when they would see each other today, for she was confident that she held him in the palm of her hand. As she made her way across the bailey, she encountered a redheaded male. Though he was far from being ugly, she realized it must be Tina's brother. She saw his eyes light with speculation and smiled warmly. "You must be Duncan Kennedy. I hear you are as expert with ships as your brother Heath is with horses."

His glance swept her from head to toe, clearly liking what he saw. "I don't consider the Gypsy my brother—Heath is merely my father's bastard."

Raven recoiled from him. "What a vicious thing to say!" Duncan Kennedy laughed, and she assumed he had been jesting. "Excuse me," she said, and quickened her steps to put distance between them.

CHAPTER 18

As Raven approached the meadow where Heath kept his mares, her steps slowed. The word *Gypsy* echoed in her head as she thought about last night. *Heath Kennedy had an amazing rapport with the Gypsies.* She argued with herself, *So did Valentina and Ramsay Douglas!* Another thought came, *Heath is handsome and swarthy enough to have Gypsy blood.* She suddenly remembered the tarot cards in the night table, and the pentagram etched on his knife blade. Her steps came to a halt as she recalled that on their very first encounter he had mistaken her for a Gypsy girl. *No, it cannot be!* she argued, but the more she rejected the idea, the more plausible it became. And what about Duncan Kennedy's other accusation? Was it possible that Heath was only Rob Kennedy's bastard? The shocking word stirred her memory further. The first time she had seen him, hadn't she called him a filthy Scots bastard? And what was it he had replied? Her brow furrowed, trying to recall his exact words. *"I will not cavil at 'bastard,' but I do object to the word 'filthy.' I bathed in the River Eden last night."* Valentina had never even hinted that Heath Kennedy was a Gypsy bastard. She had always treated him as a beloved brother. Nevertheless, Raven began to believe that she had just learned the shocking truth.

Raven was devastated. Why had he not told her? Why had no one told her? Blood of God, she had given herself to him last night! It would kill her mother if she ever found out what Raven had done. She closed her eyes and covered her face with her hands. *Dear God, how could I have been so reckless? So willful? So wicked and wanton?* If the truth ever came out, it would break her father's heart!

Her head had ever been at odds with her attraction for the dark devil; why hadn't she been guided by her instinct? Raven swore aloud, "Death and damnation!" It had been her *instinct* that had responded to him and betrayed her! She should have allowed her common sense to guide her. Bad enough that he was a Scot and a Borderer; anathema that he was baseborn and had Gypsy blood! Raven cursed herself, for now that she knew he was Gypsy, his attraction had undeniably doubled. Why was the forbidden so damned irresistible and tempting?

He has me in his power! Raven told herself. *He bound me to him by healing my hands.* None of the blame for what had happened could be laid at her door. Heath Kennedy had taken complete and total advantage of her when she was most vulnerable. Suddenly her own words from the past mocked her. *Darling Heath, thank you for forcing me, it took all the responsibility out of my hands!*

Raven's innate honesty made her admit the truth to herself. He had taken her captive, but she was to blame for what had happened between them. She had as much power as Heath Kennedy, perhaps more, for he fancied himself in love and she did not. Her hands dropped from her face. Anger at him and at herself bubbled up inside her. She would confront him and immediately dissolve the bargain to which she had so recklessly agreed.

As Raven had supposed, Heath was with his mares in the meadow down by the river. When he saw her, he stopped what he was doing and remained motionless, gazing at her as if spellbound. She walked a straight path to him, and only when she had covered half the distance did she realize that this was how he handled horses; he remained still until they came to him. Well, it was the last time he would treat her like a filly. He had made her eat out of his hand, he had gentled her, overcome her fears, and yes, he had finally ridden her! Well, it was the last time, Raven vowed.

She stopped about three feet away from him; too far for him to touch her, but close enough for her to see his eyes and gauge the expression in them. "Do you have Gypsy blood?"

Raven saw proud defiance. "I do."

"Are you Lord Kennedy's bastard?"

He slanted a black brow. "So it is rumored."

"Why didn't you tell me?" she demanded furiously.

His heart constricted and his blood slowed in his veins. "I assumed you knew. It is no secret." He took a step toward her.

"Don't touch me! It is over!"

Heath's face hardened. He pulled her roughly into his arms. "It is over when I say it is over, Raven!"

Her body was rigid in his arms. She looked coldly into his eyes. "Lord Kennedy has arrived. He is asking for you."

Heath was surprised. He had left their tower at sunrise to see Ram and his moss-troopers leave on Border patrol, and at that time there had been no sign of Rob Kennedy. With reluctance he released Raven. "Is Lady Kennedy with him?"

She shook her head briefly, without speaking, and watched him head for the castle. Heath's question made Raven realize that Elizabeth Kennedy would not look kindly upon the presence of her husband's illegitimate son, and apparently she wasn't the only one.

Heath smiled inwardly at the domestic scene he found in Eskdale's hall. His father was holding Tina's baby son, proud as a dog with two tails to be the grandsire of twins. A second look at his father, however, told him that Rob looked haggard and not in the best of health. A cold finger of apprehension touched him, and he hoped it wasn't a premonition.

When Rob saw Heath, he handed the baby back to Valentina. "I need tae talk wi' ye in private."

Heath exchanged a quick glance with Tina, then nodded to his father. "Come upstairs."

Before he had climbed half a dozen steps, Heath saw that his father was winded. Rob's florid face deepened in color as he gasped for air. "Rest a minute," Heath ordered, masking alarm.

"I'll be restin' soon enough if that bloody woman has her way!"

Heath assumed he was speaking of Elizabeth, for Rob constantly complained of his wife whenever he had a captive audience.

When they arrived in the tower chamber, Heath sat his father in a chair and poured him a whisky.

Rob Kennedy downed half the whisky in one gulp and wiped his mouth on his sleeve. "Old Meg put a curse on me, an' I want ye tae order her tae remove it!"

"A curse?" Heath was slightly bemused. "There's no such thing."

"There is, there is! It's a Gypsy curse!"

"Father, she takes pleasure in torturing you. Curses can have no effect unless you are foolish enough to believe in them."

"Foolish? Och aye, I'm a fool alreet—I shoulda hanged the old witch years ago! Now it's over late! The curse has begun its evil, an' ye are the only one can stop it!"

"Father, calm down!" Heath knew he would have to listen to Rob's fears and try to soothe them. "Tell me of the curse."

"Lizzie left me an' took wee Beth tae Carlisle. I was poorly, felt my heart was bein' squeezed in a vise. Bothwick sent fer Old Meg an' she told me I was cursed! Not just me—my whole family! The old witch told me my heart would kill me, but not afore I saw my male line die out. She told me my wife had left me, an' Beth would make a disastrous marriage like Tina. I argued wi' her, told her Valentina had a happy marriage an' was havin' a bairn. She shook her haid, said she saw *two* coffins an' red hair! *Two*—she knew there'd be *twins*! An' how did she know about the red hair?"

"Now there's a mystery," Heath mocked gently.

Rob shook his head impatiently. "There was a great storm on Duncan's return voyage from Flanders; the *Thistledoon* was damaged bad an' Duncan near swept o'erboard. That's when I made up my mind tae find ye an' force Old Meg tae remove the curse. We sailed tae Carlisle an' the bloody English burned the *Galloway* an' all the winter fleeces. The curse'll be the death of me and mine!"

"And this curse is because of me? Because you got my mother, Lily Rose, with child?"

Rob looked at his son beseechingly. "Heath, I loved Lily Rose, I swear it tae ye!"

Heath believed him; he also believed Rob Kennedy's obsession with the curse would kill him if he didn't get a grip on himself. He appeased him by telling him what he wanted to hear. "I'll order Old Meg to remove the curse, Father. Nothing more will happen—be easy in your mind."

"Ye'll leave today? How will ye find her?"

"That's easy. I was with the Gypsies last night in Hawick." Heath let Rob believe Old Meg was there.

"Why are they in Hawick?"

"They followed the court. Margaret Tudor wed Archibald Douglas yesterday."

Rob recoiled. "No good'll come of it. They shoulda' packed the English bitch off tae her brother, Henry Tudor!"

"If Margaret went back to England, she'd try to take her son with her. Young Jamie Stewart is Scotland's king; the last thing we want to do is deliver him into the hands of the King of England."

"Politics is a deep an' dirty business. Bad cess tae the lot!"

"Be careful with your curses, Father."

"Aye, well, amen tae that."

Heath noted his father's color was not as alarming as it had been. "Finish your whisky; I'll see they plenish a chamber for you, and I'll ask Mr. Burque to cook something special for your dinner."

Heath found an Eskdale steward readying a chamber in the wing that ran from his own tower. "I think it would be better to give Lord Kennedy and Duncan the empty tower, so they can have adjoining chambers. His health isn't what it should be and it would be best if Duncan could keep an eye on him." The steward readily agreed and went off to plenish the tower. Heath had accomplished what he intended. He did not want his and Raven's privacy compromised this night. Feeling a measure of satisfaction, Heath went down to the kitchens for a word with Mr. Burque.

When Raven returned to the castle, she found the ladies had retired to the solar. Tina was quizzing Beth about what had happened between their mother and father, while Ada was doing her best to keep a straight face as Beth ingenuously let all the dark cats out of their bags.

"We left Mother at Donal's; she absolutely refused to go to Castle Douglas. She told Father that you had Ada and wouldn't welcome her interference. At mention of Ada, Father let her stay."

"I'll bet he did." Tina winked at Ada, and they both dissolved into laughter.

Suddenly a bell began to peal, and they looked at each other in surprise. "The swans!" Tina and Raven said in unison.

"I don't believe it!" Ada knelt on the window seat and opened the casement. There were the swans, tapping the bell with their orange beaks, making the rope swing, which in turn rang the bell. "Well, I'll be damned; they've learned to ring the bell when they want to be fed. Raven, you are so clever!"

Heath, who had been searching everywhere for Raven, heard their laughter and stepped into the solar. Relief washed over him, for he had feared that she had fled. "I asked the steward to put Father and Duncan in the north tower," he informed Tina.

His sister looked from Heath to Raven and back again. She knew they had been intimate last night, so naturally he wanted their father at a distance from his own tower. She should have thought of it herself. "Very good. Now where shall we put Beth?"

"I would love to have Beth share my chamber," Raven invited.

"Oh, thank you, Raven, I would love that too." Beth was eager to talk about Heron Carleton.

Tina glanced quickly at Heath and saw his mouth harden. *Oh God, the consummation didn't go well.* Tina glanced at Raven and saw her look of victory that she had thwarted Heath. *They are not yet bound lovers.* She recalled the consummation of her own union with Ram; it had been utter disaster. She opened her mouth to speak, but Raven spoke first. "There is a small matter of a door off its hinges. Heath, do you suppose I could impose upon you to set matters right?"

His jaw clenched like a lump of iron, and he did not trust himself to speak. If Raven thought she had outmaneuvered him, she was deluding herself. She could evade him all she wanted, but the fact remained that she was his. She belonged to him body and soul, and if it took a forced marriage to convince her, then so be it! Heath withdrew from the solar and went directly to his tower. As he lifted the heavy oaken door and set the iron pins to hold it in place, his thoughts were consumed by Raven.

When Rob Kennedy looked from the window of the north tower and saw Heath leave the stables mounted on a fine black stallion, he assumed his son was riding to Hawick to lay down the law to Old Meg. Rob felt so weak with relief that he had to sit down. *Nobody knows more about horses than Heath*, he thought with pride. Then a wave of guilt washed over him. *No thanks tae me! I loved Lily Rose, but when she died in childbirth, I blamed the bairn! I let Old Meg have him because I didn't want him.* He got to his feet, sighing heavily, then poured himself a large whisky.

Heath rode with slow determination toward the ancient stone church at Kirkstile. Though it lay a few miles from the castle, it was on Douglas land, and the priest owed his living to Lord Ramsay Douglas. Heath tethered Blackadder and entered the church. When he did not see the priest, he walked toward a door at the back that led into the holy man's living quarters. The priest must have heard someone enter, for before Heath could knock, the priest opened the door and joined him in the church.

"Father, I need you to perform a wedding ceremony. Today," Heath added firmly.

The priest was a typical Borderer—square-built and dark, with an ungodly look about him. "Where is the bride?"

"She's at Eskdale—you'll have to come to the castle."

"I see," he said shrewdly. "Is she no' willin'?"

"Not completely," Heath admitted.

The priest stared at him with hard eyes, and silence stretched between them before he spoke. "Have ye lain wi' the lass?"

"I have," Heath said solemnly, knowing this would carry weight with the priest.

He nodded. "I'll come."

Both heads lifted as a crash of crockery came from inside the living quarters. Such a guilty look came over the priest's face that Heath became immediately suspicious. He moved to the door and threw it open. Heath's eyes widened in surprise. "You!" His dagger was in his hand before he finished uttering the word.

"I'm hiding him from the English—he's a Scot!"

"Blood of God!" Heath cursed.

"Take not the name of the Lord in vain!"

"Take not a bloody Douglas fugitive into your protection! This piece of offal was my prisoner. He escaped when the Eskdale stables were deliberately set ablaze!"

"He's a Scot!"

"Aye, he's a Scot—an Armstrong—yet he plotted to murder Lord Ramsay Douglas."

The priest, incensed, did an immediate about-face. "Ye shoulda' hanged him!"

"Rope costs money." Heath advanced upon the ugly fugitive, who stood rooted to the spot with fear. Blood lust gripped Heath as he thought of Raven's burns and the horses who had lost their lives.

"Mangey wanted me dead! Me own brother! He fired the stables!"

Heath paused. If this was Mangey's brother, he knew much more than he had ever admitted. Heath sheathed his knife and trussed his prisoner's hands behind his back, then he waited for the priest to gather the things he would need and saddle his pony. They rode back to Eskdale, with the prisoner walking between them.

This time Heath had no compunction about putting Armstrong in irons in Eskdale's dungeon; it would help loosen his tongue. Heath didn't expect Ramsay back until tomorrow night. When Douglas moss-troopers went out on Border patrol, they were usually out two days at a time, unless they encountered trouble on a large scale. Heath felt sure that if he and Ramsay confronted Armstrong together, he'd be intimidated enough to babble all.

Heath, not in the best of moods, led the priest up to his tower. He could hear the voices of Beth and Raven through the adjoining door that he had set back in place. He opened it and saw that they were unpacking Beth's clothes and hanging them in the wardrobe. Both females glanced up as he opened the door. Heath fixed Beth with a piercing look and jerked his thumb. She took his meaning instantly and, used to obeying male authority, hurried out. Heath motioned for the priest to come into the room, then he turned the key in the lock and slipped it inside his doublet.

"What the devil are you doing?" Raven's glance swept from Heath to the priest and back again. Her look of panic told Heath she knew exactly what he was doing.

In two firm strides he was beside her and took her hand. She snatched it away, and roughly he took it back again. He nodded to the priest. "Her name is Raven Carleton."

"This is a forced marriage!" Raven cried out to the priest.

"Has Heath Kennedy lain wi' ye, lass?"

She stared at him in dismay, not wanting to admit to the priest that they had been intimate. Then her eyes blazed with anger. "Yes, but—"

"Then it is right that ye marry."

Raven lifted her head with pride and raised her eyes to Heath's. "No, it is *not* right, that I am given no choice in the matter. It is *not* right that you are taking away my freedom. It is *not* right to misuse your power in this way, Heath Kennedy."

Heath closed his ears to Raven's protests. She was his woman, the only one he would ever want. He nodded curtly to the priest and imprisoned her at his side in a vise grip.

"We are gathered taegether in the sight of God, tae join this man and this woman in holy matrimony. If any man can show just cause why they may not lawfully be joined taegether, let him now speak, or else hereafter forever hold his peace."

"I *will not* marry you!"

The priest ignored Raven's interruption. "Heath Kennedy, wilt thou have this woman tae thy wedded wife, tae live taegether after God's ordinance in the holy estate of matrimony? Wilt thou love her, comfort her, honor, and keep her, in sickness and in health; and, forsaking all other, keep thee only untae her, so long as ye both shall live?"

"I will." Heath's voice was implacable.

"Raven Carleton, wilt thou have this mon tae thy wedded

husband, tae live taegether after God's ordinance in the holy estate of matrimony? Wilt thou obey him, and serve him, love, honor, and keep him, in sickness and in health; and, forsaking all other, keep thee only untae him, so long as ye both shall live?"

"I *will*—" Heath's mouth came down on hers, cutting off the word *not*. Raven struggled in vain. When Heath lifted his mouth from hers, she cried, "I *will not!*" but the priest continued.

"Repeat after me: I, Heath Kennedy, take thee, Raven Carleton, tae my wedded wife, tae have and tae hold from this day for'ard, fer better fer worse, fer richer fer poorer, in sickness and in health, tae love and tae cherish, till death us do part, according tae God's holy ordinance; and thereto I plight thee my troth."

Heath looked down at Raven and knew he loved and cherished her too much to force her. His terrible pride had ruled him. He had thought he was showing her his strength, but suddenly realized that he was showing her his weakness. He had never felt as protective of her as he did at this moment. The only thing she wanted from him was her freedom, and he knew he would give it to her. Heath brushed the back of his fingers across her cheek. "I promised that if you let me woo you, I *would* give you the choice." He searched her face. "Forgive me, Raven." Heath reached inside his doublet and offered her the key.

Raven's eyes flooded with tears as her fingers closed over it.

A loud hammering came at the door. "Raven, are you all right? I know what's going on in there! Open this door!"

"Heron!" Raven paled.

"You cannot proceed with the marriage! I am her brother, and I object on the grounds that Raven is betrothed to Chris Dacre!"

Heath closed his eyes and cursed beneath his breath.

Raven dashed away her tears and unlocked the door. "Marriage? Heron, what in the world are you talking about? Beth, did you think we sent for the priest to marry us?" Raven laughed prettily. "The father is here to bless the twins. Heron, how lovely of you to come and escort me home!" She smiled at Beth. "Brothers— we rage against them, then suddenly they do something wonderful."

CHAPTER 19

"Heron, how did you find out I was here?" Raven walked beside her brother as they left the tower and descended the stairs.

"Mother insisted I go to Blackpool Gate. Our grandmother told me you had gone to Bewcastle with Chris Dacre. When I went there, Christopher told me everything!"

"What exactly do you mean by *everything*?"

"He told me you had been kidnapped—that his father had ransomed him, but that you were still being kept at Eskdale against your will. He didn't want scandal attached to your name—said it would be best if everyone thought you were a guest here, because of our father's kinship with Lady Kennedy."

"I *have* been a guest here," Raven said firmly.

"What the devil were you doing in a locked bedchamber with Kennedy and a priest?"

"Heath Kennedy asked me to marry him."

"*Asked?*"

"Yes, *asked*. My answer was no."

"Do you still intend to wed Chris Dacre?"

"I don't know," Raven replied truthfully.

"He says he intends to wed you, and insists that's the reason he doesn't want scandal attached to your name, but I think it was unconscionable of him to leave you here."

"Did you ride to Eskdale alone, Heron?"

"What choice did I have?"

"I would rather our parents didn't know about all this, and not just for selfish reasons. I don't want to hurt them."

"Mother would run mad!"

"I have become good friends with Valentina, Lady Douglas. She just had twins, and I was able to help a little."

"Her sister, Beth Kennedy, seems to be a lovely young woman."

Raven smiled wickedly. "Delusional though—seems to think you a lovely young man!"

Heron shook his head and laughed. "Raven, how the hell do you get into these scrapes?"

She recalled Heath's words when he had taken her captive, and tears threatened. "I was in the wrong place at the wrong time." Raven smiled brightly. "We'll dine in the hall tonight. You'll love it, and you will especially enjoy Mr. Burque's cooking."

Raven wanted to be alone; her emotions were in turmoil. Heath had almost succeeded in forcing her to marry him, then at the last moment he had relented, allowing her to make a choice. His gesture touched her. Belatedly, he had acted with honor. Heron had shown up at the worst possible moment, but she knew it had taken courage for her brother to ride alone into Scotland to rescue her. She touched his hand. "Thank you, Heron."

An hour later, dinner was served in the hall. It was a far smaller gathering than usual, for Ram and Gavin Douglas and the bulk of their moss-troopers were out on Border patrol. Rob Kennedy, who had slept most of the afternoon, was flanked by his daughter Valentina and Ada. Raven sat with Heron, while Beth and Duncan Kennedy sat across from them.

Raven's glance traveled about the hall, searching for Heath. She saw that he was sitting at a trestle table with the priest and the Douglas men who had been left behind to guard Eskdale Castle. The food was exceptional; both Heron and Duncan remarked on the fact several times during the meal. Raven, however, could taste nothing. She replied politely whenever Duncan Kennedy tried to engage her in conversation, but her attention wandered, and her glance kept straying to the trestle table further down the hall. She reminded herself that she must think with her head and not her heart. Tomorrow she would regain her precious freedom and leave this place forever, and it would be best to forget about it.

When the meal drew to a close, and one by one they stood up to leave, Rob Kennedy staggered on his feet and fell against the table. Tina and Ada grabbed him and sat him down again. Heath was on his feet immediately, striding down the hall.

Beth's hand flew to her mouth. "Father's ill," she whispered.

Duncan Kennedy cursed. "He's no' ill, he drinks too much. He's been at it all day!"

Heath gave Duncan a level look. "He's feeling his age." He swept past his half-brother and went to aid his father. "I'll see him to bed," he told Tina. He picked up Rob Kennedy and carried him from the hall.

The next morning, Raven donned her own riding outfit and went to bid Valentina and her babies goodbye. Tina told her that Heath had arranged an escort to ride with them to the English Border, and Raven realized that she would not be able to bid him goodbye. Under the circumstances, she knew that was best. Her brother, however, lingered over his goodbyes to Beth Kennedy, and Raven suspected that the young couple were becoming attracted to each other.

The trio rode from Eskdale to Liddesdale and crossed the Border at Liddel Water, where their Scots escort turned back. The minute she was on English soil, she threw back her head and cried, "I'm free, I'm free! Oh, Heron, freedom is the most precious thing in the world!" Raven refused to go to Bewcastle, so Heron agreed to ride to their grandmother's at Blackpool Gate. When they arrived, he sent a message to Christopher Dacre that he and Raven were traveling home to Rockcliffe the following day.

Ram Douglas and Heath Kennedy unlocked Eskdale's dungeon and stepped inside. Douglas carried a torch that illuminated the cell, showing its furnishings were a bucket, a straw pallet, and a table. There was neither chair nor stool to sit upon. Kennedy carried a jug of ale, which he set upon the table next to an empty stone jar and a tin plate.

The prisoner immediately arose from the straw pallet and

shielded his eyes from the light. When he saw the two dark faces of his visitors, so grim and threatening, he took a step back.

Heath Kennedy pierced him with a stare. "What's your name?"

"Sim Armstrong—Mangey's me brother."

"Well, Sim," Ram Douglas said matter-of-factly, "piss around with me, and I'll hand ye yer balls in a jar of ale."

Armstrong licked lips that were bone dry.

"Your mission was to dispose of Ram Douglas and make it look like an English raid. Why?" Heath demanded.

"Clan Douglas holds too much power." Armstrong's voice quavered.

"Why me?" Ram probed. "Why not Archibald Douglas, the new earl and head of the clan?"

Sim Armstrong again licked his lips, but this time his tongue was dry too. "I'm a dead mon if I rat!"

Ram unsheathed his knife. "Ye're a dead man if ye don't."

"Archie Douglas can be bribed!"

"And Henry Tudor knows I cannot," Ram concluded.

"So Dacre is the go-between?" Heath prompted.

Armstrong nodded, and fear made his words spill out. "Mangey and Dacre are thick as thieves. They fired yer stables tae silence me because I know too much! Ye saw Mangey silence Hob Armstrong at Bewcastle, but I didna believe he'd murder his own brother!"

Heath and Ramsay exchanged a look. Heath pushed the jug of ale across the table toward Armstrong, then they withdrew.

"A piece of the puzzle doesn't fit." Ram shook his head. "If Henry Tudor wanted me dead, why did the bloody Armstrongs go tae so much trouble tae take ye tae England? Would it not be better fer the king and Dacre tae make it look like the Scots did the deed?"

"Perhaps that was Mangey Armstrong's idea, so we couldn't track them down easily."

"Or perhaps it was somebody else wanted me dead," Ram mused. "I believe I'll have a quick ride tae Glasgow tomorrow, and have a word with the partner of the late Moses Irvine. Master Goldman is the lawyer's name, if I'm not mistaken."

"You are seldom mistaken, my friend. Don't ride alone."

"I'd ask ye tae accompany me, but I know ye wouldn't wish tae forego visitin' with yer family," Ram jested. "I'll take Jock."

When Raven and Heron arrived home, her brother made himself scarce by taking his dogs into Rockcliffe Marsh to hunt, leaving his sister to answer the flurry of inevitable questions from their mother. Raven unpacked the clothes she had never worn and saw that they needed pressing before they were hung back in her wardrobe. Lark, curious as a cat, followed her to the kitchen and plied her with questions about Christopher Dacre. As Raven heated the irons, she managed to evade answering her sister, but when her mother came on the scene, Raven knew she would have to be more forthcoming.

"How was my mother? Still living in her own little world, I suppose." Kate often asked a question, then answered it herself.

"Dame Doris was very well indeed, Mother."

"Why she insists that you call her Dame Doris, instead of plain Grandmother, I'll never know!"

"She doesn't mind at all when I call her Grandmother, though I imagine she would object to *plain* Grandmother," Raven said lightly.

"Did she quiz you about your marriage plans? I warrant, it's none of her business."

Raven nodded as she gazed into the kitchen fire waiting for her iron to heat, and heard her grandmother's words: *He's a Borderer, I hope. I want a real man for you, Raven. Better someone wild and fascinating like a mountain ram than someone tame and uninteresting like a craven lapdog.*

"Did you tell her that we have great hope of betrothing you to Lord Dacre's heir, Christopher?"

"Yes, I told her about Chris Dacre."

"Did she get to meet him? Really, Raven, you would exasperate a saint. Why can't you tell us from beginning to end what happened? You act as if it's a deep, dark secret!"

Raven lifted the iron from the fire and cried out as the handle

burned her sensitive palm. She closed her eyes and felt Heath's healing touch.

"Surely I've taught you better than that, Raven!" Her mother
thrust an oven pad at her. "If you spent less time with those wild
birds and more time learning to run a household, your chances of
catching a husband would be vastly improved!"

Raven hung on to her temper. Her mother took such little interest in her "wild birds" she had no idea that Raven had lost Sultan
and Sheba. *Nor would she care if she did know.*

Tenacious as a terrier, Kate went back to the subject she had
been pursuing. "I want to know how matters have progressed between you and Christopher Dacre. After all, you only went to
Blackpool Gate because it was close to Bewcastle."

That's true. How long ago it seems. "Chris Dacre invited me to
visit Bewcastle, but of course I didn't go."

"You didn't go?" Kate was incredulous.

"I told him it would be most improper for me to visit Bewcastle
unless we were betrothed."

"Clever girl! Did that prompt him to propose a betrothal?"

Raven did not want to think about it, let alone talk about it.
"Mother, Chris Dacre and I went out riding one time, and one time
only. Matters have not progressed beyond that."

"You should have made the most of your opportunity!"

Raven looked at her mother through new eyes. "You mean I
should have seduced him."

Kate glanced at her younger daughter, Lark. "I mean no such
thing. Watch your language, Raven."

Raven suddenly realized that was how her mother had managed
to snare Sir Lancelot Carleton. Female sexuality was a powerful
force indeed.

"Mmm, Lord Dacre will be returning to Carlisle for the Border
Wardens' Court meeting next week. Since your father will be presid-
ing at the court, perhaps we should accompany him to Carlisle."

"I should be training the new pair of young merlins—"

"Don't you dare mention hunting birds to me, Raven! It is high time you got your priorities in order." Kate Carleton left her daughter to her ironing.

Her sister, however, lingered. "*Did* you try to seduce him?"

"No, it was the other way about."

"Did he succeed?" Lark asked avidly.

Raven couldn't believe it. Her sister was actually asking her if she was still a virgin. "This conversation is over," Raven said with finality.

Ramsay Douglas, along with Jock, his second-in-command, set out at dawn and rode to his castle at the town of Douglas, forty miles from Eskdale. They had a quick meal, changed horses, and rode the remaining twenty miles to Glasgow in two hours. The smoke from the city's chimneys created a pall that hung over Glasgow, making darkness arrive early.

He went straight to the offices of Irvine and Goldman and was asked to wait. He cautioned himself not to pace, but to compose his temper. Jake Goldman opened his door and effusively welcomed his visitor inside. "When I was told a Douglas was here tae see me, I had no notion it was Lord Douglas. How may I serve ye?"

"I understand that Moses Irvine died shortly after my uncle, the Earl of Angus?"

"Sadly, that is so, but I have taken over the practice, and hope to serve the Douglases as well as my late partner did."

"Irvine named you successor in his will, I presume?"

"Indeed he did, my lord, never dreaming his demise would come about so soon."

"Aye, it was abrupt." *Too bloody abrupt!* "Angus filed his will with Irvine; has it been read yet?" Ram watched Goldman's eyes; when they widened in surprise, Ram knew Archibald had conversed with Goldman since the wedding.

"Ye are mistaken—there was no will, Lord Douglas."

"I am seldom mistaken. There was indeed a will; you mean there was no will *found*."

"Exactly. There was no will found on file. But that presented no problem, since Angus's son Archibald was his legal heir."

Ye found the fucking will, all right, and it must have presented a horrendous problem. Ye eliminated Irvine before he had a chance to file it in court. Ramsay wanted to pull the swine across his desk and cut out his lying tongue. "Very good. The new Earl of Angus told me all this; I just wanted tae make certain he gets his legal due."

Ramsay joined Jock, who had been holding the horses. They rode to Angus's town house in Garrowhill, where Ram opened the door with his own key. Angus's majordomo greeted him with genuine affection.

"Ye got my message, my lord!"

"No, I got no message; I'm in Glasgow on business. Did ye send the message tae Douglas?"

"Aye, my lord."

"That explains it. I've been at Eskdale awaiting my wife's delivery." Ram grinned. "Tina gave me twins, a lad and a lass!"

The majordomo beamed and shook his head. "Congratulations, Lord Douglas! If only the earl was here tae celebrate yer good fortune."

"What was yer message?"

"We were broken into a fortnight ago. The earl's bedchamber and library were ransacked, but as far as I know, naught was taken."

"Were any papers missing from his desk?"

The trusted servant looked startled. "I wouldn't know, my lord. I'm no' privy tae the contents of his desk. The house is filled with valuable paintings and art objects, but none are missin'."

"Has Archibald been here since his father died? The town house is his now."

"No, my lord, but ye were the only one Angus trusted wi' a key."

"Archibald doesn't have a key?"

"No, my lord, there are only two keys—yours and the earl's, which I now have in my possession."

Ram knew that whoever had broken in had come for Angus's

copy of the will. He went straight to the library and searched the
desk, but as he fully expected, he found no will. Ram and his lieutenant ate in the kitchen, then the majordomo gave Jock a chamber
next to his own. Ram took his saddlebags up to the master bedchamber and began to pace. If *Archie destroyed the will, and* if *he conspired
with Goldman tae murder Moses Irvine, the amount of gold involved must
be considerable.* He stopped pacing and looked about. The paintings
and art treasures in this mansion-of-a-town house were worth a fortune. Why hadn't Archie come to claim it?

Ram glanced at the walls covered with pale green watered
silk, and at the great bed with its padded silk headboard, and knew
he needed to bathe before he could sleep there. Fortunately, the house
had a bathing room with piped-in water. Ram made short work of
the bath, then, wrapped in a towel, returned to the master chamber
and lay upon the bed with his hands behind his head.

The ceiling above depicted Aphrodite, Greek goddess of love,
rising from the sea, with one hand cupped beneath a delicate breast.
Her red-gold hair reminded Ram of his beautiful wife and of the
passionate nights they had spent in this bed. He chuckled as he recalled the very first night they had spent here, when Tina had locked
the door to keep him out. He had used the statue at the top of the
stairs to batter down the door and in so doing had damaged the figure almost irreparably. Ram realized he had just passed the statue on
his way from the bathing room, and, curious to see how it had been
mended, arose from the bed.

Ram ran his hand over the hairline fracture in the marble that
ran on a diagonal slant across the figure's ankles. From the front it
was almost indiscernible, but the back had sustained greater damage,
and Ram's fingers could feel the clumsy repair. He lifted the figure
from its pedestal so that he could see it better, and almost dropped
the statue when he saw the document nestling in the hollowed-out
surface of the plaster pedestal.

Ram snatched up the paper, carefully replaced the marble
statue, then picked up the towel that had fallen from his hips.
Naked, he hurried back to the master bedchamber, lighted all the

candles, and spread the document out on the bed. Scribbled across the top was a notation that read: *I shall take the precaution of concealing a second copy of my will, in addition to the one in my desk.*

Ram pored over the thick, bold writing of the document before him.

> *This is the last will and testament of Archibald Douglas, 5th Earl of Angus. I nominate, constitute, and appoint Lord Ramsay Douglas to be the Executor and Trustee of this my Will with full power and absolute discretion to carry out my wishes as laid out herein, and to execute all documents necessary for that purpose.*
>
> *I bequeath my fleet of ships to the Crown of Scotland.*
>
> *To my son, Archibald, Master of Douglas, I bequeath my title and estates of the Earldom of Angus. These encompass all lands and castles in the County of Angus, and all lands and castles in the County of Perth.*
>
> *To my nephew, Lord Ramsay Douglas, I bequeath all lands and castles which lie south of the Firth of Forth, to include Tantallon, Blanerne, Drochil, Cavers, Morton, Drumlanrig, and my town house in Garrowhill, Glasgow. In addition I bequeath said nephew all gold and sterling on deposit with my goldsmiths.*

Ramsay Douglas could read no further; he sat stunned, trying to take in the magnitude of the inheritance Angus had entrusted to him. Ram lowered his eyes to the paper and read it again. Angus had left his son only property in the Highlands. Everything in the Lowlands and the Borders had been left to him. Ramsay examined the seals and signatures; all looked in order and, ironically, Goldman, the junior partner, had signed as one of the witnesses! Ramsay read further. It charged him to pay all of Angus's just debts and to generously reward all those in his service. Ram's eyes dropped to the two codicils.

To Valentina Kennedy Douglas, wife of Lord Ramsay Douglas, I bequeath the Douglas emeralds and rubies.

To Heath Kennedy, half-brother of Valentina Kennedy Douglas, I bequeath one hundred acres of land which lie along the River Dee, and are adjacent to Castle Douglas, in the County of Kirkcudbright.

Once again Ramsay was stunned. Angus had given no reason for these generous gifts. The first was easy to explain, of course. Angus had loved and admired Valentina. The second gift was far more amazing, for land was precious and seldom passed out of the clan. The bequest went a long way to confirming the rumor that Angus had fathered Heath's mother.

Ram paced again, thinking best on his feet. *No bloody wonder Archie wanted me dead!* In light of what he now knew, it had been a tactical mistake to visit Goldman and reveal that he was in Glasgow. Like a canny Scot, Angus had not named the goldsmiths who held his gold and sterling, but Ram would bet a penny to a pinch of shit that he would be followed. Come morning, he had to let Sam Erskine see the will, then without delay it must be filed with the Court of Scotland. He slipped on his leathers and went downstairs to warn Jock of the impending danger.

At an early hour, before full daylight came to Glasgow, Jock, dressed in Lord Ramsay Douglas's best clothes, set out from Garrowhill on foot. Within two minutes, Ram Douglas saw that his lieutenant was being followed. He smiled grimly, knowing Jock could be trusted to lead the spy on a merry chase, while he set out for the goldsmith's.

Ram showed the will to Samuel Erskine and asked him to make two copies of the document: one for himself and one for Ram. As he waited, he warned Erskine of the danger. Sam, as he had been instructed by the Earl of Angus, then gave Lord Ramsay Douglas the names of the other goldsmiths who had Angus's gold and sterling on deposit. One was in Edinburgh; the other surprisingly was in Carlisle, England. Erskine, as did all goldsmiths, had guards of his own. Two of them accompanied Ram to the courthouse on Strathclyde. He presented the will and waited until it was registered as being received, then he tucked the receipt into his doublet, dismissed Erskine's guards, and returned to Garrowhill, where Jock awaited him.

"I dinna think we'll be followed again, my lord."

CHAPTER 20

When Christopher Dacre received Heron's message that he and his sister were returning home, he went straight to his father and told him he had made up his mind about marrying Raven Carleton.

Lord Dacre nodded with resignation. "I'll see Lance Carleton at the Border Wardens' Court next week and suggest a betrothal."

"Dispatch a letter today and invite the Carleton ladies to stay at Carlisle Castle during the session. I've wasted enough time."

When the letter arrived at Rockcliffe Manor, Sir Lancelot handed it to his wife with satisfaction. "There, I told you to stop pushing and allow matters to proceed more slowly. It looks like Christopher has been able to bring Lord Dacre around."

Kate Carleton was pleased beyond belief. "I can't believe it! I was on the verge of writing to Rosalind, hinting that we would like to accompany you to Carlisle during the Border Wardens' Court, and like magic, Thomas Dacre himself pens us an invitation and suggests we start making plans for a betrothal!"

Kate summoned her daughters and gave them the wonderful news. Lark seemed far more excited than Raven and immediately asked for a new dress. Raven appeared to be more subdued and didn't react at all the way her mother thought she should.

"Don't tell me you're coming down with something!" Kate felt Raven's forehead, found it cool, and pronounced her diagnosis. "You have a case of the jitters. You have wished for this betrothal for so long that now it is within your reach, you are suddenly unsure of yourself."

Raven couldn't have agreed more. She was unsure of herself and unsure of Christopher Dacre, yet she saw that her parents had no reservations whatever. Before she had been forced to go to Scotland, she had been completely sure of herself and knew exactly what she wanted for the future. Now her assurance had vanished, her thoughts were in disarray, and her peace of mind destroyed. *Damn you, Heath Kennedy! Damn you!*

Whenever she could, during the days that followed, Raven escaped from the endless discussions about which day dresses, evening gowns, and shoes must be packed for Carlisle. She spent many hours on Rockcliffe Marsh, flying the young merlins and reflecting upon her future. Raven found her thoughts chasing in circles, for each time she tried to think of the future, she found herself dwelling on the past.

Two days after Lord Thomas Dacre's letter arrived from Bewcastle, Raven received one from Christopher at Carlisle Castle. Her mother's face looked radiant, and her father's well pleased, when he handed it to Raven, and she saw the knowing glance they exchanged when she excused herself to open it and read it in private.

My Dearest Raven:

Words cannot express how much I miss you. I am so very sorry about what happened. It was entirely my fault; I never should have taken you riding in dangerous Border territory without an adequate escort of guards.

You were extremely brave to try to effect my escape, but I was so deeply concerned for your safety, and so hesitant about leaving you behind, that my attempt was easily thwarted.

I have told no one about your being taken against your will to Scotland, and am determined it shall remain a secret between you, Heron, and myself. Try to think of the episode as a visit with your relative, Lady Valentina Douglas.

I cannot wait to see you next week. Until then, please know that you have all my affection, devotion, and admiration.

YOURS ALONE,
Christopher

Raven read the letter again. She concluded that it was a nice letter and could find no real fault with it. Christopher had both apologized and taken the blame upon himself for what had happened. Raven had seen little of his concern for her safety, or his hesitancy in leaving her behind on the night of his thwarted escape, but to give him the benefit of the doubt, she could not possibly know his thoughts or the extent of his fears that night. She read it one more time, then burned it, because she knew that Lark's curiosity would not allow her to leave the letter unread.

That evening, Raven knocked on her father's study door. She found him behind a desk piled high with paperwork and reports concerning some of the cases that were coming up at the Border Wardens' Court. Standing before her hardworking, dedicated father, she felt ashamed about deceiving him and guilty over her reckless behavior. "Father, I came to speak with you in private."

"Come in, my dear. I hope you will always want to share your thoughts with me."

Raven, for the first time, noticed that his fair hair was mostly gray and his face was lined with care. "It . . . it's nothing really." She had been going to tell him that she was uncertain about the betrothal, but now changed her words. "I don't mind being betrothed to Chris Dacre, providing we don't marry right away. I simply don't want to be rushed."

"I understand completely, my dear. You want to be sure."

Her heart went out to him. "Yes, I'm in no hurry to marry."

The night before the Carletons were to travel to Carlisle, Raven was suffering with a headache. She brewed herself some chamomile tea and went to bed early. She hadn't slept well since she had returned home, but the mild sedative effect of the chamomile soon made her drowsy, and the next thing she knew, she was dreaming.

Heath Kennedy was standing in a lush green meadow, by a river. She could hear his voice distinctly. "I won her in a knife-throwing contest." Then suddenly, Raven remembered: She was in a Gypsy camp, dancing around a fire, without a care in the world, when all at once she became aware of undercurrents. Two males who had been admiring her began to circle each other like dogs with raised hackles. One was Heath Kennedy, the swarthy Gypsy, whose white teeth flashed when he smiled. The other was Christopher Dacre, the classically handsome, fair-haired Englishman.

"Keep your eyes from her, you bastard, she is betrothed to me!"

"Possession is nine-tenths of the law; she is my property!"

"All Gypsies are thieves, liars, or worse—you stole her!"

"I'll buy her from you!" The white teeth flashed. "How much?"

"Three hundred pounds."

"Three hundred it is, if you throw in your horse."

"Damn you both! I know a cockfight when I see one, and I have no stomach for them," Raven cried.

"I challenge you to a knife-throwing contest—the winner takes the girl." Heath Kennedy unsheathed his dagger.

"I have no knife; I'll destroy you with fire and sword!"

"No, no! Take my herb knife, Christopher." She pressed her small dagger into his waiting palm.

A target was quickly set up, and the two males took turns throwing their knives. It was no real contest, for the Gypsy hit the bull's-eye every time. White teeth flashed as the Gypsy swaggered over to claim his prize, and carried her to his bed.

Raven stubbornly refused to yield to the Gypsy.

"You wanted me to win. You knew he would lose when you gave him your knife. You have drawn your own blood with that knife, and know that it will respond to no hand but yours."

She melted into his arms, lifted her mouth for his ravishing, and yielded herself up to him. "Love me, Heath!"

When Raven awoke in the morning, the details of the dream were still with her. The knife-throwing contest in the Gypsy camp seemed just that—a dream. The part where Heath Kennedy had made love to her, however, seemed real. To Raven it felt as if he had been in the bed with her; she had touched him and tasted him. When she raised her arm to her nose, she could even smell his male scent that lingered upon her skin. Raven knew he possessed power, but was it such mystic and magic power that he could come to her at will? No, she must not allow herself to believe such things, for therein lay the power. If she firmly believed it was impossible, then it was impossible!

She told herself that the past was past. Today was the first day of her future. With resolution, she put Heath Kennedy out of her mind and stopped thinking of him. This day she was going to Carlisle Castle, where she would see Christopher Dacre. She owed a duty to her parents, who had always loved her and wanted only what was best for her. She knew she must be receptive to a betrothal. She would not think of marriage just yet; a long betrothal would give her time to be sure.

When they arrived at Carlisle Castle, the two Carleton sisters were given the same bedchamber as before. Raven opened the wardrobe and saw the red Gypsy dress she had worn to the masquerade, hanging exactly where she had left it. She quickly covered it with her own clothes, then unpacked for Lark. It evoked memories, not only of the night she had worn it, but also memories of the Gypsy camp where she and Heath had danced with such abandon. Why was the forbidden so tempting? Why did she suddenly long for the freedom of a Gypsy girl? She tore her mind from her fanciful notions and warned herself that she must start dealing with reality, not fantasy.

Heron Carleton went off to seek Chris Dacre, and was amazed to find he had only just arisen from his bed.

"*Quelle heure est-il?*" Chris asked, showing off his French.

"It's five o'clock; have you been ill?"

"Hardly." Chris gave him a conspiratorial look and lowered his voice. "Too bad you weren't here yesterday, old man; we went out on a raid and didn't return until dawn."

"Where did you go?" Heron thought of Beth Kennedy, and the idea of the English raiding into Scotland was now anathema to him.

"Are you mad, asking such a thing? You are just in time to help me dress." He winked. "Tonight is a very special occasion."

After Raven unpacked, she took a solitary walk, exploring the castle where she had lived and played when she was a young girl. Lord and Lady Dacre's apartments took up only one wing of the ancient fortress, whose history was fascinating to Raven. The son of William the Conqueror had won Carlisle from the Scots in the eleventh century. He had rebuilt the ruined city and built the original castle, and as a result some of its nooks and passageways were ancient. When she returned to dress for dinner, she found her mother awaiting her.

"Raven, you try my patience beyond reason! Why can't you be more like Lark? She has used her time to select a special gown for dinner and to fashion her tresses in the latest style. I hope you intend to do something with that wild, untamed mass you call hair."

Raven's hand went to her head, and a rebellious feeling inside threatened to erupt. She schooled her temper and promised to hurry. "Please don't wait for me; I shall be down soon." She chose a gown of deep, sapphire blue, with a matching snood for her hair, decorated with blue stones. When dark curls escaped from its confines to frame her face, Raven sighed and shrugged a shapely shoulder. It was too late to do anything about it now.

Raven arrived in the dining room only just in time to be seated. She avoided the look of censure on her mother's face and turned to greet Christopher Dacre, who was already holding a chair for her.

"I am sorry, Raven," he murmured low, "I have never seen you look lovelier." The look in his eyes told her that his words were sincere.

Raven gifted him with a smile of appreciation and sat down. She felt his hands caress her shoulders briefly before he took his place beside her, and it prompted her to steer the conversation away from personal topics to more general ones. When she looked along the table, she saw that Christopher's mother was positively beaming as she watched her son's gallantry. It was clear that she not only approved of the match, but desired it.

Raven's glance moved to her own mother, whose critical look had been replaced by one of benign approval for her willful daughter. When she looked at her father, she saw that he was in deep conversation with Thomas Dacre, and concluded that they were talking of Border affairs rather than hers. Her brother Heron's eyes were hooded, his face noncommittal, while Lark sat gazing at Chris Dacre with a look of unconcealed adoration upon her face.

When the meal was finished, Raven was relieved, but as the hosts and guests arose from the table, Christopher took firm possession of Raven's hand and addressed everyone present. "I have a confession to make. I recently visited with Raven while she was staying with her grandmother. I proposed marriage to her, and I am pleased to announce that Raven accepted, and agreed to be my wife."

A buzz of voices filled the air. Her mother looked delighted, while her father looked surprised. Raven felt numb. In essence, Christopher had not lied, but she would have much preferred that he had not made such an announcement to their families. Her glance met her father's with a plea for help, but his look was puzzled, as if he wondered why she hadn't told him the truth.

"Well, I think Sir Lancelot and I had better discuss a formal betrothal." Lord Thomas Dacre picked up a decanter of whisky from the sideboard and led Lance Carleton into the library.

For a moment, Raven had the sensation that the walls were closing in on her, and she felt trapped. Then Rosalind Dacre was kissing her and welcoming her into the family. With sinking heart, Raven took her courage into her hands. "We don't want to rush into anything. Chris and I agree that marriage is a most serious step to take, and we favor a long betrothal."

"What nonsense!" Christopher laughed and slipped his arm around her, hugging her to his side.

Raven smiled up at him, and said sweetly, "Could we walk along the gallery, Christopher?"

"Whatever you wish, my love."

When Raven was absolutely sure they were out of earshot, she stopped walking. "What the devil did you mean by all that?"

"I mean to have you for my wife, Raven."

"Whether I will or no?" she demanded.

"When we were riding to Bewcastle, I told you to consider yourself betrothed. You knew I was asking you to marry me."

"A lot has happened since then."

"This is what your parents want; it is what I want."

She searched his face. "If we are to be betrothed, it will be on my terms."

He masked his inner thoughts, lest she read them. "Agreed."

That same night, Ram Douglas returned to Eskdale and found Valentina and the twins on their wide bed in the Master Tower. He kissed his wife and tickled the babies' bellies, all the while weighing just how much to divulge. There would likely be more trouble before everything was settled by the courts, and he did not wish to unduly worry her, yet he wanted to share the news of their amazing good fortune.

"I found a copy of Angus's will at the town house and registered it with the courts. Archibald will likely contest it, and mayhap even the Crown, but once it is validated, I think it will stand. Angus was shrewd enough tae bequeath his fleet of ships tae the Crown and leave his son Archie all lands and castles connected with the Earldom of Angus."

Tina's golden eyes widened in curiosity, but she held back the questions that were on the tip of her tongue, so that Ram could tell her in his own words that which he was bursting to disclose.

"If the will stands, we'll have enough castles for our children and our children's children, as well as properties for Gavin and Cameron tae oversee."

"Splendor of God! I always knew Angus loved you more than he loved his own son."

"Nay, he was simply aware of Archie's weaknesses."

"And you have no weaknesses."

He brushed the fiery curls back from her brow, "Ah, there yc're wrong. Ye are my weakness, Tina . . . and now these two."

"Let's put them to bed, then you can prove to me that I am your weakness, devil-eyed Douglas."

Later, when she lay replete in his arms, she thanked God for all the blessings he had heaped upon her. A small shadow of apprehension hovered—had she been given too much? Would something be taken away? Her arms tightened around Ram; he was her strength, her bastion against the Fates.

"I'd like ye and the babes safe at Castle Douglas when I go tae Carlisle for the Border Wardens' meeting. Do ye think they're old enough tae travel?"

"Ada and I have already started packing. We'll have the christening there in the chapel. I think it best if the twins and I sail aboard the *Doon* with Duncan and Father to Kirkcudbright."

Ram kissed her brow. "How can anyone so beautiful be so practical?"

"I'm a Kennedy, is not our motto 'Consider the end'?"

"Kennedy be damned! Ye're a Douglas, and never forget it!" His arms tightened possessively, and he squeezed her until she squealed with laughter.

In the morning he closeted himself with Heath before they went to the hall to break their fast. Ram told him that he had found Angus's will and had registered it with the courts. "Believe it or not, Goldman signed as witness. He had me followed, but the unfortunate wretch reckoned without Jock."

"So it was Archibald who ordered your death."

"I warrant it was, though Dacre arranged fer the Armstrongs tae do the dirty work. My guess would be Archie destroyed the will and conspired tae have Goldman eliminate Moses Irvine."

"What will you do about Archibald?"

"If the courts validate the will, I needn't do a damn thing. He will get the punishment he deserves. Angus left me all the Douglas properties below the Firth of Forth, plus all his gold!"

Heath went very still, like a stag who scents danger. After a full minute had gone by, he gave Ram an intense look. "Archie will need money, and he will turn to his wife and Henry Tudor. He has something to sell for which Henry Tudor will pay any price."

"Young Jamie Stewart! Ye're right; the King of England would stop at nothing tae get his hands on the young King of Scotland. I must send a dispatch tae France, tae John Stewart, the Duke of

Albany. He is the little king's closest male blood relative, and would make a better regent than Margaret, whom we Scots must never trust."

"Angus had no illusions about his son. He left you the bulk of his holdings because he knew you wouldn't squander them."

"Oh aye, I forgot. In his will, he bequeaths ye a hundred acres along the River Dee, by Castle Douglas."

"Me?" Heath wondered if Ram was jesting.

"Aye, ye." Ram's black eyes glittered with amusement. "The drawback is, this likely means we're related by blood!"

As the stunning news sank in, Heath's first thought was of Raven Carleton. He was no longer landless. He owned a dozen mares who would foal within the year, and now he owned his own land to graze them on. Why in the name of God had he let her go?

"I want ye beside me at the Border Wardens' Court. I can't wait tae see the look on Dacre's face when we produce Sim Armstrong. Tina and the twins are sailin' tae Castle Douglas with Duncan and yer father. Ye can go with them or ride with my moss-troopers. We'll be stoppin' at Castle Douglas before we go on tae Carlisle fer the weeklong meeting."

"I'd prefer to ride," Heath said with a grin. "I'll get to see my land faster that way."

The two men went into the hall together for the first meal of the day, and Heath was pleased to see that Rob Kennedy had arisen early for breakfast and was looking much better. The food had only just been served when a grim-faced Cameron Douglas, accompanied by one of Donal Kennedy's land stewards from Kirkcudbright, burst into the hall and shattered the congenial atmosphere.

An icy cold hand gripped Heath Kennedy's heart the moment he saw his brother's steward.

"What's amiss?" Ram asked his youngest brother.

"Terrible news! Donal Kennedy was raided two nights past. I took men from Castle Douglas, but we couldn't catch the reivin' swine . . . we were too busy puttin' out the fires!"

Rob Kennedy was on his feet, his face engorged with blood. "Donal! Is my son Donal safe?"

"Donal's dead, my lord," the steward blurted. "Four of 'em, burned tae cinders in the stables!"

Rob Kennedy clawed the air for breath, then grabbed his chest and fell across the table.

CHAPTER 21

A s Duncan Kennedy sat stunned at the terrible tidings, Heath moved swiftly toward his father. He lifted Rob from the table and sat him down, keeping his hands clamped to his father's shoulders to keep him erect.

" 'Tis the curse," Rob whispered, "the bloody curse!"

Heath placed his hand over his father's heart and felt that its beat was so rapid, it was racing out of control. "Don't talk! Take deep breaths!" he admonished.

"Ye don't understand!" Rob cried, " 'Tis the curse!"

Heath grabbed the front of his father's shirt and shook him. "The curse will *kill you* if you don't calm down. Now, fill your lungs with air. Breathe deeply, slowly," he ordered.

Valentina and Ada arrived on the scene, and Ram told his wife about the raid at Kirkcudbright, purposely omitting the grisly details about her brother Donal.

"Are the women safe . . . Mother, Meggie, and the baby?"

The Kennedy land steward spoke up. "The fire didna' touch the dwellin', but the stables, the wool sheds, and all the fodder suffered the same fate as Donal!"

"Donal, my son an' heir, is dead!" Rob moaned.

Tina's face drained of blood, and Ram put a powerful arm about his wife in case she fainted.

Heath's hands restrained his father; his eyes sought Tina's. "Maybe they haven't positively identified Donal's body—he may have gone after the reivers who were driving off his sheep." Heath was clutching at straws to calm Rob and Tina and give them hope.

Ram turned to Jock, his second-in-command. "We're ridin'. We'll take half the moss-troopers and leave the others here with Gavin." Jock left to inform the men who were not already in the hall.

Heath's and Ram's eyes met. "I'll be there at the Border Wardens' meeting one way or another," Heath said. "I'll bring Armstrong, if you like."

Ram nodded, "Ye're needed here fer now. I'll see ye in Carlisle." He spoke to his wife. "I'll leave Gavin in charge here at Eskdale. Go tae Castle Douglas as soon as ye can, love."

Heath carried his father up to his tower and put him in his own bed. Heath's heart was heavy. What had happened had nothing to do with any bloody curse, yet he was likely the cause of it. Every instinct told him it was Dacre's vengeful reprisal against the Kennedys for kidnapping his precious son and holding him ransom.

Duncan Kennedy came into the tower room and challenged Heath. "Who the hell put ye in charge, Gypsy? Ye're no' even a member of this family."

Rob glared at Duncan. "Cease yer clatter!"

Heath looked at Duncan and said evenly, "If you'll stay with him, I'll go to the stillroom and get him something for his heart."

Heath couldn't find what he wanted, so he went into Valentina's walled garden to pick foxglove and lily of the valley, which he took to the kitchens. Mr. Burque helped him to make a distillation by boiling the plants' juice with watered wine. "Kirkcudbright was raided two nights past; Donal Kennedy is feared dead," Heath told him.

"*Mon Dieu!* Nothing will keep Tina here. Tell her I shall be ready to leave in two hours' time."

"Lord Douglas and his moss-troopers have already gone. Tina won't be leaving today. Our father is ill, and she has her babies to think of. We'll go tomorrow, if it is at all possible."

Mr. Burque stirred in honey and poured the hot wine into a pewter jug, then handed it to Heath. "The Lord of Galloway can be an old swine, but give the devil his due—he loves his children." Burque realized his faux pas immediately; Kennedy loved his *legitimate* children.

When Heath returned to his tower with the decoction for his father, Rob looked askance at it. "Ye wouldna give me the poison Old Meg give me? It griped my bowels terrible!"

"This will soothe you and stop your heart from racing."

Rob felt he could take Heath at his word and swallowed his medicine, but he fixed Heath with a glare. "The old Gypsy witch dinna obey ye and remove the curse! I'm goin' tae Kirkcudbright the morrow."

"We'll see," Heath said firmly.

"He'll be fine," Duncan Kennedy said with authority. "He can rest aboard ship."

"It's getting him to the ship that I'm worried about."

Duncan motioned Heath into the adjoining chamber. "If Donal's dead, I'm now heir. I'll give the orders in the Kennedy family."

Heath looked him straight in the eye. "Father isn't dead yet."

Valentina and Beth came to see how their father was faring, and Ada, who had always had a soft spot for Rob Kennedy, accompanied them. Tina's eyes were red from the tears she had shed over Donal, and the lump in her throat threatened to choke her. She took her father's weathered hand and stroked it.

Rob grabbed her hand and said urgently, "Wee Robbie—ye must take especial care of him!"

Duncan told Tina, "He's just been dosed; he's makin' no sense."

Tina, however, knew that her father was referring to her baby son. She didn't have the heart to tell him she had chosen the name Neal. "I'll take care of him, Father."

"The curse will wipe out the Kennedy male line!" Rob insisted.

"He's ravin'," Duncan said, then looked at Heath. "What the hell did ye give him?"

Ada stepped between the two half-brothers. "Heath knows all there is to know about herbal medicine. I'll sit with Lord Kennedy; you must have pressing things you need to do."

Duncan stalked from the tower and Heath put his arm about Valentina's shoulders. "We'll see this through together. The easiest way to get Father to the ship anchored in the Solway is down the River Esk in one of the boats. There would be plenty of room for you and the twins."

"Will you come too?"

He shook his head. "I have to take a prisoner. Mr. Burque intends to go; he and Ada will see to Father."

Tina nodded. "We have everything packed and ready. If Father's well enough, we'll go tomorrow. I'll speak to Duncan; he's being abrupt because he feels useless right now."

When everyone but Ada had departed, Rob Kennedy continued fretting about the curse. Over the years, the two had been intimate upon occasion, and the Lord of Galloway felt he could trust Ada, insofar as he could trust any woman. "Old Meg put a curse on me when her daughter, Lily Rose, died in childbed. I loved Lily Rose; why does the old witch point the bloody finger of guilt at me?"

"Many women die in childbirth, Rob; it wasn't your fault. It was before you wed Elizabeth; you have naught to be guilty about."

Her words did not soothe him. "Do ye believe in curses, Ada?"

Though she hesitated, Ada was the sort of woman who seldom lied. "I'm an English Border woman, Rob, superstitious to the bone. Logic tells me there are no such things, yet I believe there is a terrible power embedded in curses."

"Can they be broken?" he persisted.

"Curses are evil; they can be overcome with goodness, I warrant, but few of us are capable of unadulterated virtue."

Heath went below to the dungeons, lit a torch, and unlocked the cell door. He set the torch in a wall bracket and waited until Sim Armstrong's eyes adjusted to the light. "I have more questions. Truthful answers will earn you better treatment."

When Armstrong nodded warily, Heath continued. "Mangey controls the Armstrongs. How many? How many will ride if Dacre pays?"

The prisoner shrugged. "Hundert, more or less."

"What other Scots clans would raid their own for gain?"

"Plenty!"

"I want names."

"Grahams . . . controlled by Long Will. They raid both sides o' the Border an' take refuge in the Debatable Land."

"Come on. You can wash in the river and I'll give you some clean clothes."

"Why?" he asked suspiciously.

"Because you stink, and because we're going to the Border Wardens' meeting shortly."

Armstrong recoiled in fear. "Nay, nay! Christ almighty, ye might as well hang me now!"

Like a wolf, Heath drew back his lips to expose his teeth. "Rope costs money."

At Carlisle Castle, Sir Lancelot Carleton and Lord Thomas Dacre bargained over the details of the legal betrothal between Raven and Christopher. "The bride's dowry is so modest, I ask you to consider throwing in a piece of land. How about the Burgh, that lies south of the River Eden? 'Tis only marshland, after all."

"Raven's dowry may be modest, but her beauty and virtue are such that she needs no dowry at all. Your wife brought you nothing, as did mine," Lance Carleton countered.

"We were hot-blooded devils, led by our pricks rather than our brains. If you will put the Burgh Marsh in your daughter's name, to be held for her children, then we have a bargain."

Carleton grudgingly agreed, knowing that if Raven predeceased her husband, the land would go to Christopher Dacre.

Finally, when the betrothal agreement lacked only the date of the marriage, and the signatures, Lord Dacre opened the library door and asked the couple to join him. Kate Carleton took Rosalind Dacre's arm and said pointedly, "Surely you will not deprive us mothers of being present at such a joyous time?"

When everyone had filed into the library, Lord Dacre, playing the role of affable host, said, "All we need settle is the wedding date, then we can sign the betrothal."

Christopher caressed Raven with a look of adoration. "Tonight would be my choice."

"So impetuous, but so romantic," Raven's mother remarked.

"Need we choose a date yet? I would like a little time," Raven said.

"If this is to be a legal betrothal, we need a date," Lord Dacre said decisively.

"If Raven needs time, I am willing to wait until after the Border Wardens' Court, say the end of the month," Christopher offered generously.

The month is more than half over! Raven refused to be pushed. "I was thinking the end of the year."

Chris laughed good-naturedly. "Raven is having fun with us."

"My dear, you are not serious?" Rosalind asked anxiously.

"Of course she isn't!" Kate snapped. In a panic, she compromised by adding a few days onto what Chris Dacre had suggested. "August is a lovely month, Raven; there is nothing more romantic than a summer wedding!"

Lord Dacre's eyes narrowed. Nothing annoyed him more than a woman who wanted her own way. Raven Carleton would have them jumping through hoops. Clearly the female needed mastering! "Well, as your father said, your beauty and your virtue are such that you need no dowry, but a little consideration would not hurt."

Raven flushed with embarrassment; not only was Lord Dacre remarking on her virtue and her small dowry, he was accusing her of being inconsiderate. "I'm sorry," she said softly, "I will sleep on it and let you know tomorrow."

Lord Dacre motioned for his son to remain after everyone else departed. "That girl needs a good fucking and a good beating!"

"Don't worry, Father, I intend to give her both."

Dacre envied him. "I would advise sooner rather than later."

Raven went straight upstairs, and Lark, who had been longing to know what had gone on in the library, followed her to their bed-chamber. "Are you officially betrothed?"

Before Raven could answer, Kate Carleton swept into the room. "I don't believe it! I simply do not believe it! For months we have worked toward one goal, to get a commitment of marriage from Christopher Dacre, and just when it is in the palm of your hand, you act as if you are completely indifferent, and almost let it slip through your fingers. The time for being coy is long past! I thought you were an intelligent young woman. You must seize this opportunity imme-diately, or we shall find our long campaign has been for naught!"

"Mother, Christopher and I understand each other. He knows if there is to be a betrothal, it will be on my terms."

Kate took a step backward and gasped. "*Your* terms? You willful girl! You may have young Dacre panting after you, but I can assure you Lord Dacre has the whip hand here. A man who rules the Borders certainly rules his own household. He could betroth his son and heir to any young woman in England. He could have an heiress, a *titled* heiress even. He doesn't have to settle for the daughter of a castle constable!"

She means crippled castle constable! "Father is an appointed judge of the Wardens' Court," Raven said proudly.

"Yes, and who has he to thank for that appointment? You selfish girl, do you not realize Lord Dacre could have it off him in a mo-ment if you offend him?" Kate's voice cracked, and she suddenly burst into tears.

Raven, who had never seen her mother cry, was appalled. The tears touched her far deeper than all the recriminations Kate had heaped upon her. She felt guilty and contrite. "Mother, I'm sorry, please don't cry."

"I'll have Chris if Raven doesn't want him," Lark offered.

"Oh, my innocent lamb! What a comfort you are," Kate said through her tears. "You were always such a good girl."

And I'm the bad girl! Raven had to bite her tongue. "I need to speak with Father." She went along to the chamber her mother and father occupied, and knocked quietly.

Lance Carleton opened the door. "Come in, child."

"I've made a mess of things . . . Mother's crying."

"Tears usually get a woman what she wants," he said dryly.

"You are not upset with me?"

"Raven, it is your life. If you want to wait, it should be your free choice."

The word *free* struck a nerve. *There is really no such thing as free choice*, Raven thought cynically. "For argument's sake, let us say I chose to marry a Scot, a Borderer. Would I still have free choice?"

"When you sit as judge at a Border Court, you realize there is little difference between Scot and English. Human beings are human beings the world over. So, in theory, you would have free choice."

"What if he were illegitimate, and had Gypsy blood?"

"Now you are being ridiculous. Under such circumstances I would be derelict in my duty as a father to allow you free choice."

"A Gypsy would not be good enough for a Carleton?"

"The blood has little to do with it. Such a man could not provide you and your future children with the comfortable home and life that I would wish for you. Raven, this theorizing is all very well, but you must come to a decision about a wedding date, or call it off altogether."

"And break my mother's heart? I could hardly do such a selfish and willful thing." Raven smiled brightly. "Thank you for listening to me, Father."

When she returned to her own bedchamber, Raven hugged her mother. "I promise to set a wedding date tomorrow."

"Oh, Raven, my dear, you won't regret this, it is such a big step up in the world for us."

Raven undressed and as she hung her sapphire blue gown in the wardrobe, her hand brushed against the Gypsy dress. Its vibrant red color stayed with her as she climbed into bed, murmured good night to Lark, and blew out the candles. She lay staring up into the darkness, and pictured Heath Kennedy lying in his bed, doing the same.

At Eskdale, Heath lay in the adjoining tower room, listening to his father's even breathing. The foxglove and lily of the valley, both strong heart medicines, had slowed down Rob's heart and taken away the heavy pain. Tonight, Heath's own heart was pained. He was saddened by his father's ailing condition, and grieved over Donal, who was one of the world's innocents. He cursed himself for bringing misfortune upon the Kennedys. In hindsight he regretted taking Chris Dacre and holding him for the ransom of his mares. The only thing he didn't regret was Raven. Tonight he ached for her.

Heath pictured her lying in bed, her sensuous black hair spread across the white pillow, her lavender eyes gazing into the darkness. He focused his full attention upon her until the world fell away. He breathed deeply, rhythmically, until his very blood slowed in his veins, then his soul reached out to touch her. "Come to me, Raven."

She turned her head on the white pillow and saw him there in the bed with her. His shadowed profile turned toward her and she saw his intimidating dark eyes compelling her. She reached out her hand to see if he was real, and touched solid flesh and blood. Her fingers trembled as she brushed them across his dark skin, and his intoxicating male scent stole to her, dizzying her senses. She saw that he held the black raven's feather in his hand, and she moved closer, drawn by his compelling, irresistible power.

Leaning on one elbow, he raised himself above her and traced her delicate features with the feather. He brushed it across an eyebrow, then a cheekbone, and finally, her lips. His mouth followed the feather's path with worshipful kisses. Then he threaded his fingers into her black curls, holding her captive for his mouth's seduction.

Raven gazed up at him, wanting to commit every detail of him to memory. His brows were thick and black, his lashes tipped with gold, over eyes the color of dark whisky; his slanted cheekbones were prominent and cast their shade upon his cheeks. Though he had shaved closely, she could still see the blue-black shadow beneath his tanned skin. His lips were carved, his mouth generous and ever ready to flash with a smile that could steal your heart. The cleft in his chin drew her fingers, then she trailed them down his corded throat and across his muscled chest. Boldly, she touched his armpits and loved that the black hair felt like silk. His masculinity staggered her senses.

Heath stroked the backs of his fingers across the swelling curves of her breasts, knowing it aroused her, and when his roughened fingertips felt her nipples become erect, he smiled with delight that the secrets of her body were becoming known to him. He captured her mouth, so that when his hands moved lower, he would feel her gasp of pleasure. When his finger slid up inside her, she arched her mons into his hand and whispered his name against his lips. He circled the tiny bud inside the folds of her cleft, and almost came out of his skin when she thrust her tongue into his mouth, showing him what she really desired.

By the time he covered her lush body with his, her lavender eyes had darkened to smoky purple, and she clung to him fiercely with a passion she had never known before. When he thrust into her, his throbbing fullness branded her and she cried out as he began to plunge and unleash the animal maleness that made him so potently irresistible to her.

After the tumult, they clung to each other, murmuring endearments, enjoying the deep satisfaction and contentment that enveloped them in the darkness. She lay against his hard length, with her arms entwined about his neck, while his powerful arms held her safe. In each other's arms like this, they felt complete, whole. Their quiet time had a mystic aura about it.

She knew the hour approached when he must go. "Leave me the raven's feather; I will cherish it always."

"No, I must keep it. The raven's feather is the talisman that enables me to come to you."

"Heath, this is the last time we can be together. You must never come to me again!" Her nails dug into his shoulders with the intensity of her words, forcing him to understand.

"Raven." His lips brushed her brow, then he was gone.

In the morning when she awoke, Raven was covered with guilt over her wanton behavior. She also was filled with a sense of panic. Her dreams of Heath Kennedy were becoming more real than the times when she was awake. She actually searched the bed for the black feather, yet when she did not find it, it allayed none of her disquiet. She feared that he was becoming an obsession, her dreams a persistent disturbing preoccupation.

Raven believed there was only one sure way to put a stop to them: she must set a wedding date. She would tell Chris Dacre that she would marry him in August.

CHAPTER 22

The large wooden boat carried its passengers down the River Esk toward the Solway Firth. Rob Kennedy, who had flatly refused a mattress, reclined against cushions, morosely watching the red sandstone banks of the river, as a Douglas boatman steered the craft. Mr. Burque sat beside Kennedy with a supply of the herbal medicine for his heart.

Tina had wrapped her twins warmly and placed them together in one cradle. She had no need to rock it, as the boat bobbed about in the water; rather, she had to keep her hand on the cradle to keep it steady. Ada catered to everyone, covering Rob's knees with a lap robe, and offering dry biscuits to Beth when she began to look green about the gills. Ada had anticipated what they would need on the boat ride, while everything else they were taking to Castle Douglas was packed on wagons and would go overland, with some of the household servants.

Earlier that day, Heath Kennedy had taken Sim Armstrong from Eskdale's dungeon and provided him with a surefooted garron. He himself was astride Blackadder for the ride to the Solway, where the Kennedy vessel was anchored. Duncan, mounted on the horse that had brought him to Eskdale, assured Heath that his new ship had plenty of cargo space and could easily accommodate their mounts. Gavin Douglas had dispatched two guards to accompany them, but once they boarded the ship, the pair would ride back to Eskdale.

When Duncan boarded and the Kennedy crew reported there had been no trouble, he heaved a sigh of relief. It was a good thing his father had insisted they drop anchor on the Scottish side of the

Solway, near Gretna, rather than an English port. Heath secured Armstrong in a small area next to the galley, where food was stored, then took their three mounts down into the cargo hold. Duncan ordered all three cabins be prepared to receive passengers, then went up on deck to impatiently await the boat from Eskdale.

When it finally arrived, Beth was heaving, and Mr. Burque gallantly carried her aboard ship, where she insisted upon going straight to bed. Tina and Ada each carried a twin down to the cabin that all the females would have to share. Heath helped his father up the gangplank, but Rob refused to go below until the ship had weighed anchor. As Duncan shouted his orders, in a hurry to catch the tide, he suddenly became entangled in the line of the foresail and almost went overboard. He nimbly saved himself by catching hold of the jib stay, but watching him, Rob Kennedy had once again been badly shaken. " 'Tis the bloody curse—now do ye believe me?" he demanded of Heath.

Rob was persuaded to go below, but he sat on the edge of the berth with his head in his hands. "Donal's dead—an' Duncan won't be far behind. Fate is toyin' wi' me. I'm dyin', but I'll live long enough tae see the Kennedy male line die out." He raised his head and stared at Heath. "It'll be up tae ye tae carry on the Kennedy line. The curse doesna touch ye."

"Why doesn't it touch me? Am I not your son?"

"Aye, ye are my son," Rob declared.

"Father, did Old Meg curse you because you kept it secret that you and Lily Rose were handfast?"

"Where did ye hear such rubbish?" Rob stared long and hard at Heath while he waged an inner battle. His face was haggard with grief and fear. "Lily Rose an' me were never handfast."

Heath believed him. He and his father had many differences, but he had always taken the Lord of Galloway at his word. It settled the rumor he had pondered for years. Heath wished it could have been otherwise, for his mother's sake, but he was wise enough to know that facts were facts, and wishes could not alter them.

Through the wall they could hear the wailing of a baby, and Heath realized the child had been crying since they entered the cabin. He went next door and found conditions less than ideal. Beth was spewing into a bucket held by Mr. Burque, who looked ready to share her fate. Tina paced the cabin, white faced, trying to soothe her wailing baby son. The sea was so choppy that she too felt like retching. Only Ada and the dark-haired baby girl she was rocking to sleep were unaffected. As Heath stood at the cabin door surveying the scene, Rob Kennedy pushed past him. "I knew it was the wee bairn; what ails my laddie?"

"I don't know, Father. I tried to feed him, but he won't suckle. The wet nurse who helps me with the twins' feeding is traveling to Castle Douglas by wagon, with the other servants."

"Come intae my cabin—it stinks in here," Rob ordered.

Heath placed a steadying hand at the small of Tina's back as they went into the next cabin. He laid the backs of his fingers on the baby's forehead and found him fevered.

"Give him tae me." Rob Kennedy scooped up his grandson and held the precious burden against his heart, fiercely, protectively. The baby's red hair stood up in tufts, and his face was ruddy from wailing so long; the resemblance between grandfather and grandson was unmistakable. Rob's face set in grim lines as he came to a fateful decision. "I will no' let this bairn die! Sit down, both of ye, I have somethin' tae tell ye."

Tina sat on the berth, while Heath took a chair beside her.

"I believe Old Meg put a curse on me because of what happened long ago wi' Lily Rose an' Heath. She swore she didn't . . . vowed I was the cause of my own curse. She swore she couldna remove it; said I had tae do that my own self. But she was right about one thing—guilt is the deadliest poison there is. It surrounds yer heart an' squeezes until it bursts!"

"Well, you never did right by Heath. He was your natural-born son and should have lived with you, not the Gypsies," Tina told him bluntly.

Rob shook his head in remorse. "When Lily Rose died, it broke my heart. I blamed the bairn . . . I couldna stand the sight of him, so Old Meg took him. It was wrong!" Rob looked at Heath. "Lily Rose an' me were no' handfast, we were legally wed."

Tina was aghast. "Oh my God, Father, Heath is your legitimate firstborn son? How could you have let him think he was a bastard all these years?"

"It was easier all round. Lily Rose had always insisted we keep it secret tae shield me from the wrath of my father, so when she died I kept my mouth shut. Then my father fell ill an' insisted I wed before I came intae his title as Laird of Galloway. Do ye think yer mother wouldha' wed me if her son could no' be my legal heir?"

Heath sat quietly as he absorbed the truth of his father's words. It meant that his mother was not a Gypsy harlot, but a respectable wifc, and his heart overflowed with joy that it was so.

"But think of the harm you've done to Heath!" Tina declared.

"What harm? Look at 'im! He's a real mon: strong on the outside, an' on the inside where it counts. 'Tis obvious he didna need me as my other sons did. I love all my children, but Heath's the one I'm proudest of. I'm glad it's out in the open; he'll make a powerful Laird of Galloway."

Heath sat stunned as he realized his father was declaring him his legal heir. He would decline, of course. He had been sustained by pride his entire life, and had far too much to swallow it now. He was, however, most grateful that dishonor had been removed from his mother's name.

Rob hoisted his grandson to his shoulder, and the baby promptly vomited on him. Tina took her son from her father and realized he had stopped crying. "I think he's cooler." She touched the baby's face, and he gurgled happily.

"God's passion, the curse is broken!" Kennedy declared, totally convinced that it was so. He stroked his grandson's head with a tender hand. "You feed 'im an' we'll take a turn on deck."

Heath's eyes met Valentina's and she nodded imperceptibly for him to go with their father. A stiff breeze hit them in the face as they emerged from below deck. Heath steadied himself with the rail, but Rob, who had the best sea-legs in Scotland from years of pacing the decks of his merchant vessels, walked with ease.

"Father, what you just did took a great deal of courage."

"Nay, it was cowardice. Fear of the curse, fear of the wee bairn dyin', an' fear of Lily Rose hatin' me forever."

"It was courage"—Heath's glance traveled to Duncan at the ship's helm—"and it will take a hell of a lot more courage before you're done. Are you sure?"

"The Kennedy motto is 'Consider the end.' " He half grinned, half grimaced at his eldest son. "I've considered, an' I'm sure."

"Are you sure?" Lance Carleton asked his daughter.

"Yes, I'm sure." Raven took her father's arm and they descended the stairs that led to the first-floor library, where Lord Dacre conducted his business.

When they arrived, Thomas Dacre summoned his son, who arrived almost immediately, demonstrating that he was eager to get matters settled. Dacre read the document aloud, stipulating the amount of Raven's dowry, and adding that Burgh Marsh would be put in her name the day she married, to be held for her children. Then Dacre looked at Raven and raised his eyebrows. "The wedding date?"

"August," Raven said rather tentatively.

"August first," Christopher said firmly.

Raven glanced at him quickly, as if she would argue, but she held her tongue, and Lord Dacre wrote down the date and offered her the pen for her signature. When the document bore all four signatures, Christopher walked with Raven to the library door.

"I want to show you which apartments will be ours," he said.

"Oh, that will be lovely." Raven had happy memories of Carlisle Castle. "I'll just run up and tell Mother the deed is done," she said lightly, "and meet you in the gallery." Raven ascended the stairs, but before she reached her mother's chamber, she encountered Heron, who appeared to be waiting for her.

"Did you really go through with it?" he asked cautiously.

"Yes. I'm officially betrothed. What's bothering you?"

Heron hesitated, then blurted, "Chris mentioned going on a raid. He wouldn't say where, but obviously it must have been across the Border. As Head Warden of the English Marches, Lord Dacre is supposed to keep the peace, not harry Scotland."

Raven frowned. "The Border Wardens' Court that starts tomorrow is held to discuss and resolve disputes between English and Scots. Surely the Dacres wouldn't countenance any raid into Scotland, especially on the eve of the Wardens' Court." Though Raven spoke with confidence, she was unsure, and resolved to question Christopher about the matter.

A short time later, when she arrived in the gallery, she found Chris waiting for her. He murmured an endearment, kissed her hand, and kept possession of it as he led the way to an apartment on the opposite side of the castle from that of his parents. It was not cramped, but spacious, and Raven liked that they would have their own small dining room and not have to eat with his parents. She also liked that it was high, just beneath the battlements, and looked out over the castle's meadow. At the moment, the meadow held the tents of those who would attend the Border Wardens' Court.

Chris indicated the tents. "They'll be gone in a week, and we'll have the meadow to ourselves for a couple of days, before I take you to Bewcastle for our honeymoon."

Ram Douglas will be attending the Wardens' Court. Raven bit her lip and stopped her thoughts before they went further. She had vowed that she would not think of Heath Kennedy.

Christopher's lingering glance roamed over her modest neckline, then lowered to her breasts. "When we are married I would like to see you in more fashionable, low-cut gowns. In the not too distant future, we will be traveling to London, to the royal court."

Valentina's words echoed in her memory. *The royal court is like a dead mackerel on the beach—it shines and it stinks. The English court is even worse.* Raven guessed that her groom-to-be had known his share of immoral court ladies, yet strangely her emotions were untouched by the trivial thought. She had far more important matters on her mind. When Chris took her by the waist and was about to draw her close, she placed her hands over his to stay him. She raised her eyes to his. "Were you on a raid?"

His gray-green eyes widened. "A raid indeed. Two nights ago

we were out on patrol when we encountered such a bloody and vicious raid, it was enough to sicken hardened soldiers. When the Scots pour across the Border intent on plunder, they are like madmen. Nothing is sacred to them, not churches, not even women or children. Raven, I would rather not speak of it; I would shield you from learning of such atrocities."

"Do these raids happen often?" she persisted.

"Too often. Thank God you are off the beaten track and protected by the marsh at Rockcliffe, but Longtown is constantly set ablaze, and some of the bold devils raid as far as Carlisle." He pointed through the window. "That bastard Kennedy reived a herd of our horses from that meadow below us. He didn't hesitate to slaughter the guards on the gates."

Raven closed her eyes. No wonder there was such bad blood between them. "When you are at Bewcastle, do you raid the Scots in retaliation?"

"We are kept too busy patrolling the Borders around Bewcastle, protecting the people who live there." He did not need to remind her that her grandmother was one of them. "Raven, I don't want you to be sad today." He cupped her cheek tenderly. "Let's look through all these chambers in this part of the castle and see if there are any furnishings you fancy."

She smiled brightly to banish the darklings. "We'll go on a treasure hunt."

"I've already found my treasure." He dipped his head and kissed her. Raven did not pull away, but she did not respond the way he wished. He wanted her arms about his neck, wanted her soft body to press against his, inviting his advances. Why was she playing the cold little bitch, when even her young sister had hot eyes for him? His gut knotted with jealousy, wondering if she'd played the whore with Kennedy. The filthy Borderer had wanted her, all right, but surely the beauteous Mistress Carleton had too much disdainful pride to stoop so far beneath her. Well, he would worship at the altar of her beauty until he got the ring on her finger, then he would take perverse pleasure in dragging her from her pedestal to her knees, where she could worship him, and lavish him with the attention he deserved.

Duncan navigated the ship into the mouth of the River Dee and dropped anchor at his brother Donal's tower castle, where the stench of burned wool still hung in the air. A Douglas vessel was docked close by; Ramsay was there to meet the ship, and he went aboard to help Valentina with the twins. "Yer mother's in hysterics, and Meggie hasn't stopped cryin'. Ye'll have yer hands full, my love."

Splendor of God, Tina thought, *Mother will have hysterics when she learns that Heath is Father's heir.* Tina did not mention that their baby son had been unwell; Ram had enough to worry him.

"I'll tend to Elizabeth," Ada said firmly. "I'm used to her ladyship's temperament."

Rob Kennedy followed Ada down the gangplank with a sure gait, ready to face whatever awaited him.

"Do you have a secure place where I can put Armstrong?" Heath asked Ram.

"Put him aboard the *Revenge*; Jock will guard him overnight. We'll have tae sail tae Carlisle in the mornin'; the Border Wardens' Court starts tomorrow, so we'll miss the first day." Ram hoisted the empty cradle on a broad shoulder and followed his family into the Kennedy tower castle.

Heath turned Armstrong over to Jock, who manacled the prisoner in the hold of the *Revenge*. "We didna catch any of the English swine, and we have no idea how many sheep and cattle they drove off. All we could do was clean up the mess. Ram brought men from Castle Douglas tae rebuild what's been burned."

Anger at the English almost choked Heath as he entered the tower castle. He saw Beth Kennedy and Lady Elizabeth sobbing in each other's arms, while Tina was quietly consoling Donal's young wife, Meggie. Ada pulled Beth's arms from around her mother's neck.

"Come on, my lady, let's get you to bed, and I'll have Mr.

Burque brew you a posset to comfort you." Ada led Elizabeth away and a purposeful Rob Kennedy began to follow them.

Suddenly he turned back to speak with Heath. "Will ye represent the Kennedys at the Border Wardens' Court, and lay the charge where it belongs for this unspeakable raid?"

"I am honor bound to do so," Heath pledged.

Rob unclasped his silver dolphin brooch that bore the Kennedy motto, and pinned it to Heath's doublet. His arms went around him for one fleeting moment, then the Kennedy patriarch followed Ada.

Ram signaled to Heath and Duncan Kennedy to follow him. "Lady Kennedy and Meggie couldn't bring themselves tae look at the charred bodies. The two of ye will have tae see if ye can identify yer brother Donal."

The three men went below to the foundations of the tower castle, where the charred bodies lay on sheets. Four hewn wooden coffins stood against the wall waiting to receive the grisly remains. Heath knelt down and peered closely. None of the bodies had hair left, nor faces that could be recognized. One corpse was bigger than the others, and could have been Donal, but Heath's sixth sense told him it was not his brother.

Duncan, however, identified the body as Donal's immediately. "These boots have irons on the soles; Donal wore boots like these." Though the identification wasn't positive, the men agreed that the bodies should be buried without delay, and Heath said he'd take care of it. The minute Duncan left, Heath told Ram what he had learned from their prisoner. "He told me a hundred Armstrongs would ride if Dacre paid. I asked about other clans; he named the Grahams led by Long Will, who'd raid both sides of the Border."

Ram whistled. "Christ, that's three or four hundred. Dacre would pay them in sheep or cattle, which explains this Kennedy raid."

"Only in part; we both know this raid is in retaliation for my taking Christopher Dacre. They won't retaliate against Douglas for fear of exposing a connection between Dacre and Archibald."

"Well, the whoresons will learn that if they strike a Kennedy, 'tis the same as striking a Douglas! Do ye think we could sail on the evenin' tide? Will Rob be all right if ye leave him?"

"My father will be fine; he's suddenly become a well of strength and will soon be back to ruling the Kennedy roost."

"I'll have a word with Tina, then I'll have my moss-troopers start taking their mounts aboard."

Ramsay pulled Valentina into an empty chamber next to Meggan's. "It's been like a madhouse here. Will ye be all right if we sail tonight?" He took her in his arms and held her tightly.

She pressed her face against his shoulder, and felt his hand stroking her hair. "Father's taken over, and Mother's finally asleep. Meggie is so diverted by the twins, she has temporarily dried her tears." She raised her eyes to his. "Was it Donal?"

"Duncan thinks so. . . . Heath does not."

"Should I have a look?"

"No, Vixen. Heath will have them buried by now. I want ye tae take the babies and go tae Castle Douglas as soon as ye may. The wagons from Eskdale will be arrivin' tomorrow. Don't let yer family drain all yer strength, love."

Valentina knew that when her father told his wife and Duncan about Heath, there would be hell to pay. The storm he would unleash would be nothing short of tumultuous. Her mother would be more than hysterical; she would throw a bloody fit, and Duncan would be ready to kill. "Yes." She smiled gently. "I will go home to Castle Douglas, I promise."

When Heath took Blackadder from the hold of the Kennedy vessel, he mounted him and gave him a run along the banks of the River Dee, before he loaded him onto the other ship. Heath's eyes avidly scanned the land across the river, knowing that somewhere out there lay his hundred acres. He didn't have time to explore them today, but he promised himself that he would bring his mares to graze on his own acres as soon as it was feasible. It was the first land he had ever owned, and it meant more to him than he could put into words.

That night the wind was with the *Revenge* as it sailed up the

Solway, and the pink dawn had just begun to lighten the sky as the vessel entered the mouth of the River Eden. They anchored close to Carlisle and rode into the city, which overflowed with both English and Scottish Border Wardens and their men, who had come to attend the Wardens' Court. It was being held in the great hall at Carlisle Castle, and the streets that ran north from the market cross to the massive red fortress were clogged.

"Way fer a Douglas!" Jock shouted as Ram and his moss-troopers trotted their sturdy garrons over the cobblestones. They were all in Douglas colors today, with their badges displayed proudly on their sleeves. Ramsay was garbed as befitted the wealthiest lord in the realm. Riding beside him, Heath Kennedy, wearing black to signify mourning, rubbed his sleeve over his silver dolphin brooch.

It took the better part of an hour before they dismounted at the castle stables and turned their mounts over to the waiting grooms. Ram dispatched half a dozen moss-troopers to set up tents on the meadow below the castle, as was the custom. Heath's heart missed a beat as he recognized Heron Carleton in the bailey close by the stables. He knew Heron must be here with his father, who was an official of the court. Without hesitation, Heath strode across the courtyard to greet him.

"Is Raven here?" Heath asked hopefully.

"Yes, but—" Heron looked uncomfortable.

"But what?"

"Raven just became betrothed to Christopher Dacre. They are to wed when the Border Wardens' Court ends."

Heath's face hardened. The granitelike mask hid the scalding fury that ripped through him. So, the blood-proud beauty had made her choice. She had sold herself to the highest bidder, the one who could give her wealth and a title. *I curse Dacre to hellfire!*

CHAPTER 23

The Border Wardens' Court met four times a year, alternating between the two largest Border cities, Berwick in the east and Carlisle in the west. Ostensibly, this was where the English met their Scots counterparts so that disputes could be discussed and resolved. The English officials who sat in judgment were Sir Robert Carey, Sir Richard Graham, and Sir Lancelot Carleton; the Scots were James Elliot, David Gilchrist, and Dand Kerr.

Lord Thomas Dacre, Head Warden of the English Marches, lost no time taking the offensive. "Since spring, seven hundred cattle belonging to Dacre tenants have been taken in Scottish raids in the Middle March alone!"

Alexander Hume, Lord Warden General of the Scottish Marches, was on his feet immediately. "They were lifted orderly, accordin' tae the custom of the Borders. An' I warrant fer every beast taken, the English lifted one hundred!"

In an aside, Ram said to Heath, "These two hate each other like poison. At Flodden, Hume kept his Borderers clear of the fightin', then pillaged and plundered the victorious English of their baggage and horses."

"Your Border Wardens turn a blind eye to thieving and raiding, Hume. As Warden General your job is to control your Wardens," Dacre pointed out indignantly.

"Control the likes of Johnnie Maxwell an' Black Ram Douglas? Their idea of law enforcement is three feet of steel, an' a bloody good job it is, when we have tae deal wi' the English, who are all disobedients filled wi' dishonor!"

"Hume, you are the last man on earth who should be speaking of dishonor!" Dacre shouted with indignation.

Ram Douglas was on his feet, looking directly at Dacre. "Nay, that distinction goes to an Englishman," he said bluntly.

Dacre stared at Douglas, waiting for an accusation, but Douglas sat back down and stared back. The cat-and-mouse game went on all day, but Douglas bided his time. A dozen cases of blackmail, kidnapping, wounding, and raiding were heard, defenses offered, judgments made, and penalties decided. The punishments varied from prison to compensation, unless the offenses were committed in the Debatable Land, which was disputed territory. These culprits were let off "scot-free," because neither country would take responsibility for acts committed there.

The next day, Ram Douglas accused the English of raiding Annan and a dozen smaller villages. He named an astonishing amount of compensation he was claiming, then addressed Dacre. "These raids were made from the English West March, which you, my lord, are supposed to control. Annan and the other villages were burned to the ground, and lives were lost. Only a coward uses fire on women and children." Douglas did not accuse Dacre directly of mounting the raids, but clearly he was tightening the screws.

The third day, Douglas didn't say a word; he didn't need to. When he and his men entered the great hall, they had Sim Armstrong with them. They sat their witness between Jock and Ram Douglas, with Douglas moss-troopers all around him for safekeeping. All day it was clear that Dacre could not concentrate on the cases before the court, and when he did not refute charges brought against his tenants for illegal pasturing and wounding, the verdicts went against him.

That evening, Ram Douglas made a quick visit to the Carlisle goldsmith with whom Angus had left gold on deposit. When Ram assured the goldsmith that he was happy to leave the funds in Carlisle rather than withdraw them for deposit in Scotland, the man confided in Douglas, telling him about a rumor he had heard which the English goldsmith knew would be of great interest to the Scots lord. Ram thanked the man and told him he would make it worth his while if he remained silent and kept the rumor to himself.

On the fourth day of the Wardens' Court, the Douglas witness was nowhere in evidence. After a lull in the proceedings at mid-morning, Lord Ramsay Douglas got to his feet to set forth his accusations. It was not so much his rich attire, decorated by the bleeding heart of Douglas in rubies and diamonds, that drew every eye, as it was his dark, dominant face and deep, powerful voice.

"Gentlemen, we have a traitor in our midst. We have a March Warden who pays an outlawed Scots clan tae reive and murder and maim their own flesh and blood in the Scots Borders. The numbers would astound ye. He can call on a hundred Armstrongs tae destroy their own with fire and sword. 'Tis a shrewd and evil ploy tae make us blame the English and hate them. But it doesn't stop there. He pays an English clan tae wreak havoc in the English Borders, then blame it on the Scots. These numbers are horrific; he has two or three hundred in his pay."

Sir Richard Graham, one of the English officials, got to his feet. "Such an accusation is preposterous! Englishmen would not stoop to such vile atrocities."

" 'Tis strange ye should be the one tae deny it, Sir Richard; the English clan I speak of is Graham!"

A babble of voices filled the air. Though Douglas had not yet accused the Warden he spoke of by name, most men in the hall suspected that he referred to Thomas Dacre. Sir Lancelot Carleton banged his gavel on the table to restore order. "Lord Douglas, the accusation does seem preposterous. English Border Wardens are accountable to the Earl of Surrey, who gets his orders directly from the King of England."

Douglas nodded to Carleton. "Precisely, Sir Lancelot; ye have just made my point!"

For a full ten minutes, pandemonium reigned, and it took another ten minutes to restore order in the hall. Douglas held up a hand. "Tomorrow I will name names and bring my witness, Sim Armstrong, who will testify tae all this. Tomorrow I will bring ye proof." Ram knew that Armstrong would not testify, but no one else in the hall except Heath knew this. Douglas sat down, and Kennedy took the floor.

He was garbed in black from head to foot, and the men in the crowded hall craned their necks to get a look at the newcomer. Though more attractive than Douglas, no one doubted that here was another dark, dominant Borderer, cut from the same cloth. Heath raised his head proudly and stared at the officials who sat in judgment. "The name is Kennedy. On Dacre's orders, the Armstrongs raided Eskdale and lifted a dozen breeding mares from me. I took Dacre's son and held him for ransom. My breeding mares were restored and I turned Christopher Dacre over to his father. That should have been the end of the matter, but it was not. In retaliation a Kennedy merchant vessel, with its cargo of wool, was destroyed by fire while it was docked here in Carlisle. Then, only a few days ago, a massive raid was mounted in Kirkcudbright against my brother Donal Kennedy. Cattle and sheep were lifted, the sheds of wool set ablaze, and my brother Donal burned to death. Need I remind you that under Border law, reprisal raids are forbidden, and that Dacre controls the West March?"

Dacre was on his feet denying the accusation before Heath Kennedy stopped speaking. "These are filthy lies! My son was never taken for ransom by this Kennedy by-blow! The tales of stolen brood mares, fired ships, and Kirkcudbright raids are pure fabrication. He claims Armstrongs raided Eskdale; need I remind you they are Scots, not English, and that Douglas controls the Scottish West March?"

Lancelot Carleton jumped to the defense of the young man who was about to become his son-in-law. "Do you seriously expect us to believe that you held Christopher Dacre ransom for a few mares?"

"I grant you my mares were worth far more than a Dacre, but if you doubt that Dacre's son was my prisoner, I suggest you ask your own son, Heron Carleton." Heath directed his next words to the three Scottish officials who sat in judgment. "I speak for my father, Rob Kennedy, Lord of Galloway. We ask compensation for livestock lifted and goods destroyed, and we ask that a charge of murder be laid against Lord Thomas Dacre."

Silence blanketed the hall for one full minute before voices erupted in shouting and cursing. Grim-faced, Heath Kennedy, Ramsay Douglas, and all his men filed from Carlisle's great hall. Outside, Ram Douglas grunted with satisfaction. "We gave the whoreson a one-two punch in the gut. When I purposely didn't name him, Dacre knew I was blackmailin' him. Before the light fully fades from the sky, I wager we'll hear from him."

Heath grimaced. "I never bet against a sure thing."

It was just at twilight that a messenger came to the tents, asking for Ramsay Douglas. He carried no note, only a verbal message. He cast a wary glance at Heath Kennedy, and they knew he had been told not to speak in front of witnesses. When Heath stepped outside, the messenger said, "Lord Dacre awaits you, *alone*, my lord."

As Ram Douglas entered Dacre's library, his confidence surged and he decided to up the amount of the bribe he would demand for withdrawing his charges. But Dacre had a surprise up his sleeve.

"Tell Kennedy that he will have to withdraw the charge of murder against me. His brother Donal is alive." Dacre's smile was malicious; there were few men he hated more than Ram Douglas.

Ramsay's hope soared. Valentina would be joyous! His pewter black eyes were hooded, however; his emotions hidden from view. "If ye took Donal Kennedy prisoner, it proves ye were raidin' in Kirkcudbright."

"Not so. He was raiding across the Border in England, and captured in the Debatable Land. A dozen Grahams will swear it."

Ram was ready to negotiate. "I could be persuaded tae tell the court that my witness is unreliable, and that I have no proof of the claims I made today, in exchange fer Donal Kennedy."

Dacre smiled slowly. "I hold the whip hand, Douglas."

Ram's dark, forbidding features looked chiseled from stone.

"Unless you tell the court tomorrow that you have no witness, nor proof of your rash claims, and unless you turn Armstrong over to me tonight, your wife's brother Donal will die."

Ram's eyes bored into his enemy as he weighed the odds of knifing him on the spot. Dacre was a coward and would have guards waiting outside the door to kill him, and kill his prisoner, Donal Kennedy. So it was a standoff. Douglas nodded once and turned on his heel.

Back in the tent, he gave Heath Kennedy the news. "Donal is alive; Dacre is holding him prisoner."

"Thank God!"

"Don't thank him yet. I tried tae negotiate; I offered tae withdraw all claims and charges in exchange fer Donal. Dacre laughed in my face. Unless I agree tae tell the court I have no proof of my rash claims, and unless I turn Armstrong over tae him tonight, he threatens tae kill Donal. I believe he'll do it."

"Then we have no choice . . . I'm sorry."

"Nay, I have no problem withholdin' the proof that Dacre is payin' the Armstrongs and Grahams. The damage was done when I accused him; all now suspect it is the truth."

Heath's thoughts raced about, seeking an answer to the dilemma. "Sim Armstrong is *my* prisoner. I'll turn him over to Dacre."

Ram eyed Heath. "Don't do anythin' reckless. I was tempted, but managed tae curb my blazin' temper."

Heath nodded curtly and went to Jock's tent, where Armstrong was being heavily guarded. "Come with me," he told the prisoner, whose arms were trussed behind him.

Sim Armstrong looked terrified and ready to bolt. "Do ye want me tae come with ye?" Jock asked Kennedy.

Heath fingered the handle of his dagger in its sheath and shook his head. "Nay, I think Armstrong and I understand each other."

It was full dark as the two figures made their way toward the castle. Kennedy walked behind Armstrong, and prodded him with his blade whenever his steps became reluctant. When they reached the shadow of the wall, Heath reached out and cut the rope that bound his prisoner. "Get the hell out of here," he said low.

It took Sim Armstrong a minute to comprehend his meaning. The next minute, he was gone.

Heath Kennedy concealed his knife in his boot, expecting to be challenged when he walked into Carlisle Castle. "Take me to Lord Dacre; we have business." Two more guards were posted outside the library door, fully armed with knives and swords. When they knocked, Dacre opened the door himself and admitted Kennedy.

"You are wasting your time; I won't bargain."

"I think you will."

Dacre's eyebrows went up in surprise at Kennedy's audacity.

"You and your son would far rather have me for your prisoner than Donal Kennedy. I'll take his place if you will release him."

Dacre stared hard, wondering if he had heard right, suspicious of some ruse. He went to the door and asked the guard to summon Christopher, never taking his eyes from Kennedy. "Where's Armstrong?" he demanded.

Kennedy spread his palms. "Escaped," he said blandly.

When Christopher Dacre entered the library and he saw who was with his father, his lips curled with hatred. Then he said with relish, "There is no amount of money will ransom your brother."

Dacre cut in, "He isn't offering money—he's offering himself."

Chris Dacre's eyes widened with disbelief.

Heath Kennedy repeated his offer. "I'll take Donal's place if you will release him." He watched the expression in Chris Dacre's eyes change to avidity, and he knew the deal was done. Dacre lusted to have him at his mercy.

It seemed to take a long time for the guards to produce Donal Kennedy, and Heath surmised that was because he was imprisoned deep in the bowels of the castle. When he was brought into the library, Heath saw that there was blood on his clothes and that he had a decided limp, but at least he was upright and could walk.

When Donal saw his half-brother, Heath, he could not hide his surprise. "You ransomed me?"

"I did," Heath answered quickly, before anyone else could speak. "You will find the tents of Ram Douglas and his men in the meadow, set up next to the Maxwells."

"You are free to go," Dacre informed Donal. "Tell Douglas that I am holding his wife's brother until he withdraws all claims before the Wardens' Court tomorrow."

Donal Kennedy seemed to be in a daze, but when a guard opened the door for him, he went through it as quickly as he could.

Chris Dacre ordered the guards to seize Heath Kennedy, but his father uttered a quick warning. "Search him first. He would not come here without a concealed weapon." When they discovered the knife in his boot, Chris Dacre held out his hand. "I'll take that." Then he made a mocking bow. "After you, gentlemen."

With a guard on either side holding his arms and Chris Dacre following behind, Heath was taken to a dank prison cell beneath Carlisle Castle. He marked the winding passages down which he was dragged and knew he was being lodged in the most ancient, seldom-used part of the fortress.

Dacre lit a torch so that the guards could shackle his prisoner's arms in metal wall rings.

Heath cursed silently, knowing he would not be able to lie down. Then he laughed at his own folly, for of a certainty he had not expected to be treated in a civilized manner.

When Dacre was certain Kennedy was fully secured, he told the guards, "Leave us!" He lifted the torch so that the light shone on his prisoner's face, and suddenly Kennedy's proud, dark beauty filled him with fury. "You arrogant bastard! You are nothing but a Gypsy by-blow, yet still you stand there looking down on me!"

"Look down on you? You should be honored I'm looking at all."

Dacre's fist slammed into Kennedy's face. "I'll be back tomorrow night. We'll see how arrogant you are after you've been standing for twenty-four hours."

Heath licked his split lip and tasted his own salty blood with perverse satisfaction.

Ram Douglas was quaffing a jar of ale when Donal Kennedy limped in. He set the ale down and wiped his mouth on his sleeve. "How the hell did Heath gain yer release when I failed?" Suddenly comprehension dawned. "Christ's holy wounds, he took yer place!"

Donal nodded. "How did ye guess?"

"The reckless fool did it for me once."

"Dacre says he'll hold him until ye withdraw all claims before the Border Wardens' Court tomorrow."

Ram knew Dacre's word meant nothing, but once he had withdrawn the claims, Ram could think of no reason for Dacre to hold Heath Kennedy indefinitely. Moreover, Dacre knew that if aught befell Kennedy, Douglas would avenge him. Ram threw up his hands at his friend's brash courage. "We'll get ye home tomorrow. 'Tis not only yer women who will weep tears of joy. Yer father will kill the fatted calf when ye return!"

At Carlisle Castle, Heron Carleton's father was in a less jubilant mood. Sir Lancelot summoned his son to his chamber. "I did not see you in court today."

"No, Father. Raven was being fitted for her wedding gown, and Lady Rosalind and Mother set me a dozen tasks, not the least of which was measuring the length of the aisle in Carlisle Cathedral."

Lance Carleton was not diverted. "If you had sat in on the session, you would have witnessed Heath Kennedy accuse the Dacres of deadly reprisals because he had held Chris Dacre for ransom of some mares. When I challenged him, asking if he expected us to believe such a thing, the arrogant devil suggested that if I didn't believe it, to ask my own son!"

Heron licked dry lips. "Mmn, yes, Christopher did mention something about a kidnapping for ransom." Heron was torn. He wanted to tell his father that he believed the Dacres had raided in Scotland, but he didn't want to involve Raven.

"How was Heath Kennedy so certain you knew about it? Were you involved in this?"

"No, Father, but I believe it happened. Kennedy is your kin; why would you not believe him?"

"Heath Kennedy is no kin of mine. He has been a thorn in the side of my cousin Elizabeth since her wedding. He is Rob Kennedy's illegitimate son by some Gypsy girl!"

Raven opened the chamber door. "Oh, sorry, Father, I thought you were alone."

Sir Lancelot stared at her, as he suddenly remembered something she had said a few nights ago. *For argument's sake, let us say I chose to marry a Scot, a Borderer. What if he were illegitimate and had Gypsy blood?* "Come in, Raven, and close the door."

She glanced at Heron, and his expression put her on her guard. The silence in the room stretched to the breaking point. "Father, is there something you wish to say to me?"

"Two words: Heath Kennedy."

Raven's cheeks blushed the color of roses. "You told him?" she asked her brother.

Heron replied quickly, "Yes, I told him that Chris had mentioned that he was kidnapped and held for ransom by Heath Kennedy."

"Do I look like a gullible fool?" their father demanded. "Would you like to tell me the whole sordid story?"

"No, Father," Raven said quietly. "There is nothing to tell."

"A conspiracy!" Carleton declared.

"As a dutiful daughter, I have agreed to wed Christopher Dacre. Let that be an end to the matter. Leave it alone, Father."

Raven spoke with such quiet dignity that as he looked at her, Lance Carleton realized his daughter was no longer a girl, she was a woman in her own right. He bowed to her decision. "So be it."

As they walked back to their own chambers, Raven asked her brother, "Why was he asking about Heath Kennedy?"

"His name must have come up at the Wardens' Court today." Heron had not told her earlier that he had seen Heath Kennedy, and he was not going to tell her now. "You handled Father very well."

Inside her own chamber, Raven leaned back against the door, feeling dreadful over the way she had spoken to her father. *Let that be an end to the matter,* she had said. But it wasn't an end to the matter. In two days' time she had agreed to marry Christopher Dacre, but how on earth was she going to go through with it, when she did not love him? When she was at Eskdale she had talked incessantly about her freedom. Raven wanted to scream at the irony of it all. She had been far more free in Scotland than she would ever be again.

Marriage to Christopher Dacre was a prison from which there would
be no escape.

Yet she knew she must go through with it. All the arrangements
had been made. She had been fitted for her wedding dress, which
now hung ready and waiting in the wardrobe. The banns had been
read in Carlisle Cathedral, the guests had been invited, and their
apartment in the castle had been refurbished.

Christopher had been particularly indulgent with her, allowing
her to choose rich, oriental carpets along with whatever furnishings
caught her fancy. He seemed ready to give her anything her heart
desired, yet all she wanted from him was her freedom.

Christopher was an eager bridegroom, but whenever he got
playfully amorous, she froze on the inside. She had managed to
avoid intimacy, insisting that he wait until they were married, but
time was rushing upon her so quickly that soon the hour would be
upon her when she would no longer be able to deny him. Her complacent demeanor belied what she was feeling on the inside. Her
heart was beating and fluttering like the wings of a bird against the
wires of its cage, but she knew there was no escape.

Raven put her hands over her ears to stop the echo of her
grandmother's words. *Your heart is the doorway to your soul, my lovely.
Always remember that your soul has the final say. When your soul talks to
you, you must listen.*

CHAPTER 24

It was the final day of the Wardens' Court, and Ram Douglas sent Donal Kennedy and half of his moss-troopers to the ship to speed up their departure once he and Jock had attended the last meeting. There were no more cases to be heard, only loose ends to be tied up, except for Ram Douglas and his promised witness. The men gathered in Carlisle Castle's great hall anticipated the clash of wills between the long-standing enemies, Douglas and Dacre.

When Douglas took the floor, the silence was so great that the crowd could have heard a cockroach fart. "Since he is gravely incapacitated, I speak on behalf of Heath Kennedy today. The charge of murder against Lord Thomas Dacre is withdrawn." A murmur went up among the crowd. "*However,*" he emphasized, then repeated, "*however,* it can be reinstated at any time by me, since Kennedy and I have a bond of blood." Ram knew by the look on Dacre's face that he understood the threat. "A claim for compensation fer the loss of the Kennedy merchant vessel and fer the loss of their Kirkcudbright wool fleeces will be sent tae the Crown of England. It will not be submitted through Dacre or Surrey, but sent directly tae yer king's paymaster, Cardinal Wolsey, informin' him that there is more theft and extortion by the English West March than all the Scots in Scotland!"

A cheer went up from the Scots seated in the hall. "Now on tae my own business," Ram Douglas declared. "I do humbly beg the Court's pardon fer wastin' yer valuable time yesterday." Laughter broke out, for Douglas had never been humble in his life, nor was he a man to beg for anything. "It seems my witness has mysteriously disappeared along with the proof of my rash claims. I'm sorry . . ." Everyone held his breath, not believing that Douglas was actually apologizing. "I'm sorry there's a traitor in our midst, who can't be brought tae justice, *at this time.*" Douglas looked as if he would sit down, then he bethought himself of something. "Where are my manners? On behalf of the Scots, I would like tae extend our appreciation fer Dacre's hospitality here at Carlisle Castle. No other host can compare with him." Ram Douglas began to clap his hands, and the others joined in with laughter, hooting, and mocking applause.

Heath Kennedy was not enjoying Dacre's hospitality. The torch in the wall bracket had soon burned out, so he accustomed himself to the darkness, and from the silence he could tell that none of the cells hereabout were occupied. Wisely, he had pressed his back into the stone wall to keep some of his weight from his legs, and he had changed the position of his long limbs often during the endless night to maintain his circulation. Fortunately, with focused concentration and determined willpower, he was able to separate himself from the pain and misery of his body for long periods of time.

The only way he could tell that it was morning was when the torch was relit and he saw that the guard had brought him bread and water. With his keys the guard had unlocked the barred door of his cell, but he did not unlock Heath's manacles. Fortunately his chains were just long enough for him to hold his food and reach his mouth. Heath was completely passive while the guard was present, and did not eat until he was alone. The guard locked the cell and retreated, but not far; he was still in the vicinity.

Heath realized it would be a long day, but he knew that when evening fell, Christopher Dacre would not be able to resist visiting him. The only reason he was being held prisoner was so that the sick swine could indulge his revenge, and the only reason Dacre needed revenge was Raven Carleton. How ironic it was that though the beautiful female had chosen Christopher Dacre and was about to become his wife, he was so unsure of her that he was riven with jealousy. Heath pitied him, for he would never possess one small part of her love.

Heath knew how easy it would be to immerse himself in thoughts of Raven and lose himself in drugging fantasy to pass the endless hours of the day, but he knew he must not do it, not now, not yet. Instead, he would separate his mind from his physical being and think about Donal sailing home to his family. When she saw him, his wife, Meggie, would be delirious with joy, and Heath pictured Donal picking up his little girl and lifting her high with exultation. Lady Elizabeth would weep tears of happiness when she saw her eldest son, and Rob Kennedy would rejoice that he had found the courage to tell the truth, which broke the curse and resurrected Donal from the dead.

When Raven awoke, her first thought was that it was the last day of July and that tomorrow was the first day of August. Her heart sank. She glanced over to her sister, who was still asleep, and remembered that Lark had been absent last night when she had gone to bed. Fleetingly, Raven wondered where she had been, then thought, *What does it matter?* Raven got up listlessly and wondered, *What does anything matter?* For days she had been going through the motions of preparing for her wedding, but she was strangely detached from it all. Actually the momentum was being carried by her mother and Lady Rosalind Dacre; she was simply following their lead.

She joined the two women in the Dacres' small private dining room for breakfast, but the food was so unappealing she could not eat, and simply toyed with it on her plate. Finally, Lady Rosalind stopped her incessant chatter about the wedding and the important guests who had been invited. "Raven, my dear, is something wrong?"

"She's daydreaming again," Kate Carleton declared. "I swear it is a condition that afflicts all brides in the days before the wedding. Stop playing with your food, Raven, and contribute something to the conversation."

"Perhaps she's daydreaming about going to the English court one day soon; I'm rather excited about it myself," Rosalind admitted.

"The Tudor court in London?" Kate asked, thoroughly impressed. "What is the occasion?"

"Oh, I don't know any of the details; it is all hush-hush at the moment, but Thomas assures me I may go along, when the time comes. Did Christopher mention it to you, Raven?" Lady Rosalind inquired.

Raven looked at her future mother-in-law blankly, then a faint recollection stirred her memory. "Er, yes, I believe he did promise to take me to court."

Her mother looked at her with reproach. "How could you have forgotten to tell me something so important and so exciting?"

"I'm sorry, I just remembered that I still have a hundred things to do before the wedding. I know you will both excuse me." Raven hurried from the room, needing to escape from the feeling that a trap was closing in on her. When she reached her own chamber, she knew she must keep herself busy. She opened the wardrobe and began the task she had been putting off all week. She took out an armful of gowns and carried them to the apartment that she and Christopher would be sharing after tomorrow. When she opened the door and stepped inside, she heard her sister's laughter. Raven went through to the bedchamber and found Lark gazing up at Christopher with adoration.

Lark jumped guiltily. "Oh, Raven, let me help you with those. I was just helping Chris bring some of his things to your new apartment." Lark took the gowns from her and laid them on the bed.

Raven looked at her bridegroom in surprise. Surely there were servants aplenty to do these things for him.

"Lark is such a sweetheart, she cannot do enough for me," Chris said with affection, and received another adoring look from Lark.

If only I could look at him like that, Raven thought sadly. *Lark fancies herself in love with him, and sooner or later he will hurt her.* She suddenly remembered her sister's empty bed last night and wondered if she had been with Christopher. Raven was appalled at her suspicions.

Lark was nothing more than an innocent girl; it was Chris Dacre who spawned her suspicious thoughts! "I'll be back with more of my things," she said breathlessly.

Raven knew she must get outside in the fresh air. She needed to escape for a little while to sort out her tangled emotions. Her thoughts were in disarray, her feelings were in chaos, and her tranquility had completely vanished. If only she could ride Sully through the Rockcliffe Marsh and along the banks of the River Eden to the shore of the Solway. But she didn't even have a mount she could ride here in Carlisle. She went to the stables anyway and asked one of the grooms to saddle Lady Rosalind's horse for her. Christopher's mother was ever kind and generous toward her, and Raven was sure she would not mind.

Raven rode west, away from the castle and away from Carlisle. It seemed strange that she had been so listless lately, when usually she was bursting with vitality. As the palfrey galloped into the countryside, and she felt the sun on her face and the breeze blowing her hair behind her like a banner, Raven suddenly felt alive for the first time since she had left Rockcliffe. She followed a winding stream and watched a pair of otters playing in the water. When they scampered off, she dismounted, removed her shoes and stockings, and waded into the steam. As small silver fish darted away from her splashing feet, she laughed at the thrill of losing herself in the glory of nature.

She sat down on a fallen log amid the tall reeds and grasses to watch the birds as they circled and arced across the blue sky, then a dragonfly captured her attention. It was caught fast in a spider's web, and when she freed it with a gentle finger, she felt a moment's happiness. As the heaviness of her heart lifted, her emotions began to untangle themselves, and her thoughts became crystal clear. Her soul was talking to her, and she was finally listening. Raven knew in her heart that she could not marry Christopher Dacre.

As she rode back to Carlisle Castle the sun had begun its descent in the sky, and she was surprised that she had lost track of time for most of the afternoon. Raven was aware that her mother would be extremely upset with her, and that she also would be disappointing her father, but her resolve was firm and unwavering. She did not love

Christopher Dacre; she wasn't even sure she particularly liked him. It would be wrong to marry him simply because he was heir to wealth and a title; when she weighed those things against happiness, they meant absolutely nothing.

Raven returned Lady Rosalind's palfrey and hurried up to her chamber. She had lost her stockings, the hems of her skirt and petticoat were wet and bedraggled, and her hair was disheveled from the wind. She would wash and change, then go directly to Christopher Dacre and tell him that she had changed her mind. A swift, clean break would be the kindest and the most decent way to handle this. She would tell him first—she owed him that much—then she would explain her decision to her parents.

Raven went along to the newly appointed apartment, hoping to find him there. She found the chambers empty, however, and made her way to Christopher's own rooms in the family wing of the castle, hoping to catch him before he went down to dinner. She knocked lightly and entered, but soon realized that he wasn't here either. Her glance fell upon some personal articles that he must have been gathering to transfer to the other apartment. One of the items was a knife that looked familiar. Raven stepped over to the desk and picked it up. She slid it from its black leather sheath and saw the pentagram etched on the blade. She knew instantly that the knife belonged to Heath Kennedy!

Chris Dacre made his way down to the prison cells in the ancient part of the fortress. He felt the blood in his veins surge with anticipation; he had been looking forward to this moment for the last twenty-four hours. He found the guard at his post at the end of the ancient cell block and ordered him to light the torch so that he could see his prisoner. Dacre peered through the bars to make sure Kennedy was still securely shackled, then he motioned for the guard to unlock the cell and withdraw to his post.

"Good evening."

Heath Kennedy raised his chin, which had been resting on his chest, and looked into Dacre's glittering, gray-green eyes.

"Do you know what day this is?" Dacre asked softly. "It is the eve of my wedding to Mistress Raven Carleton." He paused to let the full impact of his statement penetrate Kennedy's brain. "And tomorrow, after we have exchanged marriage vows and Raven is my wife, do you know the very first thing I am going to do?"

Heath waited impassively for the sadistic details that Dacre was about to impart.

Christopher laughed. "No, no, I am not going to fuck her immediately; I will have all night to do that. The very first thing I am going to do with my wife, Raven Dacre, is bring her down here to look at you. She saw me when you had me at your mercy; now she will see that I have you completely at my mercy. It will be her first lesson in learning that I am the master, that I hold the whip hand." He raised his arm so that Kennedy could see the whip he held, then he lashed out once at his prisoner leaving a gash across his cheek and down his neck.

"We will have our own private celebration. I shall kiss the bride for you, then perhaps I will undress her and initiate her right before your eyes. If you see me put my brand upon her, you will learn once and for all time that Raven is my property."

You don't love Raven, you hate her! Heath Kennedy closed his eyes and mentally blocked Dacre's voice. He needed to focus and gather his inner strength and his power without distraction.

Chris Dacre suspected his prisoner had lost consciousness, and decided to withdraw. What pleasure was there in taunting an enemy who could no longer hear you?

In actual fact, all of Heath's senses were acute at the moment, especially his sixth sense. He had been successful in separating himself from the pain, and the bone-deep ache in his legs for most of the day, and had even slept for short periods, perched on one leg like a crane. The silence of the empty dungeon helped him to concentrate, and he allowed his pain to wash back over him as a spur to accomplish the task that lay before him. Focusing on the god stone he wore around his neck, he pressed his body into the ancient stones, attuning it to the energy within. Then he made an invocation for the stones' power and strength to come inside him. He also absorbed the essence of time that lay within the ancient stones to give him calm and patience.

A picture of Raven came into his mind, and he focused on every detail, seeing her beautiful face, touching her silky black hair, hearing her lovely laughter, scenting her unique woman's fragrance, and tasting the honeyed sweetness of her mouth. His pain receded and was kept at bay by his vision. He tapped his iron chains against the stones. *One to seek her, one to find her, one to bring her, one to bind her.* He went deeper within, concentrating on his sixth sense. All he had to do was conjure her. *Come to me, Raven!*

The moment that Raven realized she held Heath Kennedy's knife in her hand, her thoughts were filled with him. She had no idea how the dagger had come to be in the possession of Christopher Dacre, but the desire to find her fiancé faded from her consciousness. She took the weapon back to her own chamber and lit the candles. Then once again she drew the knife from its sheath to look at the symbol on its blade. She traced the outline of the pentagram with her finger and was filled with a sense of its mystical power. As she gazed at it, the candlelight reflected on the polished metal in the very center of the five-pointed star, making it glow. She stared at it as if entranced. *Come to me, Raven!*

She did not actually hear the words, she sensed them. She sheathed the knife, then held it against her heart, and a great feeling of comfort stole over her. Holding something powerful that belonged to Heath seemed to connect them in a way that made her feel his presence. She opened the drawer of the dressing table, took out her hag stone, and laid it beside his dagger. Heath's presence became so strong, it almost felt as if he were in the room with her. A desire to communicate with him overwhelmed her. She wanted to tell him that she was not going to marry Chris Dacre.

Memories of their time together flooded her mind; his dark face, his laughter, and his male scent filled her senses to overflowing. She saw them together at the Gypsy camp, and knew that had been the happiest night of her life. Raven went to the wardrobe, pushed aside the wedding gown that she would never wear, and took out the Gypsy dress.

In minutes she stood before the dressing table mirror in the red dress, amazed at the transformation she saw. The female in the mirror was filled with vitality and a reckless passion for life. Then from the deep recesses of the glass she saw Heath Kennedy's face reflected. He was looking at her through iron bars, and instantly she had a revelation. Heath was here; he was imprisoned somewhere within Carlisle Castle. *Come to me, Raven!*

She snatched up his knife and her hag stone and hurried from the chamber. She had an intimate knowledge of this old fortress, yet her instinct told her that Heath would guide her. She went down to the main level of the castle, then descended another floor and took a long passageway that led into the ancient part of Carlisle. It was filled with gloomy darkness and eerie, intimidating shadows, yet Raven did not hesitate as she descended another set of stone steps that took her into the bowels of the ancient keep that had been built by the Conqueror's son in the eleventh century. With every step she took, Raven gained confidence that she was drawing closer and closer to Heath Kennedy.

"Who goes there?" The guard was hoping to be relieved, but when he saw that it was a female, he challenged her.

"Can you not guess?" Raven asked in a teasing voice, keeping the knife hidden at her side, in the folds of her skirt. "Tonight everyone in the castle is celebrating tomorrow's wedding . . . everyone except you," she added, laughing. "The other guards sent me down to entertain you. Light the torch, so that we can both see what we are getting."

The guard set his sword and scabbard on his stool and lit the torch in the wall bracket.

Raven tossed her hair and pirouetted before him. Her red skirts flared out, revealing her bare legs.

"I could use a little entertainment. Is it true what they say about Gypsy girls?" He leered.

"That we are hotter than fire?" She licked her lips and drew close. "That is something you will have to discover for yourself. Is it true what the guards say about you?" she teased.

"What's that?" he asked, joining the game.

She touched his thigh. "That you can stand at attention longer than any soldier in Carlisle!" She danced away as he tried to grab her. "Ah, no, you will have to show me. I want you to show me the prisoner you are guarding too. It excites me."

When the guard looked reluctant, she taunted playfully, "Don't be a coward. Let's have a look at your prisoner, then I'll go and fetch us a wineskin and teach you some wicked tricks I can do."

He could not resist the double promise of woman and wine, and led the way down the line of cells to where the prisoner was incarcerated. As she moved against him he became erect.

The guard lost his erection fast enough when he felt the knife between his ribs. "Make one sound and you are a dead man. Do you understand?" When he nodded, Raven ordered, "Unlock the cell." Dark shadows cloaked the prisoner, but Raven could feel that she was in the presence of Heath Kennedy. She kept the knife pressed into the side of the guard as she waited for her eyes to adjust to the darkness. When she saw how Heath was chained to the wall, she gasped in horror. The blade point went through the guard's uniform, piercing his skin, as she ordered, "Unlock his shackles!"

The moment Heath was free of the arm rings, he let out a long, slow breath. "Thank you, Raven." As he rubbed his wrists, he said, "We'll need a gag for our friend here."

By the time she had ripped a strip from her petticoat, Heath had the guard locked in the shackles. He gagged him securely, then they withdrew from the cell and he turned the key in the lock. Raven went into his arms. "However did you come to be here?"

"They had Donal imprisoned; I took his place."

She stared up at his bloody face in outrage. "You took your brother's place, when they have never even treated you as one of the family? Dear God, how could you do that?"

"Donal has a mother, and a wife and child. How could I not?"

His words touched her heart. His selflessness was astounding.

CHAPTER 25

Come, we must hurry," she urged.

"I can't hurry yet, Raven. I have no feeling in my legs."

"Then we'll go slow." She was careful to not show him pity; he was far too proud to accept pity from a woman—or anyone else for that matter. When they got to the end of the cell block, they turned right, then stopped dead as they heard footsteps approach.

Heath realized it was time to change guards, and was fully prepared to use his knife.

Without a word, Raven slipped her hand into Heath's and urged him to go left. They crept along silently, turning first one way, then the other in the darkness. Heath pulled her to him and, cupping his hand to her ear, whispered, "This is the wrong way. I memorized every turn in every passageway."

Raven put her lips to his ear. "I played here as a child. Trust me."

Heath was torn. He should go back and silence the guard before he raised the alarm. Then he felt Raven squeeze his hand and he made a difficult decision. He would give control over to her and place his trust in her. He whispered, "You lead, I will follow."

They moved along with stealth through what seemed like a never-ending labyrinth of stone walls, then finally Heath could tell that the floor began to slope upward. The feeling was returning to his legs, but it brought with it excruciating pain. They stopped to listen for the footsteps of anyone that might be following them, but the silent darkness stretched all about them like black velvet.

"Almost there. Stay close." Raven climbed up onto a large

stone slab, then jumped down into a shallow pit. It took Heath longer to accomplish the maneuver, but finally he was beside her. "Keep your head low," she directed as she took his hand and ducked beneath a ledge of stone. Suddenly they were outside in what seemed to be a field.

"A secret passage!" Heath murmured with admiration.

"Not really. In the last century it was the castle privy, which emptied into this open field."

Heath, suddenly overcome with amusement, leaned against the castle wall and began to laugh. Raven joined in, exhilarated by their escape. Then she sobered. "We still have to get through the city gate."

"The Irish Gate that leads north won't be guarded close. Since early morning, Borderers who attended the Wardens' Court will have been leaving through it." He stroked her hair and flashed his grin. "They'll pay no attention to a couple of Gypsies."

"We'll go to Rockcliffe; it's only five miles away."

Heath massaged a cramp from his thigh. "We'll need a horse."

"Oh dear." Raven looked dismayed.

Heath grinned down at her. "That's no problem, my beauty, I'm an expert horse thief from way back!"

In less than an hour they had passed through the gate of the walled city of Carlisle and were mounted on a sturdy Border pony. They rode bareback without a saddle, with Raven mounted in front of Heath. There was no bit or bridle either, only a rope with which the animal had been tethered. "Thread your fingers into his mane and hang on," Heath told her.

The pony, responding to Heath's light touch and persuasive voice, plunged forward with surefooted eagerness. Raven, cradled between Heath's muscled thighs and held secure by one whipcord arm, reveled in the wild ride. As the crescent moon rose, bathing them in her pale silver light, Raven knew there was nowhere else on earth that she would rather be tonight. She gave thanks to the moon goddess for their freedom. This was paradise!

An hour's ride brought them to Rockcliffe. The stablemen, awakened by the excited barking of Heron's dogs, stared openmouthed at the dark Borderer with the bloody face and Sir Lancelot Carleton's black-haired daughter garbed in a scarlet Gypsy dress. Raven tossed her head and lifted her chin in a defiant gesture, but offered no explanation. When a stableman came forward to take the pony, however, Heath thanked him with quiet civility.

When they entered Rockcliffe Manor, they were met by both the steward and the housekeeper, who also had been roused by the dogs. The servants assumed it was the family returning home, but when they saw only Raven accompanied by the dangerous-looking, unkempt man, they could hardly credit it.

"I want hot water for a bath—lots of it," Raven directed.

"Will the family be returning tonight, mistress?" the steward inquired, raising an eyebrow at the way she was dressed.

"God, I hope not, Crawford!" Raven gave a whoop of laughter. "Hot water, if you please, and hurry!" She turned to Heath. "Go on upstairs, I have to get some things from the stillroom."

Heath tried to keep the amusement from his face as he noted the housekeeper's look of outrage, but she clearly saw the twinkle in his eye. He turned and began to limp up the steps.

"Mistress Raven, that's a *man*," the housekeeper said primly.

"Aye, Mrs. Hall, that's something he'll never be able to disguise. And not just a man, but a *real* man!" Raven winked at her. "If I were you, I'd go to bed and plug my ears."

In the stillroom, Raven selected some powdered yarrow, and a flacon of almond oil into which had been mixed marjoram, betony, and all-heal. She stopped by the kitchen to pick up honey and wine, then carried all upstairs to her spacious bedchamber, where Heath had lit the candles. She drew in her breath as the light illuminated what the lash had done to his face. "Who did this?"

"It doesn't matter, Raven."

By refusing to name him, she knew immediately that it was the cowardly act of Christopher Dacre. His words came winging back to her from the night she tried to help him escape from Eskdale. *I swear I will avenge myself against him, and against every Kennedy breathing. I will destroy them with fire and sword.* Suddenly, in a revelation, Raven realized that the Dacres were behind the fire in which her hands had been burned and also were behind the raid in which Donal Kennedy had been taken prisoner. She cursed herself for being so willfully blind. She touched his cheek tenderly. "I think I must stitch it," she said, half to herself.

"No, Raven, it will heal without stitches."

She pushed him down onto the bed so that her eyes were on a level with his face. Then she removed his bloodied shirt to examine the lash on his corded neck. "It won't heal without a scar," she protested.

"Of course it will . . . you have healing hands." Heath drew them to his lips and kissed her fingers.

"My God, don't start kissing me yet. I have things I must do."

"Such as?" His glance roamed with hunger from her lips to her eyes, then back to her mouth.

"I'm going to bathe you."

"Forgive me, love, I forgot how unpalatable I must be."

Raven groaned. "You're not unpalatable; you're absolutely edible." She heard servants in the hall and went out to them. "I want you to carry the big bath from the bathing room into my bedchamber." They did as she directed, then poured their buckets of hot water into it and went downstairs to get more.

Raven could feel Heath's eyes on her as she poured a goblet of wine and mixed in some of the powdered yarrow, then she came to the bed and moved between his thighs. She dipped her fingers into the wine and cleansed the long, open cut with the astringent liquid. "This will have to do; actually, your face had far too much beauty for a rough Borderer." She dipped her fingers in the wine and anointed him again. "Death and damnation, the scar will make you even more attractive."

She felt the bulge between his legs enlarge and harden against her soft belly, and smiled into his eyes. "I have all night to play nursemaid."

He slid his hands around her to cup her bottom cheeks and rub her against his erection. "We have all night to play, but it won't be nursemaid, my beauty."

Her gaze turned imperious. "I rescued you, and claim my rights to play whatever games I wish with you. Only when I have exhausted my imagination will I allow you to choose the games." She cushioned her breasts upon his chest as she put her lips to his ear. "Let us hope that one of them is Gypsy Prince."

Heath groaned. "You can read my mind."

Raven heard the servants behind her empty four more buckets of hot water into the tub, and mischievously stayed where she was between Heath's thighs. She noted with satisfaction that he did not lose his erection. When the men left, however, she got up and closed her bedchamber door, then she returned and knelt down to remove his boots. It was a struggle because his feet were swollen, but finally they came off. Then Heath stripped off his breeches. His cock sprang forth from the confining material, and Raven rolled her eyes playfully. "Gypsy Prince indeed!"

She watched Heath climb into the tub wearing only his phallic god stone, and she experienced his pain as he submerged his legs in the hot water and sat with his eyes closed until the excruciating cramps eased from his muscles. Then she lifted off the red dress and torn petticoat and came to the side of the tub wearing only her busk. When Heath opened his eyes he could not tear his glance away from the fetching little garment that nipped in her waist and thrust her tempting breasts upward and outward.

When Raven threw in a luffa and soap, the luffa floated, but the soap sank. As she groped about for it between his legs, she murmured, "I promise to be a most sensual nursemaid."

Heath lay back in the water, viewing her through narrowed eyes. "What you once told me is true, Raven. Danger does excite you!"

She trailed her fingers up the inside of his leg. "What excites you, ma braw Scot?" She cupped his cock and balls. "Och, it feels like ye have a set o' bagpipes between yer legs. If ye taught me to blow a tune on it, I warrant that would excite ye!"

The skin at the corners of his eyes crinkled with laughter, and in a fair imitation of Ram's accent, he said, "I warrant ye are enjoyin' havin' yer wanton, wicked way with me!"

"Do ye reckon?" She rested her breasts on the edge of the tub and teased, "How about a pair o' round haggis on a platter, or does only Mr. Burque's haggis excite ye?"

In a flash, Heath's powerful hands gripped her about her waist and he lifted her into the water on top of him. When she screamed, he grinned down at her. "Quiet, or yer screams will excite Mrs. Hall. I dinna want tae have tae pleasure both of ye!"

He unfastened her busk and let it drop from his fingers beside the tub. As her breasts spilled onto his chest, he palmed her bare bum cheeks and slid his fingers into the deep cleft. "Heath! Heath!" she cried, wild with excitement. He covered her mouth with his and tasted his name on her lips.

They clung and kissed until the water grew tepid, then Raven recalled that she had promised to bathe him. She reached for the soap and lathered his body, then he pilfered it from her and returned the favor. When she reached beneath his arms and felt the silken hair, she whispered, "I've done this before, in a dream." When he looked at her quizzically, she said, "Don't feign innocence; you know you have brought me to your bed many times."

"We are the masters of our own dreams, Raven. If you had not desired me, you would not have come."

"Conceited devil," she murmured happily. "Come, the water grows cool, and I've not finished with you yet."

"I've not started with you." He helped her from the water, then stepped from the tub. He dried her first. "I've done this before, and not in a dream."

She stood on tiptoe to kiss him. "I remember . . . I remember everything you have ever done or said to me, Heath Kennedy." The towel dropped to the floor, forgotten, as she led him to her bed. She pushed him down and he reached for her. "No, no, I want you to lie back so that I can massage your legs."

It was a novelty for Heath to be pampered, for he had been raised to do everything for himself his entire life. He reclined, folding his arms behind his head, and watched with fascination as Raven, naked, brought the flacon of oil, took out the stopper, and poured some into her palm. The fragrance of almond and something spicy permeated the air. "I smell marjoram," he said.

"Yes, there is marjoram in the oil, which prevents muscles from cramping; there also is betony to take away the bruising, and all-heal to ease the ache in joints." She stroked her palms from his ankles to his knees, repeating the long, soothing motion over and over. Then she knelt on the bed and moved her hands up to his thighs. After she had smoothed on the oil, she began to massage and manipulate the hard, knotted muscles with her fingers.

After the pain he had endured in his legs, her ministrations felt heavenly to Heath. "You know as much about herbs as I do, but you have the hands of an angel." He watched, fascinated, as she bent over him and her hair fell forward to touch and tease his flesh. In the candlelight it looked like ebony silk and fire. "Raven, you are so exquisitely beautiful to me."

She lifted her eyes to exchange an intimate glance, but her hands never left him. The tantalizing rhythm of her fingers was so seductive, it aroused sensations in both of them that left them breathless with anticipation.

"Higher, the ache is higher." Fire snaked through his groin, igniting his passionate need to be touched by her.

The corners of her mouth went up playfully, and graceful as a cat she straddled him and sat on his belly with her back to him. Then she carefully positioned herself so that his erect cock lay against her hot cleft. She poured more oil into her cupped palm, and stroked down his legs from this new angle. As she moved forward, then back, the friction became a torment that had them both reeling with need.

Heath's hands held her bottom as she moved to and fro. The curve of her back was breathtakingly lovely, and her skin was like cream velvet. Raven was the answer to a lifetime of dreams that he had thought could never be. He loved her with every beat of his heart, and vowed he would cherish her forever. Heath came up from the bed behind her and gathered her in his arms. He shuddered as he weighed her lush, full breasts in his hands, and he felt her shiver as he nuzzled her hair and whispered in her ear, "I love you, Raven."

He knew that with one driving thrust he could be inside her, unleashing the dark erotic passion she aroused in him, but Heath wanted her facing him, wanted them to look into each other's eyes as he worshipped her with his body. He wanted to drink the sweetness from her mouth and watch her cry out her pleasure. He lay back down and, lifting her, turned her about. He teased her woman's center with his thumb. "Open for me, Raven."

She knew what he wanted, for she wanted it too. She moved over him on her knees, then slowly, sensually, she took the head of his cock inside her and began to squeeze. The hot, wet pull of her sheath drew him all the way inside her, and she held her breath at the fullness and the pulsing power that made her want to yield not only her body, but her heart and soul to him too.

They both began to move at the same time; he thrust up as she sank down, and their bodies fell into the natural rhythm of the mating dance that had held lovers in thrall since the beginning of time. He whispered intimate endearments: fierce, loving words; soft, tender words; hot, dark, erotic words; promises and vows that melted her very bones. Raven could not speak, she could only feel. She wanted him buried deep inside her forever.

Raven knew that Heath was a man who would never hurt her, but would cherish her forever. She knew that she could place her life in his hands and he would keep her secure for all time. She yielded everything to him, willingly, generously, showing that she trusted him with her body, especially at this most vulnerable moment when he lay deep inside her. She abandoned herself to him, and was rewarded with a magnificent implosion like a sunburst. They clung to each other as if nothing on earth would ever separate them again, then slowly a delicious languor spread through her and she lay sprawled full upon him savoring the feeling of fulfillment.

They enjoyed the quiet time together, not moving, not talking, yet absorbing each other's essence, as the thirsty earth drinks the rain. Finally he stirred, then rolled until she was beneath him. As a pledge of his love, he took the god stone from around his neck and placed it around hers, so that the phallic symbol lay between her breasts. Then the kissing began. Softly, sweetly, temptingly at first, but soon desire inflamed them as he made love to her mouth with his, just as he had made love to her body. His tongue thrust inside the hot, dark cave in imitation of what he intended to do, if they could ever leave off the clinging and kissing.

She cupped his cheek and sighed, all aquiver at the closeness of their bodies. "Oh, Heath, I forgot the honey. It will keep your wound from leaving a scar." She reached over the side of the bed and dipped her finger in the honey, but as she brought it to his cheek, he took possession of her finger and slid it into his mouth, sucking off the sweetness.

"I can think of better things to do with honey." He dipped his own finger into the pot, then anointed her lips and the tips of her breasts, and proceeded to lick off the heather-flavored delicacy with his rough tongue. Their love games went on into the night, as if they would never have enough of each other.

Even in sleep, Raven and Heath touched. They lay curled up spoon-fashion, with his long body curving about her and her dark head tucked beneath his chin. Tonight they had no need for dreams.

In the morning, Raven slipped on a bed robe and went down to the kitchen to prepare them breakfast, then she brought it upstairs and climbed back into the big bed. They fed each other between kisses, laughing like two children who had no cares in the world. Raven brought him one of her father's linen shirts and watched avidly as he dressed. Simply looking at him gave her pleasure.

As Heath pulled on his boots, he said, "I will go and saddle Sully while you pack your bag."

Raven went still. Then she found her voice, and chose her words carefully. "Heath, I can't go running off."

"What do you mean?" He looked at her blankly, not comprehending.

"I can't run away with you. I've already done that once to my parents. I have to stay and explain my reasons for not marrying Christopher Dacre."

"To lowest hell with Christopher Dacre and with explanations! I'm taking you to Eskdale so we can have the priest finish marrying us."

"Heath, please try to understand. When I ran away from

Carlisle, I left a bridegroom standing at the altar. I owe my parents an explanation."

His eyes narrowed. "Leaving bridegrooms standing at the altar is becoming a bloody habit with you, Raven. I assumed you wanted to wed me." He stiffened with pride.

"Heath, I didn't say I wouldn't marry you!"

"No, but you didn't say you would either, did you, Raven?" Heath was no stranger to rejection; his earliest memories were laced with it, and it mauled his pride that the woman he had chosen to be his wife might not think him good enough to become her husband. Unable to hide his anger, he laughed bitterly. "It's my own bloody fault for laying my heart at the feet of a fickle female. I deserve my fate!"

"Heath, stop it! I intend to tell my parents all about you. I want them to give us their blessing. I know I can persuade them to accept you, when I explain to them how I feel about you."

"Persuade them to accept me, a Scots-born Gypsy, for their precious daughter? You are deluding yourself, Raven! I already had a confrontation with Sir Lancelot at the Border Wardens' Court. Do you think I'd give him the chance to look down his English nose at me again?"

"My father isn't like that," Raven flared. "He is the most understanding, gentle man in the whole world!"

"Ah, now we come to the crux of the matter; he's a gentleman and I am not. They will never in a million years put their blessing on our union. Come with me now, Raven!"

"Why are you being so stubborn and pigheaded about this? Why can't you put yourself in my place and understand that I cannot come with you now? My parents love me and want only what is best for me. I am honor bound to await their homecoming, to let them know that I am safe, and to explain why I want to marry you instead of Christopher Dacre."

When he heard her say the name of his enemy again, Heath was more than furious, he was livid. Beyond a shadow of a doubt, she was the most exasperating female he had ever met. "I will never again ask you to marry me, Raven. You have turned me down flatly twice; I will never, ever, give you the chance to turn me down a third time." His eyes glittered with rage as he drew himself up to his full height. "When you discover that you have made the mistake of a lifetime, and come running after me, it is you who will have to do the wooing, you who will have to do the proposing, aye, and on bended knee!" He bowed stiffly. "I bid you good day, Mistress Carleton."

CHAPTER 26

When the *Revenge* dropped anchor in Kirkcudbright, Ram Douglas cautioned Donal Kennedy. "Remember, yer family is in fer a shock. They buried ye last week."

Donal nodded his understanding, and the two men made their way down the gangplank. The men who were putting the finishing touches on the new wool sheds they had built suddenly stopped what they were doing and began to cheer. Donal waved to them, then he entered the tower castle and began to climb to the first floor. His wife, Meggie, who had just begun to descend the stone stairs, gave a little scream, then flung herself down the rest of the steps, never doubting that Donal would catch her in his arms. He lifted her in a bear hug, high against his heart, and whispered her name.

Meggie immediately buried her face in his neck and began to sob. In spite of his bulk and barrel chest, Donal was ever gentle with his little wife. He stroked her hair tenderly. "Dinna cry, lass, dinna cry . . . yer tears break my heart, Meggie." He carried her back upstairs, and Ram Douglas followed on his heels.

When Elizabeth Kennedy saw her son, one hand flew to her throat, the other to her heart. She stood rooted to the spot, hardly daring to believe that her prayers had been answered. Donal set Meggie down, but kept hold of her hand as he walked over to his mother and bent to kiss her cheek. She touched Donal's face to make sure he was real, then she looked over at Ram Douglas with genuine gratitude in her eyes. Elizabeth had never liked the Douglas family and usually avoided them at all costs; now, however, she felt ashamed of her past behavior. "Lord Douglas . . . Ramsay . . . I thank you from the bottom of my heart."

"Nay, Lady Kennedy, all I did was bring him home. Ye have Heath Kennedy tae thank fer Donal's deliverance."

"He's right, Mother. I was a prisoner in Carlisle Castle—Heath took my place on condition they free me."

Rob Kennedy, standing quietly in the doorway, heard what Donal said and was humbled by his son Heath's selflessness. He didn't deserve such good fortune. He had been an indifferent, even negligent father to his firstborn, yet his son had always shown him love and respect. Rob intended to make up for the past of course; he had already sent to Ayr for his lawyer so that he could change his will and set things right. Only one thing remained for him to do. Once the family had celebrated Donal's return, Rob Kennedy, Lord of Galloway, would tell them that Heath was his rightful heir.

Duncan, aboard the new ship when the *Revenge* arrived, came to hear if the Kennedy claim for damages had been accepted at the Border Wardens' Court. When he walked in and saw that his brother Donal had been resurrected, he felt as if he had received a blow to his solar plexus. He stood mute as he examined his true feelings. Finally he admitted to himself that though he was truly pleased that Donal was alive, nevertheless he was sorely disappointed that he was no longer heir to the Lordship of Galloway.

"Donal, I don't understand why you didn't demand to see Lord Thomas Dacre when you were taken to Carlisle. He was a dear friend of my family before I married your father."

Everyone in the room looked at her in utter amazement. "Lizzie, it was Lord bloody Dacre who ordered the raid on Kirkcudbright; it was on Dacre's orders that Donal was seized. It was Dacre who ordered my ship an' the Kennedy wool burned. Ye have the daft idea that because he's English, he's a gentleman. Once an' fer all, will ye get it through yer head that he is our enemy?" Rob, purple in the face, was in danger of another seizure.

Elizabeth looked at her husband thoughtfully. "Then I think perhaps you were right in forbidding me to betroth Beth to his son, Christopher. You have a shrewd head on your shoulders, Rob."

Her husband rolled his eyes at her naïveté, yet he was secretly pleased that she had given him a compliment.

"Join us for dinner, my lord," Elizabeth invited graciously.

"Nay, I shall take the welcome news about Donal tae Valentina as soon as I give Lord Kennedy a report on the Wardens' Court. Castle Douglas is only a stone's throw up the River Dee, Lady Kennedy; don't be a stranger tae Tina and the twins."

Ram advised Rob to make out a full claim for all the Kennedy losses and to submit it to the Crown of England. "If ye send the claim directly tae Cardinal Wolsey, the king's paymaster, he'll most likely settle it. King Henry Tudor wants tae preserve the illusion that he desires peace between our two countries."

"The Border Wardens' Court is just a farce then?"

Ram's smile was cynical. "It serves tae confirm that in the Borders, crime pays. Sheep get eaten; only wolves survive."

Rob's voice was suddenly intense. "What about Heath?"

Ram shook his head. "Heath is neither sheep nor wolf. Ye bred yerself a wild black stallion; they'll never be able tae hold him."

During dinner, Rob Kennedy pondered the best way to go about breaking the news, which he knew would be so unwelcome to his family. Should he tell them separately, or should he gather them together for the announcement? In the end he realized that there was no best way, so he decided to get it over in one fell swoop; that way there would be only one collective explosion. The meal had been a celebration of Donal's return, with more than one toast to their good fortune. Rob set down his empty whisky glass and stood. "Before ye leave the table, there is summat I must tell ye." All looked at him with only mild interest as contentment stole over them. "Try tae hear me out, before ye start interruptin'."

He looked at Lizzie, then Duncan, and finally Donal, and a measure of calm descended upon him as he began his confession. "A long time ago, I did summat that was wrong, and I never did anythin' tae set it right. Instead I lied, an' swept it under the rug as if it had never happened, thinkin' that was the best an' the easiest fer all involved. But fate has a way of makin' us pay fer our lies, an' I've finally come tae realize that what I did turned out fer the worst an' the hardest fer all involved."

Rob saw that he had their full attention now, and it pained him that he must destroy their contentment. "Ye are all well aware that Heath is my firstborn. It was a grievous sin on my part tae let ye believe he was illegitimate. What none of ye know is that I was married tae his mother, Lily Rose, which makes Heath my rightful heir."

Elizabeth gasped and cried, "No!"

Duncan cursed and knocked over a goblet of water in agitation.

Donal sat absolutely still.

Beth got up and ran from the room.

Meggie slipped her hand into her husband's.

The blood drained from Elizabeth's face as she stood up to confront her husband. "Damn you, Rob Kennedy! I always knew that you loved Lily Rose more than you ever loved me, but I told myself that *I* was the one you married, not *her*, and that was what saved my pride. Now you have stripped it away!"

"Lizzie, I cared enough about ye tae deny my first marriage, an' tae deny my firstborn son his rightful place. I knew ye were too prideful tae take second place tae another woman, but pride is a deadly sin we must pay fer, as I've learned at great cost."

"And now *my* firstborn son has to pay for your sins! Your noble confession strips everything from him. You have ruined his life!"

Donal stood up quietly. "Mother, that's not true. I've led a privileged life since the day I was born. Father not only had wealth, land, castles, and ships, he had strength and power that he seldom abused. I've long worried that I could never measure up to Father and fill his shoes, so in a way it is a relief tae know I'm not the heir."

Duncan's chair crashed to the floor as he stood up to face his brother. "Yer a useless weaklin' tae no' fight fer yer rights! Surely tae Christ ye'll no' hand everythin' tae that half-breed Gypsy? I'm the one who shouldha' been born the Kennedy heir! I hope the bastard rots in Carlisle prison—better yet, I hope Dacre hangs the son of a bitch!"

Donal's beefy fist shot out, smashing his brother in the face. Duncan was unconscious before he hit the floor.

Castle Douglas had been built so close to the water that Douglas vessels could sail right into the bailey. Valentina had been watching for the *Revenge* all day, and was waiting when Ramsay climbed over the ship's rails and jumped down beside her. He took her in his arms, kissed her once, then looked into her eyes so he could watch her reaction when he gave her the good news.

"Tina, Donal is alive! I just delivered him tae Meggie."

Her golden eyes were luminous and her face turned radiant. "Oh, Ram, how wonderful! Is he all right? Where did you find him? Was he taken in the raid?"

"He has a slight limp, but other than that, he's in fine fettle. Come, I'll tell ye the whole tale over dinner. I hope Mr. Burque has prepared somethin' special fer our homecomin'." Ram wanted to save the bad news about Heath until Tina had eaten something.

"I'll have it served in our chamber. Will that be special enough for you?"

"Good. I don't want tae share ye with anyone tonight."

By the time he had visited the twins, picking both up at the same time and singing a Scottish lullaby in a deep baritone, the food had been delivered to their adjoining bedroom in the great Master Tower. Ram put his babies in their cradles and joined his wife in the magnificent chamber, which boasted polished pink granite from floor to ceiling, and a huge fireplace that took up an entire wall. The floor was carpeted with black sheepskins, and the bed was covered by a lynx fur, so large it spilled to the floor.

While they ate, he regaled her with all that had happened at the Border Wardens' Court, and Tina listened attentively, picturing the whole thing in her mind. Finally she grew impatient. "But you haven't told me about Donal. I gather my brother was taken in the raid and was being held by that swine Dacre in Carlisle Castle. Did you ransom him?"

"I tried negotiatin', I tried blackmail, I even contemplated murderin' the whoreson, but as Dacre reminded me, he had the whip hand; he had Donal."

"Then how did you gain his freedom?" she asked breathlessly.

Ram wiped his mouth and threw down his napkin. "I didn't. It was Heath negotiated his freedom."

"But how on earth did he . . . oh dear God, he offered to take Donal's place, didn't he?" She remembered that he had done the very same thing for Ramsay once.

"Ye know he has more reckless courage than any mon breathin'." Ram came around the table and put his arm about his wife. "He'll find a way tae get free; he did before."

"I can't believe he did it; he has so much more to lose now."

"What do you mean, love?"

"Father confessed that he was legally married to Heath's mother, Lily Rose, before he married my mother. Heath is heir to the Lordship of Galloway . . . didn't he tell you?"

Ram whistled. "He never said a word." Ram recalled that Heath had worn the silver dolphin badge. "I do know he feels responsible fer Dacre's reprisal raids on the Kennedys."

"He is a noble fool if he feels guilt over displacing Donal as Father's heir. He has been cheated his whole life; the Lordship of Galloway is his birthright!"

"And he will live to fulfill that birthright, never doubt it for one moment, Tina." Ram's arm tightened about her shoulders to lend her strength. "I made sure Dacre understood what his fate would be if any grave harm befell Heath Kennedy."

"In light of Heath's courage, I'm ashamed of my own cowardice. I came to Castle Douglas as soon as you left; I didn't want to be around when Father told the family about Heath."

Ram hooted. "Judas, we'll feel the shock wave any minute. Do ye think these granite walls will hold?"

"For generations." Valentina lifted her face for his kiss. "I always feel safe here."

"I'm glad, fer I'm off again tae Glasgow tomorrow. I visited the goldsmith in Carlisle where Angus deposited money fer me, and he tipped me tae a rumor he'd heard that a shipment of gold was on its way from London fer Archibald Douglas."

"Oh, that reminds me, you have a letter." She brought it from his desk and handed it to him.

When Ram read it, he nodded with satisfaction. "John Douglas, Duke of Albany, has set sail fer Scotland. If Queen Margaret's spies have passed this information tae her, it could goad Archie tae take action sooner. I'd best go straight tae Edinburgh."

Tina gave a mock sigh. "These babies will be grown up before they ever get a chance to be christened."

He took her in his arms. "I promise ye a christening the minute I return, Vixen. It'll be bigger and better than aught they've ever seen in these parts!"

"Why does everything connected to Douglas have to be bigger and better, you swaggering devil?"

He quickened against her soft belly. "Because I *am* bigger and better. Did I not give ye twins tae prove it?" he teased.

Valentina arched a perfectly plucked brow. "I thought they were my gift to you, devil-eyed Douglas!"

"And so they were, a priceless gift indeed. I love ye, Tina."

In preparation for her parents' return to Rockcliffe, Raven scrupulously erased all signs that a male had stayed there overnight. The big tub was moved back to the bathing room, the sheets and towels they had used were washed, the red Gypsy dress was hidden away, and Heath's bloody shirt was burned. She had no illusions that the servants, especially Mrs. Hall, would keep her secrets, but for appearances' sake Raven wanted everything to be in order when her family arrived home.

She took particular care with her own appearance. She chose a simple dress of cream linen with long sleeves and a modest neckline. Then she brushed her hair back smoothly and tied it with a ribbon. The mirror showed her that she had achieved her objective of looking more like a saint than a sinner, and hoped it would prompt her parents to forgive her.

She watched and waited apprehensively for the carriage, and when it arrived she went down to the entrance hall to greet her family. Raven imagined her mother had been worried sick about her disappearance and that when she saw that Raven was at home, safe and sound, her mother would be more relieved than angry. Raven, however, imagined wrong.

Kate Carleton sailed through the front door like a battleship with her cannon primed. "So, here you are at home, looking serene as a novitiate in a convent, while we have had to face the wrath of the Dacres! You are a selfish, willful girl, who has no regard whatsoever for her parents, or for her poor spurned bridegroom! Have you any conception of the humiliation you have heaped upon your family, to say nothing of the Dacres' humiliation? I will never live this down if I live to be a thousand!"

Raven was forced to take the defensive before the rest of the family had even entered the manor. "I am sorry I ran off without telling you, Mother. I had no choice, and hoped you would understand when I explained."

"Explain? Perhaps you can explain what I was supposed to say to a furious bridegroom, to a tearful Lady Rosalind, to a livid and abusive Lord Thomas Dacre! Perhaps you can explain why you ran off on the eve of your wedding, discarding a gown that cost the earth, and disregarding over a hundred invited guests!"

"I couldn't marry Christopher Dacre," Raven protested, "because I don't love him."

"You don't love him because you only love yourself, Raven Carleton!" her mother cried.

"Kate, let's discuss this in a rational manner," Sir Lancelot implored.

"Rational? There is nothing rational about the girl. She has acted like a lunatic, like someone unbalanced!"

"Can we at least be civil?"

Kate turned on her husband. "You are to blame for this. You have spoiled her, indulged her, and allowed her to run wild, so that she has no notion of duty or responsibility, and on a mere whim she has ruined her family, spoiled her sister's chance for a good marriage, and turned us into a laughingstock!"

"That is enough, Kate!" Lance Carleton roared. "If you are more concerned with what people think than the state of your daughter's mind, then you are a shallow woman indeed. You have been talking, nonstop, since dawn. Kindly be quiet long enough to allow Raven to explain, and let's not stand out here in the hall like uncivilized barbarians."

Lance Carleton led the way into the living quarters, where he and Heron remained standing until the ladies were seated. Kate pressed her lips together. No doubt her husband's remark about uncivilized barbarians was directed at her, since she had been born and bred in the Borders. When silence descended, all eyes turned expectantly to Raven.

She took a steadying breath. "Mother is right. I am to blame for everything that has happened. I knew a long time ago that I did not love Christopher Dacre, did not particularly like him even. I should never have agreed to a betrothal. I should have ended it between us. But out of a misdirected sense of duty, I thought I could go through with it and become his wife. I knew how happy this marriage made you, Mother, and how devastated you would be if I called it off." Raven looked at her father. "I also knew you were not displeased with the match. When I began to have doubts, I tried to postpone the betrothal, thinking that if I had more time, I could grow to care for Christopher."

Raven licked dry lips. "Postponement seemed to offend Lord Dacre, and Mother pointed out to me that you owed your appointment on the Border Wardens' Court to Dacre and we could not afford to offend him, so I compromised and did what everyone else wanted. At the time it seemed the easiest thing to do."

"My appointment was the result of service to the Crown of England, given to me by the late king. I do not owe my position to Dacre, and a damn good thing too, since our opinions differ and our principles seem to diverge in opposite directions lately."

"Oh, I'm so glad to hear that, Father," Raven said earnestly.

"Dacre is supposed to keep peace along the Borders between the English and Scots, but I believe he harries Scotland to keep our two countries forever divided."

Heron jumped into the conversation. "Raven is right. I can no longer stomach the things Chris Dacre brags about to me. I know they go on raids into Scotland, reiving, burning, and even killing. I'm glad Raven finally saw him for what he is."

"We are not discussing politics, we are discussing Raven's behavior!" Kate Carleton protested.

"All right, Mother, I'll leave politics out of it. I could not marry Christopher Dacre, because I finally listened to my soul."

"What nonsense is that?"

"Your mother told me to listen to my soul. When I did listen, it told me that I loved another." As she spoke the words for the first time, Raven realized it was true. She was madly in love with Heath Kennedy. "I love a Scot, and I want to marry him."

"Intermarriage?" Kate gasped. "You expect us to countenance intermarriage?"

"Scotsmen have been marrying English ladies for centuries. Margaret Tudor married a Scot!"

"But he was a king!" her mother pointed out.

"Margaret just married Archibald Douglas."

"Speaking of Margaret, Rosalind told me that she would be entertaining the queen shortly, and that you and she were to accompany the royal court on a journey to England. Raven, how in the world could you forgo such an honor?"

Raven wanted to tell her mother that she had already met Margaret Tudor, but she held her tongue.

Heron spoke again. "Englishmen marry Scottish ladies too. I myself took quite a fancy to Beth Kennedy when I met her in Carlisle a couple of months ago."

Kate was momentarily diverted. "Why, Heron, Beth Kennedy is the daughter of your father's cousin. We would have no objection to such a fine match; her father is the Lord of Galloway!"

Raven's hope soared. "The man I love, and wish to marry, is

from an equally important family. He has asked me to wed him many times, but I told him that I wanted your blessing."

"It's Heath Kennedy, isn't it, Raven?" Her father's voice was terse, his face set in disapproving lines.

She refused to lie. She lifted her chin and said proudly, "Yes, Father, it is Heath Kennedy."

"Heath? Isn't that the name of the illegitimate son that Rob Kennedy had with a Gypsy girl called Lily Rose, years ago?"

"Yes, that's the one," Lancelot confirmed.

Raven's eyes were blazing. "Being natural born is no fault of his, and Gypsy blood is every bit as good as ours!"

"Eeew, you prefer a Gypsy to Christopher Dacre?" Lark cried.

"Yes, I do. He is a man of honor, while Chris Dacre has no honor. He was trying to seduce you. If he didn't already succeed, he soon would have!"

Lark blushed at learning that Raven knew what had been going on.

Kate looked at her daughter with new hope dawning. "My dear, if you aspire to a match with a Kennedy, Lady Elizabeth has a son who is yet unmarried. I'm sure your father would be happy to write to his cousin and sound her out about uniting our families."

Raven's mouth fell open as a full-blown picture of redheaded Duncan Kennedy came into her mind. Then her temper exploded. "You don't understand a thing I've been trying to tell you, Mother! You don't even listen! I am in love with Heath Kennedy. I don't care that he will not inherit the Kennedy wealth, I don't care that he is a Gypsy. Don't you understand, Mother? We are lovers! We are bound lovers!"

CHAPTER 27

Raven threw up her hands in utter frustration and ran from the room. Upstairs, she slammed her chamber door, tore the ribbon from her hair, and removed the demure cream linen dress. She pulled on her old riding clothes and boots, then ran back downstairs and out to the stables. She didn't bother with a saddle for Sully; she simply mounted her pony and galloped out to her favorite place, where the River Eden emptied into the Solway Firth.

She rode along the shore, knowing this was the only antidote to her feeling of being trapped. Her need for freedom had always been restored by a gallop along this seacoast that divided England from Scotland and offered magnificent open vistas of the sea and the purple mountains beyond. Today, however, it only served to emphasize that she and Heath were separated and were now in two different countries.

Why didn't I go with him? her heart cried out. *He told me my parents would not listen to me. He told me I would never be able to persuade them to accept him as my husband! Heath was right, but I wouldn't listen. I put my parents before my love for him, and it hurt him deeply.* When they reached the end of the beach, Sully stopped and Raven sat gazing out across the sea, feeling lost and forlorn, and divided from her love by a gulf as wide as the Solway. Her fingers sought the god stone beneath her shirt, and the weight of the phallic stone brought her a measure of comfort.

She looked back down the shore and smiled wistfully as memories of their first meeting came back to her. She had ridden down this beach at full gallop toward him, and he had planted his feet firmly, refusing to budge, and had laughed at her folly. She realized that was the moment she had lost her heart to him, but had obstinately refused to acknowledge the truth of it.

Raven looked down at the god stone and realized she was wearing the same shirt that Heath Kennedy had so audaciously plucked from her during that first encounter. She threw back her head and laughed with delight. Upon a few moments' acquaintance, he had actually undressed her; she should have known then that she had met her match.

Raven relived the race they'd had along this same shore, and wished with all her heart that they could do it again. If only he would appear at the far end of the beach and come riding toward her, but Raven knew it was only wishful thinking. Heath would not come back for her. She had raked his pride so deeply that he regretted laying his heart at her feet. She knew he would never give her the chance to trample upon him again.

Though a measure of calm had settled over her, the ache in her heart was unbearable. She knew that she must keep busy and occupy her mind and her hands with something that she could focus her attention upon. It was both ridiculous and fruitless to mope about feeling sorry for herself.

She went back to the stables, fed and watered Sully, then gave her black pony a good currying with his brush until his coat shone. Then she went up into the mews, pulled on her leather gloves, and lifted the two young merlins from their perches. She took a lure with her and walked out into Rockcliffe Marsh to continue their training. She spoke softly to the birds, praising their beauty and giving them her full attention.

Raven cast them again and again, exercising the greatest of patience the entire afternoon as she gave the small falcons a lesson in hunting. More often than not, they missed their prey, but the young falconer had done a good job in training them to return to the lure. Finally, when the afternoon shadows lengthened, one merlin caught a small rodent, and the other returned with a dead mackerel it had picked up on the beach.

Instantly, Raven was reminded of Valentina's words that likened a dead mackerel to the royal court. She thought of Margaret Tudor and the whispered plans of Rosalind Dacre to entertain her. Suddenly, Raven went icy cold. Why was Margaret's visit to England shrouded in secrecy? Raven could think of only one reason. Was it possible that she was taking her son, King Jamie, out of Scotland and delivering him to her brother, King Henry Tudor? The more she thought about it, the more convinced Raven became that there was an evil plot afoot. The Dacres were involved, and to Raven that spoke volumes.

Her very first instinct was to tell Heath of her suspicions. If the little Scottish king was in danger, Heath and Ramsay Douglas would know what must be done to protect him. Raven took a deep breath and examined her motives. Was she using this as an excuse to go running after Heath Kennedy? She acknowledged that he was right, she had made the mistake of a lifetime by not going with him, but it was a mistake she would try to rectify. If aught befell young Jamie Stewart because she was too proud to run after Heath Kennedy, that would be a mistake she could never rectify. When Raven returned the merlins to the mews, her mind was made up: she was going to Eskdale!

This time she did put a saddle on Sully, and as she left the stables she looked toward the manor and scanned its windows. She did not dare go back into the house for food or clothes in case her parents prevented her from leaving. If anyone had seen her from the windows flying her hawks, they would not expect her back until almost dusk. She headed for the edge of the marsh, to give her cover, then turned Sully north, keeping the sinking sun on her left.

Raven had no idea how many miles it was to Eskdale. Then she reminded herself that there was no guarantee that Heath was there. Her fingers closed over his god stone, and she put her trust in its power to take her to its owner. She suspended all disbelief and told herself there was an invisible, mystical thread that bound them. She had found him whenever he had called to her, and now put her faith in the belief that it would work if she called to him.

Raven did not gallop at breakneck speed; it was a long journey and she did not want to tax Sully's strength. She stroked his neck, holding him at an easy pace, and every once in a while she bent to whisper in his ear, "Find Heath, Sully, find Heath."

The sun set, which was followed by dusk, then a lingering twilight. She deliberately skirted Longtown, recalling stories of raids. The inhabitants would not look kindly upon a night rider. When dark descended all about her, Raven was not afraid. She loved the outdoors and nature, and night had its own breathtaking beauty, from its nocturnal noises to its inky shadows.

When she heard a river, she carefully guided Sully to its banks. She knew that the river that ran along the Border was the Esk, and logic told her that if she followed the Esk long enough, it would take her into Eskdale. Deciding this was a good place to stop and rest, she dismounted, removed Sully's saddle, and led him down to the river to drink. She bathed her face with the cool water, then cupped her hands and quenched her own thirst. She tethered her pony so that he could crop the long grass beneath the trees, and sat down with her back against the saddle.

Raven did not close her eyes, but she rested her body. She felt hungry but tried to stop thinking of food, because each time she did, her belly began to rumble. An hour or so after dark, the new moon appeared and began its climb up the sky. Raven gazed at the beautiful crescent shape and repeated the incantation her grandmother had taught her.

> When I see the new moon,
> It becomes me to lift mine eye,
> It becomes me to bend my knee,
> It becomes me to bow my head,
> Giving thee praise, thou moon of guidance.
> Give me the means to find my love,
> I have the power, and know how to use it.

She believed that the moon goddess ruled the subconscious instincts and intuition. Raven lifted her face and opened her mind, like a night-blooming convolvulus. Tonight her spirit felt psychic, in tune with the forces of nature and the power of the human mind.

She resaddled Sully and allowed the faint silver light of the moon to guide her.

When the sun rose, she stopped again and found a wild thicket of blackberries to assuage her hunger. She knew that she was in Scotland, and she imagined that she could feel herself drawing closer to Heath's presence. The dales were dotted with sheep, and after a short respite, she climbed back into the saddle and urged Sully forward. As often happened in the hills, sudden rain clouds gathered, and a summer downpour began. The sheep huddled together beside the stone walls of Langholm as Raven became soaked through to the skin. Though her pace was much slower, she kept going from Ewesdale into Eskdale, not daring to become discouraged or she would be defeated.

Finally, when she came to a place where she recognized her surroundings, and rode down the dale toward Eskdale Castle, the clouds dispersed, the sun came out, and Raven began to smile.

Heath Kennedy had a wretched night. Sleep had eluded him completely and his body ached with desire for the woman he had left behind in England. Yet it was not simply a physical restlessness that consumed him, but one of the mind and the spirit. His longing for Raven knew no bounds; she consumed every waking thought. The galling part was that he knew she was so physically attracted to him that she shared her body freely and without reserve, yet she would never marry him. It had been so ingrained in her that she must marry for wealth and a title, that she could not bring herself to go against her parents' wishes.

Three times during the long night he had been on the verge of invoking his power and bringing her to his bed. He held the black raven's feather in his hand; all he had to do was focus his mind and his spirit completely upon the object of his desire and intone the words *Come to me, Raven.* Yet each time some inner instinct had stopped him. At his core, Heath realized that it would gain him naught if he brought her at his bidding. For it to have any meaning,

Raven must come of her own free will, or it would be better for her not to come at all.

In the morning when Heath arose, he had come to a firm decision. He would take his breeding mares to his own hundred acres that lay in Kirkcudbright on the far side of the River Dee. It was not only close to Castle Douglas, but close to Kennedy landholdings as well. He knew his father's health was deteriorating, and knew he would feel better if he kept an eye on him.

In preparation for their trek across country, he would have to reshoe most of his mares. He went out to the meadow and brought two of his horses to the bailey. Then he went into the forge and lit the fire. When a sudden cloudburst brought a torrent of rain, he brought the horses into the shelter of the forge and took the Douglases' blacksmith up on his offer of help. The two men sized the mares' hooves, then sorted through piles of iron horseshoes to each find four that matched in shape and weight.

The forge became hot and Heath stripped off his doublet as he cleaned his mare's hooves, then heated a metal shoe in the fire. After he had hammered the first pair of horseshoes in place, his shirt followed his doublet, before he continued with the sweltering job. Heath grinned at the blacksmith as he kept pace with him; physical activity always made him feel better. His teeth were a startling white against his sweat-streaked, blackened face.

By the time the two mares were fully shod, the downpour had stopped and the sun came out. Heath led the two horses into the bailey, intending to check their gait as they clopped across the cobbles. He looked up in surprise as a woman rode into the bailey. "Raven!" Heath's heart soared with happiness.

"Heath! Thank heaven I found you."

He ran to her side, lifted her down from Sully, then hoisted her into the air and swung her around. "Raven, I can't believe you came!" His heart was bursting with pure joy.

"I came because I fear there is a plot to kidnap the young king! I knew I must get word to you and Ramsay Douglas of my suspicions."

Most of the joy drained from Heath's heart, and an iron carapace closed about it to guard it from her. She had not come because she loved him and could not live without him, she had come to deliver bad news. He masked his disappointment and set her feet to the cobblestones. "You are soaked to the skin. Come, you must get dry." He turned to the blacksmith and asked him to tend the pony.

"Sully and I are not only wet through, we're starving too." Raven knew that now she had found him, all her worries would be over. Heath would know if her suspicions about little Jamie Stewart were correct, and he would set everything right. She led the way into Eskdale Castle and began to climb the stairs to Heath's tower rooms as if she had never left.

"Did you ride all this way by yourself, Raven?"

"Yes, but of course I couldn't have done it without you. I shall tell you all about it."

Heath took a poker to the fire, making the flames blaze high, and when he turned back to her, saw that she was already stripping off her wet garments. He went to the wardrobe, brought her his bed robe, and held it while she slipped her arms into the sleeves to cover her nakedness. He was amazed to see her plop her bottom onto his bed and lift her leg so that he could remove her riding boot. He watched, fascinated, as the corners of her mouth went up. "You are a devil, Heath Kennedy. I'm here only five minutes and already you have me naked."

Heath, wary as a wolf who had once fallen into a trap, suspected that Raven was quite ready to resume their physical relationship, without the full commitment of marriage. Though she was easily the most alluring female he had ever known, he would be damned if he would settle for anything less than her heart and soul. He set the fireguard before the crackling flames and hung her garments to dry. He asked one of the maids to bring Raven food from the kitchen, then he handed her a towel to dry her hair, and stepped a safe distance away from her.

Raven was mildly surprised. Usually, Heath couldn't resist drying her himself, especially her hair. He had always used any excuse to entangle his fingers in her black curls.

Heath dragged his gaze from her wet tresses with difficulty. He poured water from the jug and washed the grime from his face and hands. Then because being naked from the waist up made him vulnerable to Raven's charms, he put on a clean shirt. "Mr. Burque has gone with Tina to Castle Douglas, so don't expect anything spectacular," he warned lightly.

"Is Lord Douglas not here either?" Raven looked alarmed.

It was the second time she had mentioned Ram Douglas. "Can you not tell me about this plot?"

"Of course. Why on earth do you think I rode through the night to get to Eskdale?"

I hoped there was no plot. I hoped it was a ruse, an excuse to come riding after me to tell me you had made the mistake of a lifetime to let me leave without you.

The maid brought thick mutton broth and freshly baked bread, and Raven began her story as she ate. "I suppose I had better start at the beginning. You were right about my parents. When they arrived home, they were incensed over what I had done. I told them that I could never wed Chris Dacre because I neither loved him nor liked him. I told them about you, I catalogued all your virtues"—she cast him a teasing smile—"but they wouldn't listen."

"It must run in the family," Heath murmured.

Raven ignored his taunt. "I was angry and went for a gallop along the shore, and gradually things that had been said in Carlisle came back to me. I am sorry that I didn't pay more attention at the time, but I honestly didn't have much interest in the Dacres' plans. It began as hints at first, and came to me in bits and pieces from both Christopher and Lady Rosalind. Yesterday, when I put it all together, it suddenly became obvious to me. Tell me if you agree." Raven relayed the information, point by point. "After the wedding, Christopher was taking me to Bewcastle, where we would receive some important guests. Lady Rosalind was all atwitter because she would shortly be entertaining these same important nobles at Carlisle. Soon after the wedding, we were to travel to the English court in London, but the whole thing was shrouded in secrecy. Then yesterday my mother let it slip that it was Queen Margaret who was going to Carlisle and that the Dacres would be accompanying the royal court to London."

"Archibald Douglas and Margaret are taking her son, King Jamie, out of Scotland and turning him over to her brother, Henry Tudor! Your suspicions are correct, Raven. Ramsay Douglas and I knew that Archibald would need money and might plot with Henry Tudor to sell him King Jamie, but we had no idea their plans were imminent!"

"Can you get the information to Lord Douglas?"

"I have no idea where he is. I'll have to act without him. Fortunately, Ram left about twenty moss-troopers here with Gavin." He looked at her with admiration. "It was most courageous of you to ride through the night alone, Raven."

"I wasn't alone, Heath. Your spirit was with me every step of the way, and I had your god stone." She caressed the phallic symbol that rested between her breasts, then lifted it off over her head and brought it to him.

With difficulty, Heath gathered his thoughts. He took her hand in his and looked at what lay in her palm. "I'm going to need more than the help of a stone to discern the answers I need; there are so many unknowns. Little King Jamie resides in Edinburgh. When did they leave the capital? At which castles will they break their journey? Perhaps only at Douglas strongholds where Archie feels safe. At all costs we must stop them from crossing the Border into England. While common sense dictates it will be slow traveling with a child not yet three, my instincts tell me they will travel as fast as they can while the moon is in its dark phase. I fear we have little time to waste."

She watched with avid eyes as he went to the wardrobe for a doublet. "I will go and alert the men to be ready to ride on a moment's notice."

Heath went down to the hall and spoke with the moss-troopers who were just finishing their midday meal. There was a scuffle and a loud altercation in the entrance, and when he went to investigate, Heath saw that Gavin Douglas held a man by the scruff of his neck.

"This is your bloody prisoner! How the hell did he escape?"

Heath was amazed to see that it was Sim Armstrong. "He served his purpose; I let him go. More to the point, what the hellfire are you doing *here*, Armstrong?"

"My firkin' brain must be addled, thinkin' ye'd listen!" Armstrong cursed.

"Let him go," Heath told Gavin. "We'll listen."

"Could I ha' a wee dish of broth?" Armstrong wheedled.

Heath knew the Borderer must be starving to risk asking for a favor, and signaled to a server. He unsheathed his knife, cut off a chunk of bread, then stuck the weapon in the table close to hand. "Start singing for your supper."

Armstrong eyed the knife as he reached for the bread. "My information should be worth a few coppers tae ye. There's a plan afoot tae smuggle the rightful King of Scotland across the Border tae England!"

"Your information is worth nothing so far. We know about the plot. What we need to know is when and where."

"They arrive at Hawick tonight. Then, under cover of dark, Mangey Armstrong will lead them through the Border Forest tae England, where Dacre's men will be waitin' tae take the king an' his mother tae Bewcastle!"

"How do we know it isn't a trap?" Gavin asked Heath.

"We don't," Heath said flatly. "But the information tallies with what Raven knows, and Hawick makes sense."

"Why would he betray Mangey Armstrong?" Gavin asked doubtfully.

Heath shrugged. "Revenge is a sweeter dish than mutton broth, especially when it's against a brother who has betrayed you."

Gavin thought about his own brother and knew he would not want to be on the receiving end of Black Ram's wrath, if he and the Douglas men did not do all in their power to foil this plot.

"We'll have to ride to Hawick now and lie in wait for them."

Gavin agreed with Heath and ordered the moss-troopers to fully arm themselves and ready their horses.

Upstairs, Raven wondered what was keeping Heath so long. She buried her nose in the sleeve of his bed robe to inhale his scent.

She sighed with appreciation and moved restlessly to the window. When she saw men moving about the bailey with great purpose, she knew they were preparing to leave. She ran to the fireguard to feel her garments. They were still somewhat damp, but she asked herself what choice she had. She dressed quickly, tossed her disheveled hair back over her shoulders, and ran down to the hall. Her steps faltered as she saw Heath in conversation with a rough-looking, unkempt Borderer.

The unsavory devil looked up at her as she approached, and she recognized that it was the brute Heath had taken prisoner the day he had captured her and Chris Dacre near Bewcastle. She watched Heath give him a silver coin, and her eyes widened in amazement as the unpalatable devil winked at her, then scurried off like a rat.

Heath closed the distance between them and placed his hands on Raven's shoulders. "Sim brought us confirmation of the plot. He claims the royal party is to arrive at Hawick tonight under cover of dark. Cavers Castle is less than ten miles from England if they go through the Border Forest. Gavin and I are taking the Douglas moss-troopers to Hawick to lie in wait for them."

"I'm coming too."

"Raven, you are not coming. You will remain at Eskdale, where you will be safe."

"Heath, I never want to be separated from you again!"

He pushed the black hair back from her cheek with a tender hand. "Sweetheart, those are the loveliest words I've ever heard, but you cannot come with me."

"But you will need a woman," she argued. "The little king is not yet three; he will be terrified by so many rough men."

"We are not so many, Raven—little more than a score of moss-troopers—and God knows how many armed guards Archibald and Margaret will have with them."

"You are Borderers, each worth three of any other fighting men!"

"You cannot get around me by flattery, Raven. If you want to help, you will remain here out of harm's way," he said firmly.

She dug her hands into her hips. "Well, I won't stay here! The minute you leave, I shall follow you!"

He grabbed her by the shoulders and shook her roughly. "If you do such a reckless thing, you will drive me to violence," he threatened. "I will give your arse such a tanning, you won't be able to sit for a week nor ride for a month!" He turned her around, gave her a stinging slap across her buttocks, and pushed her toward the stairs. "You think that because I laid my heart at your feet and told you I loved you, you have me wrapped about your fingers. Well, I am not one of your falcons, Raven, and I will never wear jesses. A woman who won't obey is not worth having!"

Something inside Raven responded to the dominant male who stood resolute, issuing his orders, telling her what she could and could not do. She looked back over her shoulder and was about to beg him to take care of himself and come back to her safely.

"Get the hell up to the tower. If you want to be of use, you can wait for me in bed!"

Raven's temper exploded. She ran up the stairs and slammed the tower door. "You went too far that time, Heath bloody Kennedy!"

CHAPTER 28

When Ram Douglas arrived in Edinburgh, along with Jock, his second-in-command, and a score of Douglas moss-troopers, he went directly to Edinburgh Castle. There he found Lord Alexander Hume and Lord David Maxwell, who also had received letters from John Douglas, Duke of Albany, about his imminent arrival. Conspicuous by their absence, however, were Archibald, Margaret, and little King Jamie.

"Where is the royal court?" Ramsay asked Lord Hume in alarm.

Hume waved a negligent hand. "Margaret an' her English courtiers are soft; they prefer the comforts of Holyrood Palace."

"I warrant they prefer by far the comforts of Westminster Palace!" Ram immediately dispatched Jock to ride to the bottom of the royal mile to see if King Jamie and the court were actually in residence at Holyrood. Then Ram proceeded to inform Maxwell and Hume about the suspected plot to deliver Scotland's child king into the hands of England's ruthless Henry Tudor.

"The Duke of Albany's ship was sighted this afternoon an' should be in Leith by mornin'. He will effectively crush any plot tae depose Scotland's rightful king. John Stewart makes no secret of the fact that he intends tae take over the regency. All in Scotland will support the late king's brother over English Margaret Tudor."

"By the time Albany arrives tomorrow, little Jamie Stewart could have been spirited away and halfway tae England!" Ram warned.

When Jock arrived back at Edinburgh Castle and informed

Ramsay that the royal court was not at Holyrood but was reportedly in residence at Craigmillar Castle, little more than five miles off, Hume was still not alarmed. Lord Maxwell, however, did not wish to face the Duke of Albany if the little bird had flown.

"I'm ridin' south," Ram Douglas declared. "They've had a head start, but I know which castles Archibald will seek out."

"I'm ridin' with ye," Maxwell declared. "A passel of English courtiers should no' be difficult tae catch."

It turned out to be more difficult than they imagined, however, for when they rode to Craigmillar, they learned that the royal court had departed three nights before.

Ram Douglas and David Maxwell rode hell-for-leather at the head of their moss-troopers, expecting to find the royal party at Crighton Castle, but when they arrived, they discovered their prey was long gone. While they took time to water their horses, Maxwell questioned Douglas about their route.

"The shortest route tae the Border is by way of Thirlstane Castle, then Roxborough Castle."

"Ye're right, but Archie Douglas is being aided and abetted by Dacre. They will head straight for Hawick, and if they reach it, they will be safe. Dacre will pay the Armstrongs tae get them tae the English Border. Bewcastle is impregnable!"

"The only castle between here an' Hawick is Newark."

Ram nodded grimly. "Newark is our last chance!"

At Eskdale, Raven stood at the high window of the tower to watch Heath Kennedy and the moss-troopers depart for Hawick. It was a thrilling spectacle of dark, powerful Borderers, armed to the teeth and mounted on their sturdy garrons. She could hear both their laughter and their curses as they turned their weather-beaten faces into the wind and rode from the bailey.

Raven waited a full half hour before she opened the wardrobe and took one of Heath's dark cloaks, then made her way to the stables. She ignored the young stableboys who had been left behind, and walked a direct path to Sully. When she saw him, a wave of guilt washed over her, and she knew she could not saddle him again when she had ridden him all night.

Instead she took her own saddle and put it on one of the Douglas garrons. A stableboy came forward to help her with the bit and bridle, and she rewarded him with a radiant smile. Then, wrapped in Heath's dark cloak, she mounted and rode from the bailey. She stayed far behind the men who rode ahead of her. It was still daylight and she had made this journey before up through the beautiful Teviot valley to Cavers Castle in Hawick. She was extremely cautious about the riders ahead of her, making sure they did not detect they were being followed. But Raven's purpose was so intent, she did not realize that she herself was being followed.

The unsavory male licked cracked lips as his shabby pony followed in the footsteps of the sturdy garron that carried the dark beauty. This woman was a coveted prize indeed. Two men hated each other and had become bitter enemies because of her. Each wanted her and would pay any price to keep her from the arms, and the bed, of the other. Sim Armstrong shook his head in disbelief, then he laughed at such folly, revealing black and broken teeth.

As he cautiously stalked her he amused himself by deciding which man would pay the most for her. It was an easy decision: Christopher Dacre had gold aplenty from an indulgent father. With grimy fingers, Armstrong fondled the length of rope he carried. He would never be without rope again. Nothing compared with rope for trussing up a prisoner, as he'd learned to his cost from Heath Kennedy. He pictured how helpless a woman would be if she were secured by a rope; there would be nothing a man couldn't do to her. Rope was indeed a wondrous weapon!

When Heath Kennedy, Gavin Douglas, and the moss-troopers rode into the bailey of Cavers Castle, the sun was starting to set. The tower castle was a Douglas holding with only a skeleton staff of retainers. Gavin spoke to the steward who came out to meet them, telling him that they were there to thwart an attempt to kidnap the young king and take him across the Border into England. He warned the steward that they could have a skirmish and a bloody fight on their hands and told him to keep the servants inside. The man waved them into the stables, then hurried back to the castle to see what food supplies he had on hand.

Heath saw that there were only two stalls that held horses. "The stable is near empty; this is a good place to conceal ourselves and our mounts. I think we should await them here."

Gavin nodded. "They will ride right into the bailey, never expecting a surprise attack."

The men tended their mounts, then made themselves comfortable in the straw-filled stalls. They left the doors open to provide light until dusk descended; though there were lanterns, they would not light them unless it became necessary.

Raven, filled with relief that she had arrived at Cavers without incident, rode into the deserted bailey. For the last hour she had been having second thoughts about the wisdom of following Heath when he had forbidden her to do so. She had been ready to obey him, until his infuriating male arrogance had goaded her. She glanced up at the lit windows of the tower castle, knowing she would have to do battle with Heath when he discovered that she was here. Still, it was a battle she would win, for she knew that he would never order her to ride back to Eskdale in the dark.

Totally unaware of what awaited her, Raven urged her mount through the doors of the stable. Immediately a dozen rough hands reached for her and dragged her from the saddle. Her cry of alarm froze in her throat as she lay on the floor and stared up at a circle of men who towered above her with their long daggers drawn.

"Raven! You willful little bitch! You could have gotten yourself killed a dozen times over!" Heath grabbed her by the arm and dragged her to her feet. "Are you alone?" he demanded.

In the face of his violent anger, she could not speak, she could only nod her head, but when she heard laughter she became painfully aware of how much her actions must be humiliating him before the other men.

"Come!" The terse order made her jump, and she imagined Heath did not trust himself to say more than one word to her. With her arm in a viselike grip he quick-marched her from the stables up to the castle. When she staggered on her legs, he swept her up in his arms with a foul curse and ran up the stone steps to the first floor of the tower castle. He deposited her on a wooden settle beside the fireplace and glared down at her. "Can you stay put?" he demanded.

"I'm sorry, I didn't mean to humiliate you," she whispered.

"Humiliate?" he repeated with disbelief. His gut was still in a knot with fear of what he had almost done to her, and she was worried about humiliating him?

As she gazed up at him she saw that the blood had drained from his face, and she realized it was concern for her safety that had affected him so profoundly. He showed anger because he could not show fear. In that moment it was brought home to her how much he loved her. Raven reached up and kissed him. *I love you, Heath!* She watched the color come back into his face, and as his eyes searched hers she wondered if he was reading her mind. She watched his anger melt to mere exasperation.

"If you think a kiss exonerates you from punishment, you had better think again." He removed her arms from around his neck. "I know I told you that you would come running after me, and that you would have to do the wooing, but not here, Raven, not now!"

The dark devil had a wicked sense of humor, but Raven did not dare show that she was amused. "I'll stay put," she promised solemnly. After he left, she removed his cloak and laid it on the settle, then she went to find the steward. She found him in the kitchens, having an altercation with the cook, who was roasting a haunch of mutton on a spit.

" 'Tis the King of Scotland we're expectin', ye daft clod. Kings don't eat lashings of mutton, they have refined palates. Don't ye recall when the royal courtiers came fer the weddin' they dined on pheasant an' peacock?"

"Aye, I recall. I also recall they brought their own fancy bloody chefs! I say if he's Scots, he'll eat mutton."

"An' I say yer a daft prick!"

The cook presented the steward with his long fork and jerked his thumb at the haunch of meat. "Prick that!"

"Gentlemen," Raven said, using the term loosely, "if you are preparing food for the little king, I think you have forgotten that Jamie Stewart is only two years old."

They looked at her blankly, clearly requiring her guidance.

"He will need something to warm him, and soothe him, and help him to sleep," she offered.

"Whisky?" they asked in unison.

"I was thinking perhaps soup, laced with heavy cream."

"Why didn't ye think of that?"

"Me?" The steward returned the fork. "Ye're the bloody cook!" He turned back to Raven. "May I get ye some wine, mistress?"

"That would be lovely, thank you." She took the wine back to the settle and sipped it reflectively as she gazed into the fire.

In the stables the men settled to their vigil as full darkness descended. Outside, the bailey remained still and quiet as minutes lengthened into hours and crept toward midnight. The waiting was tedious, since they had no light and could not while away the hours with dice. Yet there was too much tension in the air for them to doze; they did not know the size of the royal party and could not afford to be caught unaware.

About an hour past midnight, they became aware of galloping hooves pounding the ground. Borderers were expert at gauging the size of their enemy by the sound of their horses, and every man in the stable knew the party that approached was a small one. Though they cautioned themselves that a larger force could be following, their confidence soared.

As the riders galloped into the courtyard and drew rein, the racket they made was considerable. It was clear that they were making no effort to approach quietly, for the four people who had ridden into the bailey made enough noise to raise the dead. Heath Kennedy, who had stationed himself by the stable door, saw that they were dismounting outside. He gave the signal, and the Douglas moss-troopers quickly surrounded the horses with weapons drawn.

The four made no effort to fight back or even defend themselves; instead they cried and pleaded and begged for succor. By the sound of their voices, Heath Kennedy realized their captives were female, or very young males. When they herded them into the stable and lit a lantern, it revealed a distraught Margaret Tudor, accompanied by one lady and two young grooms.

Margaret recognized Heath Kennedy. "Help me, help me, I pray you!" she cried desperately.

"Where is your son, and where is Archibald Douglas?" he demanded.

"Attacked! Attacked at Newark! Terrible fighting . . . bloodshed. It was Black Ram Douglas, my husband's own cousin!" she cried with disbelief.

"Get yer horses, we're ridin' tae Newark!" Gavin ordered.

Heath swung Margaret up in his arms and carried her to the castle; her terrified attendants followed meekly.

Upstairs, Raven, who had been close to falling asleep, was roused by the racket below in the bailey. With her heart in her throat, she jumped up from the settle and ran to the window. She could make out very little other than men swarming about and pale moonlight glinting off their drawn swords. The steward came running. "Summat's happenin'," he shouted. "Is it the king? Should I go down?"

Raven blinked at him. "No, no, I think you should remain in the castle. We'll know soon enough who it is." She had the urge to go down herself because of her fierce desire to be at Heath's side whenever he faced danger, yet she had little fear for him. She had complete faith in his ability to vanquish any foe. She went to the top of the stairs and peered down into the darkness, then suddenly, as if she had conjured him, Heath appeared carrying a woman.

As he reached the top step he said, "It's the queen." He strode past her and sat Margaret down on the settle that Raven had vacated. Margaret moaned, then began to retch.

Raven's eyes sought Heath's. "Is she hurt?"

"No. She fled from Newark; she's had a hard ride. Will you look after her?"

"Of course," Raven assured him. "Where is the child?"

"Ram Douglas caught up with them at Newark. We are off to

join him in case he needs aid, but I warrant little Jamie Stewart is safe by now. I'll be back, Raven."

She watched him go, then turned her attention to the woman before her. Margaret was deathly pale, and her brassy yellow hair hung in shags about her face. Her purple velvet cape had fallen open to reveal her belly, swollen with child, and Raven's heart turned over with pity as the queen vomited again upon the floor. Her woman stood by wringing her hands, and the two young grooms were busy warming themselves at the fire.

Raven sat down beside Margaret and took her hand. "I am going to the kitchen to get you something for your nausea. Try to close your eyes and rest." She looked at the two young men. "You! Come with me." Her order was so direct, they obeyed her.

The cook and another servant were in the kitchen. "Give these boys a bucket of water and some cloths. They have vomit to clean up, and the poor lady may not be done yet." Raven addressed the cook. "What do you have for nausea?" When he shook his head helplessly, she took matters into her own hands and searched the kitchen and pantry herself. When she found a bunch of mint, she closed her eyes and offered up a prayer of thanks.

The steward came into the kitchen. "What can I do?" he asked.

"I will need some dry biscuits and watered wine, if I can ever get the retching stopped." She found a clean kitchen towel and dipped one end of it in warm water, then she returned to Margaret.

The groom who had cleaned up the mess on the floor got up from his knees and hurried out of the way when he saw Raven returning. She knelt before Margaret and gently wiped her face with the towel, but the mother-to-be was retching again. Quickly, Raven crushed half a dozen mint leaves with her fingers and held them beneath the queen's nose. "Breathe deeply, inhale the pungent smell, and it will control your need to retch." Raven slipped her hand into her pocket and drew out her hag stone, which she had forgotten about. She was now wise in the ways of healing lore and knew that performing any ritual occupied the mind enough to effect a physical change for the better.

"Hold this hag stone to your breast, center yourself, and breathe slowly and deeply. Draw from the stone's strength and mystic power and take it into your body." Raven saw that Margaret had stopped heaving, and picked two fresh green mint leaves from their stalk. "Put these in your mouth, my lady. Mint has such a clean taste, a fresh taste, and has been used for centuries to settle the stomach." She watched Margaret do as she suggested, and knew she was overcoming the nausea. Then Raven reinforced her cure with compliments to make sure her patient was done being sick.

When the steward brought the biscuits and watered wine, Raven urged Margaret to try them. Then she turned to her waiting woman. "Help her to remove her cloak and boots, and I shall find a bedchamber where she may rest."

Margaret grabbed Raven's hand to keep her at her side. "No, no, you must help me get to England!"

Raven stared at her in disbelief. "My lady, you need rest, you are unwell. You cannot travel further tonight."

"I must, I must! You are English, are you not? You must help to get me across the Border where I will be safe!"

"It is out of the question. You must remain at Hawick until the men return from Newark." She thought of Heath and trembled at what he might do if he returned to find Margaret gone, after he had trusted her to keep their captive safe.

"Have pity! Have pity!" The tears streamed down Margaret's face. "What I did was treason! The Scots will wreak a terrible revenge upon me!"

"They will not harm you, my lady; you are the sister of the powerful King of England," Raven assured her.

Margaret jumped up and began to pace, invigorated by the wine. "They will lock me up in prison and throw away the key. I could not bear to live without freedom! And only think how many convenient accidents happen to those who are locked away!"

Her words wrung Raven's heart. She could not lie to her and tell her that her freedom would not be taken away. For all intents and purposes, the poor lady was a prisoner now.

Margaret drained the wine cup and threw out her hands in

supplication. "It is the plotting of greedy, evil men which has brought me to this pass! My ambitious brother lusts to rule both countries, and my greedy husband has plotted to sell my son's birthright to Henry. What purpose will it serve if I languish for years in prison, and the baby I carry is denied its freedom?"

Raven's loyalties were almost torn in half. It was not too difficult to refuse to aid a treasonous queen, but it was almost impossible to turn her back upon a woman who was carrying a child.

Margaret took Raven by the shoulders. "I have lost wee Jamie, and I understand that it must be so, for he is the rightful King of Scotland, but for the sake of this child I now carry, can you not find it in your heart to help me?"

Raven's resolve wavered. How could she in all conscience refuse to help a woman in such a plight? She saw the fear in Margaret's eyes and marveled that though she must be exhausted, she was willing to ride further to save her child. "I will help you," Raven said softly.

"I must get to Huntford on the English Border, where Lord Dacre's men await me."

Raven recoiled when Margaret uttered the name Dacre. "I cannot take you to the Border, but I will lead you to the Border Forest."

The steward was helpless to prevent them from leaving in the face of the women's determination. He shrugged his shoulders. Only weeks ago he had served the queen at her wedding; surely he could not be expected to act as her jailer.

In the stables, one of Margaret's young grooms brought forward the white horse that she had ridden all the way from Edinburgh. Raven saw that it quivered and trembled. "This mare is spent," she said, running her hand along its belly. "I think she is carrying a foal." She spoke to the groom. "Take the queen up before you; she is in no condition to ride alone."

Raven wrapped Heath's cloak closely about her and led the small cavalcade through the deserted bailey. As she turned her mount east in the direction of the Border Forest, riding slowly in deference to the mother-to-be, she began to shiver. It was not from cold, Raven realized, it was from fear.

CHAPTER 29

Sim Armstrong, lying in the bracken beside his tethered pony, raised his head. He was aware of all that had happened that night at Cavers. He had seen the fleeing queen ride in with her pitiful number of attendants, and watched Kennedy ride off with the Douglas moss-troopers. It could only mean that the plot had been discovered and none save Margaret had escaped. His brother Mangey didn't know this, of course. Sim chuckled and fingered his rope. He had decided to wait for Mangey no matter how long it took, but now it looked like his plans would change. Perhaps for the better. Sooner or later, everything came to he who waited.

Sim did not mount the shaggy pony, but led him in a wide circle until he came to a clump of trees that gave him cover. Then he mounted and headed straight for the forest, only a few miles away. He rode swiftly, intending to reach the Border Forest long before Raven Carleton and the little band she was leading to safety. He did not slow until the forest trees closed about him; then he pricked his ears, sniffed the air, and peered through the darkness with expectant eyes. It wasn't long before he scented the Armstrongs, and he imitated the cry of a nighthawk they had always used as a signal, to separate them.

He had to ride a full four miles into the forest, close to the English Border, before he spotted Mangey, and lo and behold he was riding beside Dacre's spoiled, arrogant son, Christopher. So once more, Sim Armstrong adapted his plan to fit the situation. Sim fondled his rope and thought of Raven Carleton, then licked his lips as he wondered just how much money young Dacre had on him tonight. He hoped it was enough to make it worth his trouble. Sim gave the nighthawk signal, and watched Mangey rein in his mount, to look about him.

Then with equal amounts of daring and cunning, Sim Armstrong showed himself for a split second. It was such a fleeting glimpse, only a brother would have recognized him.

"Firk, it's Sim!" Mangey plunged after him through the trees, and a disconcerted Dacre tried to follow him, but at a much slower pace, which put a great deal of distance between the riders. Sim circled back and allowed Chris Dacre to see him from behind. Dacre, thinking he was Mangey, swallowed the bait and spurred after him. Sim chuckled; it was like leading a bairn around a mulberry bush.

Raven courageously rode slightly ahead of Margaret and her party, watching and listening for any sign of riders. She was ready to turn tail and run at the first indication of mounted men. She knew she was approaching the Border Forest, for it lay before her like a black serpent on the horizon. As she rode cautiously forward, nothing moved; all was still and deceptively quiet. When she reached the first line of trees, she slowed her horse to a walk as her eyes adjusted to the velvet darkness, and it allowed the others to catch up with her. As she urged her horse through the trees, searching for a path, she could hear her own heartbeat drumming in her ears. After long minutes of seeking, Raven at last came into a small clearing. She saw the beaten track and drew rein. "If you follow this path, it will lead you through the forest toward England."

"You cannot abandon us now!" Margaret cried. "We are supposed to be met, but clearly they haven't arrived yet!"

"Then you must wait for them here. I can go no further!"

Their voices covered the sound of the approaching animal, and Raven saw the mounted man emerge from the trees beside her before she heard him. A cry of fear erupted from her throat. The horses behind her blocked her from wheeling about; only the path that led deeper into the forest lay open. Then suddenly she sagged with relief as she recognized the ill-favored Borderer. "Sim Armstrong, thank God it is you, I feared it was—"

Before Raven could utter the name she dreaded, another man rode up behind Armstrong, and though it was too dim to positively identify him, she feared she had conjured Christopher Dacre. For a moment nothing seemed real; she knew this could not be happening, it must be a nightmare. She dug her heels into her horse's flanks, and it plunged forward along the forest path.

Christopher Dacre's pupils widened when his eyes fell upon the female who had betrayed him. He had no idea that he had been deliberately guided to the bait, no notion that the Armstrong he had followed was not Mangey. Lustful revenge for Raven Carleton consumed him, blocking out all other thought or emotion. He spurred his mount brutally and went plunging after her. Ever since she had run off with his prisoner, he had fantasized about the revenge he would take, and suddenly fate had delivered her up to him. Now he would make sure that Kennedy never got her. He would take the greatest pleasure in ravishing her, then he would indulge in the ultimate revenge and kill her.

"Wait here," Armstrong ordered Margaret and her attendants, then he urged his pony down the path that Dacre had taken. Sim Armstrong relished the euphoric feeling of control that rushed through him; he had never been in a position of control in his life before, and it was a heady sensation, akin to playing God. Raven Carleton was the coveted prize desired by two men, and he was the one to decide which man he would bestow the prize upon. Heath Kennedy had given Sim his freedom, and now he would repay him. He fondled the rope, then looped it firmly in his fingers.

Armstrong rode up close behind Dacre, then moved alongside his horse and delivered a powerful blow to the rider. Christopher, thrown off balance, ducked his head quickly at the unexpected attack, and in that moment Sim Armstrong had the rope around his neck before Dacre knew what was happening. The Borderer bared blackened teeth in a smile of satisfaction as he began to twist the rope. Dacre became unseated from his horse as he struggled to breathe, and the horse continued down the path. Armstrong galloped after it, tightening his grip on the rope so that Dacre was dragged along behind. As he reached for the horse's reins and it began to slow, Sim heard the telltale crack that told him Dacre's precious neck had snapped.

He was out of the saddle in a flash and tethered his pony and Dacre's horse to a tree. Then he knelt and, ignoring the bulging eyes and protruding tongue of his victim, slowly and thoroughly searched Chris Dacre's pockets. When he found three sovereigns, Sim began to chuckle. Three gold sovereigns and a blooded saddle horse—not bad for a night's work. But the very best part, the thing that warmed the cockles of his heart, was that Mangey would be blamed for the murder. Lord Thomas Dacre would hunt Mangey Armstrong and run him to earth like a cornered weasel. Sim removed the rope from the neck of the corpse and coiled it up with loving hands.

Raven fled into the forest as if Satan himself were pursuing her. She could not swear that the man she had seen was Christopher Dacre, but she had sensed his presence, and her fear had taken over. She imagined she could hear his horse pursuing her, yet when she glanced desperately over her shoulder, she saw nothing but the dark gloom of the forest. She left the path in a calculated attempt to escape pursuit and again looked back. Guiding the horse between the trees was slower, but she could not take the chance of continuing along the path. It was difficult to gauge the right direction, but she focused all her thoughts on finding her way back to Hawick. Eventually the trees started to thin out and she realized she was nearing the edge of the forest.

Before she rode out across the open dale, she stopped and listened, and when she heard only silence, she concluded that no one was pursuing her. She wondered if the danger had all been a flight of fancy, because of the darkness and her fear of the Dacres. Yet deep in her soul she believed she had been in the presence of evil tonight. Raven drew Heath's cloak tightly about her and rode like the wind back to the safety of Cavers Castle.

Raven opened her eyes when she heard her name spoken, and for a moment wondered where she was. She saw that she was in bed, in a strange chamber, and Heath Kennedy had just entered the room. Then everything that had happened came rushing back into her consciousness. She had not arrived back at Cavers until dawn, when she had sought out a bed and pulled the covers over her head. Obviously she had slept the day away. "What time is it?"

"I think it is time for an explanation," Heath said quietly.

Raven drew up her knees beneath the covers, feeling guilty. "First tell me if the king is safe."

"Yes, by the time we arrived at Newark, Ram Douglas had all under control. Young Jamie is being returned to Edinburgh to his uncle John Stewart, the Duke of Albany, and Archibald is voluntarily handing the regency over to him." Heath paused, waiting for her to speak, and when she did not, he said, "Raven, last night you pledged that you would stay put. I trusted you."

She took a deep breath and plunged in. "Heath, I swear I had every intention to stay put. I helped to ease the queen's nausea, but when I suggested we put her to bed, she began to cry and pleaded with me to help her get to England. I kept saying no, but before she was done, her plight melted my heart. Heath, I didn't do it because she was English, I didn't do it because she was a queen, I did it because she was a woman. The thought of her losing her freedom, being held a prisoner and having her baby in captivity, was unendurable to me. . . . I led her to the Border Forest."

"Blood of God, have you any idea of the peril you were in? The forest was crawling with Armstrongs and Dacre's men, who were to take the royal party to England." He closed his eyes to blot out the thought of her being at the mercy of the venal Armstrongs as he had once been. "Do you fear nothing, Raven? Does danger excite you so much that you enjoy risking your life?"

She closed her eyes and shuddered, just remembering. "Last night I was more afraid than I have ever been in my life. Danger does not excite me, and I will never risk my life again!"

Heath's face went taut. "What happened?" he demanded, his eyes filled with apprehension.

She could not cause him more concern; she had brought him enough trouble and worry, and she could see the lines of fatigue etched around his eyes. "Nothing happened. I was terrified of the darkness, and consumed with guilt for aiding Margaret, and afraid of what you would think of me for betraying your trust."

Heath sat down on the bed and took her hand. "I cannot fault you for having the soft heart of a woman, Raven." He shook his head remembering. "Archibald was blaming Margaret for everything last night to save his neck. It so sickened me that I too may have helped her escape to the safety of her own country."

Shortly after she arose, Raven bade goodbye to the steward and the cook before she followed Heath down to the stables. Though he looked weary to the bone, he insisted that they return to Eskdale. She watched as he put a leading rein on the white horse. "This mare is mine." He rubbed a comforting hand across her back and down her belly. "When Ram and I saw Margaret riding her at the wedding, it tipped us off that Archibald had been dealing with Dacre. Now that I have all my breeding mares back, my score with the Dacres is settled; I hope we never cross paths again."

They arrived back at Eskdale, but before Heath climbed the stairs to his tower for some much needed sleep, he cocked an eyebrow at Raven. "Will you stay put?"

She flashed him a smile. "This time I will," she pledged.

Heath undressed and crawled into bed, but before sleep claimed him, her words echoed inside his head. *This time I will.* Would she say those words before the priest if he brought him again? Raven had come to Eskdale because of the plot she suspected, not because she could not live without him. Now that the plot was foiled, would she stay with him? He suspected that she would, yet she had never told him she loved him. If he told her that he was the heir to the Lordship of Galloway, it might well induce her to marry him. Hot pride rose up within him and he immediately resolved to keep it secret from her; and he would keep his other resolve too. If they were to wed, Raven would have to do the proposing! His decision made, he fell into a dreamless sleep.

It was the tantalizing aroma of food that roused Heath the next morning. When he opened his eyes and saw that Raven had brought him breakfast, his spirit soared. If only she could be the first thing he saw every morning when he awoke, he would ask for nothing more.

He sat up against the pillows, and to his great delight she climbed on the bed and sat cross-legged with the tray between them.

"Let's do everything together today. I've been thinking of all the lovely things you did for me when I was hurt, and I have decided to repay you." She poured a small jug of cream onto the porridge and stirred in a generous helping of golden syrup. Then she dipped her finger into the bowl and offered it to him.

Heath licked the tip of her finger, completely bemused with her tantalizing performance. If he was not mistaken, Raven was attempting to woo him, and he decided it would be most pleasurable to see how far she would go. She proceeded to offer him delicious samples of the food she had prepared for him, and in doing so managed to touch and tease him in a dozen wicked ways. She managed to turn breakfast into a sensual game, and Heath decided he was ready to play his own game.

Because he had taken a figurative step backward from his pursuit of her, Raven was overtly pursuing him. It was obvious that she wanted him to make love to her as she continued with her tempting seduction. Heath hid his amusement and concentrated on keeping an iron control over his desire for her.

"It is so warm in here." Raven removed the bed robe she was wearing to reveal a short nightie that Ada had sewn. It had been cunningly designed so that flower petals cupped her breasts. The centers of the lavender flowers, however, were her nipples, bursting through tiny slits. She deftly lifted the tray from the bed and leaned across Heath to set it on the floor. When she stretched down, it hitched up the short nightgown, leaving her bare bottom temptingly exposed. When he didn't rise to the bait, she sat back up and asked, "Do you like to play games?"

"I love to play games; I'm rather good at them."

She leaned forward, providing him with a delicious display of breasts, and said intimately, "Tina says that between a man and a woman it is always a game." Raven made a little moue with her lips. "Unfortunately, I don't know many games, but I would love it if you would teach me how to play."

Heath's control slipped a notch as his fingers reached out to touch a tantalizing nipple. He caught himself and instead tucked a curl behind her ear and suggested, "Cards. In that drawer you will find tarot cards . . . we can play fortune-teller."

Amazed at his control, yet filled with curiosity about the cards, Raven slid from the bed to seek the fascinating pasteboards.

His avid eyes followed every movement she made. The lovely curves of her body were visible through the transparent material, and he marveled that the garment revealed far more than it concealed. Beneath the covers, his own body responded; his shaft lengthened and thickened and he felt his balls tighten pleasurably.

She climbed back on the bed and held out the tarot cards.

"You have the Celtic power of mystic divination, Raven. Tell my future. Lay out the cards and let me hear your interpretation."

She turned over the first card, which was the Knight of Wands, and the corners of her lips lifted in a mischievous smile. "This man looks very much like you. He is galloping at full speed. Is he aggressive, reckless, and brave enough to take what he wants?" She waited for him to snatch her up into his arms, but when he did not, she continued, "No, I see now that it is not you. It is Sir Galahad, filled with romantic chivalry rather than manliness."

She turned over another card, which was the Two of Cups. "Ah, here are a young man and woman, drinking a toast, pledging themselves to each other. He is asking her a question, and clearly her answer is yes," Raven hinted outrageously. "Could this couple be us? Do you wish to ask me a question?"

Heath shook his head. "I can't think of one. Do you wish to ask me a question?"

The minute he said it, Raven knew what Heath was up to. And it dawned on her that they truly were deep in a game—a male-female game that lovers had played since the dawn of time. The next card was the Empress. "Ah, here is a beautiful woman with a heart-shaped shield, bearing the sign of Venus! This woman is very close to you." She stroked his hard thigh through the cover. "Her gown is covered with symbols of fertility; she will give her husband many strong sons. She represents heaven on earth to the man bold enough to scale her walls and breach her defenses. She longs for a powerful

male who will force her to yield all her earthly treasures and pleasures." She looked at him from beneath her lashes. "Poor lady, I can
feel how she aches."

Heath felt his cock buck beneath the sheet, and the muscle in
his jaw looked like a lump of iron.

Raven pretended she did not notice, and turned over another
card. It was the King of Swords. "Now, this dark complexioned man
truly resembles you. Clearly he has been a lone wolf all his life and
has had to fight for everything he has ever achieved. But now he is
lonely; now he is seeking a mate. I wonder if this is you?" she puzzled. "He has a huge, erect sword and wields his weapon like a war-
rior." She pulled the covers down below his hips. "It *is* you! 'Twas
the unsheathed, upraised sword that gave you away!"

Heath growled in his throat and reached for her, but she held
up an imperious hand to stay him. "Wait, I must be sure! I shall investigate thoroughly, explore all the ins and outs, and see if it mea-
sures up to intense scrutiny." She closed her fingers around his shaft
and drew down the foreskin to expose the head of his cock. "It certainly looks like the King of Swords." Then, using both hands, she
captured it and rolled it between her palms. "It certainly feels like
the King of Swords." She looked into his eyes and deliberately licked
her lips. "I shall see if it tastes like the King of Swords; the proof of
the pudding is in the eating."

As Raven bent and dropped a kiss on the velvet head of his
phallus, Heath almost came out of his skin. Enthralled, he watched
the tip of her tongue delicately trace a circle around the heart-
shaped head. She repeated the torture three times, then sucked the
whole thing into her mouth like a ripe plum. Then she proceeded
with all the ins and outs as she had promised, and her glorious hair
cascaded in a black waterfall, pooling across his loins.

Heath's head went back until the cords in his neck stood out
like cables, and he arched his hips as the scalding heat of her mouth
made him writhe and gasp with savage need. The rough friction of
her tongue made him quiver and groan, and he felt his blood pulsing
through his veins and pounding in his temples and the soles of his
feet. "Raven, stop," he ordered, "I will spend!"

When she paid him not the slightest heed, he came up from the bed and cupped her cheeks in the palms of his hands and gently lifted her mouth from him. Then his hands slipped down her body until they grasped her waist, and he slid her up until her lips touched his, and he tasted himself on her mouth. Reeling from the passion she had aroused, he rolled with her until he straddled her, then he plunged down until his weapon was seated to the hilt. The brush of her thighs felt like silk as he thrust between them, and her hot, wet core branded him as nothing else had. It was primal and shocking as heat leaped between them. The loving was rough and uninhibited and splendidly frenzied as they slaked their sexual hunger. When her liquid tremors caused his white-hot seed to erupt, he was sheathed so deeply that they merged and became one.

Heath did not withdraw but stayed within her so he could feel every surging wave and pulsing tremor of the firestorm that their mating had unleashed. As he held her softening breasts, and felt her lips against his throat, he heard her whisper, "You are indeed my King of Swords."

CHAPTER 30

Raven took great delight in watching Heath shoe one of his mares. She focused on his hands, marveling at their strength and their gentleness. She had never known anyone before who was so attuned to the animals he cared for. It was evident that horses were Heath's passion, and that they loved him in return.

When Gavin with the Douglas moss-troopers came thundering into Eskdale's bailey, Heath went to the stables to talk with him and to help tend the horses. Raven followed him with trepidation. She dreaded the moment when Gavin and the rest of the Douglas men learned that she had helped Queen Margaret to escape to England. They were Scots, she English, and she feared they would resent her now and forever.

"I have a message for ye from Ram," Gavin told Heath. "As soon as he finishes his business in Edinburgh, he is headin' directly tae Castle Douglas. He vows Valentina will flay him alive if he doesn't get back so the twins can be christened." Gavin grinned as he glanced at Raven, then back to Heath. "Never thought I'd see the day when a Borderer would let a woman put him in leading strings." He winked. "Have a care, it could be contagious."

Heath grinned back. "No fear of that happening to a Kennedy." As he removed the saddle from Gavin's mount, the expression on his face became serious. "After being in Newark and witnessing Archibald Douglas's cowardly performance, I decided to let Margaret conveniently escape to England. It effectively separates her from young King Jamie, and puts an end to the influence that Henry Tudor would have over the King of Scotland."

"A wise decision," Gavin said with a straight face, before he glanced pointedly at Raven and began to grin. "Nothin' on earth gives as much trouble as a female in captivity . . . especially an English female!"

When Raven heard Heath take the blame and full responsibility for what she had done, a lump came into her throat and her eyes shone with unshed tears. Here was a real man, with his own unshakable code of honor. There was no sacrifice he would not make for those he cared about. She loved him with all her heart and soul, but what made her happier than any woman alive was the knowledge that he loved her. She felt amazingly blessed.

Raven slipped from the stables and returned to the castle. She climbed the stairs to Heath's tower rooms and bathed the tears from her eyes. She knew that Heath's towering pride was a result of all the hurt and rejection that had been heaped upon him since childhood. Yet she too had rejected him, not once but twice. She was certain that he would not ask her again to marry him, because he couldn't survive the pain if she rejected him. She knew he would not take the risk. She opened the wardrobe and chose his favorite dress. It was the pale green gown she had been wearing on the night that changed her life . . . the night when he had first made love to her. Raven then lit every candle she could find and placed them on the hearth and the mantel of the fireplace.

When Heath entered the tower, he wondered where Raven had disappeared to. He stopped on the threshold of the inner chamber and stared in wonder. Surrounded by lit candles, Raven had never looked more beautiful. Her face was luminous, and her bright lavender aura was a startling contrast against her black silken curls. He saw her eyes light up at the sight of him, and could not quite believe his own good fortune.

He watched entranced as Raven gracefully knelt before him.

"Heath Kennedy, on bended knee I am asking you to marry me."

He snatched her into his arms. "Raven, my own love, never kneel to me again! Blood of God, I am such a prideful swine that I have forced you to do this thing." He looked down at her lovely face in awe and brushed the backs of his fingers across her cheek with reverence. "Do you mean it, Raven? Will you really marry me?"

"I mean it with all my heart. I love you, Heath!"

He took possession of her hands, and his face became hard with the intensity of his emotions. "Consider carefully, Raven. All I own in this world are a dozen breeding mares. I have nothing to give you."

"Heath, you have everything to give me; your love is more precious than rubies!"

"Be absolutely certain, Raven. . . . I have Gypsy blood."

Her head fell back as she began to laugh and sing:

> *"Oh, what care I for my goose-feather bed,*
> *with the sheets turned down so bravely-o?*
> *Tonight I will sleep in a wide open field,*
> *Along with the raggle-taggle Gypsies-o!"*

"Will you marry me now, today?" he demanded.

"I will. Fetch the priest!"

"Nay, when I come back you might be gone. We'll ride up to the little church at Kirkstile. Come on." He clung possessively to her hand as if he feared she would vanish if he let go of her.

In the stables, he stopped before the white mare. "I want to give her to you for a wedding present; I want her foal to be yours too. Would you like to ride her? Exercise won't hurt her."

Raven stroked the mare's nose. "She's the loveliest gift I've ever received." She reached up and kissed him. "I thank you with all my heart, but I have no gift for you."

Heath covered her mouth with his in a kiss that was deliberately seductive. "I'll think of something," he murmured against her lips.

"I'll bet you will, you devil. Better saddle Sully, for I intend to race you!"

It was a dead heat to the church in Kirkstile. They tethered their mounts before the small stone building and went inside together.

The priest, who was polishing the candlesticks from the altar, turned and immediately recognized the couple.

"Will you marry us, Father?" Heath asked respectfully.

"Is this another forced weddin'?" The square-built man of God bent his stern gaze upon them.

"It is," Raven asserted. "This time I've done the wooing, and I've done the proposing! It is high time that Heath Kennedy made an honest woman of me."

Heath looked at the priest and shrugged helplessly. "She refuses to take no for an answer!"

The priest fetched his housekeeper from his living quarters to act as witness, and beckoned the couple to the altar. He charged them both, "Matrimony is not tae be enterprized, nor taken in hand, unadvisedly, lightly, or wantonly; but reverently, discreetly, advisedly, soberly, an' in the fear of God!" He stared hard at both of them, then proceeded with the solemnization of matrimony.

This time the bride did not hesitate to plight her troth. "I, Raven Carleton, take thee, Heath Kennedy, to my wedded husband, to have and to hold from this day forward, for better for worse, for richer for poorer, in sickness and in health, to love, cherish, and to obey, till death us do part."

Heath saw Raven's surprised delight when he produced the wedding ring he'd had for a long time. "With this ring I thee wed, with my body I thee honor, and with all my worldly goods I thee endow." He saw that her look was rapt; she saw no irony in his words.

The priest concluded, "Forasmuch as Heath an' Raven have consented taegether in holy wedlock, I pronounce that they be man and wife. May almighty God pour upon ye the riches of his grace, sanctify an' bless ye, that ye may please him both in body an' soul, an' live taegether in holy love unto yer lives' end. Amen."

Outside the church, Heath gave a great whoop of joy and lifted Raven for his kiss before he sat her in the saddle. Without another word, both knew the race was on! They galloped together over the dales toward Eskdale. As they came to the River Esk, Heath suddenly shouted, "Raven, look!"

She lifted her face to the sky and saw a pair of hunting birds circling high amid the afternoon clouds. The newlyweds drew rein, the race forgotten. "Could it possibly be?"

The raptors circled lower and Raven's trained eye saw that they were peregrine falcons. "Oh, it is! It's Sultan and Sheba; I can't believe it!"

The hawks had seen the riders, and the female perched atop a tall fir tree while the male swooped down to investigate. Raven began to laugh with sheer happiness as Sultan dived and plunged about them, and Sheba spread her wings and bobbed her head in excited recognition. "Perhaps this is a wedding gift from the Goddess of the Hunt; a mystic sign that our union is blessed and right!" Raven said with wonder.

Heath saw the radiance on her face and knew that Raven was his gift from the gods. "I can fashion you a lure," he offered.

"Oh no, I cannot take them back into captivity. I want them to be wild and free, and together in love unto their lives' end . . . like us," she added.

Heath dismounted and lifted Raven down into his arms. "That's exactly how I feel. Sweetheart, I have a confession to make. It isn't exactly the truth that all I own are my breeding mares."

She gazed up at him trustingly, ready to hear his secrets.

"Archibald Douglas, the late Earl of Angus, bequeathed me a hundred acres of land in his will."

"Why would he do that?"

" 'Tis rumored that my mother, Lily Rose, was his love child. I haven't seen the land yet, but it lies beyond the River Dee in Kirkcudbright and runs parallel with land that belongs to Castle Douglas."

"How wonderful!" Raven saw the longing on his face as he spoke of the land. "Why don't we take your mares to graze on your own land? We can visit your sister Tina, and may even get there in time for the twins' christening!"

"That's what I planned to do before you came back to Eskdale; that's why I've been shoeing the mares. If you'd arrived a day later, I could so easily have been gone."

"See? It was preordained; we were meant to be together. My grandmother wanted a Borderer for me." Raven smiled her secret smile. "I shall tell you tonight what happened when she initiated me into the Craft."

"I always suspected that you bewitched me. Tell me now." Heath pulled her down into the long grass to lie beside him.

"Alas, I cannot. It must be on the stroke of midnight," she teased. They shaded their eyes watching Sultan and Sheba until they disappeared. "Can we leave tomorrow?"

"We can if you are willing, love. It's a long trek, and herding horses can be slow work. Will you mind sleeping outdoors?"

The corners of her mouth went up. "I love nature. It will be most romantic to lie beneath the stars."

"Are you sure you won't find the ground too hard?"

"I'm not sure . . . perhaps we'd better try it and find out." They turned to each other and made love in nature's perfect setting.

The next day, Heath and Raven joined Gavin and the moss-troopers in the hall for breakfast and broke the news that they had been married yesterday.

"Why the devil didn't ye say somethin' last night? We couldha' celebrated till dawn!"

"That's exactly why we kept it secret. We're leaving today; taking the mares to my land on the River Dee. It was our last opportunity to sleep in a real bed for a while."

"And did ye sleep?" Gavin asked with a straight face.

"On and off," Heath replied solemnly.

Raven hid her blushes and bade them all goodbye. She had grown to love Eskdale; she had been happier here than anywhere else. She had a moment's misgiving about what lay ahead, but it melted away as she acknowledged that it wasn't Eskdale that had made her happy, it was Heath Kennedy.

The journey west was a leisurely one. Heath and Raven rode side by side, allowing the mares to set their own pace. It took them two days before they crossed the River Annan and another day to reach Dumfries. Heath was more than satisfied that they were able to cover eight miles a day, and the relaxed pace gave the newlyweds time to talk and learn things about each other. Whenever they found a stream where the horses could be watered, they bathed and swam together, laughing and playing like children. Heath suspected that they would never be able to be this carefree again, and knew for a certainty that in the future they would never be alone together this long.

Raven reveled in her newfound freedom. She marveled at Heath's ability to feed and shelter them. He was expert at snaring small game, catching fish, keeping them dry in rainstorms, and gathering bracken and fir boughs to make them a cozy bed. He taught her some of his secrets about horse handling, and she was delighted that sometimes the mares followed her and nudged her affectionately as they did Heath.

At night, as they lay enfolded in each other's arms, Heath told her about Donal and Meggie and how deeply in love they were. "You and Meggie will like each other; she has a sweetness that is special, and their little girl will steal your heart."

"Valentina will be overjoyed when she sees you."

"And when Tina sees that you are with me, she will be like the cat who has swallowed the cream. She was as determined as I that you were the perfect wife for me; soul mates I think she called us."

"Are Castle Douglas and Donal's tower castle far apart?"

"Nay, the land runs together. The Kennedy tower castle stands at the mouth of the River Dee where it empties into the Solway; Castle Douglas lies a few miles upriver."

"So we will reach Castle Douglas first, and your own acres? We need not take the mares further?"

Heath read Raven's thoughts and realized she was nervous about visiting the Kennedys. "We must go and see them." He took her into his arms. "My darling, you have already met my father. I know he can be fierce and overbearing at times, but you must never be afraid of him. He admires those who have courage. Valentina is his favorite because she has the guts to stand up to him. When he learns of your bravery in rescuing me from Carlisle Castle, he will be like butter in your hands."

It took them two more days of traveling to get to Castle Douglas. When they entered the massive hall, it was beginning to fill up for the evening meal. Tina scattered the rushes as she flew to her favorite brother's side. "Thank you for riding to Ram's aid in Newark. He told me you had escaped from Carlisle Castle, but I wasn't worried for a moment. I knew if you could escape the Tower of London, Carlisle would be like child's play to you. What the devil took you so long?"

"It was Raven who rescued me from Carlisle," Heath explained.

Valentina turned to Raven and stared horrified. "What the devil have you done to her, you madman? She looks like a damned Gypsy!"

Heath laughed. "We brought my mares from Eskdale."

"You've been living rough and sleeping outdoors? My God, only look at her delicate skin . . . the sun has turned it brown!" Tina was outraged. "She's wearing rags! Ada, come quickly, we must do something about Raven." She turned to Heath. "Any woman who would do this for you must love you enough to marry you. Have you asked her yet?"

"I have," Heath declared.

Tina turned to Raven, "And have you finally agreed to wed him?"

"I have," Raven declared.

"Oh, how marvelous, I have a wedding to plan!"

"As a matter of fact, Tina, we are—"

Raven put a quick finger to her lips to stay his words. Tina was the most generous woman in the world, and if her heart was set on having a wedding, Raven would see that she got her wish. Surreptitiously, she took off her wedding ring and slipped it into her husband's hand.

Heath repeated, "As a matter of fact, Tina, we are looking forward to being married in your chapel here at Castle Douglas."

Ram entered the hall with his faithful wolfhound, Boozer, at his side. When the fierce creature saw Heath, he loped toward him and stood with both his front paws on Heath's shoulders, barking loud enough to raise the rafters. Ram laughed. "Anyone would think he was glad tae see ye." He turned to Raven. "Have no fear, the Boozer's bite is worse than his bark."

"I brought my mares to pasture on the land that Angus gave me. I haven't even seen it yet, but we'll take them first thing in the morning." He turned to Tina. "We brought Indigo; would you like to ride out with us?"

"Oh, thank you so much, Heath; I have missed her dreadfully. I can think of nothing more invigorating than a morning gallop. Ram, you must send a message to my father immediately to let him know that Heath is here, safe and sound."

"I sent him a message days ago that he was safe and sound; I warrant Rob would prefer a visit tae another damned message."

"We will go downriver as soon as we get the herd pastured," Heath said.

"We?" Tina repeated archly. "You may go by all means, Heath Kennedy, but Raven cannot go to meet her future family until I have transformed her back into a lady!"

Heath looked helplessly at Ram. He certainly didn't want to be separated from his bride.

"My God, don't look at me fer help, she's yer bloody sister, and ye know she rules Douglas with an iron fist," Ram jested.

Tina looked at Ram and Heath impatiently. "Go over there and eat with the men; we have a wedding to plan."

As the two men walked apart from the women, Heath told him that he had allowed Margaret to escape to England. Ram laughed. "Let Dacre look after her; it will cost him a pretty penny. She has obscenely expensive tastes."

"What about Archibald?" Heath asked.

"Poor Archie cannot escape tae England. Henry Tudor would have his balls along with his head. Takin' Tudor gold and then not deliverin' the goods is very bad fer the health! My cousin will have tae withdraw tae the Braes of Angus in the Highlands; 'tis the only place he has left. I just got word from the courts that the will I submitted has been accepted and validated."

"Congratulations! Thank God old Angus is up there pulling the strings. If they hadn't accepted it, I would have no claim on the land across the River Dee. Things are looking up for both of us. Raven and I got married before we left Eskdale, but Tina has it in her flaming head to plan our wedding, and Raven wants me to keep my mouth shut so Tina won't be disappointed." Heath rolled his eyes.

"Yer secret's safe with me. She'll be in her glory plannin' a christenin' and a weddin'. All Kirkcudbright, Wigtown, and Galloway will be invited. She wants tae show off the twins, and we're still arguin' about the bairns' names."

After dinner Heath approached Tina and his wife, who were in deep conversation with Ada and two waiting women. He managed to catch Tina's eye. "Which chamber can we have? We want one where we won't be disturbed."

"You may take the chamber next to Cameron's. You won't be disturbed at all, for Raven is sleeping in my wing, so she may use my bathing tub and get fitted for some new gowns."

"You are wrong; I am greatly disturbed! I want Raven to sleep with me."

"And so she shall . . . after the wedding. A bride-to-be needs sleep, not what you have in mind."

"What I have in mind is throttling a certain redhead. I don't know how the hell your husband puts up with you!"

Ada said dryly, "It's because Black Ram Douglas has such a sweet nature, coupled with an extremely mild temperament. You would do well to emulate him."

Heath glared at the female conspirators and threw up his hands in surrender.

CHAPTER 31

Heath found his bed extremely lonely and the night interminable. He arose at the crack of dawn and made his way to the spacious Douglas stables to visit his stallion, Blackadder. When he saw Heath, the huge black horse began to kick the sides of his stall, indicating that he needed exercise. Heath saddled him and trotted outside to the paddock where he had left his mares. As Heath expected, Blackadder began to rear with excitement the minute he scented the females. "I know how you feel," Heath muttered sympathetically as he gentled him and brought him under control.

As he dismounted Blackadder and tethered him, Ram joined him and they went back inside the stable, where Ram saddled Indigo for Tina. "I take it the ladies intend to grace us with their company," Heath said. "I had better saddle Sully."

Ram hid his amusement. "Yer voice seems tae have an edge tae it this fine morning. Doesn't marriage agree with ye?"

Heath threw back his head and laughed, his good nature restored. He turned as he heard female voices, and stared at the beauteous creature who accompanied his sister. Raven was garbed in a fashionable riding dress of pale peach trimmed with apricot braid, and a fetching hat in a matching shade perched atop her dark curls. He immediately closed the distance between them and lifted her gloved hands to his lips. "You look ravishing, or good enough to ravish," he whispered intimately. "Though lovely, your dress is grossly impractical."

"For ravishing or riding?" Raven lifted her mouth for his kiss.

Heath's lips twitched with amusement. "Only a few hours with

Tina and already her sauciness has rubbed off. The only way I can tell you apart is by the color of your hair."

"What a lovely compliment," she teased. "Will you be this attentive after we are married?"

"Speaking of weddings, when is ours to be?" Heath smiled and tried not to grind his teeth.

Valentina jumped in with the answer. "We have decided it shall be the same day as the christening, since all the guests have already been invited."

"How many days?" Heath's voice was measured, his words deliberate.

"Such impatience. . . . I am tempted to postpone it just to see how long you can hold out."

"Tina!" His tone clearly told her he was in no mood for games.

"This Sunday, which gives us only four more days to sew a wedding gown and complete a new wardrobe for your bride."

"Four days?" It sounded like a life sentence to Heath. He took Raven's hand and drew her aside. "I cannot stay under the same roof with you for four days and remain celibate. I shall go downriver and visit my father for a few days."

Raven looked at him longingly and wished she hadn't entered into the game. She reached up on tiptoe and kissed him. "We mustn't let it spoil our joy in taking the mares to our own land."

He held her close. "I love you, Raven."

"Fer Christ's sake, Tina, will ye get in the bloody saddle before he tumbles her in the hay?"

Heath took the mares from the paddock, then he and Ram led them upriver along the bank of the Dee. For now, Valentina and Raven were content to follow where their men led.

"The river narrows about two miles from here. I warrant that would be the easiest place tae cross. Yer acres start where the Dee widens and deepens," Ram explained.

When they reached the place Ram had described, they herded the mares across with little trouble, but the moment Tina's Barbary got her dainty hooves in the water, she turned skittish and began to sidestep. Ram laughed at his wife. "Ye're out of practice."

"That's because I've been shackled to your bed, making babies for you, Douglas!" Indigo turned around and headed back, and in an effort to stay her, Tina's lovely amethyst-hued riding dress became splashed with muddy water.

"Mayhap ye're too heavy fer such a dainty mount." Ram was enjoying himself. "Why don't ye climb down and lead her across?"

Tina did just that. She loved the Barbary far too much to risk her long, slim legs. She cared nothing for the ruined boots and dress, and when she reached the far bank where her husband sat laughing, she was ready to join the game. "You are an uncouth, uncivilized swine, Ram Douglas. You need touching up with a riding crop." She jumped into the saddle and tore after him.

"Catch me if ye can," Ram called over his shoulder.

Sully, surefooted as ever, brought Raven across the river without incident, and she rode up beside her husband. "You would never guess she was the mother of twins."

"They enjoy baiting each other. Ram knows damned well the Barbary will catch him."

"But he also knows Tina won't beat him with her riding crop."

"It wouldn't be the first time she's taken her whip to him; how do you think he got that scar on his cheek?"

Raven shuddered. She completely understood the passion a woman could unleash when a man she loved drove her to it. The mares had begun to wander, cropping the rich green grass beside the water, so Raven helped Heath herd them together and they set off up a great incline. They seemed to climb forever, then finally they saw Tina and Ram awaiting them at the top of the dale.

When they arrived at the peak, they saw that the land sloped down into a long, lush valley, and below them to their right, the River Dee widened out into a loch. "This is it," Heath said, not needing to be told he was on his own land.

"What a magnificent view." A lump came into Raven's throat, for she knew this was the first land that Heath had ever owned, and she could only guess at the deep emotions he must be feeling as he watched his mares break into a gallop and thunder downhill into the valley.

Suddenly, Valentina bent over double with laughter. "I don't believe it!" She turned to her husband, with a triumphant look on her face. "This is Kennedy land! This is the land that you and Angus cheated my father out of as part of my dowry! And now it has come full circle back to the Kennedys! This is the way it was originally: Douglas land on the far side of the Dee, and Kennedy land on this side."

"Where do your hundred acres end?" Raven asked Heath.

"They don't," Tina asserted. "Kennedy land stretches from here to the Atlantic Ocean, and from Port Patrick all the way up to Ayr. We own half of Kirkcudbright, all of Wigtown, and all of Galloway!"

Raven stared out across the landscape in wonder. It was difficult for her to comprehend that one family could own land as far as the eye could see, and then beyond, all the way to the sea. She was suddenly overcome with a burning anger. If Heath's father owned all this land, why in the name of God had he never been able to spare a few acres for his firstborn son?

Heath saw her eyes flood with tears, and read her mind. "I was too proud to ask, Raven," he said softly. "Be happy for me, love."

Raven dashed the tears from her eyes and bestowed a radiant smile upon him. "I'll race you!" She thundered down into the lush valley, and Heath followed her, whooping with joy. When he caught up with her, he dismounted in a flash and lifted her into his arms. Raven had already lost her fancy hat, and by the time Heath had finished swinging her in circles and they sprawled to the ground, the pale peach riding dress was in total ruin.

They picked out the best place to build the stable to shelter the mares over the long winter months, and selected the spot where their own modest shieling would go. The building materials of stone and timber were plentiful and Ram promised manpower from Douglas, but Heath and Raven had no illusions and knew they would have to start out small until the herd doubled, and doubled again.

On the way back to Castle Douglas, the men took their wives up before them in the saddle. The riderless horses followed. With

Raven nestled in his arms, Heath was happier than he had ever been in his life. He didn't have much to offer her beyond his love and protection, but she had made it abundantly clear that this was enough by actually marrying him twice. No man breathing could ask for more. "Enjoy the next few days and let them pamper the bride-to-be. I'll be back in lots of time for the wedding with all the Kennedys in tow." He kissed her tenderly. "Always remember that I love and adore you."

When Heath arrived at the Kennedy Tower Castle, he could hardly believe the welcome he received. Meggie flew into his arms and kissed him as tears of love and gratitude streamed down her cheeks. "Donal refuses to tell me what he suffered while imprisoned in Carlisle, and that proves how terrible it was."

"I wasn't there five minutes when Raven Carleton, the girl I love, helped me to escape. Valentina is planning a wedding for us on Sunday in Douglas Chapel, after the twins are christened. I hope you and Raven will be friends, Meggie."

"You are marrying Raven?" Beth cried, overjoyed. "Father is negotiating a betrothal for me with her brother, Heron. Oh, Heath, please use your influence with the Carletons and persuade them to accept me as their daughter-in-law!"

"Sweeting, I have no influence with the Carletons. I warrant they hate me for stealing their daughter." When Beth laughed as if he were jesting, Heath wished he could make her understand.

Rob Kennedy entered the hall with his wife, Elizabeth. The father and son exchanged a quick glance that spoke a thousand words. Heath saw relief, and pride, and love on his father's face, and he was happy that his father looked so much better than the last time he had seen him.

Lady Kennedy stepped forward and placed her hand on Heath's arm. "Would you walk with me?"

It was the first time his father's wife had ever touched him; one of the few times she had even acknowledged his existence. Though Heath did not want her thanks, he had too much self-respect to act boorishly toward her. With her hand on his arm they walked apart from the others down the long hall.

"Because I was jealous of your mother, I treated you with aversion, abhorrence, rancor, and even hatred. I objected to your very existence. Yet you have repaid me with my son's life."

Heath rejected her thanks by making it clear he had not done it for her. "Lady Kennedy, Donal was taken prisoner because of bad blood between me and the Dacres. It was my responsibility to gain his freedom . . . and it cost me so little."

"Heath Kennedy, if it had cost you your life, you would have paid it. I have a confession to make." She bent toward him. "I would give all I have if you were my son."

Heath was astounded that Elizabeth had opened her heart to him; he had always believed that she had no heart. Her words had meant to compliment him, and his pride prompted him to compliment her in return. "My father is looking so much better. I know I have you to thank for it, and I am most grateful."

She looked at him coyly. "Most grateful, no doubt, that I have taken him off your hands!"

"Why, Lady Kennedy, you have a sarcastic wit!" Heath smiled with appreciation.

"Where do you think Tina gets it from? Call me Elizabeth."

Heath roared with laughter, for never in the memory of man had there been a more disparate mother and daughter!

"Thank God, ye can laugh again." Donal had walked down the hall to meet him. "Thank God my . . . our family can laugh again." Elizabeth Kennedy left them alone to talk. "Words are not enough; 'tis deeds that count, as ye showed me. I will try tae be a true brother tae ye, from now on."

Heath felt stiff and awkward and wanted to reject his thanks.

"They didn't put me in the wall irons, but I've had nightmares that they used them on ye." Donal's eyes were anguished.

"No," Heath denied quickly, "no . . . perhaps they lost the key."

"Thank God!" Donal muttered. "Father wants a word with ye."

Rob Kennedy awaited him, and there was no escape. Heath took a deep breath, then strode down the hall. "Let's go in here, so we can be private. There's summat I have tae say." Rob led the way into a small chamber off the great hall.

Heath looked his father directly in the eye. "For Christ's sake don't thank me! I've just had a revelation. I didn't do it for any of *you* . . . I did it for myself! I did it out of sheer, unadulterated pride, to demonstrate I had more reckless courage, to prove I was the better man, to show that I had more guts than any Kennedy breathing. I did it so that I could throw your thanks in your teeth, along with your offer to make me your heir!"

"Are ye done, lad?" Rob asked dryly.

Heath nodded once.

"Good. 'Tis a wonder ye dinna choke on yer own self-righteousness." Rob shook his head. "God's passion, ye get more like me every day! Towering pride is not only a deadly sin, it's bloody insufferable. I had tae swallow mine, an' ye'll do the same!"

"What do you mean?" Heath was wary.

"Tomorra, my lawyer's commin' tae change my will. We're all in agreement—well, all but Duncan—so ye have no say in the matter. I'm also expectin' Kennedys from all the other branches of the family; they're invited tae my twin grandchilders' christenin'. There's the new Earl of Cassillis, head of the clan, there's Callum Kennedy of Newark, Keith Kennedy of Dunure, an' Andrew Kennedy, Laird of Carrick. 'Tis time they got tae know the rightful heir tae the Lairdship of Galloway, an' ye'll no' shame me by throwin' it in my bloody teeth!"

Heath, refusing to argue, changed the subject. "Tina has planned a wedding for Raven Carleton and me after the twins are christened." He almost added that they were already married, but his father's words forestalled him.

"Well, there's Providence fer ye! I've begun negotiations wi' Sir Lancelot Carleton tae betroth his son tae my wee Beth, an' I've invited them here tae finalize the matter!"

"They're coming here?" Heath felt a touch of panic.

"I sent Duncan tae fetch them aboard the *Doon*. Only think how honored they'll be tae see their daughter wed my firstborn son!"

Heath's panic increased.

" 'Tis a good thing ye aren't wed yet; it'll give me a chance tae negotiate a sizeable dowry fer their daughter."

Once more Heath's pride raised its towering head. "You'll do no such bloody thing! I wouldn't take an English farthing from them. Besides, Lance Carleton has only a comfortable living; he's not filthy rich like you."

"Dinna get yer kilt in a knot! Oh aye, an' speakin' of kilts, we're all bein' fitted fer new Kennedy dress plaids afore we go tae Douglas. The blood-proud swaggerin' swine will no' outdo us!"

The following day the Kennedy clan began to arrive. Members from every branch of the family were coming to honor the Lord of Galloway's twin grandchildren, and all were eager to get to know Heath Kennedy, whom it was rumored was no bastard after all, but the rightful heir.

Heath struck up an immediate acquaintance with John Kennedy, the new Earl of Cassillis, whose father had been killed at Flodden. The old earl had bred the finest horseflesh in Scotland, and over the years Heath had managed to get his hands on a couple of his animals, most notably Tina's Barbary, Indigo.

"Horses were my father's passion," John Kennedy told Heath. "Unfortunately, I don't have the time tae devote tae long-term breedin'. My new wife, Alexandra Gordon, brought me twenty thousand head of Highland longhorn cattle, an' I don't have room fer both."

Heath wondered how on earth anyone could prefer cattle to horses. He had never allowed himself the luxury of envy, but at this moment Heath admitted that he coveted Cassillis's horses.

Rob Kennedy's lawyer arrived, and the two men closeted themselves away arguing various points of law and preparing new legal documents. When they emerged from the private chamber, Rob called all the Kennedy males into the great hall and served them whisky. "Day after tomorra, we go tae Douglas fer the christening of my twin grandchildren."

Every male Kennedy raised his glass in a toast, and Rob had the servers replenish the whisky. "After the christenin', there is tae be a weddin'. My son Heath Kennedy will wed Raven Carleton." Rob beckoned Heath forward to where he sat with his lawyer.

With a feeling of reluctance, Heath walked down the room, dreading in his bones that his father was going to propose a toast to his new heir and uncertain what his response would be. He was totally unprepared, however, for his father's words.

"Heath here is my firstborn son, an' my legal heir. However, my health is indifferent an' my days are numbered. After much cogitation an' deliberation, I've decided tae pass over the Lairdship of Galloway tae him this day."

Stunned silence blanketed the hall. Heath, who had long thought himself shockproof, realized that he was not. Slowly, hot burning pride rose within him, obliterating his feeling of shock. He stared hard at the father who had rejected him all his life, from the time he was a boy, who suddenly wanted to embrace him. Every instinct told him it was now his turn to do the rejecting and take his long-awaited revenge.

Do not allow your towering pride to rule you. Heath heard the voice of his mother, Lily Rose, as clearly as if she were standing beside him. *Do not allow your unbending pride to cheat you of your birthright.* Heath ran his hand through his hair in a stubborn gesture and argued, *To accept what he offers means I would have to forgive him!* He heard Lily Rose sigh. *Heath, my beloved son, are you not man enough to forgive him?*

Heath looked at his father's ruined face, and it finally dawned on him that pride was not strength, it was weakness. He bowed his proud head. "You honor me, my lord."

As he signed the legal papers a great cheer went up among the males present, and they raised their voices and their whisky in a resounding toast: "Tae Heath Kennedy, Laird of Galloway!" A piper appeared and the Kennedys raised Heath to their shoulders and carried him about the hall. When he looked down, the first thing he saw was Donal's beaming face.

The next two hours were spent poring over maps and deeds with his father and their lawyer, showing him the extent of his domain. "I needed tae do this while I'm still alive tae guide ye in yer responsibilitics as Laird of Galloway. Have no regrets, ye're the right mon fer the job."

"I have no regrets, Father."

That night, Heath Kennedy could not sleep, did not even want to sleep as he thought about the life-changing events of the day, and all that being Lord of Galloway encompassed. All Kennedy holdings were now in his name: vast tracts of land, half a dozen castles and peel towers, a merchant shipping empire, and untold herds of live-stock. The wealth was immense, as were the responsibilities. There were at least a score of towns and villages on Kennedy-owned land, and his decisions would affect hundreds of lives. Then there were Kennedy tenants who worked the land, and Kennedy crews who sailed the ships. Heath knew he would have to be decisive and reso-lute, but he vowed to be flexible and, above all, fair.

First thing in the morning he would speak with the lawyer and have legal papers drawn up to benefit his brothers. He wanted Donal to receive all the revenues derived from Kennedy sheep and the ex-port of Kennedy wool. Heath, aware of Duncan's resentment, de-cided that he should get all the revenues derived from the Kennedy merchant shipping business, and hc would also put the vessels in Duncan's own name.

The rest of the night he spent thinking about his beautiful wife, Raven, and the unbelievable wedding present he was about to be-stow upon her. The title was only important to him because Raven would now be Lady Kennedy.

CHAPTER 32

The chapel at Castle Douglas could not hold all the Kennedys and Douglases who had descended en masse to celebrate the christening and the wedding. Ramsay and Valentina, each holding a twin, stood at the stone christening font with the priest, who was flanked by Ada, acting as godmother, and Rob Kennedy, doing double duty as grandfather and godfather.

As the priest intoned the baptismal prayers in Latin, Ram and Tina's redheaded son began to crow and screech with delight at the strange-sounding words, and his twin sister joined in the fun. Rob Kennedy loudly cleared his throat in a not-too-subtle hint for the priest to get on with it. When the priest did not immediately take the hint, Rob stepped forward, placing the entire weight of his bulk on the holy man's foot.

"Christus!" he swore in Latin, but decided that speeding up the ceremony would be the fastest way to get the ungodly Kennedy out of his church. The priest took the baby girl into his arms and turned to Ada. "Name this child."

Ada's clear voice rang out, "Tara Jasmine Douglas!"

As a collective gasp went round the chapel at the fancy name, Valentina and Ada exchanged a conspiratorial smile.

The priest glared at Ada, then intoned, "Tara Jasmine Douglas, I baptize thee in the name of the Father, the Son, an' the Holy Ghost." He made the sign of the cross on the child's head with holy water and passed her back to her mother. Then he took the baby boy into his arms and turned to Rob. "Name this child."

Rob's grating voice was loud, challenging, and filled with pride. "Ramsay Robert Douglas!"

This time it was Valentina's turn to gasp, for she had told them all firmly that her son's name was to be Neal Ryan. As the priest baptized her baby boy, she saw her husband and her father exchange a conspiratorial wink. When Ramsay Robert Douglas grabbed hold of the priest's rosary and chucked it in the font, the holy man muttered, "Firk!"

"My thoughts, exactly!" Tina responded, her sense of humor restored.

When the baptismal ceremony was over, Valentina took her twins from the chapel and turned them over to their adoring nursemaids, then she turned to Raven, who was anxiously waiting outside the chapel for the signal that the marriage ceremony was to begin. Her wedding gown of cream lace had a train in the latest fashion, and exquisite trailing sleeves. Her flowers were lilies and roses, which she had chosen to honor the memory of Heath's mother.

Tina kissed her cheek. She was privy to the surprises that lay in store for Raven and thanked all the saints in heaven that the brother she loved so dearly had found his soul mate. "Life will never be the same again after today," she predicted.

Raven gifted her with a radiant smile. "That's true, for you will be my sister."

"There's the piper!" Valentina gathered up Raven's train and they glided up the nave of the chapel toward the altar.

Raven had eyes only for Heath. He was so handsome in the Kennedy dress plaid and fitted black doublet that her heart turned over in her breast. When she reached his side, he took hold of her trembling hands and saw the lilies and roses. He raised her fingers to his lips and murmured, "I love you, Raven."

She could not follow the Latin prayers of the priest and was glad that she had understood the words the first time they were married. Raven was unaware that a beam of sunlight pierced the colored glass of the oriel window and formed a vivid halo of light around her head, but all crowded into the chapel could see it.

The priest switched to English to ask Heath if he would love, comfort, honor, and forsake all others, and when he vowed, "I will," his deep voice sent a shiver up Raven's spine. When the priest asked her the same, adding the words *obey* and *serve*, Raven's "I will" rang out like a crystal bell.

When the priest asked, "Who giveth this woman to be married to this man?" Sir Lancelot Carleton stepped forward. "I do." He took his daughter's hand and placed it in Heath's.

Raven was so surprised, her knees turned to water, and she swayed noticeably. Heath's arm went about her to steady her. The tender smile he gave her told her that her father's presence was no surprise to her husband.

The priest was again speaking. "Repeat after me: I, Heath Kennedy, Laird o' Galloway—"

Raven drew in a swift breath at the priest's mistake, but when her husband repeated, "I, Heath Kennedy, Lord of Galloway," she began to feel as if everything were unreal, and either she or those about her had lost their mind. Everything became a blur, until she found herself clinging tightly to Heath's hand as they ran from the chapel back to Castle Douglas. Raven didn't recall plighting her troth or receiving the wedding ring, but she clearly remembered the priest saying, "Ladies and gentlemen, it is my great honor tae present to ye Laird and Lady Kennedy."

There was no time for explanations as they were surrounded by Douglas and Kennedy clansmen in the great hall. As the bride lifted her mouth for her husband's kiss, she knew that she would have to wait until tonight to learn the whole amazing story. She could clearly see that Heath was happier than he had ever been, and to Raven that was all that mattered.

Kate Carleton embraced her daughter and whispered, "You are such a clever girl, Raven! I warrant my mother must have inducted you into the Craft. Promise me you will do all in your power to see that they betroth Beth Kennedy to Heron?"

Raven's father, Sir Lancelot, claimed the first dance, and Rob Kennedy claimed the second. After that Raven had so many partners begging for dances, it made her dizzy. The Douglas men were dark, the Kennedy men red-haired, and other than that Raven could not tell one from the other. The music and feasting and drinking went on until after midnight, but long before that Heath spirited his bride upstairs to the Master Chamber, which Tina had prepared for the newlyweds.

By the time the door closed on the sumptuous chamber with the pink granite walls, Heath and Raven were in a fever of longing. Once their clinging and kissing began, explanations were postponed. Heath undressed his bride with reverent hands, then he proceeded to anoint every inch of her silken skin with worshipful kisses.

Raven lay naked upon the luxurious lynx fur. Heath's lovemaking was gentle and slow, and heartbreakingly tender. He honored and cherished her with his body as he had promised in his wedding vows, and his hands and his lips made her feel utterly beautiful. When she experienced her final rapture, he gathered her close in a tender embrace while they shared every last pulsation. She was amazed at the enormity of the love she felt for him. She experienced a sense of perfection and rightness as contentment filled her heart and her soul.

When they lay still with only their heartbeats intermingling, he poured out his love. "You have bound me eternally. I pledge you my love now and forevermore, Raven. I have never felt this way before. You are more precious to me than my own life." He pushed up the pillows behind them, then scooped her up to cradle her between his long legs. He cupped her softening breasts possessively and told her everything that had happened to change their lives. "I had known that I was my father's legal heir for some time, but when he passed over the Lordship of Galloway to me, it came as a complete surprise."

"You had known for some time? Did you know when you made me propose to you?"

Heath's grin flashed forth, "I did, but you don't understand, at that time I thought I might refuse his generous offer."

Raven stroked his thigh. *I do understand, Heath. It was your pride that prevented you from proposing to me, and pride that prompted you to refuse his offer.* "What made you change your mind?"

"It was thoughts of my mother . . . and you. She was my father's legal wife, and the lordship is my birthright. But more than anything, I wanted to bestow the title of *lady* upon you. It means nothing without you, Raven." His arms tightened about her as he told her of his plans.

"I am going to buy the Earl of Cassillis's herds of thoroughbred horses. I want us to travel across every mile of Kennedy land, visit every town and village and meet the people who live there. Beyond the River Cree is a Kennedy castle on the shores of Loch Ryan. If you love it as much as I think you will, that's where I would like us to live. Between the castle and the River Cree lies a vast stretch of land called The Moors, which should be ideal for horse breeding. Loch Ryan opens into the sea, which will be a great asset when we have enough horses to export."

Catching his enthusiasm, Raven added, "It sounds like a marvelous place for me to breed hunting birds."

Heath couldn't resist teasing her. "I don't think that's a suitable occupation for a lady!"

She jumped up from the bed and stood naked, hands on hips, ready to join the fray. "Be damned to you, Lord Kennedy. I am no ordinary lady!"

"Because you tame raptors?"

"No, because I have a Gypsy lover . . . but come to think of it, they are one and the same!"

He cocked a dark brow. "I don't cavil at being called 'raptor,' but I'll be damned if I'll have you think I can be tamed!" He lunged after her, but she ran out onto the parapet walk, and it took a minute or two to catch her.

Raven was laughing uncontrollably by the time his arms closed around her. "Standing here naked on the ramparts of Castle Douglas makes me feel most unladylike. Do you know what I've always wanted to do? Ride naked in the moonlight!"

Heath bowed low. "I am here to fulfill your every fantasy, Lady Kennedy." He returned to the chamber for his cloak, then wrapped it about her and drew her down the outside steps. He found the stables deserted, for even the lowliest groom was celebrating tonight.

He led Blackadder outside without a saddle, mounted him, then lifted Raven before him between his naked thighs.

When they reached the banks of the River Dee, Heath snatched away his cloak and touched his heels to Blackadder's flanks. The horse surged forward eagerly and Raven threaded her fingers through his wild black mane, feeling utterly wild and wanton. When Heath finally drew rein, he whispered wickedly, "My fantasy is to tumble an English lady under a hedge."

Raven grabbed the cloak, slid down from the horse, and began to run. She looked back over her shoulder. "What the devil are you waiting for, Lord Kennedy?"

About the Author

Virginia Henley is the author of seventeen romantic novels, including the *New York Times* bestsellers *Seduced* and *Desired* and the national bestsellers *A Woman of Passion* and *The Marriage Prize*. Her work has been translated into fourteen languages. A recipient of the *Romantic Times* Lifetime Achievement Award, she lives in St. Petersburg, Florida.